The Fallen Woman's Daughter

The Fallen Woman's Daughter

A NOVEL

MICHELLE COX

Published: 2024
Printed in the United States of America

Print ISBN: 979-8-9880097-0-2
E-ISBN: 979-8-9880097-1-9
Library of Congress Control Number: 2023906457

For more information, address:
Woolton Press
285 N. Cambridge Ct.
Grayslake, Il. 60030

Dedication

For all the girls who run.
May you find the home you are looking for.

April 1932

Nora

This was all Olson's fault, Nora thought bitterly, trying to fight back her tears. They had been happy enough with Ma in the shelter and then the little apartment. But then he had come along and ruined it all. It was Olson's fault, and no one else's. *His* fault that they had been taken away by these terrible people.

Nora peered out the rain-splattered window at the landscape rolling by. Not even the fact that this was her first time in an automobile could abate her rising panic. Though she was all of eight years old, she had never been outside Chicago, and she began to feel more and more afraid as the horizon opened up, the motorcar chugging along. So much open space. It was frightening.

"Where are we going?" Nora finally managed to ask.

The man driving said nothing, but the lady next to him barked, "The Park Ridge School for Girls," without even bothering to turn around. Nora could only guess what that meant and clutched Patsy's hand, though she knew her little sister wouldn't be of any real help. Patsy had somehow fallen asleep, her head nestled in Nora's lap. She was six years old, but still acted like a baby. Still even sucked her thumb.

Nora wiped the tears that would not stop rolling down her cheeks. Ma had tried to hide them in an armoire, but the woman had found them anyway. Patsy had managed to escape the woman's clutches and had run to Ma, but the woman had simply pried her off, despite Patsy screaming and Ma crying and begging. In the end, the woman had had to employ the silent man she'd left leaning in the hallway to help her carry the kicking, wailing Patsy down the stairs. Nora, watching with horror, had decided she wouldn't struggle. Ma had grabbed Patsy's little cloth doll and stuffed it into Nora's pocket, fiercely instructing her to watch over Patsy until she could come get them.

Nora couldn't get Ma's eyes out of her mind. She had never seen them that frantic—that scared and trapped. It made Nora cry all the harder.

The car stopped, and Patsy stirred. Nora peered out at a cluster of stark brick buildings. "Park Ridge School for Girls" was chiseled above the front door of the main one.

The tall, angular woman opened the back door. She stood there expectantly, but when the girls didn't move, she snipped at them. "Come on, out you go. It's not so bad here. Plenty of fresh air, good food. Better than that rat-infested hovel you were in. Should be grateful, I'm thinking. Not all girls get to come here, you know. Most have to go to Dixon, which is a lot worse. You got lucky, so come on." She crossed her arms and tapped her foot. "Come on! Get out, or Larry'll drag you out."

"We're here, Patsy; wake up." Nora gave her sister a nudge. Patsy whimpered and sat up, clutching the ragged doll Nora had given her.

Nora scooted out and pulled at both Patsy and the little carpet bag they had been allowed to bring. Ma had blindly shoved some things in it, but Nora had no idea what. Shivering, she looked around at the dreary grounds. The rain had stopped, but the sky was still dull, everything soggy and ugly.

"Come on," the woman repeated brusquely and marched up the wet concrete steps. Nora's throat ached as she took Patsy's hand. For a brief moment, she considered running . . . but where would she go?

"Come on; let's get this over with," the woman said, pulling open the thick wooden door. Nora climbed the steps, Patsy in tow, but hesitated before stepping into the yawning black interior, the result of which was a swift push.

Nora and Patsy stumbled inside, Nora righting them before they fell. They were in a type of common room with thick, old wood everywhere and a winding staircase at the back, under which a set of pocket doors had been partially left open. In the room's corner, under a low, slanted ceiling, sat a massive desk guarding two more closed doors. On the walls were long rectangular photographs of groups of girls, all dressed in what looked like sailor dresses and black boots. None were smiling.

Patsy clutched at Nora's dress as she hid her face and simultaneously inserted her thumb in her mouth. Nora's right leg was trembling the way it had while they hid in the armoire. The way it did sometimes when Mr. Richardt, their neighbor, was around . . .

Brushing past them, the woman stiffly pointed to a wooden bench set along one wall. Nora obediently sat, pulling Patsy down next to her, while the woman began to pace around the room, drawing out a little watch on a chain from her pocket every so often and looking at it impatiently.

"I don't like it here," Patsy whined. "I want to go home!"

"Shh!" Nora said sharply, shrinking back from the woman's icy stare.

"Mr. Ackerman!" the woman called out loudly. "Mr. Ackerman?"

Nothing stirred. After a few moments, however, an oldish-looking man slipped through the pocket doors under the staircase. He had snow-white hair and a large flowing white moustache and wore an old-fashioned white shirt with puffy sleeves. A black vest hung precariously on his rounded shoulders. He seemed startled to see them, and for a fleeting second Nora thought he might retreat.

"There you are!" the woman said, stopping any further potential thoughts the man might have had on that subject.

"Oh, Miss Whitlow, not today," the man groaned. "Today's not a good day, and Mrs. Harvey won't like it. Can't you come back a different day?" he implored, scooting behind the desk, as if wanting to maintain a safe distance between himself and Miss Whitlow.

"Certainly not. Don't be ridiculous. Where *is* Mrs. Harvey? I've got two new ones." She gave Nora and Patsy a triumphant nod.

Mr. Ackerman afforded himself a quick look. The corner of one of his eyes twitched relentlessly.

"Well, she's out back." He slowly scratched his head. "Been a bit of a disturbance this afternoon, you see."

"A disturbance? What sort of disturbance?"

Mr. Ackerman glanced back at the girls. "Well, I don't think I should say. In the present company, that is."

"Oh, for Heaven's sake! Where's Mrs. Dubala, then?"

"Well, she's most likely out back, too . . ."

"Who is it, Jacob?" a loud voice boomed as the pocket doors banged open. A large bull of a woman stormed through.

"It's Miss Whitlow." Mr. Ackerman tried to shift out from behind the desk, but the bulk of the woman blocked him. She stared at Nora and Patsy, hands on her hips.

"What's this?"

"You know very well, Mrs. Dubala," Miss Whitlow said evenly, not at all cowed by Mrs. Dubala's hostility. She fished in her handbag for an envelope, which she then thrust at Mrs. Dubala. "Court order. Just this morning. You should have already received a telephone call from the circuit court."

"Well, we didn't."

Mr. Ackerman shuffled from side to side, still trapped behind the desk.

"I can't help that," Miss Whitlow went on crisply. "It's my job to round them up. And that's what I do. Now here they are. My part of it's done."

"We're full-up. Not a single bed open." Mrs. Dubala said it coolly, as if the two were engaged in a card game and Mrs. Dubala had just put down an ace.

"Not my business, I'm afraid," Miss Whitlow responded, laying down a trump. "Clearly, you have a problem in your communications." She waved a hand at the desk. "If you have issue with Judge Schaefer's ruling, I suggest you take it up with him. Good day." She turned on her heel and strode toward the front door.

"They permanent?" Mrs. Dubala called out.

"Probably, from the look of it," Miss Whitlow answered without looking back.

Nora felt a strange panic at the disappearance of Miss Whitlow, even though the woman had not given them one drop of kindness. Mrs. Dubala seemed infinitely worse somehow as she stuffed her thick fingers into the envelope. Roughly, she pulled out the letter inside. Her tiny black eyes darted through it. "Stand up," she barked as she read.

Nora stood, pulling Patsy to her feet as well.

"Leonora and Patricia De Lor-en-zo," Mrs. Dubala sounded out. She shot them a glance. "That you two?"

Nora nodded. She considered telling her they were never called those names, but she didn't dare.

"When it rains, it pours, eh, Jacob?" Mrs. Dubala snapped irritably as she tossed the letter onto the desk.

Mr. Ackerman made a move to pick it up and insert it neatly back into the envelope, which she had also tossed on the desk. "Yes, ma'am, I reckon so," he answered meekly.

With one deft movement, Mrs. Dubala grabbed a bit of Nora's hair, roughly pulling her head down. With the other hand, she did the same to Patsy, who let out a little yell.

"Just as I thought. Lice," she said with disgust, then wiped her hands on the apron that squeezed around her large stomach. "I hate Italians. Take them to the bath chamber."

"Then what?" Mr. Ackerman asked. "Ain't no openings, just as you said."

Mrs. Dubala sighed, thinking. "Take them to Solomon," she said finally. "They'll have to share a mattress on the floor."

"Mrs. Morris ain't gonna to like that. Maybe we should ask Mrs. Harvey."

"You do as you're told, Jacob. I'll handle Mrs. Morris."

With a heavy sigh, Mr. Ackerman finally managed to squeeze his way past Mrs. Dubala's large girth and led the girls out.

CHAPTER 2

April 1932

Nora obsessively smoothed her navy uniform skirt one last time and tucked a stray bit of hair behind her ear. Then she chanced a glance at Patsy and quickly swiped her sister's thumb out of her mouth.

The girls had indeed been placed in Solomon Cottage under the direction of the grim Mrs. Morris, who was twice as bad as Mrs. Dubala. Though Solomon Cottage was for eight-to twelve-year-old girls, Mrs. Morris made no exception for the fact that Patsy was only six, having fervently protested taking the two of them in the first place. Mrs. Dubala had insisted, saying that as sisters they could share a bed, and, anyway, there was no other place. This command from on high naturally did little to put Nora and Patsy in Mrs. Morris's good graces.

After the two of them were sent to bed without dinner two nights in a row—Nora for not properly tying the red neck bow of their uniforms and Patsy for sucking her thumb while Mrs. Morris was speaking—Nora began to learn the endless rules, which no one ever bothered to explain. Sometimes a few of the girls would whisper hints or reminders, but others seemed to enjoy watching the two new girls get punished. Worse than any of this, however, was that Nora still didn't understand why they were even here. Why Ma didn't come to get them.

Obviously, there had been some terrible misunderstanding. *House of prostitution*, Miss Whitlow had said the night she came to get them. Nora had barely heard it in the confusion, but she had pondered it many times since, trying to make sense of what had happened. She didn't know what *house of prostitution* meant, but whatever it was, Miss Whitlow made a mistake. They weren't a house of anything.

Visitors were only allowed at the Park Ridge every other Sunday, the girls explained, and it was their "tough luck" that they had just missed one the day before they had gotten there. Nora had painfully counted down the days until the next one, today, and had spent the whole of this morning not only doing her required chores *and* Patsy's—she couldn't take any chances—but also making sure their uniforms were perfect.

"Don't suck your thumb, Patsy!" Nora hissed as she heard Mrs. Morris clipping down the hallway now. No matter how many times Nora reminded her sister of the rules, Patsy never remembered them. But then again, Patsy barely understood where they were, much less what was expected of them, and cried every night for Ma.

"Stand up straight!" Mrs. Morris barked as she entered the long, low bedroom. All giggling and chatter ceased instantly as the girls stepped into place, shoulder to shoulder in front of their beds, their arms held stiffly at their sides, eyes straight ahead.

Nora bit her lip and focused on the wall across from them as the matron clipped closer, praying that Patsy was doing the same. Knowing her, however, she was probably staring up at Mrs. Morris with those big blue eyes.

Though they were sisters, the two girls looked nothing alike. Nora was tall for her age with thick black hair and dark eyes, while Patsy was tiny and fair. Often Nora wished she had taken after their mother, as Patsy obviously had, but instead she had been dealt their father's looks. She hated her black hair and frequently tried to hide it by tying it up in a bun, but strands of it were always coming loose. She was tempted to pull them back, but she made herself stand still.

"I won't have you shame me like you did last Visiting Day," Mrs. Morris quipped, walking down the row. "Imagine the horror of having Mrs. Harvey—*Mrs. Harvey!*—comment on the state of Solomons' shoes. 'Awfully scuffed' were her words. 'A-w-f-u-l-l-y scuffed!'"

Nora tried not to breathe.

"Margaret, your handkerchief is sticking out of your pocket. Honestly!" Mrs. Morris moved to the next girl, Abigail, but apparently found nothing. "Agnes, your tie is crooked. Again." Out of the corner of her eye, Nora saw Agnes hurry to adjust it as Mrs. Morris continued down the line.

Fortunately, or unfortunately, she found no other faults to decry before she came to the end, where Patsy and Nora were trying their best to stand at attention. Mrs. Morris hovered in front of them.

"Patricia De Lorenzo, stand up straight," she finally snapped. Mrs. Morris refused to call them by anything but their full names, which was a problem for Patsy, who had never been called Patricia in her life. Her non-responses had already earned her the reputation of being willful, as well as inattentive, distracted, and flighty. When Nora had finally worked up the courage to inform Mrs. Morris of their nicknames, Mrs. Morris had punished her by putting her on extra dish duty up at the main hall.

Nora braced herself.

"Your shirt is untucked," Mrs. Morris continued. "Your stockings are falling down. And good Lord—your shoes are scuffed!"

Nora bit her lip again. She was tempted to look over, but she didn't dare. She had polished Patsy's shoes herself just this morning!

"I've a mind to cancel Visiting Day for you," Mrs. Morris snipped. "Girls who can't keep themselves presentable don't deserve to have visitors."

"No!" Nora blurted before she could think.

"What did you say?" Mrs. Morris asked slowly, stepping in front of Nora.

Nora tried not to cower. "Please, Mrs. Morris," she begged, staring at the silver buckle on Mrs. Morris's thin black dress belt. "I . . . it was my fault. I . . . I forgot. I'll polish them right now. Please don't cancel visiting day. Please let us see our Ma." She made herself look at the woman's pinched face, if only for a moment, before dropping her gaze again to the buckle.

Mrs. Morris did not immediately respond, and in the ensuing silence, Nora felt her right leg begin to tremble.

"Very well. But see that it doesn't happen again. You can stay behind and sweep," she said, pointing a long, bent finger at Patsy. "And don't do it for her, Miss Goody-Two-Shoes," she snipped at Nora. Nora wanted to argue that the cottage floor was already immaculate in preparation for Visiting Day, but she stopped herself.

"Yes, Mrs. Morris," Nora answered. Patsy looked up at Nora questioningly, but Nora gave her a small shake of her head. Patsy looked back up at Mrs. Morris. Nora could tell she was about to put her thumb in her mouth, so she quickly reached out and grabbed her hand.

"And you can carry the trash to the burn barrels behind the main hall."

"Yes, Mrs. Morris."

"If there's time after that—and only after that—you can join in Visiting Day. If anyone turns up, that is."

As soon as the girls of Solomon Cottage were released to the main hall, Nora ran to the supply closet in the kitchen and grabbed the tin of black polish and the rag, already full of black smudges. She scooped out some of the thick polish with a clean corner and quickly ran it across Patsy's shoes. "Pick up your feet when you walk, Patsy," she scolded. "Otherwise, they get scuffed."

"They're heavy," Patsy complained, affectionately patting Nora's bent head.

Nora knew what Patsy meant. The thick black ankle boots did feel heavy compared to the worn-out Mary Janes they had been given at the shelter; before that, they had usually gone without anything, roaming around barefoot.

"Well, you'll get used to them. You'll be thankful in the winter. Now, come on! Ma's coming today. You sit there while they dry, and I'll sweep."

Patsy obediently wiggled herself up onto a chair while Nora did the most precursory of sweeps and then led Patsy out back, expecting that the garbage would have already been done this morning. The sight of newspapers stacked up and overflowing rotting food in the crates, then, both surprised and infuriated Nora when she remembered that this chore had initially been assigned to a girl named Priscilla, who was not only very mean but, Nora was slowly learning, Mrs. Morris's especial pet.

Nora stood for a few moments, fuming, before she hurried over and grabbed some of the newspapers. This was no time to be angry. It was already ten o'clock, the official start of visiting hours, and Nora didn't want to keep Ma waiting.

"Here, take these," she said, thrusting them into Patsy's little arms while she picked up the heavy crate. "And don't drag your feet!" she scolded, wishing she had saved the polishing for last.

As it turned out, they were only fifteen minutes late to the main hall, Nora slowing their steps as they entered the building, not wanting to be punished for running. Mrs. Morris was thankfully nowhere in sight, so Nora took Patsy's hand and led her toward the main parlor. She paused in the doorway, not wanting to simply barge in. Instead, she looked for Ma, and when she didn't immediately see her, took a few tentative steps inside so that she could see into the corners.

Ma wasn't anywhere.

Biting her lip, she retreated back to the little lobby, wondering what to do next. She could see through the big open doors to the grounds beyond, where some girls were strolling with their families, and wondered if Ma might be there. As strong as the urge was to dash outside, she made herself stand her ground, calculating that Ma, after waiting only fifteen minutes, wouldn't have just gotten up to stroll the grounds on her own.

She glanced over to the main desk. Mr. Ackerman was leaning back in the desk chair, his thumbs resting behind his suspender straps. He looked to be enjoying this easy assignment.

"Mr. Ackerman?" Nora asked timidly. The man did not respond, seemingly caught up in a daydream, his right eye twitching. Nora cleared her throat. "Mr. Ackerman?" she said, more loudly than she meant to.

Mr. Ackerman plopped his chair down and observed them over the top of his spectacles, which had slid down his nose. "Yes?"

"I'm . . . we're looking for our mother. Is she here, do you know?"

Mr. Ackerman blinked his eyes sleepily. "Don't reckon so, if she's not waitin' there," he said waving a wrinkled hand absently toward the lobby. "Name?"

"Nora DeLorenzo."

"No, not you. Yer Ma."

"Oh, it's Mrs. DeLorenzo. Gertie DeLorenzo," she said, hope filling her chest as Mr. Ackerman picked up the guest book splayed in front of him and turned it around to read it.

"Nope. Not yet," he said, tossing it back down. "See?"

Nora looked at the signatures under today's date and was relieved to see that they hadn't missed Ma after all.

"You sit over there and wait," he said, nodding toward the benches along the walls where other hopeful girls were sitting. "She'll be along."

Nora pulled Patsy toward the benches where they had sat just two weeks ago, dumped by Miss Whitlow, but there was no more room. They would have to stand, Nora realized, not daring to sit on the floor even though there were no teachers around. Maybe they went into town, happy to have a break from their charges. Or maybe they were all sitting in a lounge somewhere discussing who the worst girls were.

Maybe it was *better* they were standing, Nora thought as she leaned against the wall. From this vantage point, they were the first to see people enter the building. Ma would be here soon anyway, and then she would fix this. Nora was sure of it.

A woman with a bruised face nervously entered, and the girl beside Patsy let out a little squeal of delight as she got up and threw her arms around the woman's waist. Nora watched, her stomach clenching, as the woman bent and kissed the girl on the head, tears in her eyes. She wondered if Ma would cry when she saw them. The woman was whispering something in the girl's ear, probably some exchange of love, but Nora made herself look away before she could see the girl's reaction and turned her attention to more practical matters. Hurriedly she plopped herself down in the girl's empty place and squeezed Patsy in beside her, who immediately began to swing her feet. Nora considered stopping her, trying to remember if there was a specific rule against that, but she finally just let her go. No one around them seemed to care.

Nora watched as the woman and the girl walked out into the grassy quad, trimmed neat and perfect by the older girls in Wordsworth. Nora noticed now that not only was the woman's face bruised, but her arm was bandaged, too.

Since their abrupt arrival at The Park Ridge School for Girls, Nora had been able to piece together that all of the girls here came from broken homes, a fact which only served to further confuse her. Their home hadn't *seemed* broken. Nothing had been wrong. Which is why, Nora thought bitterly, it must have something to do with Olson. Ma was different when he was around. Always fretting, roughly trying to braid their hair before he came, and telling them to smile and be nice. Pretending to laugh at his jokes, which weren't even funny. At least to Nora.

Well, whatever the reason they had been taken, Nora was sure that it was a big misunderstanding. No, Ma would sort it out and maybe even take them home today. It was the reason Nora had yet to unpack the carpet bag. No need.

Seven hours later, Nora was still sitting on the bench, her eyes strained and bleary as she watched the clock's second hand slide into place onto the twelve, the hour hand firmly on the five. The lobby was deserted now, but Nora could hear a few people in the parlor next door, saying their goodbyes. She willed them to stay where they were, to give Ma a few extra minutes to turn up. Someone had closed the big, thick outside doors hours ago, but Nora could see from one of the tall, narrow windows that the sun was setting, coloring the sky with oranges and pinks. Patsy rested heavily on her, asleep, her thumb in her mouth.

Nora dared not look at Mr. Ackerman, afraid that if she caught his eye he would shoo them off. He had already suggested several times that they go wait in their cottage. "I'll come git you if yer ma turns up. No need to sit on that bench all day. Go on an' git some fresh air." But Nora hadn't wanted to leave, even for a second. She couldn't take the chance that there would be yet another mix-up.

Nora winced, then, when she heard his chair creak and what she assumed were his knees cracking as he stood up. She kept her eyes on the clock as he shuffled toward them. Her throat began to ache.

"'Fraid visiting hours is over, girls. Best get on back to yer cottage before yer matron finds you missing."

He stepped directly in front of Nora, blocking her view of the clock.

"Can't we wait just a little bit longer, Mr. Ackerman?" she asked timidly, her voice hoarse from lack of use.

"'Fraid not." He thumbed over his shoulder at the window. "Almost dark. Be suppertime soon. Best git on."

"But . . . but . . . I *know* she's coming. Please."

Mr. Ackerman scratched his head. "Don't think so, by the look of it. Go on, now." He made a shooing gesture. "You know what Mrs. Morris's like, an' I got ta lock up."

Nora looked around desperately and saw someone else's mother pass through the lobby, her heels clicking on the black-and-white checked tile. She gave them a pitying look before opening the big lobby doors, which then closed softly behind her with a thud. That was it; she was the last one. Tears stung Nora's eyes. Oh, where could Ma be? Something terrible must have happened!

"Sure she knew about Visiting Day and such? Maybe she is un-in-formed," Mr. Ackerman said, drawing it out, as if it were a difficult word to pronounce.

Uninformed? A new fear suddenly gripped Nora's heart. *Did Ma not know about Visiting Day?* Maybe that was the problem! But could Ma really not know where they were? The force of this realization nearly crippled Nora.

"I . . . I don't know," Nora mumbled, hastily wiping her eyes.

"Why don't you write her a letter? Girls here is always writing letters. It's my job to give 'em all to the mailman every day. Lot more goin' out than comes back, though."

A letter? Nora had not thought of writing Ma. But then again, she hadn't thought she would need to.

"Come on, Patsy." Nora gave her sister a little shove. "We've got to go."

"Is Mama here?" Patsy said sleepily, sitting up.

"No, she's not. But we've got to go."

Patsy instantly let out a loud deep wail, causing Nora to grit her teeth. "I want Mama!" Patsy cried and then began to sob.

"I know that, Patsy," Nora said sternly, holding her own tears at bay. "But she couldn't come today. Come on," she said in her best grown-up voice as she took Patsy's hand and pulled her off the bench. "She'll come next time," Nora promised and led her out, determined to have a letter written before she went to sleep.

CHAPTER 3

May 1932

As it turned out, Nora wrote a total of three letters before the next visiting day, each one more pleading than the next.

April 19, 1932

Dear Ma,

Where are you? We are at a place called The Park Ridge School for Girls. It is very far away. The teachers are mean. When are you coming to get us? Visitors can only come every other Sunday but I think you can come take us home any day you want. Patsy cries all the time and sometimes I can't get her to stop. We both miss you. Please hurry.

Love,
Nora

Nora had no idea how long it would take for a letter to get to Ma, so, after only a few days with no reply, she decided to write another.

April 23, 1932

Dear Ma,

Did you get my last letter? I forgot to say that I love you and that you are the best mother ever. I'm trying to take care of Patsy like you asked. I'm sorry for anything bad I did, Ma. Sorry that I wasn't nicer to Mr. Olson. I'll be the best girl in the world when you come get us, Ma. You'll see. Please come two Sundays from now. It's the Park Ridge School for Girls. Do you know how to get here? I love you, Ma. Please come get us. We're scared here.

Love,
Nora

And then a third.

April 27, 1932

Dear Ma,

I don't know if you will get this in time, but I forgot to say that the school is on Prospect Avenue. Do you know where that is? And visiting hours start at ten. We'll be waiting for you. We love you, Ma. We miss you. Patsy still cries at night. Sometimes I do, too.

Love,
Nora

Nora was about to insert this last missive into an envelope when Patsy interrupted her by handing her a drawing from under her pillow.

"Here. Thend this to Mama, too." Patsy said. They were alone in the long, low bedroom.

Nora examined the drawing. It was a picture of a carnival. Neither of them had ever been to a carnival, of course, but plenty of times they had sat and watched the one in the parking lot of St. Sylvester's every Fourth of July from behind the fence. Once they had asked Ma to go, but Ma had frowned and said, "Carnivals aren't a nice place for little girls." It was an answer which had confused Nora, as she saw plenty of little girls, and boys, for that matter, running around happily.

"What's this?" Nora asked, pointing to the drawing.

"Thas where Ma is," she answered, not bothering to take her thumb out of her mouth.

"No, it's not, Patsy. Don't be silly."

"Yes, it is." Patsy stared at her with her big innocent eyes.

Nora sighed. "Fine." She supposed it wouldn't hurt to include it. Maybe it would make Ma smile, which she rarely did, except when Olson was around. But she didn't want to think of that now.

Time dragged along, Nora religiously counting down the fourteen days until the next visiting day when Ma would surely come and take them home. Nora was tempted to be more lax in following the rules, knowing that it would soon not matter, but she didn't dare lose visiting privileges and thus remained vigilant, not only of herself but of Patsy. In fact, she watched Patsy like a hawk—keeping her in line, secretly doing her chores for her, endlessly polishing her shoes.

When other girls sometimes made friendly overtures, offering to share a bit of candy they had squirreled away or asking them questions about where they were from, Nora did not reciprocate beyond the simplest of answers. So much effort and concentration was required to keep her fear at bay that she had very little left inside of her to share, even if she wanted to. In any case, there was no need to make friends. They would be gone soon.

When not doing chores, the girls were required to attend school, which served to take up time, if nothing else. Nora was mildly interested, though she didn't put forth much effort, and all Patsy seemed to do in her baby class was draw pictures and sing songs. Back at the apartment, Nora had only spottily gone to school, as most of the time she had stayed home to watch Patsy while Ma was working. Next year, though, Ma had warned her several times, Patsy would be old enough for them to both go. "You need to at least know how to read," Ma had said. "Some people don't, you know, and life is hard for them."

Despite her sketchy attendance, Nora had already learned to read and write. She liked to read, in fact, but there was never anything much around *to* read, just one old storybook that Ma possessed. It had scribbles in the margins, but Nora could still read the words, which she did, over and over, during many a rainy day in the apartment.

Nora was secretly thrilled, then, when she was handed new books by one of her Park Ridge teachers, though she feigned indifference. They were lovely. Not new, exactly, but not frayed and tattered like the storybook. One was called *Swiss Family Robinson* and another was called *Black Beauty*. She liked that title. *Black Beauty*. She wondered if she would be allowed to take them home after Ma came to get them. Probably not . . .

Nora adjusted her tie and gave Patsy one last look-over, licking her fingers and smoothing down a lock of Patsy's hair that seemed to have a mind of its own. Visiting Day had finally arrived again, and Nora was leaving nothing to chance. She had carefully repacked the few possessions that had managed to creep out of the carpet bag in the almost month they had been here, including Patsy's ratty doll. It was an old thing, given to Patsy by one of their neighbors, Mrs. Kennedy. It was made of dishcloth and had once been white, though it was gray now and patched in various places. It no longer even looked human, with only one button eye and a line of x's where the mouth should be. Nora had often wondered why Mrs. Kennedy hadn't stitched the mouth into a smile. Would the appearance of happiness have taken that much longer? But Patsy didn't seem to care, carrying it everywhere. It even smelled like her. It was the first thing Nora made sure she packed, knowing what a fuss Patsy would cause if they left without it.

"No sucking your thumb, Patsy," Nora warned, knocking it out of her mouth. "Ma's coming today, and we have to be ready." She attempted to say it authoritatively, but it came out more pleading than anything else. She tried not to think about why Ma had not responded to any of her letters. Perhaps she meant to surprise them?

"But thas what you said the lass time." Patsy's lower lip stuck out.

"Well, that's because she didn't know about Visiting Day. She does now. So stand up straight, and don't make Mrs. Morris mad!"

Nora gripped her sister's shoulders and roughly placed her in line beside a girl named Celia and then stepped in place herself just as Mrs. Morris entered the room.

"Stand up straight!" Mrs. Morris barked, which Nora recognized now as her opening command. All of the girls shuffled into place and sucked in their chests.

"Fortunately, none of you managed to shame me last time in front of Mrs. Harvey. God only knows how. But don't think that means I'm paying one bit less attention this week. Agnes, straighten your tie, for Heaven's sake," she snipped at the first girl in the row.

Mrs. Morris again proceeded down the line, making comments here and there, but nothing too extreme, and Nora dared to hope that she was perhaps in a lenient state of mind today. Mrs. Morris gave Celia only the most cursory of glances before moving on to Patsy. Nora bit the inside of her cheek.

"Eyes straight ahead, Patricia. Pull your stockings up!"

For once, Patsy obeyed, though Mrs. Morris remained in front of her. Nora could feel the perspiration beginning to build under her collar and on her upper lip, but she remained rigid, eyes forward. Finally, Mrs. Morris moved on. Nora forced herself not to exhale and instead held the air in her lungs, making her chest burn a little. She kept her eyes locked on Mrs. Morris's buckle.

Finally, Mrs. Morris let out a little sigh. "You'll do, I suppose," she muttered, the disappointment in her voice obvious.

Nora quietly released the breath she was holding, her heart pounding.

Mrs. Morris turned to walk back up the line. "Now, girls, you must all—" she began and then stopped not far from Patsy. "What is that?" she hissed, and Nora, despite the rules, could not help but turn to see what had caught Mrs. Morris's attention. Her stomach clenched when she saw the limp leg of Patsy's doll sticking out from under her pillow.

Oh, Patsy! When had she gotten it out of the bag?

"I told you to get rid of that filthy thing!" Mrs. Morris made a sudden move towards the bed. "I'm sure it's crawling with lice, just as the two of you were. No wonder we can't get rid of them!"

Before she could reach the doll, however, Patsy ran and grabbed it, pulling it tightly to her chest.

"Give me that!" Mrs. Morris demanded, holding her hand out.

Nora rushed to step protectively in front of Patsy. "I . . . I washed it, Mrs. Morris. It's clean now."

"No wonder Solomon is called 'the lice cottage,'" Mrs. Morris hissed. "I'm the butt of the other matrons' jokes, I'll have you know. Give me that!" she demanded, giving Nora a little shove out of the way.

"No!" Patsy cried loudly and hurdled over the nearest bed. Within seconds, she had bolted out of the bedroom.

"Patricia De Lorenzo! You come back here!"

The only response was the bang of the cottage's front door.

"Right," Mrs. Morris snapped. "The closet it is," she said matter-of-factly, which caused an immediate eruption of horrified murmurs. "Go get her," she commanded Priscilla.

"Yes, Mrs. Morris," her pet said sweetly and shot out of line, her face one of glee.

Panic erupted in Nora's brain, and she didn't know what to do first. She wanted to run and find Patsy herself, but there was a larger threat to face . . . the closet. Nora had heard about it from the other girls, several of whom claimed to have been locked inside it overnight for various infractions. It was the old coal chute in the cellar, but the girls called it the Carrie Cort, after the first girl who had found herself imprisoned there. Up until this moment, Nora had suspected it was just a tall tale meant to scare the new girls. Now, however, she was accordingly filled with terror.

"Please, Mrs. Morris," Nora begged. "Please not that. I . . . it was my fault. I . . . I should have gotten rid of the doll. I know it now. Please don't put Patsy in the . . . in the closet." She wasn't sure if she should call it the Carrie Cort out loud. In complete desperation, Nora sank to her knees in front of Mrs. Morris, causing a few snickers.

"Get up, you stupid girl. Of course, she'll have to be punished. She needs to learn a lesson. I'm tired of being trifled with. Get up, I said!"

"Got her, Mrs. Morris!" yelled Priscilla as she came back into the room, pulling a kicking, screaming Patsy behind her. Roughly, the girl released her with a shove.

Nora quickly got to her feet and ran to Patsy.

"Oh, Patsy, why?" she asked angrily, only to feel a wave of compassion at the sight of the little girl's tear-stained cheeks and heaving chest. "Shh," Nora said, putting her arms around her. "It's okay."

A hand grabbed her by the back of the collar and pulled her away from Patsy. "That's enough," Mrs. Morris spat. "You," she said, pointing at Nora, "will spend the day peeling potatoes. And you"—Mrs. Morris snatched the doll out of Patsy's hand— "will spend the day and the night in the closet. Here." She pinched a tiny bit of the doll between her finger and thumb and handed it gingerly to one of the girls. "Throw this on the burn pile for Mr. Ackerman."

"No!" screamed Patsy and drew back her leg to kick Mrs. Morris, but Nora, seeing what was about to happen, leapt back in front of her. "You can't take that! It's mine! Stop her, Nora!"

"Patsy, shh." Nora again wrapped her arms around the struggling girl. "Don't worry. We'll get it back. Shh." Nora couldn't think straight. Everything was happening at once and going from bad to worse.

"Come on, you," Mrs. Morris said, grabbing Patsy by the arm.

"No!" Patsy screamed, trying to pull back, her legs locked stiffly.

Mrs. Morris slapped her firmly across the face. "That's enough, you hellion. Shut your mouth!"

Stunned, Patsy immediately stopped fighting and was pulled along by Mrs. Morris toward the cottage's small pantry, where a door was cut ingeniously into the floor. Priscilla ran ahead to pull it open, revealing the yawning black cavern of the cellar. With a nod of appreciation to Priscilla, Mrs. Morris banged down the wooden planks, pulling Patsy behind her. The girls all rushed to follow, leaving Nora somehow to bring up the rear, unable to push her way through the throng of girls.

By the time she reached the dirt floor below, Patsy had already been imprisoned and was beating on the door of the old coal chute.

"Let me out!" she screamed. "Let me out!"

Between her extreme fear and the moldy air, Nora suddenly felt like vomiting. She looked around desperately for someone, anyone, to appeal to, but there was only Mrs. Morris and the girls lined up on the stairs, their eyes big with morbid excitement in the glow from the pantry light above.

"I hope you both learn a lesson from this," Mrs. Morris shouted over Patsy's screams. "And don't think you're going to sit down here and mind her," she said to Nora. "You get upstairs and start the potatoes. The show is over," she barked at the girls huddled on the stairs. "Get on with your work before visiting hours begin, or I'll rescind them for the whole cottage."

Visiting hours! Nora's heart sank. In the current crisis, she had forgotten.

The girls scurried up the stairs, and after giving Nora one final glare, Mrs. Morris stomped up herself. At the top, she switched off not only the one bulb that hung from the low cellar ceiling, but the pantry one as well, so that the only light to be had was what trickled in through a little window, no bigger than a bread box.

"Nora!" Patsy cried, her voice so high-pitched and frightened that Nora winced. "Nora, are you there?"

"Yes, I'm here, Pats," Nora shouted.

"Nora! Get me out! I'm scared. It's dark in here! Nora!" she screamed, high and long, like a wounded animal. She banged wildly on the door with her little fists. Nora put her mouth close to the door.

"Patsy!" she shouted. "Patsy, calm down!" Her voice shook. "Patsy, I'm right here. I'm right here. Just on the other side of the door." There was no use trying to open it—it was padlocked shut—but Nora jiggled it all the same.

"Nora! I'm scared!"

Nora frantically ran her fingers along the thick planks of the door, searching for she knew not what . . . a hole maybe? But there was none. She slid down onto her knees and wedged her fingers under the door, wiggling them. "Here, Patsy. Take my fingers."

"I can't see them."

"Down at the bottom of the door. Reach down. Feel them?" She wiggled her fingers wildly until she felt the soft tips of Patsy's hand. "See? I'm right here. That's not so bad, is it?" she asked, trying to calm herself as well. "It's just like the armoire at home. Remember? How we used to hide sometimes? It's just like that."

"But there might be spiders in here!" Patsy cried, the panic welling up again.

"There's no spiders, Patsy," she said sternly, but couldn't help but imagine them crawling all over her little sister. She shuddered.

"I'm scared, Nora. Don't leave me here. Please. Don't leave me!"

"I won't, Pats. I won't," she promised, though her arm was already beginning to ache, strained as it was with her fingers wedged under the door. She lay down on the dirt floor—what did it matter now if her uniform was dirty?—so that it was easier to hold onto Patsy. She laid her head on her arm and listened to the girls leaving the cottage one by one, banging out the screen door into the fresh, warm air. Nora longed to be one of them, free, but she couldn't possibly leave Patsy here alone in the dark. But what about Ma? She couldn't just leave Ma standing alone in the lobby. What would she do when they didn't turn up to greet her? Would she turn around and go back home? *Oh, Ma!* Surely not!

"What about Mama?" Patsy asked suddenly, as if reading her thoughts. "How will Mama find us down here?"

"I don't know, Patsy."

"I want Mama!" Patsy screamed, and for a moment, Nora was tempted to do the same.

"I'll figure it out. But you have to be quiet," she scolded. "Be brave."

"I don't want to! I want Mama. And Baby," she cried, referring to her doll.

"Patsy, calm down. Crying isn't going to help. Be quiet, and I'll tell you a story," she offered desperately. She said it to silence her, but now Nora wondered if it might have a second purpose. If she could get Patsy to fall asleep, she might be able to sneak off to the main hall.

"Once upon a time there was a . . ." Nora paused, trying to decide which story to tell. . . "there was a very good girl who was made to do all the chores by her evil stepmother. Her name was Cinderella. But she was very beautiful, and all the woodland creatures loved her and helped her do her work . . ."

Nora told the whole of that story and then another and still another until she was pretty sure Patsy had finally fallen asleep, because there was now no sound from inside the Carrie Cort besides a light wheeze.

Nora, still lying on her stomach, allowed herself to feel a moment of relief before considering what to do next. What if Patsy woke up, and she wasn't there? She would be hysterical, Nora knew, and memories of what had happened the last time she had left Patsy alone back in the apartment began to surface . . .

She shuddered and pushed away that horrid memory, but the thought of Ma, sitting in the front parlor, looking at the clock, pacing around, was nearly as terrible. Slowly, Nora pulled her fingers from under the door and stiffly sat up. Patsy remained quiet. She would be fast, she decided, and got to her feet. She paused, though, when she heard the cottage door open and footsteps above. Maybe someone had forgotten something? Nora decided to wait until whoever it was left, but the footsteps came closer, toward the pantry. They stopped just above her.

"Nora?" called a soft, hesitant voice. Nora didn't completely recognize it, but she thought it might be Celia, the girl who slept next to them.

"Nora?" the voice repeated. "Are you there?"

"Yes," Nora whispered, not wanting to wake Patsy.

The sound of the girl's faint footsteps was easily absorbed by the deep stone walls. Nora peered through the dim light and saw that it was indeed Celia.

"Here you go," she said, thrusting Patsy's doll at Nora.

Nora looked at it incredulously.

"Mr. Ackerman said to give it to you. He's nice, really. But don't let Mrs. Morris see."

"Thanks." Nora didn't know what else to say and avoided looking at the girl's heavily freckled face.

"And I thought you might like some company. I was in there once myself, so I know what it's like," Celia said.

"But what about your mom? Or your dad? Don't you want to visit with them?" Nora asked.

Celia twisted a lock of her dishwater hair. "My mom is dead, and my dad ran off."

"Oh."

"Usually my Aunt Rita comes, but she's sick today." Celia shrugged.

"Our mother is coming," Nora said firmly.

"That's good." The two girls stared at each other, Nora really *seeing* Celia for the first time. There was nothing remarkable except for a small dimple in her chin. And her eyes. They were a warm hazel and held a kindness that made Nora feel calm somehow.

"What are you going to do about her?" Celia asked finally, nodding toward the Carrie Cort.

"I . . . I don't know. I can't just leave her."

"Well, you can't stay down here forever. Don't forget about the potatoes."

The potatoes!

"I . . . I guess I forgot about that," Nora mumbled, fear rising up her throat again.

"Want me to do them for you?"

"Oh!" Nora couldn't believe anyone would be this kind. "You . . . you wouldn't mind?"

"Sure. I don't have anything better to do."

"But won't Mrs. Morris find out?"

"Nah, she's on the desk today. Don't know why. Maybe it's because Mr. Ackerman is supposed to be burning that," she said, gesturing to the doll still in Nora's hands.

Mrs. Morris was on desk duty? How would she find Ma now? Mrs. Morris was sure to see her creeping around the main hall instead of doing the potatoes. And what would happen if Mrs. Morris got to Ma first? Would she tell her that her girls were being punished? Tell her to go home and not to bother? Oh! She had to get out of this cellar . . . had to fly across the quad and find Ma before Mrs. Morris had a chance. She would just have to risk it.

Before she could even put her plan into action, however, Celia spoke in a voice that was much too loud. "How you gonna find your ma, though, if you're stuck down here?"

Nora quickly raised her finger to her lips to shush Celia, but before she could say anything, she heard a tiny mewing voice from inside the Carrie Cort.

"Nora?" squeaked Patsy, and with this tiny sound, any hope that Nora had of finding Ma was bitterly crushed. "Nora?" Patsy called, louder this time.

"I'm here, Pats," Nora said heavily, her own eyes finally filling with tears. She couldn't fight them any longer.

"Sorry," Celia said quietly, seeming to sense her error. "I didn't know she was sleeping . . ."

Nora didn't say anything. Her throat was aching.

"Listen, I'll try to get the potatoes done real fast, and then I'll sit down here with your sister. Then you can go look for your mom. How about that?" she suggested.

Nora gave Celia a sad little nod. She knew she should probably thank Celia, but no words would come out.

"Nora! I want to get out!" cried Patsy.

"I'll come back as fast as I can!" Celia banged up the wooden planks. "Don't worry!" she shouted down through the gaping hole, but Nora, alone in the dark, save for Patsy, helplessly entombed in the Carrie Cort, could do nothing *but* worry. She sank to the ground, trying to fight her own terror.

"Nora?"

"Yes, I'm still here, Pats," Nora answered wearily.

"Did you send the letters to Ma? Did you put in my carnival picture?"

"Yes." It was a simple, meaningless question—one of Patsy's many, but this one struck an odd cord, causing goosebumps to suddenly appear down Nora's neck. "Why?"

"Ma will know."

CHAPTER 4

May 1923

Gertie

"Step right up, step right up, ladies and gents! See the finest show on Earth. Only a quarter to get in. That's right. Twenty-five cents is all it takes to see the wonders of the known world! You'll be amazed, educated, titillated and stunned. In short, you'll be astounded. You won't regret a single penny. It will be the talk of your friends and neighbors for years! Don't miss out on this chance to see what few people on Earth have *ever* seen!"

The announcer stood before them on a small dais, loosely gripping a podium. He was tall and thin and dark. *Swarthy* was the word that came to Gertie's mind, with equal parts fascination and fear. Yes, that was it. Swarthy. He was dressed in an old-fashioned black frock coat with tails, under which was a shiny gold vest and a red sash. Gold braiding ran down the side of his pantaloons, which were tucked neatly into shiny black knee-high boots, and a matching shiny black top hat graced his head. He looked marvelous.

"A quarter apiece gets us in to see everything?" Pa asked with a slight tone of incredulousness as he pushed his own dull brown derby back on his head, revealing his thinning hair beneath. Having just come from church, they were all dressed in their Sunday best. Each of the Gufftason children had managed to make it to the wagon this morning before Pa had had to take up his switch. It wasn't an idle threat; all of them, even Felix, the runt, had felt the lash of Pa's belt, or worse, a hickory branch more than once.

"No, my good man," the showman replied, stepping gracefully from behind the podium. "But I can see you are a man of sense. A man of business, perhaps. A mere twenty-five cents allows you to enter these magnificent gates and see for yourself all that lies within," he said, gesturing widely. "Plenty to see, I guar-an-tee it."

Gertie tried to see beyond the makeshift fence that had been erected around what the showman was proclaiming to be almost hallowed grounds. She could see the top of the carousel and hear its melodious music. Also in view were several large red-and-white striped tents, and Gertie shivered to think what they might hold. How was it possible that all this could have been built in a matter of days in what had essentially been an empty field on the edge of Eddyville, Iowa? The thought of it took her breath away. Such a wonder of ingenuity and modernity.

Gertie had never been to a carnival before, but she had seen the poster in town, a little shiver rippling through her as Carl and Ernie pulled at her dress. All of it looked just splendid, but what had especially intrigued Gertie was the performers, the singers in particular. Patsy Montana and the Cowboys would be there, which she could hardly believe. They were her very favorites.

The Gufftasons were too poor to own something as extravagant as a radio, but their neighbors, the O'Reillys, two shacks down, had one. Keystone had only recently been wired, and the O'Reillys had been the first to purchase a contraption that actually required electricity. Pa said it was an awful waste of money, but Gertie marveled at it and crept over to the O'Reillys most evenings to listen.

At first, Gertie had been disappointed that all Mr. O'Reilly seemed interested in listening to was *The Grand Ole Opry* and *The Rodeo Boys*, both of which weren't to Gertie's liking. She would much rather listen to *Amos and Andy* or *Your Hit Parade*, but beggars couldn't be choosers. As time went on, however, she came around and grew nearly as enchanted as Mr. O'Reilly was with the lore of the West. Adventure. Gold. Train robbers. Noble steeds. Shiny rifles. Heroes. This was the stuff that fueled her imagination now, and she chattered about it endlessly, so much so that Maman said she'd never known a girl so given to flights of fancy. But they weren't flights of fancy, at least in Gertie's mind. She honest-to-goodness meant to see the West someday! Get away from this Godforsaken mud pit.

"There's lions, an ape or two, a tiger that's one hundred percent guaranteed to be ferocious, and even a man-eating grizzly," the showman continued. "That's all to be eyeballed for the price of a quarter. You should count yourselves lucky, in fact, because in Des Moines we're charging two. But you all here are lucky. Blessed I'd even say." He shifted his gaze from Pa to Maman, but she quickly looked away. "No," the showman continued, "you won't find no better deal nowhere. A whole afternoon's entertainment, and one which you'll be talkin' about and discussin' for years."

"That include the carousel?" Pa asked, squinting up at the man, the creases in his face deep and chiseled.

Gertie desperately wanted to ask about Patsy Montana, but she didn't dare speak.

"Now, my good man," the showman continued, "the carousel is an extra five cents. But you won't want to miss it. Straight from the Chicago World's Fair. Won't get no better thrill. But suitable for the ladies, of course." He tipped his hat at Maman, who was still staring at the ground and gripping Pa's arm. "Eminently suitable. And for those who might be looking for an extra thrill," he went on, looking at Carl and Ernie, "those that don't frighten easily, that is, you might want to buy a ticket to the House of Freaks."

Gertie held her breath. She would positively love to see the House of Freaks!

"Now, I'll bet you my very life, you ain't never seen what lies inside that bastion of exotica," the showman said, then hunched forward in a conspiratorial sort of way. "I tell you, not one hundred yards from where you're standing, there exists such curiosities as the bearded lady; the sword swallower; the floating, talking head; the snake woman; the three-legged man; the two-headed baby, and, of course," he said, standing up straight and gesturing widely, "the Great Romanov, fortune teller extraordinaire. These are just *a few*—let me repeat, ladies and gentlemen—*a few* of the freaks, the oddities of nature, the truly strange, the *abominations* that can be beheld inside. Only an extra dime to see over fifty-two unbelievable, anatomically misshapen, and in some cases downright grotesque monstrosities!"

"No, Anders," Maman spoke up suddenly. "I'm not going. I won't be a part of this." She tugged on his arm. "Especially on the Sabbath."

Gertie, who had been practically salivating at every word that came from the showman's mouth, felt her stomach clench. Maman hadn't wanted to come in the first place, saying all manner of evil could be found at a place such as this, which, shamefully, had made Gertie want to come all the more.

"Now, now, now," the showman interrupted. "The House of Freaks certainly ain't for everyone, that's to be sure, but there is plenty of good wholesome fun to be had, all the same. Cotton candy and popcorn, too. Why, not just a moment ago, a preacher and his wife bought two tickets and went right in, happy and excited. Wished me a fine good day, they did. Mighty kind of them." He absently rubbed his nose.

"Reverend Chambers?" Maman asked.

Gertie held her breath, and as she did so, the showman suddenly flicked his gaze at her. It was as if he could see right through her, and she felt naked and exposed. Just as quickly, however, he shifted his gaze back to Maman.

"I do believe that was his name. Said he was heading for the lemonade stand and then to the bandstand to hear some of the fine musical acts we have lined up. I reckon if the minister and his good wife thought it proper . . ."

"Please, Maman," Felix whined, pulling at her skirt.

"Yes, please, Maman," chimed in Carl and Ernie.

"Come, Lisbet," Pa said gruffly. "We're here now. And I'd like to get a look at that bear. We won't go anywhere near the freaks. Reckon that's all a lot of hooey, anyway." He kept his eyes on the showman, as if he expected some last-minute trickery.

"Alright, then," Maman muttered with a deep sigh, her forehead crinkled. She refused to meet the showman's eyes and instead looked furtively at the crowd milling about, as if perhaps to spot Rev. Chambers herself.

Pa fished quarters from his pocket and begrudgingly paid the entrance fee for just the nine of them, as her oldest brothers, Arnie and Bjorn, were coming separately. After all, they were already down the mines and earned their own money, though neither of them had yet reached twenty. They were expected to give their wages to Pa, but he allowed them to keep a bit.

Gertie fiercely wished she had her own pocket money. She had begged to be allowed to get a job in town, but Maman had insisted she attend school, which she herself had not been allowed to do, something she had always regretted, she always said. Maman's mother had died when she was still very little, so she'd had to stay home and cook and clean for her father and brothers. Though this old story did not sound particularly nice, Gertie had long ago decided that it was preferable to her situation. She hated school with a passion and longed to be done with it, but her mother had been adamant. Gertie thought this unfair, especially as neither of her older sisters, Signe and Astrid, had been made to finish; they had gotten married instead.

The Gufftasons shuffled through the gates. Only Gertie looked back at the showman, but he had already turned his attention to the next group of people.

"Where do we go first, Pa?" Kerstin asked.

"Yeah, Pa," Frida added. "Can we go see the tigers?"

"I want to go on the carousel!" Carl shouted.

"For shame!" Mama chastised. "Pa's already paid for all of us to get in. You should be happy with seeing the sights. We don't need to be riding on that machine."

Pa stared sternly at each of them in that way of his that made them tremble. But instead of adding to Maman's repri-mand with his own particular brand of chastisement, which was swift and quietly ferocious, he instead fumbled for something inside his tiny inner jacket pocket, which was difficult on account of his permanently blackened fingers being so thick. Finally pulling out a small stack of dimes, he placed one in each of their hands. An astonished round of gratitude followed.

"When it's gone, it's gone," he said emotionlessly. "I'm gonna take Maman to see that there bear." He held out his arm to Maman as if they were at church, which was the only time he ever did.

Maman took it with what seemed a trace of hesitation and then held out her other hand. "Come, Felix; you stay with us."

"Can I come, too, Pa?" Frida asked. Pa gave a gruff nod, and Frida hurried to grab Felix's other hand.

"The rest of you stay out of trouble. Meet back here at sundown. Understand?"

"Yes, Pa!" they all said excitedly.

"Let's go to the carousel," Carl suggested as soon as they had disappeared.

Ernie and Ingrid and Kerstin excitedly agreed.

"But doesn't anyone want to see the House of Freaks?" Gertie asked. No one answered, instead filing after Carl, who was walking toward the spinning carousel. Not knowing what else to do, Gertie followed, but after a few steps, she shouted her question again.

"Ingrid, don't you want to see the House of Freaks?" Gertie asked, tugging the sleeve of her sister's dress.

"No, I want to go on the carousel and then buy some popcorn," she said defiantly and pulled away.

They had reached the whirling machine now. With its bright paint and flickering electric lights, it was certainly a thing of beauty. Slowly, the Gufftasons shuffled to join the line that wrapped all the way around it, feeling the churning music in their very chests. The melody was louder here, and even Gertie was mesmerized as she watched the ornately carved animals spin past. There were horses, a bear, a giraffe, a dolphin, and even a dragon, each bearing an innocent child with only a leather strap holding them down. Gertie decided she would mount one of the steeds . . .

But, no! she cautioned herself. She didn't want to spend her dime on the carousel, spinning endlessly and going nowhere. She would spend her money on the freaks and then seek out the bandstand.

She gazed back toward where the tents were staked, wondering if she dared go see the freaks all by herself. As she did, however, she unfortunately spotted Warren Klein, who stood a ways off, stupidly gazing at the carousel like all the rest.

Having no desire to speak to the likes of Warren Klein today, Gertie tried to nonchalantly step behind Kerstin. Warren was her classmate at school, the boring type who was studious and well behaved, and he would only ruin things now by trailing after her and stuttering uncontrollably. Much to Gertie's annoyance, he seemed to have lately taken a fancy to her, which confused her, as she was never very nice to him. She preferred the naughtier boys who were much more amusing.

Nevertheless, Warren had started to bring her a sweet each day and now carried her books for her as far as Holler Ridge, where the Gufftasons turned off the main road and descended down into Keystone. It was just a simple thing, but it was enough, plus the fact that he lived in town, to at least cause Gertie to consider.

But now was certainly not the time to entertain any of Warren's clumsy efforts at . . . at whatever he was trying to do, and thus she stood very still behind Kerstin. Her older sister, though, noticed her immediately and smoothly stepped to the side.

"Why! Look who's over there, Gerd. It's your beau."

"He's not my beau!"

"Why not? He seems alright to me, and he sure is sweet on you. You can't exactly be choosy, you know."

Ingrid and Carl giggled.

Gertie bit her lip and crossed her arms across her chest. She knew Kerstin was referring to her skinny body and her almost non-existent breasts. But she knew she had a pretty face, not like Kerstin, who had a big mole on her upper lip. "Neither can you, Kerstin! I don't see anyone knocking for you."

Kerstin scowled and then turned to where Warren was still looking about helplessly. "Yoo-hoo!" Kerstin called out sweetly. "Warren!"

Gertie shoved her, but it was too late. Warren had spotted her and was walking over with a big grin and his hands thrust deeply in his pockets. Gertie gave Kerstin one last scowl before Warren hurried up.

"Hello, G-Gertie!" He stood awkwardly in front of her.

"Oh, hello, Warren," Gertie answered weakly, trying to compose herself after her brief shoving match with Kerstin.

"Well, go on," Kerstin urged. "Don't you have more to say to your beau than that?"

Gertie felt her face flush and saw that Warren's did, too, despite his thick mask of freckles. Carl snickered.

"Just leave me alone!" Gertie snapped at no one in partic-ular and turned and stomped off.

"Gertie! You'll miss the carousel!" Ernie shouted.

Gertie continued marching across the grounds, not real-ly knowing where she was going, though she was aware that Warren was walking silently behind her, easily keeping pace. She was bristling with irritation, absolutely full up with it, though she couldn't rightly decide with whom. Though it burned her to admit it, she knew that Kerstin was right, that Warren was a good catch and that she could do worse. Much worse. Hadn't one of Mr. O'Reilly's boys trapped her behind the mercantile only a few weeks ago and . . . well, it was lucky that Ingrid had come along when she did. Even now, she was horrified by what he had tried to do. No, she refused to get tied down with anyone in Keystone.

Keystone wasn't even a real town, just a ramshackle collec-tion of buildings surrounding a dirty hole in the ground, no different than any other of the many mining camps scattered across southern Iowa. It was ironic that Keystone's mine was called "The Paradise," as the camp sprawled out around it was anything but. It consisted of a tiny mercantile, a blacksmith, a defunct tavern, and about twenty or thirty dwellings—or "the shacks" as they were called by people in Eddyville.

Eddyville was the closest proper town to the Keystone and boasted 961 souls, or at least that's what it said on the sign coming into town. Most people in Eddyville looked down on anyone from "the shacks," and Gertie couldn't blame them. Keystone didn't even have sidewalks, only planks of wood sunk into the mud. Once upon a time, she had envied her oldest sisters and dreamed of having a little house in town just like theirs. But now, thanks to Mr. O'Reilly and his radio, Gertie wanted something more than a house in town—something different. To see California, maybe, or the Yukon, even.

Only once did it occur to Gertie that she was *already* living in a sort of frontier town, but she had quickly shooed that thought away. Keystone was *not* at all like the fabled West of *The Rodeo Boys*. Keystone had not a jot of adventure, not to mention treasure or glamour. All it had was mud and misery. And as far as Gertie could tell, the men were not heroes on noble steeds, but brutes, given how often the women in Keystone walked around bruised.

No, she had decided. She would not get tied down here. She would not get serious about anyone, and that included Warren Klein, who was still following her as she stumbled over the uneven ground. Not even if Warren had strangely begun to consistently invade her dreams, which positively unnerved her. At least she *thought* it was Warren.

The dream was always the same. A boy calling out to her to wait for him. To take him home. His pleading was always desperate, and it tore at her heart so much that when she awoke she was always left feeling helpless and trapped. She could never quite make out the boy's features, as they were fuzzy and indistinct, but it *seemed* to be Warren. Did that mean they were connected somehow? That they were meant to be together? But surely that was wrong. She knew she didn't love Warren, though she suspected by the way he looked at her that he might love her. Or thought he did, anyway. How could anyone really know? Maybe she would grow to love him, the way Maman had with Pa.

Maman always told the story of how her marriage to Pa had practically been arranged back in Sweden after Pa had finished his duty in the cavalry. Gertie thought this barbaric, but

Maman said that it hadn't really been so bad. They were little more than strangers when they married, but they had grown to love each other in their own way. "Sometimes others can see things you can't. Anyway, here we are, eleven kids later," she said with a little smile. But Gertie didn't think that was proof of anything, certainly not love.

Pa, thankfully, was not the type that beat his wife, but Gertie often heard equally disturbing things coming through the thin wall that separated the only two bedrooms of their shack. Every night it was the same. Pa begging and Ma saying no until finally Pa got his way. Every night! It disgusted Gertie. She used to cover her head with her thin pillow, alternately hating Pa and then, in later years, Maman. Why didn't she just give in and get it over with so that they could all get some sleep?

"Gertie," Warren finally called out, startling her.

Reluctantly, Gertie stopped and looked around, careful not to meet his eyes. They were standing very near the bandstand, a gazebo-type structure erected where the land gently sloped into a depression. Rows of brown wooden folding chairs balanced unevenly on the rough ground before it, and though its strings of electric lights barely showed up amidst the brightness of the sun, Gertie thought it looked marvelous.

A big red-and-white-striped tent was pitched to the left, which various carnies dashed in and out of. Only a few people sat in the chairs waiting for the show to start. Or maybe they were just taking a rest, Gertie thought, from all the activity. She wondered when Patsy was scheduled to go on—

"G-Gertie," Warren repeated gently.

Gertie pulled her gaze away from the stage. He was wearing the same red plaid shirt he always wore, but for once he was not wearing his overalls. "Yes?" she asked, leaning against an old crumbling fence that ran along this bit of the ridge.

"Can I buy you some p-popcorn?"

"I'm not really hungry," she said, looking back at the bandstand.

"Wh-what about seeing the ani . . . ani . . . ani—" He stopped and closed his eyes as if to concentrate. "Animals?"

"Maybe later." Gertie gave him a small grimace of a smile.

Warren was silent for a few moments while she continued to look out at the crowd and then asked, "Wh-what *do* you want to do?"

Gertie considered. "I want to see the freaks." She looked at him, curious to see his reaction. Predictably, it was one of surprise.

"The f-f-freaks? Are you sh-sure, Gertie?"

Gertie let out a sigh. "Listen, Warren, I'll see you at school, alright? I have to go."

"G-Gertie, wait." He put a hand on her arm. "Gertrude—"

"My real name is Gerda," she interrupted. "I just told people at school it was Gertrude."

"Gerda, then." He swallowed loudly, his large Adam's apple bobbing up and down. She had never been this close to him, and she could see the blond hairs dusting his chin and upper lip.

"G-Gerda, y-you must have n-noticed that I c-care for you. Very much." He thrust his hands into his pockets but then removed them just as quickly. "I . . . I want to c-court you. To . . . to speak to your f-father. Will you . . . will you let me?" he asked, ending with a soft finish.

Speak to her father? Gertie was taken aback. She knew he liked her, but she wasn't expecting this! Not something this overt, and certainly not right now.

She took a step back. "I—"

"I know you m-might not f-feel the same. Not yet. But m-maybe you'll change your m-mind in a year. I'm not asking for you to m-marry me," he added with a sheepish grin, "just to c-court. Be your beau, as your sister c-calls me."

Gertie fixed her eyes on his chest, watching it rise and fall instead of looking up into his face. She could smell his scent: clean linen and soap and maybe wood. It was a good smell, not one her brothers or father ever had about them, and she found that she liked it. Very much. But still. She allowed herself to look at him briefly before letting her eyes roam back to the bandstand. More people were milling about now. Why didn't the music start?

"I like you, Warren," she began and was annoyed when she saw a big smile break out. "But I, well, I . . . I don't want to get stuck here. I want to see places. See people," she said, waving her hand at the bandstand.

"I c-can take you places," he said earnestly. "Wherever you want."

Gertie let out another sigh. He didn't understand.

He shocked her then by taking her hand in his and holding it very gently. "Gertie—" He swallowed again. "I know I'm not m-much, but I won't be like other m-men. I'd never hurt you. N-n-n-n-n-n——" Flustered, he stopped and looked at the ground. He took a deep breath and raised his eyes again to her. "I'd n-never t-touch you unless you . . . unless you wanted me to." He looked at her with such knowing in his eyes that Gertie suddenly paused in her own internal argument. He had somehow found his way to the quick of it. Maybe he, too, observed things, understood things more than she thought he did . . .

"Let m-me try to w-win your heart. Let me c-court you, and if at the end you don't want to m-marry me, then we'll both be f-free. I p-p-promise."

Gertie didn't know what to say. She knew she should say something, reject him, but all she could do was stare at his deep blue eyes. It was like staring into a peaceful lake, and it calmed her. Her eyes fell to his lips, then, his thick stuttering lips, and she wondered whether if he kissed her, his stuttering might go away. Perhaps he was under a spell, she imagined, and then scolded herself for being so silly. Why was her mind always wandering?

"C-can I speak to your f-father?" he asked again, more hopeful this time.

Speak to her father? No, not that! She was about to tell him such when he further surprised her by lifting her hand and softly kissing it. What was even stranger was the flush of excitement that raced through her. She had *never* seen a man in Keystone— or Eddyville, for that matter—do something like that, and again she distressingly wondered if there was more to Warren Klein than she had previously thought. She felt herself dangerously wavering. He *was* handsome in a simple kind of way, with his thick blond hair and broad shoulders. But there was something else. She felt safe with him, protected.

"Yes?" he almost begged.

As if in a trance, Gertie gave him a slow nod.

"Oh, G-Gertie!" His worried face relaxed a bit. "I'm g-going to make you so happy. I p-promise."

Gertie felt herself smile back, suddenly pleased with her decision. She did *like* him, she told herself again, pushing away her many hesitations, at least for this moment. It wasn't every day that a girl got asked to be courted, and she wanted to enjoy it. If nothing else, courting a boy—a man!—made her feel grown-up. Maybe now her older sisters would give her more respect. But fat chance of that—Kerstin was sure to find something about the whole thing to criticize, probably his stuttering. Well, what did it matter what Kerstin thought? Warren was handsome enough, had a good job after school at the hardware store, and lived in town. He saw the misery of this place and said he wouldn't be a part of it. Not in so many words, of course, but that's what he had meant.

"Do you ever listen to *The Rodeo Boys*?" she asked abruptly.

"*The Rodeo Boys?*" He grinned. "That's my f-favorite show!"

"No fooling?" she asked, feeling almost giddy.

"No fooling." He squeezed her hand. "Come on. Let's g-go find your father."

Suddenly, Gertie's stomach sank. She dreaded drawing Pa's attention to her, though she was pretty sure he wouldn't care less if Warren took her off his hands. One less mouth to feed. But he always insisted on being deferred to, like some kind of king, by the suitors who came along after his daughters.

She pulled her hand from Warren's. "I don't think I'm supposed to be there when you ask," she mumbled, feeling suddenly nauseous.

Warren's brow furrowed.

"That's how my sisters' husbands did it," she said, thinking back to how Signe's beau had appeared at their shack one Sunday afternoon, wearing a very stiff collar and tie and a jacket that was a little too tight and how they had all had to leave. And Astrid's had done something similar, but she couldn't remember all the details. "He can be mean sometimes," Gertie warned.

"I c-can handle myself," Warren said confidently.

Nervous, Gertie wondered if Pa would hold Warren's stutter against him. But why would he? She wondered if Maman would have a say in it. Maybe she should go along with Warren after all . . .

There was a stirring in the crowd, then, and Gertie's attention was drawn back to the bandstand. Three men were making their way up the wooden steps, each carrying a different instrument. One of them tapped the big silver microphone in front of him, and without any further preamble or introduction, the three of them spontaneously began to play.

With the first lick of the banjo, Gertie's heart sped up. She had no idea who they were, but it didn't matter. It was wonderful.

"You go on," she said absently to Warren, her eyes on the performers. "I'll wait right here for you."

"Are you sh-sure? I'm don't think I sh-should leave you alone." Warren shuffled uneasily.

"I'll be alright. I want to hear the music."

Warren hesitated. "Well, okay. But wait right here for me. P-promise?"

"Yes, I promise." Gertie gave him a quick look accompanied by a hurried smile. "You'd better hurry before he has too much to drink," Gertie advised, knowing that her father surely had his flask on him. "Go on!"

Still, Warren lingered. "Well, w-wish me luck," he said finally. He gave her one last look and then disappeared into the crowd.

CHAPTER 5

May 1923

Finally left alone, Gertie turned her full attention to the music and relaxed, leaning her full weight against the fence as her whole body began to tingle with the rapid twanging of the banjo and the deep thud of the bass. She recognized the song they were playing—"Frankie and Johnny"—and tapped her toes. Hearing the same music she heard on the radio performed live—*and* out here in the open, where the notes practically hung in the sticky air—was just about the best thing she had ever experienced. She felt jittery and alive, and for a moment, she wished Warren had stayed to hear it.

"Pretty damn good, ain't they?" asked a deep voice.

Startled, Gertie turned to see none other than the showman from the entrance! He filled the space around her and made her feel as if she was standing in the presence of someone famous. She hardly knew what to say. What *could* she say? *What had been his question again?*

"I couldn't help notice you tappin' yer toes. Thought to myself, must be an appreciator of good music. Am I right?" he asked with a daring little wink.

Gertie blushed and tried to turn her attention back to the bandstand. But she could feel his eyes on her.

"Bet yer waitin' for Miss Patsy Montana, am I right?"

Gertie looked back at him, surprised. "Yes . . . yes, I am," she stammered.

"I knew it." The showman gave her a self-satisfied grin.

"Is she really here?"

"She sure is, darlin'."

Something about the way he said "darlin'" made her stomach queasy, which she wasn't sure was a good thing or a bad thing. His black hair hung down to his collar and his dark eyes seemed to see right through her, just as they had back at the entrance. A part of her was intrigued, yet there was an element to him she didn't trust. She crossed her arms across her chest and looked back at the bandstand.

"You wouldn't be interested in meeting her, now would you?" He stuck his thumbs in his tiny waistcoat pockets.

"Meet her?" Gertie asked incredulously.

"Course! Why, darlin', Miss Patsy's a close personal friend of mine, and I know for a certainty she'd like to meet a pretty little thing like you. Come on; I'll take you to her." He held out his arm. "She's right down yonder in that tent there," he said, nodding toward the red-and-white-striped tent. "All the performers are down there. You can meet them all. I reckon this here's your lucky day, darlin'."

Gertie's mind raced. *Meet Patsy Montana?* It was too good to be true! Hurriedly, she put her hand on the showman's outstretched arm, but then paused, wondering if she could trust him. But surely she could . . . After all, wasn't he in charge of the whole carnival? And wait till she told the others! Wait till she told Warren! *Oh, Warren!* she suddenly remembered. Desperately, she looked around the crowd, but there was no sign of him.

"I can't." Gertie pulled her arm from the showman's grasp.

"You can't? You *can't* meet Patsy Montana?" he asked, as if she were crazy to pass up this chance. "Well, fine then." He gave her an irritated shrug. "Just thought you'd be excited, is all. Not many people get to meet her, you know." He perused the crowd, as if he were looking for someone else to ask.

"Oh, no, mister!" Gertie said, hurriedly. "It's not that I'm not excited. It's just that . . . it's just that I'm waiting for someone."

The showman gave another little shrug. "Well, you suit yerself. But it wouldn't take but more than a minute to meet a woman whose next stop is the Grand Ole Opry. Now that's a chance that only comes along once in a lifetime. But if you say you can't, then you can't. But I've got to get goin', so I'll wish you good day." He gave his magnificent top hat a curt tip in her direction.

"Don't be mad, mister!" Gertie exclaimed. "I just . . . it's just that I promised Warren that I'd wait right here for him. Can't we wait for him and *then* go down and meet her?"

"Well, that's not a bad idea, darlin', but Patsy's goin' on next."

Gertie wrung her hands. "Well, maybe we could come and meet her after the show?" she suggested weakly.

"I wish that were so, darlin', but Miss Patsy Montana is rushin' off right after this performance to catch the train bound for Nashville. So, it's now or never." When she didn't immediately respond, he gave her a third shrug and turned away. "Well, you enjoy the show," he called over his shoulder.

Gertie suddenly felt an odd panic. This was her only chance! Irritated, she looked desperately over the crowd again. What was taking Warren so long? Maybe Pa had already started drinking—the more he drank the more cantankerous he would be. She looked back at the showman who was making his way down the little slope toward the tent. He was almost halfway there already. *Oh, God! What should she do?*

Well, hadn't she come to the carnival specifically to see Patsy Montana? And here was her chance to meet her in the flesh! And if Miss Montana was scheduled to go on stage next, perhaps it *would* only take a minute. And surely Warren would wait, wouldn't he? Yes, he would. She knew that.

She began running in the direction of the showman.

"Wait!" she called. "Wait!" she shouted, spurred on by the sudden fear that she might already have lost her chance.

The showman wasn't responding. She felt sure he could hear her, couldn't he? She ran a bit faster.

"Wait!" she called more loudly, causing several people in the crowd to turn and stare.

The showman stopped with his hand on the tent flap, a big grin sliding across his face, and Gertie felt something flutter inside of her. She had pleased him, which pleased *her* for some reason. Making up for her idiotic hesitation, she ran faster until she stood breathless before him.

"I changed my mind," she said, panting slightly.

"I see that, darlin," he drawled, looking her up and down. "You won't be sorry. What's yer name, anyway?"

Gertie hesitated. She hated her name, Gerda. It sounded like something someone would name a cow or a goat. And

Gertie was little better. Trudy had a certain ring to it, she decided suddenly. Maybe even a bit of a theatrical one.

"Trudy," she said, trying it out in a low voice.

"Trudy?" the showman said, his eyebrows raised in what Gertie hoped was not amusement. "Well, *Trudy*, step right up. We don't call it the greatest show on earth for nothing, you know." He held the tent flap open.

The tent was bigger than she had expected it to be. And darker. She blinked rapidly to allow her eyes to adjust. The interior was vaulted, she eventually made out, with several large poles in the middle propping the striped canvas roof. Although she was glad to be out of the hot sun, she was surprised by how stuffy it was in here. It was like a big barn, really, thanks to the mingled smell of sawdust and hay and sweat. She was expecting something more exotic, something along the lines of *Ali Baba and the Forty Thieves*, the radio show Mr. O'Reilly sometimes let them listen to after *The Rodeo Boys* was over, though he said he had no use for foreigners and their evil ways.

"This way, darlin'" the showman said as he began to lead them through the tent. Gertie was surprised that there were so many people in the tent, most of them sitting on overturned soda pop crates, drinking and smoking cigarettes. A few of them were eating, and some were even sleeping on blankets on the ground. The showman barely gave any of them notice, although almost all of them gave *him* a deferential nod.

The showman was making a beeline for a little area blocked off by standing partitions, the panels of which were made of various scraps that appeared to have been haphazardly sewn together in no apparent pattern. Several men in black cowboy hats and rhinestone-studded shirts hovered about it, and

Gertie realized, with a sudden flush of excitement, that this must be Miss Montana's dressing room.

The showman turned to her. "Ready, darlin'?" he asked with another of his sly winks. "Let's go meet Miss Montana." He held out his arm again, and this time Gertie clutched it. She was grateful that she did, as she embarrassingly stumbled over a particularly stubborn tuft of grass as they made their way around the partitions. She had forgotten that she was in actuality still outdoors.

In only a few more steps, Gertie found herself standing behind a woman seated at a little mirrored vanity, which seemed a bit absurd, even to Gertie, perched as it was in the middle of a tent.

"Got someone here to see you, Pats," the showman said.

Gertie felt her stomach clench as Miss Patsy Montana herself turned and gave her a little grin. She was older than Gertie expected, as evidenced by the tiny crow's feet around her eyes, but even so, Gertie was enamored.

"Oh, yeah?" the woman drawled. "What's your name, kid?"

Gertie was mortified to discover that she couldn't actually speak. All she could do was stand there and stare.

"Name's Trudy," the showman said. "Trudy, this here's Miss Patsy Montana."

It took all of Gertie's concentration to make her head nod in what she hoped was a polite way.

"Trudy, eh?" Patsy asked, picking up her hairbrush. "That with a *y* or an *ie*? Had an aunt named Trudy."

What kind of question was this—*y* or *ie*? She didn't have the slightest idea.

"She's a little young, Lor, even for you. Don't you think?" Patsy turned back to the mirror.

"Now, now," the showman said, "let's not jump to nasty conclusions, Pats. Give me a little bit of credit."

Patsy continued to pat her hair into place.

"I . . . I sure do like your music, Miss Montana," Gertie managed to get out. "I've heard you on *The Grand Ole Opry*. My neighbor has a radio, and we listen sometimes."

"Do ya?" Patsy asked, slowly turning to study her again. "Well, you go on over there and fix me a drink, *Trudy*," she said, handing her an empty glass. "With ice."

"Sure, Miss Montana!"

Gertie took the glass and wandered toward a big metal tub in the corner, banked with sawdust. She peeled back the thick canvas covering to reveal a block of ice. Gertie pulled out the ice pick jabbed into the block and began chipping away until she had enough to fill the glass. Behind the tub were several brown jugs that Gertie assumed to be hooch. Carefully, she picked one up, uncorked it and filled the glass with the amber liquid.

Gertie herself did not care for hootch. Bjorn had let her try some once, and she had woken the next day with a terrible headache. But it made sense that a big star like Miss Montana would drink it. She probably needed it to steady her nerves.

Drink in hand, Gertie hurried back to the partitions. The showman was bent over Patsy, whispering something, but at Gertie's approach, he stood. He had a guilty look to him, but all he said was, "Ladies," and touched the brim of his hat. He gave Gertie a little wink and then surprised her by ducking out of a nearby tent flap.

Gertie wasn't sure what to do next—should she follow him?

"That mine, kid?" Patsy asked, nodding at the drink in Gertie's hand.

"Oh, yes, Miss Montana! Here you are." Gertie nervously handed her the glass.

Patsy took a long drink. "Help me with my costume, would ya?" she asked, nodding toward a white cowgirl dress hanging from a nail pounded into one of the wooden tent poles. The dress was short and studded with rhinestones like the Cowboys', only this had fringe hanging from the sleeves. How had she not seen that when she came in? It was positively marvelous!

"Men are useless," Patsy grumbled as she stood, simultaneously draining her drink. Gertie blushed to see that her idol was wearing nothing but a cream-colored slip and white cowboy boots. Thankfully, the Cowboys had wandered a small ways off, but they were still close enough to be able to see Miss Montana. But if they *did* notice that Miss Montana was standing there practically naked, they did not seem to care.

"Come on, kid!"

Gertie snapped to attention and hurried to the costume. Gingerly, she removed it from the hanger then delicately carried it the short distance to where Patsy waited.

She was surprised when Patsy took it roughly and pulled it over her head with no more deference than one would employ in slipping on a nightgown. "Hook me up, will you?" Patsy demanded, turning her back to Gertie. Gertie paused at the sight of the long row of buttons. "Hurry up, kid, I've got to go on in a minute."

Gertie buttoned as fast as she could, but her fingers were still wet from the ice tub. Finally, however, she managed to get the job done. "There you are," she said proudly, and took a step back, clasping her arms nervously behind her.

Patsy reached for a white cowboy hat sitting on the edge of the little vanity. The Cowboys, seeming to sense that their moment was almost up, adjusted their own hats and tightened the red bandanas around their necks. Gertie could feel a nervous tension in the air now, the way she could feel a storm brewing.

"Same set, Pats?" one of the Cowboys asked lazily.

Suddenly, the showman poked his head back in through the tent. He had a cigarillo between his teeth. "Ready?" he asked Patsy.

Patsy gave him a quick nod then another to the Cowboy who had asked the question. "'cept we're gonna open with *The Prisoner's Song.* Everyone got that?" she said, glancing around. There were various murmurs as the Cowboys downed the last of their own glasses of hooch. "You stayin' to watch the show?" Patsy asked Gertie.

Gertie nodded eagerly.

"Good. I like you. Stay away from Lorenzo, though. He's a pile a trouble. Like I said, men are useless. You remember that. Ready, boys? Let's go!" she said with a whoop, then charged out of the tent flap. There was loud applause from the crowd, which, Gertie observed as she peeked out from inside the tent, had grown remarkably. Every brown chair was full, and many more people were standing.

Warren! Gertie eyed the spectators gathered along the dilapidated fence. *Oh, no! How long had she been gone?* Oh, she was forever doing this—getting distracted and losing track of time. It was one of the reasons she was no good at school.

Miss Montana was greeting the crowd, and as much as she desperately wanted to stay and listen, her mind was filled with worry. She hoped Warren was still waiting! They could watch the show together, and she could tell him all about meeting Patsy Montana.

Just as she tried to slip through the tent flap however, the showman appeared on the other side, blocking her way.

"Where *you* goin', darlin'? The show's just starting."

"But I *have* to go," Gertie begged, trying to squeeze her way past. "Please, mister." As she looked up into his face, a wisp of panic began to take hold.

"What's your hurry?" he drawled. "And you don't have to call me 'mister.' You can call me Lorenzo."

"Lorenzo, then," she said. "Please, I'm . . . I'm supposed to meet someone."

"Your beau?" Lorenzo asked with such amusement that Gertie felt a sudden urge to strike him. Why did he seem to know everything? Everything about her, as if he could read her mind. It both terrified and intrigued her.

"Well, come on then, darlin'," he said stepping aside. "Let's go find this beau of yours."

"Oh, no, that's okay." She gave him a weak smile. "I know you're plenty busy. But thank you . . . Lorenzo."

"Nonsense! Jimmy can take over for a little while," he said, signaling with two raised fingers to one of the carnies.

Gertie suddenly wanted to get away from the tent *and* him. It had been spectacular meeting Miss Montana, but now she only wanted to find Warren. What if he had brought Pa and Maman back with him?

Without another word, however, Lorenzo looped her hand through his arm. Sensing she wasn't going to get away from him, she decided it would be faster to just proceed rather than waste time by arguing. With a grin and a low little whistle, Lorenzo led her out of the tent toward the ridge. He walked slower than Gertie would have liked, sharing interesting tidbits about the carnival as they ambled along, and Gertie wondered if he was doing it on purpose.

When they finally reached the spot where Gertie was supposed to be waiting, Warren was nowhere to be seen, nor was anyone from her family. Worried, Gertie watched the people strolling by with food purchased at one of the wagons—ice cream, popcorn, lemonade, taffy apples, and, of course, pasties—and enjoying the music. Patsy and the Cowboys were in full swing, and she was upset; not only had she apparently lost Warren, she was missing the show—the very thing she had come here to see!

Where *was* he? Maybe Pa had said no after all, and he hadn't the heart to face her? But no, that wasn't like Warren . . . was it?

"Guess he's not comin'," Lorenzo said when Patsy started belting out her fourth song. He leaned against the fence, casually crossing his arms and legs. "If it was me, though, I sure wouldn't leave a pretty young thing like you waitin'."

Gertie bit her lip. She wasn't sure whether to be irritated or flattered.

"Tell you what." He was still leaning. "Why don't you come back down to the tent with me, wait for Miss Patsy to be done. You can catch up with this Warren later. He'll understand. People miss each other in crowds all the time. You can find him any ol' time, but you'll never get this chance again. Hell, I bet Miss Patsy would even give you an autograph. Imagine that. Miss Patsy's autograph!"

Gertie looked around again. She *did* feel bad about missing Warren, but for all she knew, he could be still talking to Pa. And an autograph? This was a once-in-a-lifetime opportunity; she saw that. She could rub it in Kerstin's face, for one thing, and maybe take it to school. Then maybe she wouldn't be dismissed so easily as being a bit of trash from the shacks.

"Come on, darlin'," the showman said in a sultry voice that made her feel older and free, pretty even. The fact that someone like *him* was interested in someone like *her* made her feel almost giddy, ethereal. But surely this thing, this feeling he was igniting inside of her was wrong. She had never once felt this way around Warren, and with a fresh prick of worry, she wondered if this was a sign, like it wasn't meant to be with Warren, after all.

"Come on," Lorenzo whispered, his dark, mysterious eyes boring into her. "Let's go."

"Alright," she said finally with a tiny smile and took his arm. *What harm will it do?* she asked herself.

Gertie spent the rest of the afternoon in the tent with the various performers and carnival hands. Lorenzo rarely left her side and introduced her to so many people that she soon forgot about Warren. Lorenzo offered her some hooch, but when she declined, he produced a different bottle.

"This here is mighty fine wine." He poured the contents into three glasses he had rummaged from Patsy's vanity. "All the way from California, this is," he said, though the bottle had no label.

Gertie perked up at the mention of California and eagerly took a sip after Lorenzo clinked his glass against hers. It was terrible! Dry and bitter. But Gertie was determined to finish it, especially after Patsy waltzed in and downed the glass Lorenzo gave her in one gulp.

"You still here, kid?" she said, looking Gertie up and down. "Well, I did try to warn you. Help me out of this thing, would ya?" She turned her back. "We gotta get on the road."

Gertie set down her wine and hurriedly began unbuttoning Patsy's costume. When it was finally undone enough for Patsy to peel herself out, she turned and looked back at Gertie. "Thanks, kid. Go on and fix me a drink, would ya?"

Gertie was confused. How did she have time for a drink if she was rushing off to Nashville? Well, who was she to question Miss Montana? She was happy to be of service.

Anxiously, she weaved her way through the performers to the ice tub. In her haste, however, she almost ran right into a man standing beside it. It was if he had just appeared in front of her.

"Oh, I'm sorry! I . . . I didn't see you."

The man turned, and Gertie was shocked to see how very similar he looked to Lorenzo. They could almost be brothers, Gertie decided, except for the scar running down this man's cheek. He was dressed in a long purple cloak edged in gold braiding, and a turban of sorts sat on his head. He didn't smile at all, but simply stared at her, rubbing his hands together as if he were cold. Gertie suddenly felt very uneasy.

"Do you wish me to tell you your future?" he asked mysteriously.

Gertie stared at him for several moments before it dawned on her who this man must be. "You're the fortune-teller, aren't you?"

"Yes," he said simply. "You are easy to read. There is much I could tell you."

Gertie hesitated. Surely this man couldn't *really* tell her her fortune, could he? After all, he was just a performer, wasn't he? And what if he told her she would end up marrying a miner and be stuck here all her life, or something equally dreary? No, best not to know, she decided. And anyway, wasn't fortune-telling a sin?

"You seek adventure, do you not?" he asked before she could say anything.

Gertie let out a little gasp, her curiosity piqued. She found herself giving him a little nod.

"You will certainly have a life of adventure," the fortune-teller began, closing his eyes as if concentrating or trying to see something. He was interrupted, however, by Lorenzo's sudden appearance.

"I see you've met my cousin, Roman," he said gruffly.

"There is a man in your life," Roman continued in his deep, slow voice.

"Yes, that's true," Gertie said eagerly.

"He will promise you things, but you must not listen. You must run away from him before it is too late."

"What?" Gertie's stomach suddenly bottomed out.

"I see much sorrow and suffering. I am saying this now to warn you." He opened his eyes to look steadily at Lorenzo.

"Alright, alright, Roman," Lorenzo said. "That's enough. Can't you see you're scaring the young lady?"

"I can only speak the truth. You know this, Lorenzo."

"Well, sometimes you should just keep it to yourself," Lorenzo snarled.

Gertie barely heard them argue back and forth as she set down Patsy's glass, her mind racing. Should she really run away from Warren? Surely this was just part of the fortune-teller's act. But why would he say such things?

"You'd better get back to the booth before Gideon sees you," Lorenzo snapped, and Gertie saw a flicker of something cross the fortune-teller's eyes, maybe fear?

"Farewell, Gerda," he said.

Goosebumps instantly covered Gertie's arms and neck. How could he possibly know her name? Her *real* name?

"I will see you again," he said cryptically and then shot Lorenzo a final, disapproving look.

"Thought your name was Trudy." Lorenzo gave her another one of his grins, but Gertie thought it seemed forced. "Tryin' to outfox me, eh? Well, I can keep yer secret, darlin'."

Gertie stared at the opening of the tent where Roman had disappeared, as if he might reappear at any moment. What if what he said to her *was* true? What should she do?

"Don't pay no mind to what he says, darlin'."

Lorenzo put his arm around her, a gesture which, in a remote part of her brain, Gertie knew she should protest. Perhaps it really was time to go back and find her family. She needed to think, but the wine she had drunk was very strong; it made her feel fuzzy . . .

"That's just part of his act. Him being all dramatic like that," Lorenzo said, gesturing widely with his free hand. "Don't you pay him no mind." He released her then. "You'd best get fixin' that drink for Patsy," Lorenzo encouraged with false cheerfulness. Something had changed between them, but Lorenzo seemed to be trying hard to turn it back, whatever it was.

"Yes, okay." Shaking off her unease, Gertie reached for the ice pick and chipped away at the ice. Lorenzo poured out the hooch, then together they made their way back to where Patsy was standing with the Cowboys, smoking a cigarette and laughing.

"There you are. Thought you got lost."

"Say, Pats, how about an autograph for Trudy here." Lorenzo took the drink from Gertie and handed it to Patsy.

"An autograph?" she asked as she took the glass, and Gertie suddenly felt very silly. "You mean one of those glossy snaps? Sure, kid, but I don't have none on me. You'll have to go back to the wagon," she said to Lorenzo.

Gertie thought Lorenzo might be upset at the dismissive treatment, but her answer seemed to delight him. "Now that's a darned good idea, Pats. You come with me, Trudy. I'll show you the wagon."

"That's alright, Lorenzo," Gertie said hurriedly. "It doesn't matter."

"Nonsense!" He put his arm around her again. "You look like you could use a little air."

The mention of fresh air was actually quite welcome, but when they emerged from the flap, a ray of the descending sun hit her square in the face. Was the sun already near to setting? She would have to meet her family soon!

Again, Lorenzo seemed to sense her distress. "This way, darlin'."

He led her through the crowd before she could say anything, moving much faster than he had when they had been searching for Warren. She looked for her family as they hurried along, though it occurred to her that she didn't exactly want to run into them while on the arm of the showman. How would she explain it all?

Eventually, they ended up in a small grove of pines standing sentinel at the entrance of the carnival.

"Here we are!" Lorenzo said, dramatically gesturing at what looked like a big, oversized barrel on wheels, like a gypsy caravan. Unlike the rest of the carnival's structures, the caravan was painted a dark green with no ornamentation, perhaps to help it blend in. Though it lacked outward gaiety, Gertie couldn't help but be intrigued. It looked like something out of a fairy tale, like the cottage that had appeared in the woods for Hansel and Gretel or Little Red Riding Hood . . . or, better yet, it was what she imagined the chuck wagon looked like on *The Rodeo Boys*.

After moving a battered little stool in front of the tiny door, Lorenzo stepped up, fumbling for something in his pocket. He eventually produced a key and unlocked the black padlock hanging from a chain around the door's antique handle as easily as if he were undoing a belt buckle. He pulled the chain through the handle and tossed it on the ground as easily as if he really had pulled off his belt, and Gertie was disturbingly reminded of Pa. Lorenzo dispelled this image, however, when he pushed open the door with a squeak and jumped off the stool.

"Home sweet home," he said.

"You live here?" Gertie asked tentatively.

"Well, not all the time. But when we're on the road. Go on in. I'll show you around."

Gertie peered up at the dark interior. She was wildly curious to see what it looked like inside, but a stray thought suddenly wiggled its way through her mind that she shouldn't go into a strange man's home, alone.

"I'll just wait out here for you." She gave him what she hoped as a convincing smile.

Lorenzo let out an irritated sigh. "Come on, darlin'. Don't you trust me yet?" he asked. Roughly, he stepped inside. "Fine with me if you want to be that way. Just thought you'd like to see it, is all."

The look of hurt on his face made her stomach clench. Quickly, she thought the situation through again. She supposed that Lorenzo wasn't *really* a strange man; she had spent the afternoon with him, after all. Besides, this wasn't really a house. It was so delightfully small.

"I'll be out in a minute," he snapped.

"No, Lorenzo, wait! I'll come."

"Sure?" He seemed unconvinced.

"Yes, I'm sure."

His face relaxed into an immediate grin, which irritated Gertie—his almost immediate change of mood was like that of a child who had gotten his way—but she decided to ignore it.

"Well, come on, then, darlin'. Get yourself on in here. Time's a wastin'." He reached down to help her up.

A ripple of unease passed over her, but Gertie pushed it away. With a last look behind her, she took his hand and followed him into the darkness.

CHAPTER 6

May 1923

Gertie stumbled back out into the crowd, not really sure where to go when she miraculously spotted Frida, not far off. Slowly, as if in a dream, she began walking toward her and saw with relief that her family was also near. She blushed as she approached them, her cheeks hot with embarrassment at what had just happened not five hundred feet away in the caravan.

"There you are!" said Frida, clearly annoyed. "We've been looking everywhere for you. Why's your face all red?"

Gertie felt her mother's eyes on her and fumbled for an excuse. "I . . . I—"

Blessedly, Felix began to cry over some trivial thing, and Maman's attention was distracted as she hauled him into her arms. Gertie let out a long, slow breath, grateful for once to not be allowed to finish a sentence.

"She was probably with Warren," Kerstin tittered.

Gertie felt stabs of guilt at the mention of Warren, but before she could even open her mouth to respond, Carl and Ernie began making cooing noises.

"Yeah, Gertie," chirped Frida, "tell us all about it. He came to see Pa, you know."

"W-w-w-w-Warren!" Carl crowed.

"Shut up, you lot," Pa slurred. He looked blearily at Gertie, his arm around Maman, who seemed to be partially holding him up with one arm while holding Felix in the other. Gertie could not help but think of how she resembled a pack mule and suddenly felt like crying. "Warren wants to court you," Pa said with a hiccup. "I said he could have you. That's what you wanted, wasn't it?"

"Come along, Anders. We can discuss it in the morning," Maman said, struggling under the weight of Felix and trying to get Pa moving forward at the same time.

"Here, Maman, give him to me." Frida tried to peel away a now-squealing Felix.

"Stop your blubbering, Runt," Pa shouted.

Felix obeyed and lowered his head onto Frida's shoulder, putting his thumb in his mouth as he did so.

Pa's reprimand had quieted them all. As they plodded toward the wagon, however, Gertie felt a rising sense of panic. She simply couldn't go back home now. For one thing, once they saw her in the light, albeit dim, they were sure to be able to tell what had happened. What Lorenzo had done. She blushed yet again, thinking of it. But even more than the fear that her family would find out, she was positively overcome by a desire to not be separated from Lorenzo.

Tentatively following him into the caravan, she had been delighted to find that the inside also resembled something out of a fairy tale. There was a little bed that looked as if it doubled as a sofa built into the wall opposite a table. A trunk with many travel stickers sat at the foot of it, and there were even little shelves on the curved walls for mugs and other pieces of pottery. While Lorenzo made a show of searching for something in the trunk, presumably the "glossy snaps," Gertie looked around, charmed by the idea of life on the road. She was startled, then, when Lorenzo suddenly stood up, empty-handed, and pulled her to him, planting a big kiss on her!

Gertie had never been kissed before, unless she counted Warren kissing her hand, which she didn't. Although the shock immobilized her, the sensation wasn't unpleasant, and she eventually began to feel an errant tremor dart through her as he caressed her lips, tugging at them slightly. Tentatively she dared to move her mouth as well, though it felt strange.

"That's it, darlin'," Lorenzo said hoarsely. "You're getting' the hang of it."

Gertie blushed and tried to push him away, but he didn't even budge an inch. "What are you doing?"

"Now, darlin'," he said soothingly, rubbing her cheek with the back of his fingers, which caused an instant clenching in her stomach. "Don't you play hard to get. I know what you want," he said, bending forward to kiss her again.

He was gentle this time, almost teasing, brushing her lips with his and then pulling away. Gertie felt a heat shoot through her, and every extremity began to vibrate as he continued to kiss and caress her lips. She was shocked by how immediately her body was responding to his touch. She wasn't sure what to do with herself, where to put her hands, though his seemed to know exactly where to go. When they crept down her backside, however, she grew alarmed and forced herself to take a step back.

"You don't know what I want," she panted. Part of her was terrified; she knew she was in a very dangerous situation, but a part of her was wildly attracted to him for that same reason. In a way, she was flattered that he wanted someone like her. Not only was he in charge of the whole carnival, he was friends with Patsy Montana! But more than that, he was terribly exotic, with his piercing black eyes and straight dark hair that skirted his collar—a length Pa would never have allowed on any of his sons. He even smelled different, like spices and pine trees and tobacco, and it was oddly pleasant.

But still, she felt a little electric hum of warning in the back of her mind. She knew what he wanted, and she knew she shouldn't give it to him. But how could she say no to someone such as himself? And what if he just took it?

"Oh, I think I do, darlin'. A pretty little thing like you," he said, brushing her hair back behind her ear and then leaning forward to kiss her there. Gertie felt herself stiffen as he peppered her neck with little kisses.

"You don't need to be afraid, darlin'. I won't hurt you. Don't you trust me?" he whispered in her ear. He moved his lips to hers, tugging at her bottom lip and then tentatively touching his tongue to hers, which sent a guaranteed electric current through the whole of her body.

Gertie felt herself giving in, *wanting* to give in, but she managed to break free once more, balling her hands into fists and pressing them against his broad chest. "No, Lorenzo. I . . . I've got to go."

"Go? Things are just getting interesting," he said, kissing her neck again. Again, she wavered as he continued kissing her, this time his hands brushing across her breasts. She felt a responding tug in her lower regions.

"No, Lorenzo, please," she begged, then summoned all her strength and pushed him away so there was at least one foot of space.

There was a moment of tension then, as they stared at each other, Lorenzo cool and composed, except for a lock of hair that had fallen across one eye, and her, hot and quivering.

To her dismay, he closed the space between them with one quick step and grabbed her by the upper arms, planting another kiss on her lips. A long, sloppy kiss in which his tongue fully found hers. She was shocked by how shamefully her body responded, her own passion growing by the second. His hands again found her breasts, and this time he blatantly rubbed them through her dress with his thumbs. A strangled little gasp escaped her.

When she opened her eyes, a coy smile played across Lorenzo's face as he fondled her. A part of her was disturbed by the fact that he was making no attempt to hide the pleasure he felt in seducing her, but another part of her didn't care.

"You like it, don't you, darlin'?" he cooed, kissing her again. He pressed her tightly to himself, his hands traveling around to her buttocks as his lips stroked hers. He led her back toward the bed without breaking his kiss and then pulled her down, his hands moving over her body all the while. Gertie was engulfed in pleasure, every nerve in her body firing, and she knew there was no way she could fight him now, nor did she really want to. This was a passion she hadn't known existed.

She stiffened a little, though, when she felt his hand roam under her dress until his fingers reached her underthings. "Don't be afraid, darlin'" he said smoothly, as he slipped them underneath and began to caress her. Embarrassingly, she let out a low groan. "That's it, darlin'." Breathing heavily himself, he continued kissing her neck and fondling her until she felt something begin to erupt within her. She could no longer hold it back, even if she wanted to. She let go, then, and shuddered with pleasure, crying out loudly as she did so. He continued to kiss her as her body went limp.

"Told you I knew what you wanted."

She opened her eyes and saw him grinning at her with that cocky smile. In a moment of tenderness, she wanted to reach out and touch his face, but before she could, he abruptly climbed off the bed. She wasn't sure what she was supposed to do, so she just lay there, exposed, feeling exhilarated and ashamed at the same time.

"Guess we got a little carried away, didn't we?" Lorenzo reached for a cigarillo from the pack sitting on the little table and lit it. He inhaled deeply and blew out a cloud of smoke through his nostrils.

Awkwardly, Gertie pushed her dress back down. She could feel that her underthings were sticky and wet and that her face was flushed. What had she done?

Lorenzo pulled her up and gave her a hard kiss on the lips. "You're still a virgin, if that's what you're worried about," he said huskily, again as if able to read her mind. "This was just a little taste of what the real thing is."

But she already knew what the real thing was like . . . For one thing, hadn't she heard Pa and Maman every night? And yet, Maman never seemed to get this amount of pleasure out of it, at least as far as Gertie could tell.

Lorenzo took another deep inhale of his cigarillo and roughly ran his hand through his hair. She could see he was still tightly wound, not finished. When he stepped toward her, she instinctively backed away until she felt her back pressed against the door. He stretched out an arm on either side of her head, trapping her, his stub of a cigarillo still in one hand.

"Now, darlin', you've got to promise me you'll come back tomorrow," he said thickly, dropping his arms to put a knuckle under her chin. He raised her face to his and kissed her again, softly this time. "I've just got to see you again; you understand? Promise you'll come back tomorrow." He ran his fingers along the side of her breast as he kissed her.

"I can't, Lorenzo," she murmured between kisses. "I have to go back to Keystone."

"You'll find a way, won't you? You're clever. There's so much I could show you." His hands traveled behind her, and he again clutched her buttocks, pressing her to him. She felt his hardened state and felt another rush of both fear and arousal. "You're mine now," he said sternly. "And don't you forget it. Promise me."

Gertie didn't say anything.

"I said promise," he commanded loudly and kissed her hard.

"Yes, Lorenzo," she said breathlessly, "I promise."

She had no intention of ever returning, of course, but now, as she was being led to the wagon behind Pa and Kerstin and all the rest of them, she wasn't sure she could leave. If she went with them, she was certain she would never see Lorenzo again. She couldn't go back to the shack, and she couldn't possibly be with Warren. The thought nauseated her now, as did the prospect of fielding questions and being teased.

Quickly, she moved up to walk next to her mother.

"Might I stay with Signe tonight?" Gertie asked quietly. "Or maybe until the baby is born?" she added with a stroke of genius. "I could help her with the boys."

Maman just kept walking, Pa nearly asleep on her shoulder at this point, his arm draped loosely around her.

"Maman?"

"I suppose so," Maman finally said with a sigh. "It's not a bad idea. Did you speak with Signe, though?"

"Well, not . . . not today, but she did say when we saw her last that I could come stay. You remember, don't you, Maman? She *did* say that."

"Yes, yes." Maman gave another sigh. "Yes, alright. But make sure you really help. Don't make more work for her."

"Can I go, too?" Ingrid asked from the other side of Pa. "I can help."

"No!" Gertie said vehemently, irritated that Ingrid had been listening.

"Me, too," Kerstin chimed in. "I should be allowed, Maman; I'm older."

"I asked first!" Gertie retorted, frantic that her brilliant opportunity was about to be stolen.

"Gertie and Ingrid can go," Maman said.

"But, Maman," Kerstin whined. "I'm older; it should be me. I'd be more help than those two."

"I need you at home. You can go later."

"She just wants to see Warren, Maman! Can't you see that? She probably has it all arranged!"

"No, I don't!" Gertie said angrily, feeling in this moment that she might actually hate Kerstin. But she *had* brought up a rather distressing fact. In her desperation to think of a way to remain in town, Gertie had not considered the possibility of running into Warren. She would have to avoid him somehow. Maybe he wouldn't find out. But of course he would. He would drive out tomorrow to Keystone, looking for her, and they would tell them she was at Signe's. Suddenly this plan was not sounding as perfect as she had originally thought . . .

"You'd better watch her, Maman," Kerstin said sharply. "She's a wily one. I've been saying that for years, but no one listens to me."

"That's enough, Kerstin," Maman said.

"Maman," Gertie began, deciding to gamble further, "I think I should go alone, don't you think? Ingrid will just be underfoot."

"I will not!" Ingrid said indignantly. "I can help as much as you, bossy pants!"

"Either the two of you go, or none at all." Maman's voice was weary. "Now that's enough."

"Shut up, you lot!" Pa slurred, suddenly lifting his head.

"Shh, Anders. Almost there," Maman cooed, walking toward where the wagon stood amongst a collection of others. Their horse, Betsy, was tethered a short distance away. "Help me, Kerstin," she said as she slumped Pa into the back. "Carl, get Betsy," Maman instructed.

The rest of the kids began climbing into the cart, careful to give Pa a wide berth, while Gertie and Ingrid stood beside.

"Best be off now before it gets full dark," Maman said. "Go on. Give Signe my love. Tell her and Astrid I'm sorry we didn't get to see them today."

Uncommonly pleased with herself, Gertie turned and hurried off, not waiting for Ingrid. If Gertie had known, however, that it was the last time she would ever see her mother, she might have given her a hug and told her that she loved her. Many times in the future, she wished that she could redo this moment, but alas, it was never to be.

CHAPTER 7

June 1923

Gerda Elizabet Gufftason and Norman Guglielmo De Lorenzo were married on June 2, 1923, in a late-night ceremony in the front room of the Reverend Wilson's home in Ottumwa, Iowa, which Gertie was told often doubled as a makeshift wedding chapel. Gertie wasn't sure of the Reverend Wilson's denomination, but she wasn't about to object. The minister's wife served as her maid of honor, and an elderly man who rented a room from the Wilsons was the best man. Gertie was surprised to learn that Lorenzo's real name was Norman, but she decided to ignore this, remembering that, after all, she, too, had fibbed about *her* name, initially telling him that it was Trudy. Likewise, she did not want to start her marriage on a sour note.

As it had happened, Signe had not been overly pleased to see her and Ingrid on her doorstep. She had reluctantly made up a pallet on the floor next to her two little boys then waddled back to bed, grumbling at the late hour. The morning found her no kinder—she assigned Gertie to work in the garden all day and Ingrid to help her bake.

After only an hour of kneeling in the dirt, sluggishly pulling weeds, Gertie began to regret her decision. First of all, she realized, she should have asked to go to Astrid's, as she was nicer, more like Maman. But then again, Astrid was newly married with no children yet, so it would have been harder to persuade Maman she needed help. But infinitely worse was her regret over what had happened with Lorenzo. How could she have let herself get that carried away?

She tossed a clod of dirt at the peeling fence. Her feverish excitement had dissipated into embarrassment and shame in the light of day. Somehow, she had managed to give a promise to *two* men in one day, neither of which she really wanted to keep. She wondered how long Warren had waited before he finally left. She felt terrible, but maybe it was for the best. It was clear after what had happened between her and Lorenzo that she could never be with Warren. Warren, she knew, would never be able to elicit that level of passion in her, and having tasted it now, she wasn't sure she could live without it. And even if she could, she didn't think she could face Warren, ever look him in the eye. She was too ashamed. He deserved someone much better than her, she decided nobly.

But on the other hand, it was out of the question to keep her promise to Lorenzo. Even if she wanted to return to him, how would she get away from Signe and Ingrid? And, anyway, he had probably not even meant it. What would he care if she came back when there were so many pretty performers lounging around? Surely, he had been teasing. How could he possibly be interested in a girl like her? Suddenly, she felt very small and vulnerable, the way she did in front of Pa sometimes.

She let out a deep, sad breath. She should have gone back to Keystone. Here in town, not only was she too close to both Warren *and* Lorenzo, she would have to be Signe's slave for days instead of Maman's. She wished she had been assigned to bake instead of toiling in the hot sun, as even the heat of the kitchen would be preferable to having to hear the music of the carnival, drifting across town on the heavy air. It was coming from the carousel, still spinning endlessly but going nowhere, its carved animals trapped in perpetual motion. Nevertheless, it called to her like a siren, making it nearly impossible not to think of Lorenzo—his exotic good looks, his confidence, and, if she was honest, the touch of his hands. Even now, in the hot sun, she felt a shiver run through her.

Gertie worked all morning, stopping only for the meager lunch Signe had prepared. Gertie had expected some little bit of praise for having nearly finished the weeding, but Signe barely acknowledged her effort at all and instead instructed her to whitewash the fence.

That was hours ago, and Gertie now tossed her frayed paintbrush into the pail of whitewash at her feet and put a hand on her lower back and stretched, looking in the direction of the carnival. She could just see the top of the red-and-white striped tents and a few of the electric lights. Somehow the music seemed louder, and as the sun began to set, an ache within her began to rise. Surely, it wouldn't hurt to stroll over? Absently, she began to pick off strips of the curling paint. It was certainly *not* to see Lorenzo. It was wrong, she knew, what they had done. Shameful. And even if she wasn't ashamed, which she was, she couldn't just show up like a cat in heat. She would die of embarrassment.

She rolled the paint strips around and around between her thumb and forefinger until they were little balls and then flicked them, further considering the situation. The carnival would only be here one more night before it lumbered to the next town, so shouldn't she take advantage of this chance? The more she thought about it, the more it seemed that it would for sure be a *mistake* not to go back. Miss Montana had already left for the Grand Ole Opry, of course, but she could still help the others, she reasoned, her skin beginning to prickle with excitement. It was definitely *not* to be alone with Lorenzo. She would give him a wide berth. Chances were, he had forgotten the whole thing anyway. Yes, she decided with a flurry of excitement, she would just sneak over and say hello to the performers, if nothing else.

Gertie gave the house behind her a nervous glance as she pulled off the sunbonnet Signe had insisted she wear and hung it on one of the fence's thin planks. She would go before dinner, before Signe discovered she was gone. She walked to the dilapidated old gate at the end of the yard, but just as she put her hand to it, she heard Signe's voice.

"Where do you think you're going, young lady?"

Signe was in the doorway, a big apron tied round her bulging middle, huge with her imminent third child. Despite Signe's accusatory tone, Gertie suddenly felt a pang of sympathy for her older sister, who was really no better off than poor Maman. Her husband, Mel, seemed kind enough, but Signe worked as long and as hard as any woman back in the shacks.

"I'm going for a walk," Gertie answered.

"No, you're not. You can help me with dinner if you're done back here," she said, her eyes darting along the unfinished fence.

"I won't be gone long, Sig. I just want to stretch my legs."

Signe shielded her eyes against the glare of the setting sun. "Don't you run off to that carnival, Gerd. Once is enough."

"I'm not!" Gertie could feel the blush on her cheeks and was glad that her face was in shadow.

"Ingrid told me about Warren," Signe said coolly, crossing her arms.

Warren! She had almost forgotten about Warren. "What do you mean?" Gertie said nonchalantly, wondering if he was even now on his way to Keystone to find her.

"That's why you're here, isn't it? You shouldn't chase," Signe scolded. "It will never do."

Gertie bristled. It annoyed her to no end that Signe thought she knew best, just because she was married with a family. Even now, when she obviously had no idea.

"You should wait for him to come to you, Gerd. You've heard what Maman has said."

"I just want to take a walk, Signe! It has nothing to do with Warren!"

Signe shot her a disbelieving look.

"And even if I *was* interested in Warren, which I'm not saying I am," Gertie argued, "how on earth would he be able to court me if I'm all the way out in Keystone?"

"Mel managed it," Signe said smartly.

"Oh, good for you two," Gertie snipped. "I'm going for a walk!"

"Then take Ingrid and the boys."

"No!" Gertie called, hurrying out the back gate and letting it bang behind her.

"Gerda!" Signe shouted.

"You're not my mother!"

Gertie practically ran across town, pausing only when she reached the ancient oak that grew on the edge of the field so recently breached by the traveling show. Next to the brightly colored tents and the flags whipping in the air, the old tree looked as out of place as Gertie felt, standing there in her pale blue cotton dress. From where she stood, she could see the little platform at the entrance, and, of course, she could see Lorenzo, strutting upon it in all his glory, enticing the crowd to "step right up." He was so marvelous decked out in his elegant frock coat and his bright red vest that Gertie found it almost difficult to breathe. For several minutes, she simply enjoyed watching him unawares, glad for the chance to be able to stare at him without risk of embarrassment, until she finally decided to leave the shelter of the tree.

Eventually, she began inching into the crowd, hoping he wouldn't notice her, but like a spider sensing the tiniest movement in his web, Lorenzo immediately caught sight of her. A grin crossed his lips, and he gave her the tiniest of winks as he lifted his top hat an inch above his head. She wasn't sure if he was laughing at her, but she didn't care. A dark lock of hair fell across one of his eyes, and as his long fingers pushed it back, she felt a deep pull of attraction. Desperately she wanted to go to him, but she instead stood, motionless, waiting for some sort of acknowledgement or signal.

Finally, after what seemed like several agonizing moments, he gave her the slightest backward tilt of his head, beckoning her toward him. Without reservation, she hurried toward the stage, feeling a shiver of delight when he bent toward her and said in a low voice, "Get yourself on in there, darlin'. I'll come find you," and nodded toward the performers' tent. This was all the encouragement Gertie needed.

Once inside, however, she stopped short. Miss Montana's dressing table was gone, and Gertie felt a momentary disappointment. As she watched the carnies rushing to and fro, she wasn't sure what to do. No one seemed to pay her any attention. She stood awkwardly by the tent flaps, staring at them, waiting for Lorenzo to burst through them, but he never did. Finally, after about twenty minutes had passed, she grew bored and decided that she might as well try to make herself useful.

Before long, she was also running back and forth, making drinks, holding costumes and instruments, delivering messages. It was exciting, so much so that she hardly noticed Lorenzo's absence, nor did she realize when she stopped for a moment to catch her breath that it was already dark outside!

Gertie looked around the tent for Lorenzo. Well, she scolded herself, she hadn't come for him, had she? She must have misunderstood his wink when she had run to the stage, and now she would have to go back to Signe's and face her certain anger. Still, it had been worth it, even if Signe sent her back to Keystone as a punishment. Perhaps that was for the best—

"Where you runnin' to, darlin'?" said a man's husky voice as two arms clutched her waist. It was Lorenzo!

Gertie felt her stomach flutter as she turned to him.

"You certainly are a sight for sore eyes," he said with what was becoming his familiar grin. He kissed her, then, and she tried her best to return it, though she felt clumsy. Lorenzo didn't seem to mind; in fact, he seemed encouraged, continuing to kiss her until she felt a hot flush race through her body. He took her hand and led her over to a hay bale just inside the tent flap. Gently, he pulled her down and continued to kiss her lips and then her ear and then her neck.

Every part of Gertie quivered when his hands found their way to her breasts, just as they had yesterday. Gasping aloud, she opened her eyes and for a moment was surprised to see that they were still in the tent. A couple of carnies were still working at the other end, folding up chairs and tying the flaps shut.

"Lorenzo," Gertie said haltingly, suddenly embarrassed. "We can't stay here like this."

"Why not?" he asked, as his lips returned to her neck.

"Maybe . . . maybe we should go back to the caravan?" she murmured.

Lorenzo paused to look at her for a moment before breaking into a grin. "Well now, darlin'. I wasn't sure you were that kinda girl."

Gertie felt her face grow hot with embarrassment, and she looked away.

"Hey now." He put a knuckle under her chin and drew her gaze back. "Don't get me wrong. I like that about a girl. You've got a bit of spunk to you." He gave her a fierce kiss. "Unfortunately, though," he said, breaking it just as quickly, "ol' Roman's got the caravan tonight, so we're stuck out here."

"Maybe I should get going," Gertie mumbled, feeling more than a little ashamed and beginning to worry more about what Signe would say. She started to try to think of what her excuse would be. She had gone walking with Warren and lost track of the time? She had gone to visit Astrid? She had tripped and fallen?

"Not so fast, darlin'. Ain't no cause to be embarrassed. I know just what you need. Jimmy!" Lorenzo shouted at the carnies, startling Gertie. "Beat it."

"Sure thing, boss." The carnie gave a little grin. "Come on, Mack," he said to the man next to him, and the two of them shuffled out.

"Now, ain't that better?" he asked, turning his attention back to her. They were alone in the big hollow tent, and Gertie felt a prick of fear.

"Lorenzo, I—" she uttered, but before she could finish, he kissed her. It was a surprisingly gentle kiss, followed by another and then another until her fear and shame were replaced by a rising desire to be touched and caressed again. She began to eagerly return his kisses.

Lorenzo continued his lovemaking, eventually pulling her to the hard ground, his hand again finding its way to her underthings, and he again brought her to a shuddering climax, his own need somehow suppressed within his trousers. She lay there, panting, and gazed up at him, something swelling inside her chest and threatening to burst out. He was so lovely, so manly, so . . . so . . . she didn't know enough words to describe him. Surely she was in love with him. This must be what love, true love, felt like.

Unlike last time, he remained beside her, stroking the side of her face. "Well, guess this is goodbye, darlin'."

"Goodbye?" she said, the peaceful glow she was basking in as she huddled close to him suddenly broken. "What do you mean?"

"Why, tomorrow's our last day in town, then we're movin' on. But I'll remember you, darlin'. You sure are a pretty little thing."

Gertie hurriedly sat up. "You . . . you can't just leave!" she blurted. "I thought you . . . well, that you cared about me."

"Well, darlin', I do. More than I have about anyone in a real long time, but 'the show must go on,' as they say."

"But . . . what am I supposed to do?"

Lorenzo laughed. "Well, how would I know? I reckon you're gonna marry

that fella of yours. What was his name? Walter?"

"Warren? I don't want to marry *him*!"

Lorenzo looked at her with an odd mix of gentleness and amusement. "You sure about that, darlin'?"

Panic filled Gertie's chest. She had never been more sure in her life. He was teasing her, she could see, but the thought of never seeing him again filled her with some kind of unexplained claustrophobia. "I could come with you," she said hesitantly and hoped he wouldn't laugh.

He didn't laugh, but his brow did crease. "Well now, darlin', that might be real nice, but I'm afraid Gideon don't like that sort of thing."

"Who's Gideon?"

"Why, he's the one that owns this here show."

"I thought you did," she said.

Lorenzo let out a deep laugh. "Course not, darlin'. I just run it. With Roman, that is."

"Well, maybe this Gideon wouldn't find out. If he's not around all that much . . ."

"Oh, Gideon knows everything that goes on round here, darlin'. Roman sees to that."

Gertie burst into tears.

"Well, now, don't cry, darlin'. Seems to me, there's only one way around this."

Gertie looked up at him blearily.

"You and I could get hitched," he said conspiratorially. "What would you think of that? Then Gideon couldn't say anything."

"You mean get married?" she asked, wiping her eyes with the back of her hand. It seemed preposterous.

"That's what I said."

Gertie stared at him. "Are you . . . are you teasing me?"

"Course not, darlin'. I never tease. That's for the weak. I say what I mean, don't you know that by now? Come on, whaddya say? You and me was meant to be. Seein' the world together," he gestured at the big empty tent interior. "I'll take you on the biggest, best honeymoon there ever was."

Gertie's heart was racing. Marry Lorenzo? It seemed ridiculous, but wasn't this, or some version of this, what she had always wanted? A life of adventure? A stray specter of a thought of Warren attempted to wiggle its way into her mind, but she pushed it away. Warren had no place in her mind now, or her life, for that matter. He was a nice boy, she would give him that, but he was clearly not the man Lorenzo was.

"So what's it gonna be, darlin'? Yes or no?"

"It's going to be yes," she said with a little laugh, hardly able to believe he was going to be her husband.

Gertie tried her best to keep her impending marriage a secret, thrilled by the sheer wildness of running away to Ottumwa to get married. In the end, however, she found she had no choice but to confide in the unsuspecting Ingrid.

As predicted, Signe was indeed furious when Gertie had eventually slunk home and had scolded her severely, her anger further fueled by Gertie's irritatingly sly smiles. She had ended her small tirade by declaring that she and Ingrid would have to walk home in the morning, that she wasn't about to put up with this sort of tomfoolery when she had enough to do as it was besides mind the two of them.

Ingrid begged to be allowed to stay on her own. After all, she whined, why should she be punished for Gertie's bad behavior? Signe would have none of it, though, which resulted in Ingrid not speaking to Gertie all through breakfast. Immediately following, Gertie had benevolently offered to go to the market for Signe before they left. Signe eyed her suspiciously before reluctantly acquiescing, but only on the condition that she take Ingrid. Gertie was about to protest this clever parry, but then thought better of it.

The two sisters set off, then, both quiet as they trudged along—Ingrid fuming, and Gertie scheming. This wasn't how she had planned her escape, but Gertie thought it just might work anyway.

Dutifully, she marched into McKenna's and bought the various items requested by Signe, but instead of turning left out of the shop to return to her sister's, she turned right and headed down the main street.

"Gertie!" Ingrid called from behind her. "Wait! Where are you going? We shouldn't dawdle. Signe's already mad, thanks to you."

Gertie didn't respond but marched into Linden's, the shop bell tinkling gaily, and gazed at the array of ladies' gloves, hats, and underthings. She had never been in a shop like this, and it was lovely. Lorenzo had told her where to find it. In the back were a few pre-made dresses, and she made her way toward them.

"Gertie" Ingrid hissed, trailing behind her. "What are you doing in here?"

Gertie finally turned. "I'm buying my wedding outfit," she said simply, wicked delight coursing through her at the look of utter shock on Ingrid's face, her buck teeth sticking out ridiculously.

"Your wedding outfit!" Ingrid sputtered. "What do you mean? I thought . . . I thought maybe you'd changed your mind about Warren. He turned up last night, you know—"

"Warren? No, not him! I'm getting married to Lorenzo. Tonight, as it is." Gertie gave her head a little toss.

"Lorenzo?" Ingrid asked, mystified. "Who's Lorenzo?"

"He's the showman."

"The showman?"

"Yes, you know," Gertie said, her exasperation growing. "The carnival barker? His name's Lorenzo."

"Oh, Gertie, no," Ingrid responded, horrified, her hand traveling to cover her teeth. "Why on earth would you want to marry *him*? You can't mean it."

"Well, I *do* mean it. Here, hold this." She thrust the marketing basket into Ingrid's arms.

"Gertie!"

"Ingrid, don't be such a child," she retorted, trying to ignore the look of hurt on her sister's face. "You don't understand these things." She turned away and began to rifle through the small selection of dresses.

"Gertie, please," Ingrid begged. "What's gotten into you? What about Warren?"

"What about him?" Gertie managed to say, though in all honesty, the thought of Warren made her feel slightly nauseous. If she hadn't met Lorenzo, Warren might have been alright, but as it was, how could she ever be with Warren now, dream or no dream? Especially after what she and Lorenzo had done together. She couldn't imagine doing something like that with Warren; she was sure he wouldn't have the faintest idea about how to please a woman in that way. Hadn't he said he wouldn't touch her? And, anyway, what about what Roman had said? How he had warned her away? She wasn't sure she trusted Roman, but, on the other hand, what purpose would he have in lying to her? And then there was the fact that he had known her name, so he must have *some* psychic ability.

"How can you do this to him?" Ingrid pleaded. "He loves you, you know. He even asked Pa for your hand!"

Gertie was surprised by the appearance of small tears in the corners of Ingrid's eyes. Did *she* fancy Warren?

"Ingrid, it's hard to explain." She pulled out one of the dresses to examine it more closely. "I have to do this. I *want* to do this. Warren will be better off without me. Why don't *you* set your cap for him?"

"How can you say that, Gerd? How can you say he'll be better off? You're going to break his heart."

"I can't explain it, Ingrid. I love Lorenzo; it's as simple as that."

"You don't even know him!"

"Yes, I do, Ing," Gertie said solemnly. "I know him enough."

"Gertie, I can't let you do this!" Ingrid whined. "I'm going to tell Signe! Or I'll walk all the way home and tell Pa."

"No, you won't."

"Yes, I will!"

Gertie held up the black dress in her hands. "What do you think of this one?"

Ingrid stared at the dress in utter disbelief. "For your wedding dress? Why on God's earth would you choose *black*? You know what they say, 'A bride in black, wish you were back.'"

Gertie managed a dismissive little laugh. "That's just an old wives' tale. I happen to think black is rather elegant. And then I can use it again, more so than white. I'm just being practical."

"Practical to run off and marry a carnival man? I swear to God I'm going to tell," Ingrid whispered fiercely.

Gertie gripped her sister's arm. "Please don't, Ing. For me."

Ingrid stared at her until her face finally crumpled. "Oh, Gertie," she practically cried. "What will Maman say?"

Gertie bit her lip. What *would* Maman say? She had been trying hard not to think of Maman. "Doubtless she'll be happy for me." Gertie gathered up the dress and a pair of black gloves and made her way back to the front of the shop.

"How can you say that? You'll break her heart, too. And where did you get the money for all of this?" Ingrid whispered incredulously as Gertie laid her items on the counter.

"Would Madame care to look at our hats?" the shop woman queried as she waved her hand toward a shelf with a large variety of hats and lovely hat boxes to match. She was a much older woman with a pinched face, and Gertie sensed that she, too, was disapproving of her from behind her wire-rimmed glasses.

"Why, yes, I would," Gertie tried to say importantly. "What would you suggest? Something simple, I think."

When the woman moved to select one, Gertie murmured, "Lorenzo gave me the money to buy a wedding outfit. Doesn't that prove something?"

Ingrid's face was still one of despair.

"And as for Maman," Gertie went on, "it's like when she left Sweden for a new world. For America. I'm just doing the same. I'm sure she'll understand."

"But why not tell her, then?" Ingrid begged.

"Here you are," the woman said, handing Gertie a simple black cloche. Gertie set it on her head and looked in the little mirror on the counter. She couldn't believe how grown-up it made her look.

"Yes, this will do." She handed it back to the woman.

"Very good, Madame. Shall I wrap it all?"

"Yes, please," Gertie said curtly.

"Gertie, why the haste?" Ingrid asked in a low voice. "Were you . . . were you interfered with?"

"No! It's nothing like that." Gertie felt herself blush and began fishing through her coin bag for the money Lorenzo had given her. She could never tell Ingrid any of those details! "Listen," Gertie said hurriedly, "the carnival is leaving town today. If I don't go now, I'll never get the chance. And I can't just run off with him; that would be living in sin. You wouldn't have me do that, would you?"

"Here you are, Madame." The woman handed her the bundle. "Good day."

Gertie took the package in her arms and hurried toward the front door, Ingrid following morosely. Gertie could tell she had defeated her, and for once, she wasn't proud of it. When they were back outside, the shop bell tinkling again, Gertie turned to face her little sister. "Well, wish me luck, Ing."

"Wish you luck?"

"I'm going now." She nodded at the full basket in Ingrid's arms. "Take that back to Signe's."

"What! You're leaving *now*?" Ingrid exclaimed. "But . . . but what am I supposed to say?"

"Just say I went on home. That we had a fight or something."

"But—"

"Everything will work out, Ing." Gertie leaned forward and kissed her on the cheek.

"Don't go, Gerda," Ingrid pleaded, shifting the basket and throwing her arms around Gertie's neck.

"Don't worry about me. I'm excited. Honestly. Just think, after tonight, I'll be a married woman! I expect we'll be on the road with Patsy Montana or maybe traveling west with the carnival. Might hit Wyoming by fall, Lorenzo says. That's the life for me. Adventure," she said, attempting an enthusiastic smile.

"But where will I find you?" Tears flooded Ingrid's eyes, and Gertie knew she needed to start walking or she might not have the courage to go through with this after all.

"I'll send you a postcard!" Gertie tried to say gaily. She turned away then and started walking briskly.

"I love you!" Ingrid shouted, but Gertie found she couldn't answer, even if she wanted to, her throat thick and aching. Instead, she made herself march steadily forward.

When she reached the old oak, however, she did look back, but Ingrid was already gone. Gertie brushed a few tears from her own eyes and stood staring at the spot where she had left her sister. She took a deep breath, then, before turning around to face the new life she had chosen.

The wedding ceremony was oddly short and almost anticlimactic. Not at all what Gertie had been expecting. The Reverend

Wilson did not drone on as Father Kristoff was wont to do every Sunday at St. Mary's, and there was very little ritual. Just a quick exchange of vows and a blessing of sorts, and that was it. Afterwards, the minister's wife served them orange juice in pretty crystal glasses. Gertie thought that maybe someone would give a speech or maybe even a toast, but no one did. The minister's wife seemed dreadfully tired, if her excessive yawns were any indication, and, taking the cue, Lorenzo handed the minister an envelope and then declared that they should probably get going. The best man was already asleep in the corner, but the Reverend and Mrs. Wilson wished them luck as Lorenzo helped Gertie into his battered truck.

Neither of them said much on the short drive, Gertie not sure exactly where they were headed. She was delighted then, when Lorenzo—her husband (it was so strange to call him that!)—pulled up in front of what Gertie was sure must be the nicest hotel in Ottumwa, The Carlton. It was unfortunately too late to dine, so they proceeded directly upstairs to the wedding chamber.

Lorenzo, Gertie soon discovered, was eager to begin the consummation. Gertie felt shy as she accordingly began to undress in front of him, especially with him looking on while taking several long swigs from the flask he had extracted from inside his jacket. She had wanted to buy a frilly nightgown to go along with her wedding outfit, but she hadn't had enough. It was either the nightgown or the gloves, and though she longed for something exotic and risqué, she was hesitant to purchase such a thing in front of Ingrid.

As it was, all she had to come to him in was her shift, which didn't stay on long anyway, further justifying her more practical purchase. His eyes had a certain wolfishness to them tonight that both excited and frightened her, and she tried not to think, especially in this moment, about Warren's deep blue ones and the gentle wistfulness they always held.

Lorenzo was perhaps not as tender with her as she had been led to expect, given their two previous rendezvous, and he did not tonight take time to pleasure her the way he had in the caravan and then in the tent. Still, she managed to eventually find *some* enjoyment in the act and was thrilled when he murmured that he loved her. Lorenzo kept her up all night, wanting to do things she had never imagined before, until Gertie was utterly exhausted and sore. In the wee hours of the morning, he finally turned away and fell asleep, lightly snoring every so often.

Gertie rolled onto her side, and though she was dreadfully tired, she found she couldn't sleep. Images of Maman and Ingrid, and even of Warren continued to force their way into her mind. Tears rolled down her cheeks, and she tried to stop them by shutting her eyes tight. Doubtless, things would look better in the morning, she told herself. She wondered if she might have the dream tonight. For once, she wanted to have it, but try as she might to conjure it, it eluded her.

Lorenzo was awake surprisingly early the next morning, throwing back the thick damask curtains of the window that looked out over Main Street to let the sunshine in. For a moment, Gertie was startled to find herself in a bed with no clothes on before she remembered that she was now a married woman. And as if to further cement that fact, Lorenzo, upon seeing her stir, threw himself on the bed with a whoop and proceeded to make love to her yet again.

Eventually the newlyweds rose to bathe, Lorenzo going first and asking her to wash his back. Her doubts from last night had thankfully scattered, though as she squeezed water across Lorenzo's back, she wondered if all their mornings on the road would begin this way. She felt a fresh niggling of a doubt attempt to resurrect itself, but she had only to think of poor Maman, up at four every morning to start the coal fire and the bread baking, to decide that this was infinitely preferable.

They breakfasted in the dining room, Gertie having to wear her wedding dress, as her blue cotton would never do in such a fine establishment. Lorenzo told her not to worry, that no one would notice, and that he would soon buy her a whole new wardrobe. As he ordered coffee for them both, Gertie silently congratulated herself yet again on making such a practical choice.

When the breakfast arrived, Gertie devoured it. She thought it very good—eggs, bacon, hash browns, beans, flap-jacks, toast, and even fresh butter and blackberry jam—but it could have been anything at all and Gertie would still have thought it lovely, as she had never been in a real restaurant before. She felt like a queen!

Lorenzo, she discovered, was not a conversationalist, at least in the morning. When they were finished eating, he lit a cigarillo and reached for the paper the waiter had set on the edge of the table, which he opened and began lazily leafing through, while Gertie contented herself with looking out the big picture window. At one point, a team of horses pulling a wagon full of miners rumbled by, and Gertie wondered if they were headed for The Royal, the mine she knew was closest to here. The thought made her think of her father and her brothers, and she guiltily pulled her eyes away and rested them on Lorenzo, still reading the paper.

"What are we going to do today?" Gertie asked finally, not wanting to disturb him, but feeling a little tired of just sitting there.

"Whaddya mean, darlin'?" Lorenzo said, looking up with only mild interest.

"Well, are we going away? Like you said? On a honeymoon?"

"Well, now, darlin', I can't rightly up an' leave the carnie at this exact moment, you know that. This is high season. Soon as fall comes an' things slow down, we'll set off on just about the best trip you ever saw. Chicago, New York, maybe even London."

"Oh, Lorenzo! Do you mean it?" Gertie exclaimed, despite the initial prick of disappointment.

"Course I do, darlin'," he said, letting the paper fall on the dirty dishes and taking the cigarillo out of his mouth.

"Well, what should *I* do?" she asked hopefully. "Want me to keep helping you in the tent? You know, with the performers?"

"Nah. That ain't respectable." He flicked ash on the remains of his eggs. "Can't have my wife hanging about for all to see and slobber over."

"But I thought we were going to be partners at the carnival . . ."

"Now, darlin', so we are, but not in these parts. Don't you see that don't make no sense? What if one of yer friends was to see you and ran to tell yer folks?"

Gertie admitted this was a good point, but still . . . "Well, we *are* legally married, so I don't see what they can do about it now."

"True enough, but they could make it not so nice for us. Ruin our special times together."

"I guess so," Gertie said, musing this over for a few moments. "Well, are we going back to the caravan, then? I could tidy it while you're out at the carnival," she suggested, albeit without a whole lot of enthusiasm.

"The caravan? Nah, that's barely big enough for me and Roman. We'll worry about that later. First, I've got someone I want you to meet. Been keepin' it a surprise. Come on now, get finished, an' I'll take you on over there."

"Someone you want me to meet?" Gertie asked, her stomach sinking. She hoped it wasn't another cousin; the first one was bad enough.

Lorenzo stood, wiping his mouth with his napkin and tossing it onto the table. "Come on', darlin'. Times a wastin'. Get yer things, an' let's go."

The last forty-eight hours of Gertie's life had been one surprise after another, but nothing surprised her more than when Lorenzo pulled up in front of what had to be, if not the biggest house in Ottumwa, then certainly the oldest. Despite its daunting size, however, it was not at all stately or grand. In fact, it was horribly decrepit and looked decidedly haunted. Several windows were broken and most of the shutters had either fallen off or hung loose, and the yard was brown and overgrown with weeds.

"Who lives here?" Gertie asked nervously.

"Why, darlin', we do," Lorenzo said cheerfully. "This here's your home now."

Gertie's jaw dropped open the same way Ingrid's unfortunately often did, and Lorenzo barked out a loud laugh. *Her home?* They weren't meant to have a home! They were meant to be on the road, traveling, not keeping up a house. And if they *were* to have a home, surely it wouldn't be this one, would it?

"Come on, darlin'. Get on out."

Dismally, Gertie slid out of the truck. As she followed Lorenzo up the crumbling concrete steps from the street, it suddenly occurred to her that perhaps this was merely a boarding house, in which Lorenzo had rented a room, or maybe a set of rooms. He must be teasing her! Yes, that made sense, although it was a little run-down, even for a boarding house. *And* there was no sign or placard anywhere . . .

When they reached the front porch, worn and peeling, Lorenzo further surprised her by scooping her up in his arms. Gertie gave a delighted little scream as he thrust open the door and carried her across the threshold. Once inside, he set her down and gave her bottom a swift little pat.

As Gertie looked around at the dilapidated interior, any hope of this being a boarding house quickly faded. The whole place was dusty and dim, and Gertie could see sheets of cobwebs in many of the ceiling's corners. The front room was only sparsely furnished, and dirty dishes and newspapers were strewn all over the floor.

Gertie panicked, shooting Lorenzo a frantic look.

He met it coolly, giving her the tiniest wink as he strode toward a dusty grand staircase.

"I'm home, Ma!" he shouted up.

CHAPTER 8

February 1924

Gertie did not think she could be more tired than she was at this moment. Slowly, she lifted the heavy tray from Madre's bedside, the old woman's small eyes watching her all the while. The whites of them were even more yellow than they were the day before, if that were possible. The old spider refused to see a doctor, but Gertie was sure she was getting worse. Or so she hoped, which she knew was a positively evil thing to think, but she couldn't help it.

Gertie balanced the tray of food, mostly untouched, on her bulging stomach and made her way down the back staircase to the kitchen. She set the tray on the stove and shoved open the battered screen door, stuck because of the frigid cold, and set Madre's nearly full bowl of oatmeal on the screened porch for the cats that roamed the back yard. Right now, the near acre of land was a frozen wasteland with piles of snow everywhere, but in spring it would return to being a wild overgrown mess, with grass as tall as her knees, and flowerbeds choked with weeds and fallen branches. Not long after arriving, Gertie had tried to pick some of the flowers still trying bravely to bloom through the overgrowth. And for a few weeks, she had even tried to pull some of the weeds, but after a while she simply gave up. It was too big of a task, and she soon had other cares anyway.

Gertie watched as one of the cats jumped through a big tear in one of the screens and eagerly began lapping up the contents of the bowl. *Well, at least someone likes it*, Gertie thought disgustedly. Her mother-in-law, or Madre as she was supposed to call her, hated her cooking. In fact, she hated everything about Gertie, though Gertie was forever trying to please her, at least in the beginning. But, like the weeds, Gertie had eventually given up where Madre was concerned and resolved to simply endure her spite, which the old woman was surprisingly able to communicate to Gertie despite not speaking a word of English.

Indeed, Madre was ingenious in getting Gertie to understand what she wanted by simply pointing her gnarled fingers or by slapping Gertie's hand when she did the wrong thing. Eventually, they had developed an elaborate set of hand gestures, and, likewise, Gertie was slowly beginning to understand various words or phrases in Italian or Romanian, or whatever it was they spoke, which made things a little easier. And contrary to what Lorenzo said, Madre *did* know a few English words, such as: *come, go, coffee, bread, stupid,* and *bitch.* However, none of those, Gertie noticed, were used whenever Lorenzo was present, which, unfortunately wasn't much.

Sometimes Lorenzo would disappear for weeks, traveling with the carnival through southern Iowa, Kansas, and even Nebraska. Gertie had begged to be taken along, especially to places where she was sure to not run into anyone from her family, but Lorenzo thought it best that she stay behind and care for Madre. Gertie had explained that she knew nothing about nursing, but Lorenzo had just laughed and said that "all women know how to nurse, darlin'. It's in their blood, don't you know that?" And so, Gertie had had no choice but to nurse the old crone, who reigned from an upstairs sitting room that she had commandeered as her bedroom.

Madre refused to have anyone from the outside world examine her except for a fellow crone who had appeared one day at the front door and brushed past Gertie as if she wasn't even there and had proceeded up to Madre's bedroom. The woman, dressed all in black, as Madre always was, had come down a half an hour later and given Gertie various sacks of herbs and powders and instructions on how to use them. It was terribly confusing, though, so in the end, Gertie had resorted to scribbling it all down in her own way—she wasn't much good at writing—in the margin of an old storybook she found on one of the shelves.

And then Gertie had discovered herself to be pregnant, which had solidified Lorenzo's insistence that she stay behind.

"The carnie ain't no place for a lady," Lorenzo said more than once, each time in a more irritated tone. "'Specially one that's expectin'. Gideon don't like it."

To this, Gertie always wanted to reply that she was hardly living the life of a "lady" here in the old McPherson place, as she had discovered this hulking house was called, nursing a shriveled up black spider, but she didn't dare. And she couldn't imagine a man like Gideon caring about who was hanging about the carnie tents, but, again, she didn't dare question Lorenzo.

Despite his gruff manner and his sometimes almost complete disregard for her, Gertie genuinely missed Lorenzo when he was away. She missed his grin and his suggestive winks, which he periodically shot at her when Madre wasn't looking. And she missed how he would, in the early days, anyway, scoop her up in his arms and carry her to the front porch, where they would drink a bottle of dandelion wine or a couple of bottles of beer as he told her story after story of his days with the carnival or his previous lives, of which he seemed to have many. Gertie lived for these moments, which were sadly becoming less and less now that Roman had started accompanying Lorenzo home. The thrill she used to feel when Lorenzo walked through the door was considerably lessened by Roman's inevitable shadow.

Technically, Roman did not actually live with them, but he might as well have. Though Gertie tried to like Roman for Lorenzo's sake, she just couldn't. On the nights he slept over, he and Lorenzo would stay up late, drinking and loudly singing folk songs outside by a fire. Or, if it was cold or rainy, they would light a fire in the library fireplace, one of the few that still worked in the crumbling old house. Lorenzo kept a stack of firewood in the library for this purpose, scattered aimlessly on the once beautiful parquet wood floor and used the few tattered books that still remained on the old shelves as kindling.

At first, Gertie had tried to sit with them, out of politeness, but Lorenzo usually waved her away and told her to get back to the kitchen or to go sit with Madre, which was infinitely worse. Madre would simply make her fetch needless items or scold her with lectures she didn't understand. It soon became clear that when Roman was around, Gertie was meant to simply serve them and that was it.

Thus, Gertie began to kindle a little hatred of Roman, and she definitely didn't like who Lorenzo became when Roman was around. For one thing, it made him rougher and more commanding; these were the nights that Lorenzo would stumble upstairs and demand to make love to her. Normally, Gertie didn't mind, even looked forward to his kisses and his attentions, but not now when she was so fully pregnant. The doctor in town had told her it would be any day, but Lorenzo didn't seem to care. "It feeds the baby," he would say with a grin as he gave her swollen, tender breasts a sloppy kiss, and she would have no choice but to endure it, though she was so big and uncomfortable and tired. So tired she thought she might die. *How had Maman had so many babies?* she found herself wondering more and more.

Gertie longed to be with her mother. She wanted to ask her so many questions, especially about the impending birth, to wrap her arms around her and smell her scent, which was like sweet, fresh-baked bread, and to tell her that she loved her.

But this was impossible.

For one thing, Keystone was twenty-five miles away, and for another, she was too ashamed. Pa would probably not speak to her, and anyway, she felt like a fool. She had told Ingrid she would send postcards from all the exotic locales she was to see, but the furthest she had gotten was Ottumwa, Iowa! It was humiliating. She had "made her bed," as Pa would have said, and now she had to lie in it. Not that she considered her marriage to Lorenzo to be a mistake, necessarily, but the fact that she contemplated it at all suggested something to Gertie that she didn't like to think about.

Even if she had wanted to visit Keystone, it was impossible now that it was winter, as the roads were so bad. And besides, the carnival was shut down for the season, which meant that Lorenzo was home permanently, and he was more unpleasant than ever. Gertie had never seen him like this. Grumpy and brooding, he wandered listlessly about the house, complaining about everything. That or he drank, sometimes starting in the morning and continuing steadily all the way until late, swearing that he was going to take the carnival south to Louisiana or Georgia where it was always warm. But in the morning, he never did.

That was one good thing about the mines, Gertie thought ruefully—the temperature deep within the earth did not vary. It was cool, but not cold, and constant. Still, it was no consolation for the hacking coughs nearly every man and boy eventually developed, she swiftly reminded herself.

As much as Gertie didn't want Lorenzo to go far away, especially with the baby due so soon and Madre getting worse by the day with whatever strange illness she had, Gertie worried about their dwindling stash of money, which happened to likewise be Lorenzo's most popular thing to complain about. It was going faster than usual, he claimed, and blamed it on Gertie's poor husbandry. Didn't she know how to make a penny stretch? His mother had always managed to have money *left over* at the end of the month, so what was wrong with her?

Mortified by Lorenzo's new criticisms, Gertie angrily wondered how Madre had managed the household so efficiently when she had apparently been an invalid for so many years. Also, it seemed obvious that adding another person to the house meant that the money would drain faster, though Gertie tried not to eat very much. It was hard, though, once she became pregnant. At first, she had been too ill to eat, but then she had become ravenous. And it didn't help that Roman was almost a nightly guest for dinner. Oftentimes, she herself went without meat, having to give her portion to Roman, and simply ate potatoes and bread. The more she thought about it, it positively infuriated her that Lorenzo didn't seem to understand any of this.

It also bothered her that he didn't seem to notice the looks Roman gave her whenever he wasn't looking. Long, leering looks that made her skin prickle, like he was able to read her mind and discern the innermost thoughts and desires she barely knew herself. She was secretly afraid of Roman, afraid of his abilities, especially after what he had told her in the tent that night, which now seemed like a lifetime ago.

Only once had she gotten up the courage to ask Lorenzo if Roman's psychic abilities were genuine, or if it was just part of the show—the whole of which she saw now was so horribly obvious and phony. There was no magic there at all, never had been. How could she have been so dazzled by it all? It was simply a bunch of cheap tricks and makeup. Knowing what she knew now, Gertie seriously doubted that Roman really had the power to tell the future, but a part of her wanted it to be true, *needed* it to be, because otherwise she had given up her old life—and Warren—for nothing.

So, finally, one night after Lorenzo had had his way with her, she had tentatively brought it up. Lorenzo had looked at her steadily, propped up on one elbow, and Gertie thought she saw some hesitation in his eye before he threw himself back on the pillow and casually lit a cigarillo.

"'Course he's genuine, darlin'," he said finally, lazily blowing out a long stream of smoke. "He's got what you'd call a gift. He can tell the future surer than shit. Got it from Madre's side of the family. Gideon knows it. That's why he's afraid of Roman. And you should be, too, darlin'. You should be, too," he warned.

"But . . . but doesn't he have his own home or a wife or . . . something?"

"Roman ain't like that, darlin'." Lorenzo looked over at her. "He lives free. He's one with the elements. He don't need no roof over his head."

That's because he has one here, Gertie thought irritably. "Well, what about a wife? Doesn't he want to get married?"

"Roman ain't like that, darlin'. He don't have the same kind of needs as the rest of us. Sometimes he takes a woman, if the spirits move him, but most times not. He's been known to take a man, though, too. But that was a while ago."

"A man!" Gertie exclaimed, feeling thoroughly sickened. *How could that be?*

"Darlin', there's a whole lot of life you know nothin' about, so you best listen to me. I ain't gonna steer you wrong. You don't need to worry none about Roman. I'll take care of you, and he can take care of himself."

But, Gertie wanted to say, if he could take care of himself, then why did he feel the need to be *here* so often? She didn't say it, though, and instead bit her tongue and rolled over on her side, wondering what this all meant.

She almost never had the dream about Warren anymore, which she told herself was for the best, though she sometimes imagined that Warren was somehow watching her, especially when Lorenzo was away. Sometimes this thought brought her comfort, like she had a friend nearby, but other times it unnerved her. She would be ashamed if Warren was to somehow see her this way.

Lorenzo's verification of Roman's powers only served to make Gertie more wary. She tried her best to keep her distance from him, but it was difficult. For one thing, he always seemed to be where she was, even if she tried to hide herself away in the kitchen scrubbing something that didn't really need scrubbing. Anything to keep from running into him or having to sit with Madre in her horrible bedroom, where she kept a fire burning even in the summer! *Did she not have any blood in her?* Gertie often wondered, the sweat of a hot July afternoon pouring down the back of her neck. But then again, most spiders didn't.

No, the best place to be alone, Gertie had discovered, was the kitchen, though sometimes not even that was safe. Inevitably, from time to time, she would turn around from wiping the stove, or chopping onions, or wringing out laundry to find Roman leaning against the counter with his arms folded, a big grin on his face. It would scare the life out of her! Sometimes she even let out a little scream, much to her embarrassment. He seemed to enjoy this element of surprise—or, more than that, he seemed to enjoy her *fear*. Fear and discord were what he thrived on. Sometimes she even caught him grinning whenever Madre or Lorenzo was scolding her, which infuriated her.

All told, she usually felt ganged up on by all three of them. Both Lorenzo and Roman treated Madre like a queen, almost worshipping her. Once, when Gertie had dared to question Madre's ability to cook and clean so much better than herself, even in her decrepit state, Lorenzo had actually struck her. Swiftly, across the face with the back of his hand, and with Roman looking on. Tears had immediately stung her eyes, not only because of the pain, but because of the sheer shock.

"Don't ever talk about Madre that way again; you hear me, darlin'?" he said, pointing a finger in her face.

Trembling, Gertie had managed a stiff nod and, turning her face from the scowling Lorenzo and the grinning Roman, had gone back to scrubbing the pans, her tears dripping into the dirty dishwater.

Gertie disgustedly scraped the remains of Madre's tray into the garbage and resolved that tomorrow she would serve her less. It was a sin to throw away what little food they had! Gertie would have eaten it herself, but she couldn't bear the thought of putting her lips on something that had touched Madre's.

Gertie angrily stacked the dishes in the sink and poured herself a cup of coffee. Only the dregs were left in the pot, but it was enough for her. Wearily, she sat on one of the kitchen chairs, unable to face the dishes or the lunch that she would soon have to start preparing. Though she had never been any good at sewing, she had started making a little blanket for the baby, and she supposed she should try to finish it, though a part of her wished she could simply sit in the front room with the big brown radio. Almost as tall as her, it had been covered in dust when she had discovered it. There was a small hole in the speaker mesh where it looked like a mouse had begun to chew, but she had fiddled with it until she managed to get it to work. Thus, every once in a while, when Lorenzo was gone, she would be able to catch *Amos and Andy* or *Your Hit Parade*. She had lost her passion for *Ali Baba* and even *The Rodeo Boys*, though once when she happened to hear Patsy Montana, her heart gave a little flutter. She had been tempted to switch it off as soon as she heard Patsy's jangly voice, but somehow she just couldn't. Instead, she sang along, her eyes stinging as she did.

No, she didn't have time for the radio this morning. After she did the dishes, she would have to bundle up and walk to Peterson's to get some pork or maybe beef bones for a soup. The thought of food made her feel nauseous, but she would welcome the cold air. She felt unusually warm and breathless this morning, as if the baby was sucking the very air out of her. Lorenzo had gone off somewhere early this morning with Roman, though she had tried to tell him that Madre seemed worse. What if the old witch died while he was gone? She was sure to get the blame for it.

Well, she sighed, putting her head down on her crossed arms on the table, there was nothing she could do about it. She stayed this way for a minute or two, trying to catch her breath, until she heard the sound of a bell ringing. She groaned, thinking it was Madre ringing her bell again for something, before she realized it was only the doorbell.

Feeling heavy and bloated, Gertie hauled herself up from the table and felt a pain disturbingly rip through her lower regions. She had been having dull aches all night, but she assumed it was indigestion. Cradling her big stomach with one hand, she made her way to the door and opened it, a gust of February wind hitting her hard in the face. It was only the old woman, obviously come to see Madre. There was no rhyme or reason to this woman's appearances, and Gertie had long ago given up trying to predict them.

"Oh, it's you." Gertie stepped aside and waved her in, wondering why the woman had even bothered to ring the bell. Normally, she just walked in. "She's not very good today."

"I not come for her," the woman said simply as she stepped inside and lowered the black scarf from around her head. "I come for you. It is time for baby to come." She removed her coat, an old black woolen thing, worn and patched.

Gertie was about to protest when another pain ripped through her, this time making it hard for her to stand. *Was the baby really coming right now?* she panicked. She wasn't ready!

"I . . . I have to get to the doctor," Gertie panted, cradling her stomach with both arms, wondering how the old woman had known. Horrified, she felt a trickle of water pour down her leg.

"No time," the old woman said matter-of-factly. "Baby come now. Here, I help you." She took Gertie by the arm.

"Oh, no!" Gertie exclaimed. "Not here! I need a doctor. I . . . I don't know what to do! I want my mother!" Gertie cried and was instantly embarrassed by her outburst.

"Come, come." The woman seemed impatient. "I take a care of you. I bring many babies into world. You see. It's fine. Come," she said, more gently now, leading her to the stairs. "You go upstairs, no?"

"No!" Gertie groaned. "I can't possibly make it up the stairs."

The old woman shrugged. "Then you have baby here." She nodded toward the couch in the front room. The thought of giving birth to her baby on the place where Roman sometimes slept made her almost physically ill, and so with renewed strength, she determined that she would climb the stairs to her and Lorenzo's bed. With a deep breath, she gripped the railing with one hand and the old woman's hand with the other and began to climb, having to pause every few minutes when another pain surged through her.

Finally, she made it to their room and wanted to collapse onto the bed, but the old woman made her stand and helped her take off her dress and her underthings, as if she were a little child, and put her in a nightgown. Gertie tentatively lowered herself onto the bed then, and tried to scoot back, but she could barely do it—the pain wracking her body was too intense.

"Put knees up," the woman instructed, and when Gertie obeyed, she lifted the nightgown and looked at her nether regions. "Baby come fast." The woman stood up. "I be back," she said and quickly left the room.

Gertie didn't want her to go and tried calling out, but another pain ripped through her and a loud groan escaped instead. Gertie gripped the quilt beneath her until the pain passed. Breathless, she lay back on the pillow. She could hear Madre in the room across the hall ringing her little bedside bell. *For the love of God!*

Gertie heard the old woman shout to Madre, "She have baby now! You be quiet."

The pains were coming harder and faster now, and Gertie bore down, panting in between, until, after what seemed to be ages, the old woman mercifully reappeared carrying a teacup, a large pair of evil-looking scissors, and some towels. She tossed the towels and the scissors onto the end of the bed and brought the teacup to Gertie's lips. "You drink."

Gertie turned her face away. "No. I can't drink anything."

"You drink! It help. Come. Hurry."

Reluctantly, Gertie sipped the strange tea. It was bitter, but it had a hint of mint, which made it a little more palatable. Gertie drank the whole thing down and then strained again with another pain, her knuckles white as she gripped the quilt. "Ahhhhh!" she screamed, unable to hold it in any longer. She had been determined not to scream as her mother had with every single birth, but now she found she couldn't help it, and neither did she care. She just wanted this pain to stop! *Where is Lorenzo?* she thought desperately, though what help he would be at a time like this, she didn't know.

Gertie continued this way for almost another hour, the old woman sitting beside her during the pains then shuffling across the hall to tend to Madre when they subsided. Finally, when Gertie was sure she couldn't take it any longer, her screams were joined by another's wails, as the baby finally emerged, squalling. Gertie's cries of pain turned to ones of joy as she beheld the bloody crying mess.

"A little girl," the woman said, wiping the baby's eyes and then holding her up to show Gertie. Tears poured down Gertie's face as the woman handed her the baby—a girl, her daughter! She knew Lorenzo would be disappointed that it wasn't a boy, but she didn't care. She was so beautiful! The woman stayed long enough to deliver the afterbirth and scoop it up into towels, but then hurried away, leaving Gertie to fumble to get her breast in the baby's mouth, both of them still covered in blood. When the baby finally latched on and began to suck, Gertie felt her insides contract and a deep peace flood through her. She watched, amazed, as the baby sucked, her eyes closed.

Gertie had never felt so happy in her life.

After what was probably an hour, if Gertie judged correctly, though she couldn't be sure—she seemed to exist outside of time right now—the old woman finally reappeared. She was holding a basin of water, which Gertie presumed was to wash her and the baby, who was blissfully sleeping in her arms. She remained in the doorway, however, and announced, with no preamble at all, that Madre had died just minutes after the baby had been born.

"Died?" Gertie tried to sit up without waking the baby, her nether regions throbbing. "Are you sure?"

"*Sì*, I am sure." The woman nodded sadly as she set the basin at the foot of the bed. "In *this* room, I bring life into world. Over there," she said, gesturing toward Madre's room, "I help one leave." She gave a little shrug, as if this was not an extraordinary occurrence.

"Oh, God," Gertie groaned, immediately imagining Lorenzo's reaction. Gertie, of course, was not a bit sad that Madre was gone. It was a relief, to be sure. After all, wasn't it what she had secretly wished for for months? But why today? Why on her little girl's birthday? she wondered, rubbing the baby's silky cheek as she slept, her mouth slightly open, reminding Gertie so much of Ingrid that fresh tears suddenly burned her eyes. She didn't want any blight on her little daughter's entry into this world.

"This bad omen, I think," the old woman said nonchalantly and reached for the baby.

"Don't say that!" Gertie exclaimed, clutching the baby tighter. "How dare you say that!"

The old woman shrugged. "Maybe yes, maybe no. But maybe this baby is cursed. You must pray to St. Trofimina or to Virgin."

"I don't believe all that mumbo jumbo," Gertie said firmly, though in her heart she was terrified that what the old woman said might be true.

"What you name her?" the woman asked, again holding out her arms for the baby.

"Patsy, I think," Gertie murmured with a tentative smile as she looked at the baby and finally gave her to the woman to be washed. "Or maybe Ingrid."

As predicted, Lorenzo was beside himself with grief. Even all the way up in the bedroom, Gertie could hear his loud moaning from the kitchen where the old woman was apparently telling him the bad news. He was drunk as a skunk, Gertie could tell, which was probably making his reactions even more dramatic. Finally, after what seemed like hours, she heard him mount the stairs, and she nervously smoothed out the bedquilt as best she could and then propped the baby in her arms so that he would see her sweet, scrunched face when he first walked in.

He did not come into their room, however, but instead went immediately into Madre's. She could hear him sobbing. An ache in her throat, Gertie sat waiting until she eventually drifted asleep, waking only to feed the baby when she heard her tiny mews.

It wasn't until almost dawn when Gertie opened her eyes fully to see Lorenzo standing over her bed. Startled, she struggled to sit up, fumbling to unwrap the baby nestled beside her. This was not how she had imagined presenting the baby to her Papa.

"I'm sorry about your mother," Gertie thought to say, to which Lorenzo only gave a curt nod. "It's a good thing that the old woman turned up when she did."

"That's so." Lorenzo's face was grim. "But if she wasn't bothered with you and this brat, she might have been able to tend to her better. Might have been able to save her."

"Lorenzo, I—"

"It's a girl, right?" Lorenzo interrupted.

"Yes," Gertie answered nervously.

"Then we'll name her Leonora, after mother," he said stiffly.

"But I thought we might name her—"

"Her name's Leonora," he barked and left the room.

Gertie broke down into tears.

June 1932

Nora

Nora held in her tears as she made her way down the grand staircase of the main hall. Classes were over for the week, and girls were running to and fro on the quad, a happy buzz permeating the grounds. Nora, however, could not join in their happiness. This Sunday would mark the sixth visiting day since they had been here, and with each one that passed, she had less and less hope that Ma would actually appear.

After her vigil in the cellar with Patsy, Nora had managed to get a look at the entries in the guest book and discovered that Ma hadn't in fact shown up that day. It had utterly baffled her. Surely, she had gotten her letters explaining where they were, hadn't she? Perhaps she had to work? Though Ma normally didn't work *every* Sunday, she knew. None of this made any sense.

Not knowing what else to do, Nora wrote *more* letters, each of them sad missives filled with proclamations of love or apology, declaring Ma to be the very best mother in the world and saying she was sorry if they had done something wrong. She closed each letter with a sincere apology and an offer to be good, to be a better girl, to help more with Patsy.

None of these had been answered, either, which drove Nora to the brink of despair. Perhaps Ma really *was* angry at her, tired of her surliness toward Olson. Tired of her "trying to ruin it for her," as Ma had once accused, simply because Nora hadn't thanked him nicely enough for the sweets he once bought them. Or maybe it was because she had pouted about having to take Patsy to the park whenever Olson happened to turn up. She didn't know which was worse . . . Ma being gone all hours of the night, or when he would appear at their home, forcing Nora and Patsy to sleep on the worn-out sofa rather than in bed with Ma.

Nora now regretted her behavior. She should have pretended to like Olson more. Maybe then Ma wouldn't have been so irritated? Is that why she stayed away? To teach her a lesson? *I'm sorry, Ma!*

Sometimes, late at night, when she found it hardest to control her rampant fear and guilt, her mind would inevitably stray to what Ma had said to Miss Whitlow that terrible day. Nora tried not to think about it, pulling the thin blanket over her head to block out the words, but it was no use. She still could hear Ma begging to be allowed to at least keep Patsy. "Please," Ma had cried, "she's only a baby! Please! Take Nora if you must, but don't take Patsy!" Trapped under the blanket with only her own stale breath, Nora would wonder over and over why Ma had begged to keep *Patsy* and not *her*? Did Ma hate her so very much?

"Hey! Where are you going?" someone called after her as she walked aimlessly across the quad. It was Celia, running to catch up.

"I don't know. To study, I guess."

"On a Friday night?"

Nora shrugged.

"Want to go to my Girl Scout meeting with me? You'd like it."

Nora wasn't sure what a girl scout was, but she didn't think she should go. For one thing, what would she do with Patsy?

"No thanks."

"Maybe next time, then?"

"Maybe."

"What about this Sunday?"

Cheeks burning, Nora kept her eyes locked on the ground. "What about it?" she asked, knowing full well what Celia was referring to.

"You know, if your mom . . . can't make it," Celia said, the hesitancy in her voice not lost on Nora, "why don't you and Patsy spend the day with me and Aunt Rita? She's a little bit strict, but it's better than . . ." Her voice trailed off.

Nora's head snapped up. "Better than nothing?"

The unease on Celia's face had Nora regretting her sharp retort, but she didn't apologize.

"Come on, Nora. Don't be cross. She might bring my brother, Lyle, and my dumb cousin, Billy. They're great fun, and then I wouldn't be outnumbered. You'd be doing me a favor."

Nora bit the inside of her cheek, trying to determine if this was simply charity. Ever since Celia had offered to peel potatoes the day of Patsy's first imprisonment, she had been making friendly overtures. Celia seemed like a nice girl, but Nora didn't want to make any friends. She wanted to go home.

"At least your mom's alive," Celia said, almost cheerfully.

Nora stopped walking. She had forgotten that Celia's mom was dead. She felt she should say something, but she didn't know what.

"Sorry," she finally mumbled.

"That's okay. It was a while ago now. I miss her, though."

Nora's curiosity got the better of her. "How'd she die?"

"Bringing my little brother into the world. Cal's his name. I named him," she said with a note of pride. Then she threw herself down on an iron bench positioned beneath a giant oak tree in the middle of the quad. Nora remained standing, her arms folded across her chest.

"That's sad," was all she could think to say.

Celia rested her elbows along the back of the bench and crossed her legs as casually as if she were telling Nora the most basic of tales.

"It *was* pretty terrible," Celia admitted, though her face betrayed no emotion. "I cried for weeks, but it was worse when Dad left. Just up and went."

Nora uncrossed her arms, intrigued. She could barely remember her father, Lorenzo. He, too, just disappeared one day. "He just left?"

"Yeah. Don't know why, really. I guess he got plain fed up. Got tired of taking care of six kids, so he just didn't come home one night. Went out west somewhere is what we heard."

"He just left you all?" Nora asked, gingerly taking a seat beside Celia.

Celia merely nodded. "Margaret tried her best. That's my older sister. She tried her best to take care of me and the boys on her own, but it was hard with not very much money and Cal being so little. Ralph got a job loading boxes, but it didn't pay much. Before long, though, he got fed up, too, and said he wasn't gonna get tied down changing a lot of a diapers of kids that weren't even his, so he ran off and joined the Navy."

"He did?"

"Yeah. Stinker." Celia rubbed her nose. "Lyle got a job on a milk truck, but that wasn't enough, either. Finally, Margaret got so desperate that she had to lower her pride an' telephone my Aunt Rita. That's Dad's sister. She lives all the way out in Elmwood Park. She came to our apartment in Edgewater and said what a disgrace it all was. Said no wonder Burt ran off." Celia gave a sad shrug. "We did try our best, but . . ."

"It wasn't your fault that your mom died." Nora could feel her indignation rising.

"No," Celia mused. "I 'spose that was Cal's fault. That's what Dad always said. He wouldn't even pick him up. Not one time. Margaret and me, but mostly Margaret, had to take care of him. He didn't even have a name for the longest time. We just called him 'Baby,' but then after Dad left, Margaret said he should have a name and made me pick it. I miss him terrible, Nora. I know it's Mom I should be missing, and I do, but I can hardly bear to be apart from little Cal. I'm terribly worried about him."

"Where . . . where is he?" Nora asked, fearing the answer.

"Aunt Rita put him and Benny and Frank in Queen of Angels."

"An orphanage?" Nora was incredulous. "How come she didn't put *you* there?"

"I don't know. I guess 'cause I'm too old."

"What about everybody else?" Nora had lost track of how many of them there were.

"Well, Ralph had already run off to the Navy. And Aunt Rita arranged for Margaret to become a nanny for a rich family on the North Shore. I got sent here." She gestured widely. "That just left Lyle, and he got to go live with Aunt Rita and Uncle Carroll. I think it's 'cause he was always the quietest. *And* he's the same age as my cousin, Billy, so Aunt Rita said he'd be a good playmate."

Nora considered this. "Couldn't she have taken all of you?"

"Nah. Aunt Rita is very particular, you see, and she and Uncle Carroll live in a bungalow filled with all sorts of fine things. The boys would be sure to break all of them if we were to all go there and live."

Nora did not think this was a very good reason, but she didn't say so. In fact, hearing all of this, Nora judged Celia to be remarkably forgiving. If she were in the same situation, she suspected she might be a little bitter. But at least Aunt Rita came to visit, which was more than she could say for her own mother.

Nora stood up unsteadily. "I should probably go."

"Go? Go where? You just said you didn't have anything to do." Celia sat up straight and tented her eyes with one hand.

"I have to check on Patsy."

"Want me to come along?"

"No. I . . . I can do it."

Celia's face crumpled a little.

"I'll find you later, okay?" Nora offered.

"Yeah, okay." Celia gave her a little smile.

Nora tried to return it and hurried toward Solomon. In truth, she did need to find Patsy, but another idea was uncomfortably brewing, like a storm on the horizon. Celia's story, which on some small level had succeeded in making her feel better about her own situation, had unfortunately caused another, bigger worry to surface. What if Ma had up and left, just as Celia's father had done? Gone out west somewhere with Olson to start a new life? The thought nearly strangled her. She quickened her steps and silently entered Solomon.

Normally, Patsy was supposed to return to the cottage after her morning class to nap, but she didn't always do so. Nora stood in the foyer, listening. She could hear Mrs. Morris typing away in her office at the back of the cottage.

Nora tiptoed toward the dormitory and prayed that Patsy was there, not off wandering. She paused at the partially open door and was relieved to hear Patsy's tiny voice. She peered in and saw her sister, not on her bed, but sitting on the floor, wedged between the bunk beds, her back to her, playing with her doll.

"But I don't want to stay here anymore, Ma," Patsy said in a high-pitched voice.

"I know you don't," Patsy replied in a deeper, loving voice. "I've missed you so much, Patsy. I want you to come home now and never, ever leave me again."

"Do you really mean it, Ma?" Patsy asked in the high-pitched voice.

"Of course I do. Let's go right now!"

"But what about Mrs. Morris?"

"Oh, blast her. She's an evil spider, and she can't tell you what to do anymore! She's going to jail!"

"Do you really mean it, Ma?"

"Sure I do."

"Wait 'til I tell Nora! When will it be?"

"Don't tell Nora," Patsy said in the maternal voice. "She won't believe you. She'll find out on her own."

"Oh, Momma!" said the high-pitched voice, as Patsy hugged the doll.

Nora pulled away and leaned against the wall, the desperation in Patsy's voice resonating with her own new fears. Again, her mind returned to Celia's story, this time jumping to an even worse conclusion. *Maybe . . . maybe Ma wasn't even alive.* Nora's heart began to pound in her chest. But surely someone would have told her, wouldn't they? What if . . . what if Olson had harmed Ma? Or, worse, killed her? *Oh, Ma!* Nora worried, tears blurring her eyes. She simply had to know! She *had* to know what had happened to Ma! But how?

Patsy had stopped talking to herself, and Nora peeked in again. Miraculously, Patsy had climbed up on her bed, her doll clutched tightly in her arms. There was silence except for the muffled clack of typewriter keys.

Mrs. Morris.

She would have to ask Mrs. Morris. There was no other way. None that she could think of, anyway.

Nora tiptoed down the narrow hallway toward the back office, her fingertips dragging along the wall. She paused outside the closed door, listening to the rhythmic typing, which helped to drown out the pounding of her own heart. For a brief moment, she almost lost her nerve, but before she could, she heard a shrill voice from within.

"Who's there?"

"It's me, Nora," she called.

Nora thought she heard a chair scrape backwards. "What do you want?"

Nora desperately wanted to flee, but it was too late now. She had caught the spider's attention.

"I said, what do you want? Get in here!"

Nora bit her lip and took hold of the doorknob, pushing the door open. She stood in the doorway, unsure.

"Well? What do you want?" Mrs. Morris commanded, a deep furrow etched across her forehead.

"I . . . I was just wondering . . ."

"What? I can't hear you! Come in. And speak up. You're always mumbling!"

Nora took a few tiny steps forward. "I . . . I said I was just wondering if my ma . . . my mother . . . knows where we are," Nora said, not knowing how else to begin.

"Of course your mother knows where you are, you stupid girl," Mrs. Morris said absently, looking back at what she had been typing. "She was served the papers by Miss Whitlow the night she came to collect you."

Papers? What papers?

Nora swallowed and gathered her courage, her right leg shaking. "But . . . but are you sure? Sure there wasn't some mistake?"

"Mistake?" Mrs. Morris looked up sharply.

"Maybe they forgot to put it on the paper," she faltered. "Maybe she doesn't know where we are. Maybe that's why she doesn't come to see us."

"Of course, it was on the paper! I have it right here somewhere." She opened one of the desk drawers and began rifling through the hanging files. "More than likely, she doesn't know how to read. Scarlet women usually don't."

Not know how to read? Of course Ma knew how to read! Ma had lots of stories about growing up somewhere in Iowa with strict parents who were Swedish—or was it Spanish?— and who made Ma go to school. Of course Ma could read.

"Here it is," Mrs. Morris said, opening the file. "See?" She held out a piece of paper, which Nora had to squint to read. PARK RIDGE SCHOOL FOR GIRLS, it said, with the address typed neatly beneath. Nora bit her lip, her throat aching at the effort of keeping her tears. She did not want to cry in front of Mrs. Morris.

"Satisfied?"

Nora gave a little nod.

"You're not the first, you know, to not get any visitors. Typical of the trash."

Nora felt as though she had been slapped, anger coursing through her. "Maybe she moved? Or . . . or maybe something happened to her?"

"Maybe."

"But . . ." Nora hesitated. "But what if . . . what if she's dead?"

Mrs. Morris gave a sharp little laugh, which wounded Nora as much as if she had thrust a dagger into her heart.

"I doubt it. The state would inform us—eventually, anyway. Look, I don't know why your mother doesn't come to see you. Maybe she *did* move. How would I know? It isn't any of my concern. Now go on and get back to work." She gave a stiff wave toward the door and then resumed her typing, as if nothing were wrong, as if she hadn't just crushed a little girl's last hope.

Nora stood frozen just inside the doorway, her insides caving in over and over. She couldn't think! There had to be more to it than this, but she didn't know what else to ask. She stood perfectly still, not wanting to attract Mrs. Morris's attention while she searched for something to latch onto. There *was* one thing . . .

"Mrs. Morris?" she asked timorously.

Mrs. Morris looked up, surprised. "You still here? What do you want now?"

"What's a . . . what's a *scarlet woman*?"

"A scarlet woman?" Mrs. Morris scoffed, a strange grimace, or maybe it was a smile, crossing her face. "Don't you know anything? A scarlet woman is a lady of the night." Mrs. Morris paused, waiting for Nora to understand. "Oh, for heaven's sake, she's a prostitute! Don't you know that?"

June 1924

Gertie

Everything changed after Madre died.

For one thing, Lorenzo was inconsolable and spent weeks after the funeral in a perpetual state of drunkenness. Even the fact that there was a new little life in the house did not have any effect. In fact, Lorenzo barely noticed his daughter, except to tell Gertie to shut her up whenever she cried. Roman, too, ceased his visitations, as if he couldn't bear to be in the house without Madre.

Gertie, on the other hand, was utterly consumed by the baby, who filled her with a new type of joy. Privately, Gertie called her Nora, as she refused to attach the spider's name to her beautiful little girl. She was convinced that when Lorenzo finally got over his grief, he would see how perfect she was and then they might have a real chance at being happy. She no longer cared if she went traveling with the carnival. All she wanted now was to make a nice home, like Maman had done for all of them. With Madre gone, Gertie found she was finally able to breathe deeply and started to try to fix the place up, sewing curtains and even rearranging the furniture, delighted not to have anyone disapprove or scold her.

As winter began to melt away, however, Lorenzo was still paralyzed by grief. With spring came the resurrection of the carnival, which Gertie hoped might restore him to his former self, and for once, she was glad to see Roman when he came round to fetch him. Lorenzo had dutifully followed him out of the house, but Gertie could see that his heart wasn't in it. Still, she was hopeful.

After only about a month, though, it seemed that Lorenzo had still not returned to his usual charming self in front of the crowds. Roman had accompanied him home late one night, startling Gertie when he shoved Lorenzo through the front door and accused him of being surly and foul with the crowds.

"Listen, Lor," Roman said evenly, pointing a finger at him, "it's one thing to have a beer or two with the performers, but not the hard stuff all day long." He reached into Lorenzo's red velvet vest and snatched a silver flask and pocketed it.

"Fuck off," Lorenzo slurred.

Roman stared at him, his hands on his hips. "I'm warning you, Lor. This is no way to run a business, and if you don't stop, I'm going to have to go to Gideon."

"You wouldn't dare!"

"Try me," Roman snarled. "You got one more chance." He shot Gertie a quick glance, huddled in a corner of the room, Nora in her arms, and then banged out of the house.

"You can't talk to me that way!" Lorenzo yelled at the screen door from where he stood, swaying, before he stumbled up the stairs, not saying a word to Gertie.

It didn't even take a full week, however, for Lorenzo to burn through this last chance.

Gertie stood at the stove early one Saturday morning, frying eggs and fretting because Lorenzo had not come home at all the previous night. He had begun staying out until the wee hours now that the carnival was in full swing, but he had never stayed out all night before. She wondered if he had spent the night in the caravan and if he would even bother coming home at all today. She hoped so because she had bought sausages with the last of her housekeeping money. Before she could ponder this dilemma too much, however, she heard the slam of his truck door and breathed a sigh of relief as she scrambled to toast some bread.

The screen door banged, and by the way he pounded across the front room, she could tell he was in a foul mood.

"Pack up!" he shouted as he came into the kitchen. "We're movin'."

Nora, who had been contentedly sleeping in her cradle by the stove, startled awake and began to cry.

"Moving?" Gertie picked up the baby and began to sway with her, hoping this was some kind of joke. "Where to?"

"Chicago. Now get yourself going."

Chicago? Surely this was a jest, but panic started to ripple through her just the same. How could they move to Chicago?

"But why, Lorenzo? What's happened?"

Lorenzo stared at her, his dark eyes small and mean. "Just shut up, woman, and do as I say!" he barked.

Gertie began to pat Nora, hard, on the back. "Did . . . did something happen at the carnival?" she ventured to ask. "Is that why you didn't come home last night?"

"I spent the night in a ditch, for all you care."

"Oh, Lorenzo! What happened?"

"There was a fight. The cops were called. Roman threw me out, told me not to come back. So, fuck him." Lorenzo picked up a glass sitting near the sink and hurled it across the room, where it collided with the far wall and shattered, causing a fresh burst of wailing from Nora.

"I said pack up!" Lorenzo shouted. "Now!"

"But . . . but why can't we stay here?" Gertie asked looking forlornly at the new curtains she had sewed for the kitchen window, as she swayed with Nora, trying to quiet her.

"Because Roman pays the rent on this shithole. Now get going, or so help me God . . ." He strode toward her, his fist raised, but Gertie backed quickly away. His chest was heaving, but he dropped his arm. "And don't look at me like that," he snarled and walked out.

Gertie managed to pack up their few meager belongings by that evening, which Lorenzo threw into the back of his battered truck while Gertie climbed into the front with Nora. They didn't even bother to lock the door of the old McPherson Place; they just left, and Gertie wondered if Roman would move in. The fact that he paid the rent explained much, and Gertie wished she had known that earlier on. Lorenzo gave the truck a violent crank, starting it with a choking cough, and off they went. Gertie tried not to cry. She chastised herself for being so silly. After all, wasn't this what she had always wanted? To get away?

It took two days to get to Chicago, mainly because the truck kept breaking down, forcing them to spend an uncomfortable night sleeping on the road. Lorenzo laid out in the warm spring air in the bed of the truck, while Gertie tried to stretch out with Nora on the seat. In the morning, Lorenzo was somehow able to get the truck started again, and they set off, the roads becoming more crowded with automobiles the closer they got. Finally, at a filling station on the edge of the city, Lorenzo asked for directions to Little Italy, where he said had a friend they could stay with. Gertie didn't like the sound of showing up on someone's doorstep, but what could she do? Lorenzo had barely said a word the whole of the journey. When she tried to ask him questions, he either told her to shut up or simply didn't answer.

Lorenzo's friend, a fellow Italian by the name of Mario Martino, lived in an apartment building on Halstead. Gertie, her insides churning, slowly followed Lorenzo up the stairs and stood nervously behind him while he knocked on a random door on the third floor. She wanted to die of embarrassment when the door opened abruptly and she saw the look of surprise, followed immediately by one of annoyance on the face of the man standing there. After only a few moments, however, the man managed to produce a reluctant sort of smile. He embraced Lorenzo, then, and began speaking rapidly in a foreign language.

"Lorenzo! Lorenzo! You come to see us!" he said, eventually switching to broken English. "Come in, come in! We not see you for long time. Maybe years. And who is this?" he asked looking behind Lorenzo. "This you wife? And *bambino*! Come, come. We drink. To celebrate, no?"

The Martinos were in truth very kind to them, though Gertie was humiliated to have to accept their forced hospitality, especially as it was painfully clear that they had very little to share. It was a tiny apartment, just a kitchen, a front room and two bedrooms for what appeared to be six kids and an elderly mother. Gertie was reminded of their little shack in Keystone and understood very well what a hardship it would have been if a family of three had suddenly turned up at their door. As it was, Mrs. Martino forced her two daughters out of the bedroom they shared with their grandmother and had them sleep on the floor of the front room with all of the boys so that the De Lorenzos could have their bed.

As the days passed, Gertie tried to help Mrs. Martino as much as she could, but it was obvious they were just underfoot. After a week had passed, with Lorenzo making no apparent move to find them their own place, Gertie urged him to leave.

"They don't mind," Lorenzo snapped back as they squeezed into the tiny bed. Nora was on the floor beside them while the old grandma snored away across the room.

"They do, Lorenzo. We can't just live here. We've got to get our own place."

"I know that! I'm working on it. Can't you ever be happy?" he said, rolling over onto his side.

Whether or not Lorenzo noticed Mr. Martino's increasingly forced smiles at dinner or the fact that the wine no longer flowed so readily, he finally announced one day that he had found an apartment for them on Hudson, and more than that, that he had found a job. There was much cheering to be had that night, several toasts, and the same loud, boisterous talk that had accompanied dinner on their first night.

The apartment was miles away in an area of the city called Cabrini Green. Built at the turn of the century, the building itself was a hulking structure of brown brick with three floors and six units on each side of the main door. It looked to have once maybe been respectable, but now it just seemed tired and run down. The tiny entryway's tiled floor was cracked and smudged with dirt, and the plaster along the stairs was crumbling. Still, Gertie tried to be positive as Lorenzo led her to the top floor. It was a small place, just a front room, a tiny kitchen, a bathroom, one bedroom, and a tiny back porch off the kitchen.

The whole place had a sad, abandoned feel, as if it had sat empty for a long time, but Gertie started right away to try to make it a home while Lorenzo went to his new job at Schneider & Sons Sheet Metal.

As it turned out, however, Schneider and Sons was merely the first in a long string of jobs. Born for the carnie life, Lorenzo found it hard to stay with any one thing for more than a short period. He was constantly quitting or getting fired.

When they had first arrived, Lorenzo was a bit more like his old self, and Gertie was hopeful that perhaps he was turning a new leaf, leaving his grief behind. But after he lost his second job in a month, he began drinking heavily again and his surliness returned. He rarely called her "darlin'" anymore and never Trudy. Usually, he didn't call her anything at all, except maybe "woman." He stayed out increasingly longer as the months went on. At first, he said he was working extra hours, then that he was with friends, and then he eventually admitted that he was sometimes picking up a game of cards at Bruno's, the corner tap.

Whatever the case, Gertie never really knew where he was or when he was coming home. He gave her a small amount of money at the beginning of each month, and from that she had to manage. Likewise, she did her best to be pleasant, but he seemed to find little pleasure in her company. He rarely made love to her anymore, though Gertie didn't mind, as he was becoming increasingly rough and violent during the act, and she no longer particularly enjoyed it.

She began to fear their intimacies, actually, ever since that one terrible night when she was so very ill with a flu. To make matters worse, Nora had been teething. Gertie had finally gotten her settled into the cradle beside the bed for the third time and had just crawled into bed, weary to the bone, her stomach and her throat aching, when Lorenzo had finally banged through the bedroom door, startling Nora awake as he proceeded to strip off his dirty work clothes.

"Lorenzo, you've woken up the baby!" Gertie said, feeling like she might cry herself. She lay there for a moment, letting Nora whimper, as she tried to gather her strength. Then she felt Lorenzo's hand on her breast.

"No, Lorenzo, I'm sick as a dog. Please. Not tonight," she pleaded, trying to turn away.

But Lorenzo continued, pulling at her underthings as he rolled on top of her.

"No, Lorenzo! I'm sick. Please," she cried, trying to squirm out from under him, Nora wailing now. "Lorenzo, the baby! Please. Not now." She tried to push him off, but he had already thrust himself inside her, hard and fast. Tears stung her eyes.

When he finally finished, he slapped her. "Don't you say no to me again, hear?" he snarled with a final painful thrust and rolled off her.

As it happened, Gertie unfortunately conceived a child that night. In the beginning, she hoped she would lose it, but as the birth grew ever closer, she simply prayed that it would not be an unlucky baby, having been the product of . . . well, not exactly love.

Thus, on a warm June morning another baby girl had come into the world. Again, Lorenzo was not around for it, but this time Gertie knew what to do when she began feeling pains. She went down and knocked at the Kennedys, two flights down, trying not to panic because it was at least a month before her time. Thankfully, it was Mrs. Kennedy who opened the door and not her ogre of a husband, and she promptly sent off one of her kids for the midwife.

The baby was almost out by the time the midwife got there, but she was at least there to finish the job. Being early, the baby was very tiny, only about four pounds the midwife guessed, but other than that, to Gertie's worried eyes, she looked perfect. Not deformed or unlucky at all.

Gertie was determined to name this one Patsy, and she had a persuasive speech all ready for Lorenzo for when he came home. It turned out that Gertie's efforts at crafting a winning argument were in vain, however, as when he did eventually come home, he barely looked at the little thing and told Gertie she could name it what she wanted. And so, Gertie happily named her Patricia, or Patsy, for short, though her victory did not have the exact flavor of triumph she had expected.

Though the birth had been uneventful, Gertie had a difficult time recovering. Patsy, too, was failing to thrive. When she realized just how bad Gertie was, Mrs. Kennedy began stopping by at least once a day, bringing soups and teas, or whatever else she could spare, especially advice.

"It's colic for sure," Mrs. Kennedy told her in regard to Patsy's endless fussing and crying. No matter what Gertie did, she could never get the new baby to settle. Nora had never been like this, and Gertie was nearing her wit's end. Mrs. Kennedy had provided relief, however, in the form of a "tonic" in a small brown bottle. Prying off the cork, Gertie had gingerly smelled it and thought she detected a faint whiff of alcohol. Dubious, she was hesitant to give it to Patsy, but nearing despair, she had finally tried it. The tonic worked like a charm, sending Patsy straight to sleep.

Unfortunately, in her continued desperation to keep Patsy quiet, especially when Lorenzo was around, Gertie had gone through the bottle rather quickly. Lorenzo had no patience for Patsy's crying, and continually roared at Gertie to "shut the brat up or I'll give her something to cry about." Gertie would frantically pace, shushing her over and over, which only seemed to make her cry all the more.

One terrible night, Lorenzo, drunk and fed up, came through on his threat and ripped Patsy from Gertie's arms. Gripping the front of her little nightgown in a tight ball, he held his little daughter at arm's length and slapped her across the face. Poor Patsy's little eyes widened with the shock of it before she let out an ear-piercing wail.

"Lorenzo, no! No! God, please!" Gertie shouted, pulling at his arm and trying to grab Patsy back. Nora was whining now, too, adding to the din. Miraculously, Gertie was able to somehow wrench Patsy away from Lorenzo. Clutching the baby to her, she quickly grabbed Nora's hand and ran for the back porch, hoping it would calm things down.

"Mamma!" Nora cried, pulling at her dress. "Mamma!"

Gertie gave her a little pat on the head but turned her full attention to the squalling baby in her arms, trying to assess if she were badly hurt. How could she tell? she worried, kissing her soft little forehead and trying to rock her.

"Mamma!" Nora cried again, and Gertie gave her another caress.

"Shh, Nora. It's okay now. It's okay," she said in a soothing voice, though panic was coursing through her.

Gertie stayed out on the porch, rocking Patsy and trying to tell Nora stories, for nearly an hour until she was pretty sure Lorenzo had passed out. Only then did she dare to creep back into the house, still in shock that Lorenzo had hit a helpless baby.

The very next day, while Lorenzo was still asleep, Gertie hurried down the stairs to ask Mrs. Kennedy where she had gotten the tonic from.

"From Lieberman," Mrs. Kennedy informed her, wiping her hands on her apron. "You know, the old Jew? Pulls that medicine cart? Comes through on Tuesdays."

"Tuesday?" Gertie groaned at the fact that she would have to wait almost a whole week.

When Tuesday finally arrived, she waited by the front-room window for much of the day until she saw Lieberman's old-fashioned horse and cart rattling down Hudson. She left Patsy with Nora and rushed down to buy her own little bottle of tonic out her meager household money, wishing she had enough to buy two.

Though she resolved to try to make this one last longer than the first, it had unfortunately gone just as quickly, and Gertie was again left with no resource in a matter of days.

She shifted Patsy onto her shoulder and tried rubbing her back as she paced. She was especially fussy tonight, and Gertie was desperate to get her to sleep before Lorenzo stumbled in. He had not come home at all yesterday, so he was sure to turn up tonight and probably in a very foul mood. Gertie considered bundling them all up and going for a walk around the block to avoid a confrontation, but it was raining, and, likewise, they couldn't just wander outdoors indefinitely. For one thing, Lorenzo would be furious if he returned to find no dinner waiting.

For the second time tonight, Gertie unbuttoned her dress in an attempt to get Patsy to latch on, but Patsy was having none of it. It was as if she were constantly in pain, her little legs seizing up every time she cried. Gertie again shifted her onto her shoulder when she heard heavy footsteps on the stairs.

Oh, God! The only thing she could think of was to again retreat to the back porch. Grabbing Nora by the arm, she hurried to the kitchen and fumbled to open the back door. Once outside, she turned the crying Patsy around so that the cool air hit her face straight on. Sometimes that worked for a few moments. Gertie held her breath, watching the breeze lift Patsy's blond curls. Miraculously, she quieted for a moment.

Gertie braced herself for the bang of the front door, but she was instead surprised by a firm rap. Gertie poked her head back into the kitchen, straining to listen, and heard the knock again, this time harder. Puzzled, she stepped back inside, wondering who it could be. Mrs. Kennedy would never knock, and she was the only person who ever visited.

Slinging Patsy back onto her shoulder, Gertie opened the front door and gave a little gasp to see a policeman standing outside with an assortment of Mrs. Kennedy's children behind him.

"Mrs. Norman De Lorenzo?"

"Yes?" Gertie asked hesitantly, forgetting for a moment that Lorenzo's real name was Norman.

"I'm afraid I have some bad news, Mrs. De Lorenzo," the policeman said, his forehead creased. "Your husband's been killed."

CHAPTER 11

January 1932

The girls at the Sunshine Café were in the habit of going to the new dance hall, the Aragon Ballroom, on a Tuesday night because admission was free. They were constantly urging Gertie to come along, telling her she simply *had* to see the inside of this place, as it was grander than anything any of them had ever seen, but Gertie always declined. She was hesitant to leave Nora and Patsy alone any longer than she had to. She didn't trust her neighbors, she said, and it made her uneasy. If she went, she would surely fret the whole time.

Gertie had been working at the Sunshine for almost two years now, and besides the tips and the scraps she sometimes ate off the plates stacked in the kitchen, the thing she enjoyed most was the camaraderie of her fellow waitresses. She finally had what she saw had been lacking in her life for years and years—friends.

When she had first gone to the shelter, the nuns had arranged for her to clean offices at night, and though Gertie was grateful, working nights by herself had been terribly lonely.

She had been dying a slow death from loneliness, she realized, going all the way back to her entombment in the old McPherson place with Madre. She had met a few women at the shelter, but most of them were transitory or else women of the night who weren't overly warm despite Gertie's initial attempts at conversation. The nuns were friendly, but they were busy and overworked.

"You have to live a little bit, Gert," Monica, one of the girls at the Sunshine, said impatiently. "How are you ever going to meet anyone stuck at home all the time?"

Gertie, of course, had no answer to this.

In the five years since Lorenzo's death, she hadn't ever considered being with someone else. She still felt tied to Lorenzo, as if he were just on one long trip with the carnival and would be coming home any day. She had been in a fog for months after Lorenzo's death. Though it was true that he had not at all turned out to be the man she had thought him to be, she found she missed him, at least initially.

In the early days following his hasty funeral, she had considered making her way back to Keystone. But even if she could figure out how, her prospects there seemed dismal. After everything that had happened, she couldn't just move back in with Maman and Pa, or even Signe or Astrid, not with another two mouths in tow to feed. And what would she do there? Get a job? There were no jobs there, she knew, nor even in Eddyville. At least here, she *might* be able to find something. But who would watch the girls? Mrs. Kennedy had told her once that sometimes single parents put their children in orphanages until they got on their feet, but Gertie had adamantly dismissed such an idea. She would never give up Nora or Patsy. She would just have to find some other way.

She had managed to make the meager pile of money Lorenzo left behind last for almost three months, but eventually the landlord had appeared out of nowhere to collect the rent she didn't have. Gertie tried to protest, even beg, but he didn't care, just picked his teeth with a toothpick and told her to get going or he'd physically throw her out. Crying, she had packed up as much of her things as she could carry while also holding Patsy, and made her way, clinking and clanging, down the stairs to Mrs. Kennedy's door, little Nora toddling behind.

Mrs. Kennedy had proven herself to be a saint yet again following Lorenzo's death, but even that good woman had limits, as she had her own large brood of children, not to mention her own short-tempered husband. After welcoming Gertie in for some coffee and a piece of toast and what turned out to be a good cry, Mrs. Kennedy had tenderly suggested that perhaps Gertie should seek help at a shelter. That was when Gertie had begun to really sob. "Word has it that Sacred Heart ain't such a bad one. It's safe, that's the thing. And clean," Mrs. Kennedy had explained hopefully. "You know I'd help you if I could, right?" she kept repeating. "But Ed'll be home soon, and you know how he is."

In the end, Gertie had allowed herself to be led to the door of Sacred Heart, over on Division, Mrs. Kennedy instructing her oldest, Fiona, to start the supper while she was away. "I won't be gone long," she whispered.

At the shelter, Mrs. Kennedy quickly embraced Gertie and tucked a small ragdoll she had made under Patsy's little hand, asleep in Gertie's arms, her cholic having miraculously disappeared of late.

"I was saving this for Christmas," Mrs. Kennedy said with a little smile, "but she might as well have it now." She turned to Nora, then, who was watching with big brown eyes that had suddenly grown watery, perhaps at the quick realization that there wasn't one for her, and handed her a cookie, promising that she would make her a ragdoll, too, and bring it by some other day.

As promised, Mrs. Kennedy did visit from time to time, though the periods between her visits continued to grow longer and longer. Each time she turned up, she brought a little basket of goodies, but she seemed to have forgotten all about Nora's doll. Gertie noticed, though, and resolved that by the next Christmas she would save enough money—only God knew how—to buy Nora her own.

"You know I don't like to leave the girls at night," Gertie said as she wiped the far table in the corner at the Sunshine.

"Well, we've come up with a plan," Monica called over. "My cousin has agreed to sit with the girls while you come out with us! I don't know why we didn't think of this before."

"Oh, no!" Gertie exclaimed, standing up straight. "I couldn't do that!"

"Why ever not? You've got no excuse now, Gertie. You're going to die an old maid!"

"That's impossible, seeing as I've already been married," Gertie said with a little laugh. "Anyway," she went on, her smile disappearing, "it's really not a good idea."

"You don't have to pay her, you know. She owes me a favor."

"It's not that, it's just that . . ." How could she explain? "Patsy is naughty sometimes," Gertie mumbled, thinking about how Patsy sometimes drew on the walls if someone wasn't watching her every second. "And they're not used to strangers."

"Not used to strangers!" Monica burst out. "After living in a shelter for almost a year? I'd say they were plenty used to strangers."

Gertie walked past Monica into the kitchen and tossed her rag onto one of the counters. She supposed she would have to go, she thought with a sigh. Maybe just for a few hours to appease them. Maybe then they'd leave her alone.

"You'll have to lend me a dress," Gertie shouted through the rectangular food window, past Lou, the owner as well as the cook, who was standing in front of it.

"You dames gonna work, or you gonna yak all day?" he asked, plopping two more plates through and then ringing a little bell. "Doris! Your order's up!"

"I've already got the perfect one in mind," Monica shouted back at her.

"I said get back to work!" Lou shouted.

"All right, Lou, hold your pants on," Monica called and went to take the order of a couple who had just sat down.

Gertie smiled. She *was* curious to see the inside of the Aragon. But it wasn't to meet someone, she told herself. There were plenty of men who flirted with her or asked her out at the café, but Gertie always said no. And then there were the men at the hotel, who whistled or gave her long, leering looks as she hurried past—even if she had Nora and Patsy with her! She was afraid to trust anyone after her experience with Lorenzo, even if a part of her knew that at just twenty-six, it was probably unrealistic to think that she would be alone for the rest of her life.

The interior of the Aragon was magnificent, even better than the girls had described. Gertie was amazed as they made their way past the ticket booth, her mouth agape as she looked up at the painted ceiling. She felt as though she had been transported to some foreign land as she observed the walls' tile inlay and the Moorish columns and the swirling staircases. Now *this* was what she had imagined when she listened to Ali Baba all those years ago.

The girls quickly found a table before they were all taken, and Gertie took her place among them, almost giddy with excitement when the music began. Monica ordered her a Coca-Cola, and Gertie closed her eyes as if to better hear the music. The band was doing a rendition of "All of Me."

> *You took my kisses and all my love*
> *You taught me how to care*
> *Am I to be just remnant of a one-sided love affair*
> *All you took*
> *I gladly gave*
> *There is nothing left for me to save*
> *All of me*
> *Why not take all of me*

It was utterly delicious, and Gertie soaked it up, feeling like she hadn't felt in a long, long time. The effect was soon ruined, however, by Doris, who suddenly began to giggle. It wasn't until she poked Gertie in the ribs that Gertie finally opened her eyes to see a man standing before her.

"Shall we?" he asked with a grin. Tall and well-built, he wore a trim gray suit, gold cuff links flashing.

Gertie looked over at Monica, who merely raised her eyebrows and gave her a tiny encouraging nod.

Gertie felt her panic rising. This is exactly why she hadn't wanted to come; she had no desire to dance with anyone. "No, thanks," Gertie mumbled. "I don't really know how. Honestly."

"Oh, go on, Gertie!" Doris said.

"Yeah," the other girls chimed in. "Live a little, Gert!"

Gertie bit her lip and looked at the man again. He remained planted in front of the table, as if he had no intention of moving away without her.

"I won't bite. Promise." He gave her a wide grin.

Gertie sighed and slowly stood, smoothing down her dress and shooting the girls a secret scowl. "I really don't know how to dance, you know," she said, putting out her hand and letting him lead her toward the dance floor.

"Don't worry." He placed a hand on her back and then expertly wove them out onto the floor. "Just follow my lead."

Gertie tried hard to concentrate on moving her body in rhythm with his, her heart beating fast. Several times she stepped on his feet, which caused her to blush to the roots of her hair.

"Just relax, honey. That's it," he said encouragingly. "What's your name?"

"Gertrude," she answered, pleased that she had seemed to twirl well. She looked up at him briefly. He had a firm jaw and wavy blond hair combed neat with a heavy dose of Brylcreem. He had nice eyes, she decided. Blue, though they looked a little droopy, like he wasn't able to open them all the way. Not wanting to stare, she studied his white collar and the way his tie rested against his protruding Adam's apple. His cologne was divine, and the fabric of his suit under her fingertips was a fine serge. He was so polished and primped, so different from Lorenzo! It had been ages since she had been held by a man in this way, and she couldn't help but feel . . . well, a certain little stirring of something. In a strange way he reminded her a little of Warren, though she hadn't thought of him in ages and never had the dream anymore, as if the connection to him was well and truly dead.

Over the years since she had eloped, she had sometimes wondered what had happened to him. Surely, he was married with children by now. Maybe she should write to Ingrid and inquire. But somehow, she just couldn't get the words out. She was horrible at writing, struggling to get her thoughts down on paper. And anyway, where would she begin to explain the last nine years?

"What's . . . what's *your* name?" Gertie asked timidly.

"Olson."

"Just Olson?"

"It's Ingmar Adolf Olson to be exact, but everyone calls me Olson."

"Are you Swedish?" Gertie asked eagerly. "*Känner du vägen hem?*" she asked without thinking. *Where on Earth had that come from?* It had been years since she spoke Swedish.

Olson's response was to throw back his head and laugh. He had a loud, booming laugh.

"Why are you laughing?" Gertie felt suddenly mortified.

"Honey, I don't know a word of Swedish. That's what that was, wasn't it? Or was it German?"

"I'm sorry. I assumed you were—"

"I *am* Swedish. Swedish descent, that is, but that was years ago. A few generations now, I reckon. Me? I'm a radio salesman. I work downtown at Zenith, but I travel all over."

Radio? Gertie was intrigued. "Working in radio must be terribly interesting!"

Again, he threw his head back and laughed heartily. Gertie grinned, too, though she wasn't sure why. His laugh was contagious, even though the couple beside them shot them a rude look.

"Selling radios is a little bit different than working in radio," he explained, "but it has its rewards, that's for sure. Now, I got a question for *you*," he said, his voice dropping to a more intimate level. The dance had ended, however, and though the couples around them were making their way off the floor, Olson remained, one hand sliding from her back down the length of her arm to grasp hers. "I've been wondering, you see, why you're wearing a wedding ring."

Gertie pulled her hand from his. "I . . . my husband died," she said, flustered.

"Did he, now? Well, I'm sorry about that. How long ago was this?"

Gertie thought for a moment. "About five years and eight months, I think."

"Still counting the months?" he asked, rubbing his chin.

Gertie looked away.

"Hey, that wasn't nice of me. I beg your pardon," he said, his tone sincere.

Gertie looked back. He was certainly handsome, and a part of her fluttered under his gaze.

"How'd he die? If you don't mind me asking. Heart attack?"

She rarely spoke about Lorenzo; she hadn't even told the nuns how her husband had died. They never asked. But somehow she didn't mind talking about him now with this strange man. "He was knifed in a bar fight is what I was told."

Olson's eyebrows shot up. "Gee, I'm sorry. Tough luck."

"I suppose it was. He wasn't all that nice, though," she said quietly, again surprising herself.

Olson just stared at her, and Gertie suddenly felt she had said too much. She glanced over her shoulder to where the girls were sitting, some of them watching her and whispering. When she turned back, he appeared to be weighing something over. Gertie shifted uncomfortably.

"Well, thank you, Mr. Olson, for the dance." She took a few steps back.

"It's just Olson."

Gertie gave him a curt nod, but before she could move, he spoke again.

"What would you think of me asking you out? Would that be alright?" he asked with a little tilt of his head. "Gertrude."

Gertie was stunned. What should she say? She hadn't come here prepared to meet anyone! And if she *were* to step out with someone, should it be *him*? He was the first one to come along; maybe she should be more choosy. After all, she barely knew him . . . And yet, everyone had to start out at this point, didn't they? Not knowing each other. That was part of the intrigue, wasn't it?

"You're awfully quiet," he said, his sideways grin melting her. "That a no? You sure? It won't be no cheap date. How does dinner at Knickerbocker sound? Dancing, too? Nothing serious," he added hurriedly. "I'd just like to get to know you better."

"The Knickerbocker?" Her eyes opened a fraction wider. It was so expensive! "On Walton?"

Olson threw his head back and laughed again. "There's only one Knickerbocker, honey. How about Friday?" he asked.

"Where should I pick you up? You got your own place, or did you move back with your parents when your husband died?"

"I'm at the Hirsch Hotel."

"The Hirsch? That ain't no place for a lady. How old are you anyway?"

"That's a very rude question, Mr. Olson," she said, blushing more at his reaction to the Hirsch than his question about her age.

"It's just Olson. Well, honey, I know it's a downright inappropriate question, but I don't want no trouble, and you don't look a day over seventeen."

Gertie wanted to smile, but she made herself keep it in. "I'm old enough to have two little girls and be at the Aragon dancing with a strange man," she replied coolly. She looked at him steadily and had the pleasure of seeing him look not a little bit surprised.

"You don't say? Two little girls, eh?" he asked, his eyebrows raising and something crossing his face, though Gertie couldn't read what it was.

For a moment, she regretted mentioning Nora and Patsy, but it wasn't as if she could hide them. He would have to know sooner or later, and there was nothing shameful about having them, she reminded herself. She had been a married woman.

"Well, I stand corrected. And I'll have to meet these two little girls of yours. Should we say Friday?"

"Yes, alright then," she said, agreeing before she could think it all through. What did it matter if she went out with him once? He lifted her hand to his lips and gently kissed it. Again, she was reminded of Warren and hoped it was a good sign.

Olson had dutifully turned up at six on the dot, dressed in a pinstripe wool suit with shiny black oxfords. His hair was again slicked back with Brylcreem and the scent of his cologne was even stronger than it had been at the Aragon. He presented Gertie with a small bouquet—the first she had ever received if she didn't count the few limp-stemmed daisies Warren had once given her, which she didn't. Olson also produced a lollipop for each of the girls, who were dressed in clean dresses and standing shyly by the kitchen table. Gertie scurried to get her hat and coat, not wanting to afford him even one extra second to take in her meager surroundings. If he noticed the sparsity of furniture or the peeling paint, he didn't comment, and instead stood politely holding his hat and smiling at the girls.

She was sure their one-room place looked terrible to him, but she had been proud of it when she and the girls had moved in after so many months of scrimping and saving her tips. It wasn't the best place, granted, but it was all she could afford. And though it had lost a bit of its initial luster as time went on, she was still proud of the fact that she was able to provide a home for the girls. The nuns at the shelter had not been all that approving of her choice, but they had helped her arrange it anyway.

Gertie hurried over to the girls as she pinned on her hat, nervous to leave them and feeling a tidal wave of guilt. She regretted not asking Monica if her cousin could come again, but there was the matter of paying her this time, plus she didn't want any of the girls at work to know she was going out with Olson at all.

"Don't go, Ma!" Nora whined, grasping her about the legs.

"Don't go, Mama," Patsy also said, her lollipop already in her mouth. In one hand, she still clutched her ragdoll, which had since been named "Baby." Nora's doll had already been lost somewhere in Humboldt Park, a fact that still irritated Gertie, after she had saved so long to buy her one.

"It's just for a little bit." She bent to hug them as best she could. "Get yourselves tucked in bed and look at your picture book," she said, straightening. "I'll come in and kiss you soon as I get back."

"No, Ma, please! Please don't go! We're scared!" Nora insisted.

Gertie's face flushed with both embarrassment and annoyance. "A big girl like you, Nora? You've stayed on your own plenty. Now hush up! I'll be back soon!"

She turned away from them and walked toward the door. Olson, taking his cue, opened it and shot her a wink. She gave the girls one last look, still huddled by the table, before she closed the door and locked it, irritated almost to tears that her worry and her guilt were competing with her desire to be treated special for just one night.

As it turned out, Olson *did* treat her special that night. The dinner at the Knickerbocker was the best Gertie had ever had, to the point that she wished she could lick the plate. Olson ordered wine—not just a glass, but a whole bottle!—and afterwards asked her to dance in the crystal ballroom, just as he said he would. She knew she didn't belong here, but it was heavenly to spend one night pretending. It didn't matter if she ever saw Olson again, she told herself. It was enough to be happy for just one night.

But she did see Olson again. He began turning up unexpectedly outside the Sunshine, bringing her flowers and little gifts—pastries, a necklace, and once even a radio! It was thrilling to be spoiled in such a way, and Gertie found herself falling for him. Soon they began meeting every Friday, and sometimes Saturdays, when he'd take her to dinner, to the Aragon, to the pictures, and once even to Riverside Amusement Park, which she thought was leaps and bounds ahead of Lorenzo's shabby little carnival. On Sundays, they would sometimes go to the park, and he never minded having Nora and Patsy tag along, which she thought was awfully nice of him.

From what she could tell, Olson was the perfect man, charming and sweet and always able to make her laugh. And he knew just how to kiss her. Each time he did, Gertie felt an itchy, grasping, desperate sort of longing that was becoming difficult to control. Even a simple thing such as him gently stroking her hand as they walked excited her. Sometimes while they were dancing at the Aragon, his fingertips would caress the side of her breast, causing her to flush with pleasure, and his kisses when they parted for the night left her increasingly breathless.

Eventually, Gertie suggested that he come for dinner at the apartment, that she would cook dinner for him. He seemed delighted with this idea, and Gertie began saving money to buy the ingredients. It turned out to be a simple roast chicken, as she hadn't been able to afford beef, but it came out nicely. Gertie put on her best skirt and blouse and made sure to wear the necklace he had given her. Afterwards, they all sat and listened to his radio, and Gertie felt a happiness she hadn't known in such a long time. She couldn't remember a time when she had felt this content, this safe.

Finally, she tucked the girls into bed and drew the make-shift curtain that divided the bed from the sitting area. Then she returned to the sofa and sat next to him, so close that their legs were touching. The Guy Lombardo show was on, and Olson took her hand as they listened to Bing Crosby sing.

"Want to dance?" he asked her.

She shook her head. As much as she loved dancing with him, she didn't want to interrupt this lovely moment of contentment and peace.

"God, you're one pretty woman, you know that?" he said huskily.

He stroked her cheek with his thumb, causing her insides to instantly begin melting. He leaned toward her and brushed his lips against hers, she inhaling the crisp, clean cotton smell of him, the one hidden beneath the tobacco and cologne that infused his pressed suits. He put his arms around her and pulled her close, his lips continuing to caress hers until they moved to her cheek, and then her ear, and then the hollow of her neck. Shamefully, Gertie returned his kisses, though she wasn't sure how long she could resist giving him what she knew he wanted, what *she* wanted. When she felt him fumbling with her buttons, she knew they were crossing into dangerous waters, but she couldn't seem to stop him, her chest heaving when his fingers snuck inside her blouse and ran along the top of her brassiere. Before she knew it, they had found their way underneath, and the touch of his hands on her naked breasts sent an electric bolt through her.

They continued this way, him kissing her and caressing her breasts until she felt like she might explode. The spell was broken only when his hand traveled under her skirt and brushed the outside of her underthings. She wanted so badly to give herself to him, but she knew she shouldn't. For one thing, the girls were just on the other side of the curtain, and she wasn't sure they were yet asleep, disturbingly reminding her of Maman and Pa. The sudden memory of her parents' nightly battle over sex was enough to give her sufficient pause and to muster the necessary restraint. Awkwardly, she pushed him away and held her open blouse closed at her throat.

"No, Olson," she panted. "This isn't right. We can't do this."

Olson merely chuckled. That's one thing she loved about him. He was never angry. Always laughing. "Why not?"

"You know why," she said, tilting her head toward the sheet.

"Honey, I can be real quiet. Promise," he whispered.

Gertie looked into his droopy blue eyes and felt herself wavering. Would it be so bad to allow him to make love to her?

Finally, she let out a deep sigh. "It isn't right, Olson," she said quietly, feebly trying to fix her buttons.

Olson leaned his head against his fist, his arm propped on the back of the sofa as he stared at her. "Alright, then," he said calmly. "Let's get married, and then we can."

A small, unexpected thrill ran through her at these words, though they were quickly followed by a siren of alarm. Hadn't she already fallen for this before with Lorenzo? "Married?" she sputtered, louder than she wished and shot a glance over at the curtain. "We . . . we can't just get married on the spur of the moment!" she whispered.

"Why not?" he said with a grin. "Happens every day. Here, look." He shifted so that he could reach into his trouser pocket. He pulled out a small, navy-blue box. "I can prove that it's not just a spur of the moment thing. I've been planning this for a while, and now seems the right time."

He opened the box and held it in front of her. Inside was a very tiny diamond ring.

Gertie gasped. She had never seen anything so beautiful.

"Got that at Woolworths just today," he said. "Now, I know it's small, but there's plenty more where that came from."

Tears filled Gertie's eyes, momentarily blurring her vision.

"And I'm not talking about no courthouse wedding; I mean a *real* wedding. A great big one in a church with a breakfast after and you in a pretty white dress."

Gertie's tears rolled down her cheeks as she tried frantically to assess his genuineness. Did he really want to *marry* her? More importantly, she asked herself, did she want to marry him? Truth be told, it wasn't the first time she had considered this question in regards to Olson, and her conclusion had always been *how could she not?* He was perfect. He hadn't a single flaw that she could see, but then again, she wasn't exactly an expert when it came to sizing up men.

On the positive side, Olson certainly had a good job and did not seem wanting for money. More than that, though, he was never cross with her—or with Nora and Patsy, even when Nora occasionally tried to stand between him and Patsy in a willful little way. And that was another thing, wouldn't it be good for the girls to have a father? And maybe . . . maybe she could even go back now for a visit to Keystone. Maybe with Olson on her arm—an upstanding man and a Swede at that—maybe she would be forgiven for her earlier sins . . .

Yes, she admitted, a flicker of excitement rippling through her, she could see herself marrying him. But why on Earth did he want to marry her?

"Why me?" she blurted out.

Olson laughed. "Because I love you, honey. And I'm pretty sure you love me, too, am I right?"

A small smile escaped despite Gertie's best effort to keep it in. She could count on one hand the number of times Lorenzo had ever told her that he loved her. And here was this man giving it to her effortlessly, without any cajoling or begging on her part, which she had sometimes humiliatingly resorted to, especially after Lorenzo had had his way with her.

"Well, if you don't love me now, maybe you'll grow to love me," he suggested with a little smile.

"Oh, no, Olson! I do love you," she said hurriedly, again oddly reminded of Warren for some reason. "It's just . . . well, I suppose we don't know each other all that well."

"Course we do," he said, rubbing his knuckle along the side of her breast, stirring her again. "Don't you trust me?"

"Well, yes, but . . ."

"No buts. Come on now, honey," he whispered. "You know it makes sense."

He leaned forward and kissed her, long and slow, his tongue finding hers until Gertie felt *all* of her resolve melting away. So when he slowly pulled off her underthings and slid inside of her, she didn't stop him but indeed welcomed his thrusts and groaned with pleasure.

The next morning Gertie awoke to his arm stretched across her and the sound of his heavy breathing behind her. She smiled, remembering what they had done. Olson had made love to her in a way that Lorenzo never had. Lorenzo was always hard and fast, never really concerned for her except those couple of times at the carnival, but that had only been to lure her, she unfortunately realized later. Olson, on the other hand, was slow and sensual, pleasuring her in such a way she never knew existed. She turned to look at him, snoring lightly beside her. It was so nice to have a man to snuggle up to, she thought, observing all of his features—the tiny mole on his neck, the creases at the corners of his eyes, the small indent on his chin. She was tempted to kiss him, but she didn't want to wake him.

Was this really happening? she wondered, daring to lightly rub the blond stubble that had appeared on his cheek overnight. It was so fast, although admittedly not as fast as Lorenzo. Still, three months wasn't a long time, and she prayed she wasn't making a mistake.

Easing herself out of bed, she carefully stepped over the girls sleeping on the floor. She had been uncomfortable bringing him to her bed, but Olson had helped her transfer the girls to the floor as easily as he would have scooped up two little puppies. And, as promised, he been quiet during their second lovemaking, only letting out a tiny grunt of passion as he released inside of her. Gertie looked back on her little family one last time before tiptoeing around the curtain and padding to the kitchen area.

As quietly as she could, she pulled the frying pan out of the oven and tapped a scoop of lard into it. She watched as it melted, pulling her thin robe a little tighter before cracking the eggs. She wished she had bacon instead of just bread, but it would have to do. Soon, she wouldn't have to worry about where their next meal was coming from, and she would be able to leave this dump. She wondered where Olson lived. He had never asked her to his place, which she thought was very gentlemanly of him, a sign he didn't want to take advantage.

Gertie filled the coffee pot with water and had just struck another match when she heard an odd knock on the door. She paused, wondering if it was someone pounding on the neighbor's door . . . No, it was definitely hers. She shook the match out and hurried to the front door. Who could it possibly be at this hour?

She opened the door a crack and was surprised to see a large woman with puffy cheeks and a flabby chin, her nondescript brown hair piled lazily on top of her head. A deep scowl was writ large across her face.

"Olson in there?" she asked in a deep, almost masculine voice.

"Olson?" Gertie asked, wondering how this woman knew him, and more importantly, how she knew he was here.

"Don't play dumb with me, sugar," she said. "Where is he?"

"I . . . I . . . who are you?"

"I'm his wife, dope, or didn't he tell you that?"

"His wife?" Gertie whispered, suddenly feeling as if she might vomit. "But . . ."

"Olson?" the woman shouted. "Come out, you rat!"

Suddenly, Olson appeared behind Gertie. He had put on his pants and his white shirt hung loosely over his white t-shirt.

"Is this your wife?" Gertie asked him incredulously.

"Up to your old tricks, Myrtle?" Olson asked, absently scratching his head and ignoring Gertie's question.

"*My* tricks?" the woman shouted. "How dare you!"

"Olson, *is* this your wife? Are you married to her?" Gertie demanded.

"Now, honey, it isn't what it seems," he said, turning to her. "Fact is, I *am* married, but I've been planning on getting a divorce. Thing is, she won't agree." He wagged his thumb at

Myrtle. "She's crazy, you see, but I can't get no judge to believe me. And it don't help that she's got some slimy uncle who's a lawyer."

"Crazy?" Myrtle roared. "Oh, that's a fine kettle of fish. Aren't you one to talk? This isn't the first time he's done this, sweetie. Is it, Olson? Tell her. Tell her how you like playing house everywhere except in your own." Myrtle's small eyes were boring a hole of hate into Olson, but she was momentarily distracted by the sight of Nora and Patsy, who had crept out of bed and were standing there shivering in their nightdresses.

"What's this?" Myrtle asked. "Two little girls? Aw, ain't that sweet for you, Olson? Always wanted kids, didn't you? Well, he's mine," she said snidely at Gertie.

"Ma?" Nora asked in a tremulous voice.

"What kind of woman brings a married man into her bed with children looking on? There's only one type of woman that I know that fits that description. You're not fit to be a mother, you know that? Not fit!"

"That's enough, Myrtle!" Olson said loudly, but Gertie felt a sinking in her stomach.

"You'd better go, Olson," she said hoarsely, her heart ripped open and bleeding. She backed away from him and stepped over to where the girls stood.

"But I do love you, honey," he whispered urgently, following her and leaving Myrtle in the doorway. "I hate her. I want to marry *you*. Honestly. I meant every word I said. You have to believe me. I'll get a divorce quick as I can."

Gertie stood looking at him, her arms around the girls, as if protecting them from she knew not what. She felt like her insides were shriveling up and dying all at once. How could she have been fooled again! Was she really that stupid?

"Please, just go, Olson."

"I'll be back, Gertrude. Will you wait for me? Say you will," he begged, hurriedly buttoning his shirt.

"He always says that," Myrtle crowed from the doorway.

"Shut up, you bitch!" Olson shouted, stunning Gertie. She had never heard him shout or use foul language before. He had his shoes on now and his coat, and he strode swiftly to Gertie and clutched her face with both hands and kissed her. "I meant what I said, Gertie." His voice was low. "I love you."

"I can hear you, you know!" Myrtle shouted. "You always did go for the whores. Most of 'em don't have kids, though, do they?" she said hotly.

Olson strode across the room and grabbed her roughly by the arm. "Come on!"

"You ain't heard the last of me, Madame! I have connections, you know. I'm going to turn you in!"

"To who?" Olson snarled. "Shut your fat mouth."

He slammed the door shut, leaving Gertie in a state of shock. For many minutes she just stared at the closed door, the door through which she had hoped would be a new life, and then sank to the ground.

When the girls crawled into her lap, she put her arms around them and began to rock, holding them for a long time before the tears finally came.

Olson did not appear all the rest of that day, or the next, or the next, until Gertie began to wonder, as the weeks wore on, if she would ever hear from him again. She knew it was wrong to want him to suddenly appear outside the Sunshine, as he used to, but she couldn't help it. She didn't dare to hope they had a future together, but she longed to at least know the truth. Did he really do this kind of thing all the time, as his *wife* (she could barely say it) accused? Or was Myrtle actually "crazy," as he had suggested? She hadn't *seemed* all that crazy . . . But the real question that seemed to surface more than any other was whether he had really loved her. Had he really wanted to marry her? Or had it all been a ruse?

As it turned out, Gertie *did* hear from Olson again about a month after their affair ended, but not in a way she could have ever expected. She was in the kitchen one Monday afternoon, her only day off, ironing, when a rapid knock sounded on the door. Her heart quickened just a little. Could it possibly be . . . ?

Gertie ran to the door and threw it open, half expecting it to be Olson standing there wearing his usual grin. But it was not Olson. It was a woman in a tweed skirt and jacket, her hands gripped around a clipboard. A man stood behind her on the top step, leaning against the wall, his arms crossed.

"Gertrude De Lorenzo?"

"Yes?" Gertie asked anxiously, wiping her hands on her apron. She had a terrible feeling about the woman standing before her, memories flooding her mind of the night the police had turned up to tell her Lorenzo was dead.

"I'm Miss Whitlow. I'm a social worker employed by the City of Chicago." She held up a piece of paper. "I have a court order here to remove two minors from a house of prostitu-tion," she said sternly, her eyes narrowed in disgust.

"Prostitution? I'm not a prostitute!" Gertie exclaimed. *Remove two minors?*

"I'm sorry, ma'am, but you'll have to take that up with the judge," the woman said briskly. "Meanwhile, I'm to remove one Leonora De Lorenzo and one Patricia De Lorenzo from the premises and deliver them to a court-designated facility for girls until further notice."

May 1932

The girls being taken was very nearly the end for Gertie. It crushed her to the point she didn't want to go on, and on one rainy night, just days after they had disappeared, she considered ending everything by jumping off the DuSable Bridge.

She stood looking at the black water, the wind whipping her hair into her face as she held onto a thick, twisted wire cable anchored into the steel beams. She felt utterly hopeless. Over and over the scene played out in her mind: her little girls alone and afraid in some God-forsaken "facility for girls." She could barely breathe. She stood, wavering on the edge of the bridge for several minutes before she finally came to her senses. Killing herself would not help the girls. No, she reasoned, as she began to carefully climb down. She needed to find them.

Gertie's only recourse was to confide in the Sunshine girls, who were suitably outraged when Gertie confessed all that had happened. Only Monica knew that Gertie had been seeing Olson on a regular basis, and she threatened to strangle him if she ever saw him again. Gertie showed them the crumpled paper the social worker had left behind, and the girls interpreted it for her. A Mr. Arthur Cohen was listed as the person in charge of appeals.

"You're gonna have to go down there," Monica said. "Maybe go on your lunch break."

"I can't make it all the way to State and back in half an hour," Gertie worried, rubbing her forehead and glancing toward the kitchen window, where plates were beginning to pile.

As if on cue, Lou's sweaty face appeared in the window. "Orders up, girls!" he shouted. "There's dames a mile long who'll take yer jobs in a second."

"Hold your pants on, Lou!" Monica shouted back. "You want me to go with you?" she asked Gertie in a low voice.

Gertie did in fact want Monica to go with her, but she knew that both of them would never be able to escape under Lou's watchful eye. One of them being gone for extra time would be bad enough. Better that Monica stay and try to cover.

"No, I'll be alright," Gertie answered, and hoped that was true. What's the address?"

The first thing Mr. Cohen asked her about, after taking what seemed to be ages to read through all the documents, was the charge of prostitution. Shamefully, Gertie tried to explain what had happened, how it was all a big misunderstanding, her face beet red and her hands twisting in her lap. Surprisingly, Mr. Cohen did not seem the least bit shocked by her tale and, in fact, seemed a little bored, as if he heard this sort of thing all the time.

"Listen, Mrs. ..." his eyes flicked to the file in front of him, "De Lorenzo. It's not the first time something like this has happened." He let out a sigh. "Not when Brady is the lawyer and Schaefer is the judge. Both are easily bought."

Gertie thought back to Myrtle's threat that she had connections. Is this what she had meant? "But . . . but they had no proof!" she faltered. "They can't just do that, can they?"

"They have a witness who claims to have routinely seen men coming and going from your apartment."

All the blood drained out of Gertie's face. "A witness? Who?"

Mr. Cohen examined the file again. "Says here a Mr. Richardt," he said, tossing it back on his desk.

Mr. Richardt? From downstairs? "Him?" Gertie exclaimed. "He's a creep. He's a lying little—"

"Be that as it may," Mr. Cohen interrupted, languidly waving one hand, "the judge took his word for it. It's a travesty of justice, but there you have it."

"Well . . . why didn't I get to explain my side of it? To this judge or whoever it was?"

Mr. Cohen folded his hands and leaned back in his chair. "You were apparently mailed several orders to appear in court, but you neglected to report for any of them."

Gertie tried to remember getting any letters. There were a few, maybe, she recalled, but she . . . she admittedly hadn't read them.

"Do you know how to read, Mrs. De Lorenzo?" Mr. Cohen asked with surprising gentleness. "Was that the problem?"

Gertie studied her worn shoe. "I can read a little."

The fact of the matter was that Gertie did find it hard to read more than the simplest things. The letters on a page were always jumbled, and she could never seem to sort them out into words. It was why she had always been so terrible in school. Oh! Why had she thrown those letters out? She should have taken them to the Sunshine and gotten one of the girls to read them to her. But she had always been this way . . . avoiding uncomfortable things and not wanting to face them.

"I guess I didn't think they were important," she fibbed, knowing that that was probably the exact reason why she *had* tossed them. *Out of sight, out of mind.*

"Look, Mrs. De Lorenzo, I can probably get the charge of prostitution dropped."

Gertie's head jerked up. "Does that . . . does that mean I can have my girls back?"

Mr. Cohen sighed. "That might be harder."

"But why? It was all a mistake . . . a 'travesty,' you called it."

Mr. Cohen picked up the file again. "Says here that another neighbor came forward and testified that the kids were routinely left alone all day and sometimes at night. Neither of them in school. This woman said she frequently heard them crying."

A woman? There was only one other woman in the building, her next-door neighbor, Mrs. Valentine. Gertie felt a stab to the heart. She had betrayed her, too? Granted they had never been friendly, but to testify in court that she was a bad mother? Gertie wasn't sure how much more she could take. "But I . . . I had to work," she muttered, not looking at Mr. Cohen. "I left food for them."

"Mrs. De Lorenzo, you must understand. Now that they've been removed, it's going to be all that much harder to get them back. The burden of proof is now on you. You'll have to prove that you have a fit home and that you're gainfully employed. Which you still are, aren't you?"

"Yes . . . yes, I'm a waitress."

"Well, you'd have to get a lawyer, and I could try to get you in front of one of the more sympathetic judges, but then—"

"I don't have the money for a lawyer!"

"You'd be assigned a public defender, then, but there might be a bit of a wait, seeing how this isn't an urgent case."

"Not an urgent case! It's very urgent, Mr. Cohen! Don't you see that?" Tears found their way to the corners of her eyes.

Mr. Cohen studied her for a few moments. "Look, Mrs. De Lorenzo," he said gently, "have you considered simply leaving the girls where they are?"

Leave them! "I—"

Mr. Cohen held up his hand. "Now, just listen. I happen to know a little about this Park Ridge School, and it's really not so bad. They were fortunate, really. The one in Dixon is terrible."

"Park Ridge! That's miles away from the city!"

"Well, yes, which is the advantage, isn't it? The girls have space to roam about, good fresh air. And I'm told they provide music and art and ballet lessons, trips to the cinema on Saturdays. But more importantly, they come out with a useful skill, ready to get a good job. Isn't that what you want for them?" He rested his head on his folded hands, propped up by his elbows. "Think about it, Mrs. De Lorenzo. Don't you think it would be selfish to take them from such a privileged life just because you might miss them? You need to think of their welfare, Mrs. De Lorenzo, not your own. Do what's best for *them*."

Gertie left Mr. Cohen's office feeling utterly confused. As soon as he had told her where they were, her first instinct had been to rush to Park Ridge somehow, but by the time she got home, she had already begun to reconsider. Maybe it *would* be selfish on her part to go and get them. Maybe they *were* better off at this school.

Gertie stewed for weeks, moping back and forth to work, barely talking to the girls at the Sunshine. With each sad day that passed, Gertie became more and more of the opinion that perhaps Mr. Cohen was right. The girls probably *were* better off there. Clearly, she was an unfit mother. What had she been thinking, leaving them alone for hours and hours? She wouldn't mind being here alone, working day after day, carrying heavy trays of food, putting up with Lou occasionally rubbing his fat hand across her bottom, if it meant that they were happy.

Eventually, her fevered mind began to imagine little scenes in which Nora and Patsy were truly happy at the school—well-fed and running about, playing games and singing songs. Over and over, she would conjure up these imaginings on her way to work each day, her feet dragging through the slushy snow.

Monica encouraged her, telling her that it was probably all for the best, but not all of the Sunshine girls seemed convinced.

"Kids should be with their mother," Doris called out more than once. "But that's just me. What do I know?"

"Oh, no, Doris!" Gertie tried to say convincingly, her stomach twisting. "It's a real crackerjack of a place. They've got everything there—put on plays and all that stuff. Mr. Cohen even said they were real lucky to have been taken there."

"Well, plays or not, if it was my kids, I'd be fightin' tooth and nail to get 'em back," Doris grunted, hefting a tray loaded with plates up onto her shoulder.

"Shut your trap, Doris," Monica scolded. "You're just jealous is what you are." Gertie caught Monica's nervous glance in her direction, though, and felt ashamed.

Yet as time went on, Gertie learned to ignore Doris's pitying looks whenever she told the regulars that her girls were at a fancy school taking ballet and painting.

"Can you believe it?" she would ask as she topped up their coffee cups.

Sometimes, as if to prove her point, she would bring in some of Nora's letters. Not the first ones, though. Those had been terrible. Something about Patsy crying and Nora begging. They were so devastating that Gertie had been tempted to throw them away and not open another, convinced that she was a terrible mother. But she *did* continue opening them, forcing herself to face whatever they held, and happily found that Nora's letters had begun to change. They were not so despairing now, more like lists of what they did each day. These weren't so bad, and these were the ones she took along with her to the Sunshine. The girls seemed genuinely impressed when Monica read them out loud, and Gertie was relieved to find that their occasional looks of pity almost disappeared entirely.

Eventually, however, the letters began to come less frequently, much to Gertie's disappointment. Doubtless it was because Nora was so busy, though it did hurt sometimes, as it was Nora's letters that renewed her conviction that she was doing the right thing.

She was delighted, then, to find a letter waiting for her one Saturday night after she got home from work. Linda had sprained her ankle, and Gertie had ended up working a double. She was glad for the extra money, but her feet ached. Seeing Nora's letter in the mailbox cheered her.

Plopping down on the sagging secondhand sofa, she pried open the envelope as she slipped off her worn oxfords.

She quickly perused the letter and was able to make out at least some of the words: "Ma," "Patsy," "band," "lunch," "dungeon." Dungeon? Surely that wasn't right? Gertie rubbed her eyes, trying to make them focus, but it was no use. The letters and words were still jumbled. Her eyes immediately went back to the dungeon word. She put her thumbs on either side of it, hoping it would help to block out the others, but it was no use.

Gertie studied the letter for a very long time, her unease growing. She began to pace, wondering what she should do. She glanced at the clock, hoping she might still be able to make it back to the Sunshine for Monica to help her read the whole thing. It was already past ten, though, and she knew the diner would be locked tight, everyone, including Lou, gone home. She would have to wait until the morning.

She tucked the letter into her dress pocket and went into the kitchen to make some tea, but found her hand wandering back to the letter. She took it out again and studied it. She couldn't explain it, but there was something about it that filled her with dread. She tried to reason it away. More than likely, she wasn't reading it correctly. Or maybe it was a reference to a play they were putting on. Or maybe it was part of hide-and-seek. Or maybe it was a nickname of something not-so-insidious.

Gertie wandered into the front room and looked down at the city street below, feeling the familiar black hole of despair beginning to open up inside of her again. She would go mad if she didn't know what this letter said. Maybe it was something terrible! Oh, who could she ask to read it to her?

Mrs. Valentine across the way was the only one she knew to be literate, but she refused to have anything to do with that witch, not after what she had done to her. Testifying in court that she was a bad mother!

As time ticked by, however, and Gertie's panic continued to rise, she reconsidered. What did it matter what the old witch thought? Surely, she couldn't think anything worse than she already did . . .

Desperate, Gertie marched across the hall in her stocking feet and knocked briskly at Mrs. Valentine's nicked door before she could change her mind. No one came, but she could hear a dog barking and someone trying to shush it.

"Mrs. Valentine?" Gertie called through the door. "Mrs. Valentine! It's Gertie from across the way!"

The door opened a crack, revealing an eyeball, and then the door opened fully. Mrs. Valentine had her arms folded stiffly across her chest. A little white dog beside her was yapping ferociously.

"What?"

"I . . . I got a letter from my daughter, but I . . . I was wondering if you could read it to me."

Mrs. Valentine rolled her eyes in disgust and then yanked the letter from Gertie's outstretched hand. She reached into her apron pocket and pulled out a tiny pair of wire-rimmed spectacles, which she painstakingly wrapped around each ear. The dog continued to bark, and Mrs. Valentine made no effort to stop it as she began to read the letter to herself, taking her sweet time.

"Well?" Gertie finally blurted over the barking. "What does it say?"

Mrs. Valentine peered at Gertie through the space above her spectacles. Then she cleared her throat and looked back at the letter.

"It says, *Dear Ma, How are you? We are fine. Or almost fine. We are working hard at our classes and chores, but we are wondering when you might be coming to get us. I know you must be very busy with work and with Olson—*" Mrs. Valentine stopped reading to cluck disapprovingly. "*—but can you please come get us? There is a terrible place here called the Carrie Cort. It is a dungeon in the basement where bad girls are put. I've never had to go in it, but Patsy is sent there almost every other week. There are spiders and snakes, and Patsy cries something terrible. Sometimes she screams.*" Mrs. Valentine flicked her eyes at Gertie again before going on. "*Please, please come get us, Ma. We'll be good, I promise. We love you, Ma, even if you don't. Please. Your loving daughter, Nora*"

Mrs. Valentine handed the letter back with a sniff of disgust. "Trouble seems to follow you, don't it? Well, you've made your bed, guess you'll have to lie in it," she said, reminding Gertie unexpectedly of Pa, and promptly slammed the door.

She turned and went back to her own apartment, closing the door and leaning against it, her heart racing. Was it true? Were the girls in some sort of danger? The whole illusion she had built up was threatening to crumble. Surely Mr. Cohen would not have recommended the school had he known there was a dungeon there? But maybe he *didn't* know. Or maybe he had lied to her. Had she been tricked yet again?

Gertie stayed up all night, pacing and crying, until the sun broke over the horizon. She didn't even change out of her uniform. Without even pausing to comb her hair, which she was sure was a mess, she threw on a coat and walked to the Sunshine.

Once there, she barely said hello to anyone, but marched back to the corner booth where one of her regulars was already perched, his newspaper splayed out in front of him, as he smoked his pipe.

"Jerry!"

"Well, hey, Gert. Wondered where you were," he said, looking her up and down. "You look like shit."

"You have a car, right?" she asked, ignoring his comment.

"You know I do, doll. You finally ready to take a look at it?" he asked, giving her a sly grin. He was forever asking her out, even when she had been with Olson, but she had always brushed him off. It was a little game they played. Even now that Olson was not in the picture, she continued to brush him off, determined to never be with another man again.

"Can you drive me to Park Ridge?" she asked plainly, only once looking over her shoulder at the girls who were now all watching her.

"Park Ridge?" He took a puff of his pipe. "What's out there?"

"I'll explain later. After work. Pick me up here. Six o'clock."

When they pulled up in front of the Park Ridge School for Girls, it was already dark.

"Nice place," Jerry said, peering through the front windscreen.

Gertie couldn't tell if he was being sarcastic, but she didn't care. She had barely spoken on the whole ride except to briefly tell him that her girls were going to school here and that she had received a disturbing letter from one of them.

Jerry parked, and Gertie hurriedly got out. "You wait here, okay?" she said through the open door.

"Sure? Looks a bit spooky, if you ask me."

Gertie didn't answer, but shut the door quietly, not wanting it to bang. Timidly, she climbed the steps of the main building and lightly tapped the big wooden door with the heavy iron knocker. Three times she had to knock, each time with a bit more effort, before the door finally opened to reveal a woman with a sharp scowl.

"Yes?"

"I'm . . ." Gertie hadn't thought about what she should exactly say. "I'd like to speak to someone in charge."

"Why?" the woman asked, her eyes narrowing.

"I'd like to check on my girls. They're here, I believe. I got a . . . a disturbing letter, and I . . . well, can I come in?"

The woman looked her over for a moment and then held the door open.

"This way," she said curtly then led her across the lobby to a little desk cozily illuminated by a brass lamp. After gesturing for Gertie to sit in one of the two chairs in front of it, she took a place behind it.

"Now, what's this all about?" she asked, her hands folded tightly. "What's your name?"

"Gertrude De Lorenzo."

A ripple of something crossed the woman's face.

"Ah, yes. Your daughters are Leonora and Patricia?"

"Yes!" Gertie said. "Are they . . . how are they?"

"They're quite happy, I believe. Adjusting well."

"Oh, I'm so glad!" Gertie exclaimed. "I've been so worried." Hurriedly, she wiped her eyes. "Have they gotten into any . . . any trouble?"

The woman blinked just a little. "No more so than usual. You mentioned a letter?"

"Yes," Gertie said, remembering why she was here. "It's from my daughter, Nora. She says that Patsy has repeatedly been put into some kind of dungeon." Gertie looked up at the woman nervously, not wanting to offend her. Suddenly this all seemed ridiculous.

The woman's face remained perfectly still. "A dungeon?"

"Yes . . ." Gertie rifled through her handbag. She located Nora's letter and pulled it out. "Yes, here it is. She calls it the 'Carrie Cort'?"

"May I see that?"

Gertie handed it to the woman, who quickly skimmed it before thrusting it back.

"I have no idea what she could be talking about," the woman snipped. "That's positively barbaric." A stiff smile momentarily cracked her otherwise smooth exterior. "Childish imagination, I'm sure."

"Yes, that's what I thought," Gertie agreed hurriedly.

"I'll let Mrs. Harvey know, however."

"Mrs. Harvey?"

"Yes, she's the director. She's home sick today with a very bad cold. I'm Mrs. Morris."

"Oh. She won't be in any trouble, though, will she? Nora, I mean?"

"Of course not," Mrs. Morris said, another tight smile erupting briefly. "I'll take care of this. Don't you worry."

The two women stared at each other, and Gertie hardly dared ask the next question, the one closest to her heart.

"Could I . . . could I see them? Just for a minute?" she asked, her voice suddenly thick.

"I'm afraid that's out of the question," Mrs. Morris said crisply. "We have a very strict visiting policy. It's disturbing to the girls, you see, if family members are always coming and going. And since this is a school for girls from *broken* families, I'm sure you understand what a problem that might be, don't you?" she asked, her eyebrows arched.

Gertie swallowed. "But, I've . . . I've come such a long way—"

"Rules are rules, Mrs. De Lorenzo," Mrs. Morris sniffed. "If I bend the rules for you, I have to bend them for everyone. Visiting day is every other Sunday. Unfortunately, you've missed today's, so you'll have to come back in two weeks. Now, is there anything else?"

"Oh, but surely if it was today, I could just have a few words! I won't be long."

"I'm afraid not. Visiting hours end at five. You're out of luck."

"Oh, but please."

"It's out of the question," she repeated. "You'll simply have to come back in two weeks."

"But I work every Sunday," Gertie pleaded. "Please . . ."

"I'm afraid that's not my concern. My concern is for the welfare of these girls. You'll have to make other arrangements."

"But I—"

"Look, Mrs. De Lorenzo," Mrs. Morris said, standing now. "I have a great many things to attend to before I retire for the evening. I'm sure you wouldn't want to keep me from them." She walked out from behind the desk toward the door. "Come on," Mrs. Morris commanded, holding it open.

Gertie heard her, but she couldn't think of a word to say in response. Likewise, her legs didn't seem to want to move. Finally, however, she made herself stand.

"You needn't worry, Mrs. De Lorenzo," Mrs. Morris said brusquely as Gertie stepped past her. "They're perfectly fine. Better off, I'd say. After all, they got sent here for a reason . . . didn't they?"

The door closed with a tight click, and Gertie found herself, stunned, standing once again in deep blackness. A small flame of anger flashed through her.

Without taking too much time to consider the wisdom of actually acting upon it, she slipped down the side of the stairs and made her way around the building, determined to find Nora and Patsy herself. It couldn't be that hard. There were only six cottages. She would start with the one on the far left and make her way around the semi-circle.

Gertie hurried across the wet lawn, praying no one would spot her. She successfully reached the first one undetected and stood outside it, hesitating. The front of it was dark, though she could see some light coming from the back, where the bedrooms presumably lay. Her heart racing, she crept along the side of the cottage until she was just outside one of the windows. She drew herself up, hands gripped rigidly into fists, then peered over the sill.

She could see many girls, about twelve, in what looked to indeed be a bedroom. Most were already in their nightgowns and were reading or talking. Some were already in their beds. Gertie watched for several moments, noting that they *did* seem well cared for, at first glance, anyway. Her eyes darted to each girl before she finally determined that Nora and Patsy were not among them. She slipped her head back down and made her way to the next cottage.

This one was filled with very little girls, most of whom were already in bed, and Gertie felt a rising hope that she might at least find Patsy. Desperately, she tried shifting into different positions and angles to see better, but she was interrupted when a woman dressed all in black came into the room. Quickly Gertie pulled away, her heart pounding. She remained there for several more moments, debating about looking again, but ultimately decided against it. She would return to this one later if she didn't find them in the others.

By the time she got to the fifth cottage, Gertie had not only almost given up hope, but she had begun to worry that Jerry might leave without her. But when she reached the sixth, she almost cried aloud—there they were, plain as day. Nora's back was to her as she stood talking with another girl, and Gertie wanted to bang on the window, to call out to her, embrace her. Her heart was beating so hard she felt like it might burst. What was to stop her from rushing in the front door and scooping her up in her arms? Who had the right to keep her girls from her?

She stood there for several moments, her mind racing as she tried to decide what to do, when she saw Patsy, wandering around the room in her nightgown, holding her ragdoll and sucking her thumb. Gertie felt a hot flush cover her whole body at the sight of her baby, and, almost as if she could sense her presence, Patsy turned to the window, her eyes instantly connecting with Gertie's.

Gertie knew she should duck back, but she couldn't help it. She drank in the image of Patsy as if she were a dying soul and Patsy, with her golden hair and big, blue eyes, was the elixir. For a moment there was a silent connection between them, one of love and delight and joy, before Patsy pulled her thumb from her mouth.

"Ma!" she yelled excitedly.

Panicking, Gertie pulled away, out of sight. She could hear Patsy's little voice calling "Ma! Nora, I see Ma!" and her little fist pounding on the window.

Every muscle, every fiber of her being wanted to go to them, but the rational side of her brain told her not to. *They are better off here*, Gertie said to herself, over and over. *They are better off.* Oh, why did she come in the first place? She had disturbed them, just as Mrs. Morris had said she would. No, it was terrible to have come. She saw that now. Not just for them, but for her; she wasn't sure how much more of this she could take.

Suddenly, she heard a horn in the distance. After several more loud toots, she realized it must be Jerry. It was now or never, she realized. Either she was going to burst into the cottage in a blind effort to see them for a few moments before someone discovered her, or she was going to have to go back to the city with Jerry.

Hesitating for a few more seconds, she made her choice and ran across the wet grass, slipping only once. Jerry was standing outside the car, leaning his elbow on the open door as he reached in and squeezed the horn.

"There you are! Thought they'd kidnapped you or something. Whatcha doin' out there in the lawn?"

Gertie didn't say anything, but slid into the front seat, her face red and blotchy. Jerry swung himself behind the wheel and roughly pulled the choke. He looked over at her as he turned the key and the car sputtered to life.

"Jeez, what happened?" he asked. "You look like shit again. Come on, I'll buy you a drink."

"I've got to find a way to get off on Sundays," Gertie mumbled, staring forlornly out the window.

CHAPTER 13

September 1932

Nora

"Nora, are you coming?" Celia asked, poking her head into the music room.

"Yes, in a minute." Nora gave the dented clarinet a final toot before packing it up in its little case. Music class had ended almost twenty minutes ago, but Nora had stayed behind to practice. She was hoping to join the school marching band in the spring, but, as only a beginner, she was very far behind. Still, Mrs. Clark, the music teacher, had been very encouraging, telling her that she did have talent. She was doing well in her classes, too, and had very much impressed her teachers by rising to the head of the class in almost every subject. She was second only in mathematics, but she was determined to be first by the end of the year.

The girls at the Park Ridge School were all required to take the same seven classes: history, geography, mathematics, English, penmanship, calisthenics, and spelling. In seventh grade, the girls dropped calisthenics and spelling and took up home economics and deportment instead. In addition, all girls had to take at least one additional class such as music, art, stenography, science, or literature. A few girls were allowed to take *two* additional subjects if they had proven the ability to maintain top marks in their existing classes.

Nora had chosen music as her elective, but she was determined to be allowed to take stenography, too. Likewise, she was set not just on joining the marching band, but on joining the Girl Scouts as well, who met every other Friday under the direction of Mrs. Faraday. Celia had finally convinced Nora to tag along to a meeting, and the other scouts had been very welcoming. Nora had marveled at all of Celia's badges—twelve—and longed to collect them as well.

All in all, the Park Ridge School for Girls wasn't as bad as Nora's first few weeks had seemed to portend. For one thing, the cottages were warm now that the days were getting cooler, and there was plenty to eat. Not an excessive amount, but at least she never went to bed hungry. Indeed, she was genuinely growing to like the Park Ridge School, especially now that she knew all the rules and, in particular, how to survive under Mrs. Morris's all-seeing eyes.

Nora had all but given up on Ma ever coming to rescue them, much less visit, which was a hurt that threatened to stop her heart if she let it, so she didn't. Instead she threw herself into her new life, succumbing to Celia's repeated overtures to be her "very best friend." She and Celia had *almost* the same birthday, Nora discovered—just one day off—which she was convinced was a sign that they were supposed to be friends, if a sign was even needed.

Nora continued to write to Ma once a week, but only because she was forced to participate in "Correspondence" every Thursday; otherwise, she would have stopped altogether. When her initial sad missives were not answered, she had traded them for ones that were mere listings of their daily routine—what she was studying, what her chores were, what they had for lunch.

Not knowing how to write yet, Patsy mostly drew pictures, which, in the beginning, Nora had also mailed to Ma. Now, however, Nora threw them away. Clearly Ma didn't care, or didn't care enough.

There was only one time that she had lapsed back into begging, on a particularly sad, gray day in May, one which found Nora more than a little homesick. After staring at the rivulets of rain running down the classroom windows, she decided to one more time try to pour out her heart to Ma. Picking up her pencil, she filled the blank piece of paper in front of her with a description of the Carrie Cort, ignoring her twinges of guilt in so doing. Patsy had begged Nora to never tell Ma, but she needed to in order for Ma to understand the full extent of their despair.

Nora waited on tenterhooks for weeks after, resurrecting her fledgling hope that Ma might yet appear, but after two months passed and still no Ma rushing to their rescue, much less any letter of love, Nora gave up and pushed her hurt even deeper down. It was a skill she was becoming very good at.

Nora found Celia waiting for her downstairs. The two of them walked back across the campus toward Solomon, both of them brimming with excitement. It was Friday night, Girl Scout night, and Nora had finally been granted permission to join.

"It's a useless waste of time, you know," Mrs. Morris had chided. "Marching about, studying leaves, singing songs. It's ridiculous."

"But we learn things like sewing and . . . and first aid, too. Useful things," Nora had offered.

Mrs. Morris had merely rolled her eyes and told her that while she could join the Girl Scouts if she wished, the moment her grades dipped, as they surely would after all that messing about, her privilege would be immediately revoked.

"Don't worry about her," Celia said as they walked across the campus, the cool air of dusk a welcome relief after the hot music room. "She's just a bitter old walnut."

"Don't I know it." Nora gave a deep sigh.

Celia hugged her books to her chest. "Anyway, tonight's your swearing-in ceremony, and the girls have something fun planned!"

"What is it?" Nora asked, excitement rippling through her.

"I can't tell, but you'll like it! And don't forget about Sunday. Lyle and Billy are coming again."

"Of course, I didn't forget *that*. I hope it doesn't rain, though, so we can play the game," Nora suggested eagerly.

For weeks, Celia had begged Nora to come along and meet her Aunt Rita on Visiting Day instead of sitting alone in the foyer of the big hall with Patsy, but Nora always refused. As the months had worn on, though, and it was becoming increasingly clear that Ma wasn't coming, Nora's curiosity, if not sheer boredom, had finally gotten the better of her. Despite Celia's opinion that Aunt Rita was somehow their family's savior, Nora thought she sounded more like a mean old witch.

When the day arrived, Nora made sure that Patsy's hair was braided tight and that her tattered doll was safely hidden under her pillow before following Celia to the front parlor of the main hall.

Aunt Rita was surprisingly cordial, instructing them to sit down across from her on the scratchy horsehair sofa. Nora sat stiffly, expecting to be grilled by the majestic woman as to why they had no visitors of their own, but she was relieved that, beyond giving them a close once-over, Aunt Rita pretty much focused her attention on correcting poor Celia's posture.

"For heaven's sake, sit up straight!" Aunt Rita admonished with a bit of a snort. "And stop swinging your legs. You're not a monkey, are you?" Again, Aunt Rita snorted, this time twice in quickly succession, making her sound like something was stuck in her nose. It was a nasally, rattly sort of sound.

Patsy giggled. Nora gave her a little nudge with her elbow and kept her eyes fixed politely on Aunt Rita, who gave Patsy a disapproving glance before going on to expound on the fact that there was a rip in one of the living room doilies.

"I'm sure it was Lyle," Aunt Rita declared, her voice quivering. "He's simply too rough. I've told him a hundred times that he's not allowed in the front room. You've no idea, Celia. I don't know how your mother managed. But then again, she didn't, did she? Lucille was never much of a house-keeper." Another snort.

Celia sat on her hands. "Maybe it was Billy?"

"Billy? Now why would it be Billy? He was raised *correctly*, right from the beginning. Billy? That's ridiculous!" Aunt Rita took a sip of her tea.

"Are we going to get to meet them?" Patsy blurted, horri-fying Nora.

"What?" Aunt Rita seemed startled by this interruption, as if she had already forgotten they were there.

Patsy, undisturbed by Aunt Rita's stern gaze, pointed a little finger at Celia. "*She* said we could meet them today. That we could play with them."

"Did she now?" Aunt Rita said, drawing herself up with another snort. "Well, I suppose I'm chopped liver. Driving all the way out here to sit in a dingy hall with weak tea," she declared, lifting her teacup for emphasis, "when I really should be at home canning the beans. Billy picked a whole bushel yesterday for me. Can't say as much for Lyle, of course. Very well, then. Off you go." She gave a double snort. "I'll have to sit here and amuse myself," she said, picking up a tattered copy of *Life*. "Go on. Off with you. I can't trust Lyle to behave like a decent human being indoors, so they're waiting outside. I instructed them to wait on the steps out there, but knowing Lyle, he's already run off."

Celia stood awkwardly, and Nora followed suit.

"It was . . . it was nice to meet you, Aunt Rita. I mean . . . Mrs. . . . Mrs. . . . ." Nora faltered, mortified that she didn't actually know Aunt Rita's surname.

"You may call me Aunt Rita," the plump woman said benevolently. "You'll make a nice little friend for Celia, I'm sure." She held out her arms stiffly despite the fact that she was still seated. "Give me a kiss, Celia," she instructed and waited while Celia dutifully bent and plucked her cheek with the quickest of kisses. "Here you are, then," Aunt Rita said, handing her a brown paper bag, the top neatly folded over. "It's some blackberries from the garden. Lyle picked them for you, so they might all be smashed. Heaven only knows."

Nora wasn't sure what else to say, so she gave Aunt Rita a little bow, which she was immediately embarrassed by, and followed Celia out into the foyer and down the cement steps of the main hall.

On the bottom step sat a rake of a boy, his shoulders hunched forward.

"Lyle!" Celia called. The boy stood up, gripping his cap in his hand, a small smile creeping across his face as Celia hurried toward him. "Lyle, this is Nora and Patsy, my friends," Celia said, waving a hand at them.

Lyle only briefly caught Nora's eye before he looked back at his sister, his black hair hanging across one eye. "You got the berries?" He nodded nervously at the brown paper bag.

"Yes, thanks, Lyle. You don't mind if I share them, do you?"

"No. Course not." He flicked his pale brown eyes at Nora again.

"Well, where's Billy?" Celia asked, looking around.

Lyle shrugged. "He went round back."

Before Celia could say anything, Billy came racing around the corner of the main building and ran up to them, breathing hard.

"There's a big rat back there!" he panted, his hands on his knees. "Come see it!"

"No, Billy! That's horrid."

"Aw. Spoil sport. You want to see it, Lyle?"

Lyle shifted uncomfortably and shook his head. "Maybe later."

"Who's these two?" Billy asked, his hands on his hips and big smile across his face as he looked the girls over.

"I'm Nora, and this is Patsy," Nora answered weakly. Billy had thick blond curls and enormous blue eyes with long lashes and deep dimples. He looked like a wild explosion of sunshine, almost too bright to look at.

"Well, what are we gonna do? Let's explore," Billy suggested eagerly, his big eyes darting around the grounds. "I know! Take me to the dungeon. The Carrie Cort thing."

Celia's eyes narrowed. "How do you know about that?"

"I read your letters to Lyle. How else?"

"Billy!" Lyle exclaimed, his face flushed. "I told you before to stay out of my stuff."

"Oh, be quiet, Lyle. It was a while ago now. Come on," he said sweetly, dimples exposed. "Please, Ceil," he begged.

"You have no right to read my letters to Lyle! Those are private!"

"Aw, come on! If you wrote to *me* sometimes, then I wouldn't have to resort to reading his. It's kind of your fault, Ceil."

"*My* fault?"

"Listen. It doesn't really matter, does it?"

"I think it does," Lyle said quietly. "You're always doing stuff like this, Billy. You're always taking stuff that doesn't belong to you."

"Alright, alright. I'm sorry. Okay?"

Lyle didn't respond and instead looked away.

"Look, I'll make it up to you. I'll chop your wood next week. How about that?" He looked from Lyle to Celia for approval.

Lyle turned his gaze back to him. "Promise?"

"Promise," Billy said easily. "Now where's this dungeon?"

The girls led Billy and Lyle to Solomon Cottage, but they refused, despite Billy's most charming begging, to take him inside, scared to death of what would happen if Mrs. Morris should suddenly appear. Instead, he had to be content to lie on his stomach on the grass and peer through the basement window.

"It don't look so bad to me," Billy said after a few moments, squinting back up at them.

"Well, it is!" Celia retorted. "You wouldn't think that if you had to spend all night in it."

"I wouldn't care!"

"Yes, you would, Bill Williams."

"Nah." He threw a little wink at Patsy, who had her thumb in her mouth.

"There's spiders there," she said in her little baby voice.

"I ain't afraid of no spiders." A grin erupted. "I'd catch 'em and eat 'em, that's what I'd do."

"No, you wouldn't, Billy. You're a liar!" Celia said hotly.

"I ain't no liar. But I *am* a wizard. An evil wizard!" He wiggled his fingers. "Come on, I'll show you. My lair is over in that there woods." He nodded toward the patch of trees and undergrowth beyond the cottages.

Celia threw a worried glance at Nora. "We're not supposed to go in there."

Billy laughed. "Who'll notice? Besides, it's boring just running around here. Come on!"

"I'll go," Patsy offered, taking her thumb out of her mouth.

Billy laughed again. "See? She's not afraid. Don't be such a wet hen, Celia."

Celia looked again at Nora and gave her a little shrug. Nora had no desire to be punished, but she desperately wanted to be part of the fun. Nor did she relish being called a wet hen.

"Come on!" Billy grabbed Patsy's hand and began running toward the woods.

"Patsy! You come back!" Nora shouted, running after them. "Come on, Billy! Stop!"

"Yeah, Billy, stop! You'll get us in trouble," Celia shouted, running now, too, Lyle beside her.

Billy and Patsy did *not* stop, however, until they reached a massive oak tree in the middle of the woods. Dropping Patsy's hand, Billy hopped onto a fallen log.

"This is my lair," he said, gesturing widely. "This is where I perfect my magic powers, which I use on unsuspecting victims." He made a crazed face. "I'll count to twenty and give you all a chance to hide before I come looking for you. Whoever I catch has to come back to my lair and wait for someone to rescue them."

"How do you rescue someone?" Lyle asked.

"All you have to do is touch them. Then they're free. Ready?" Billy asked, wiggling his fingers again. "Go!" he shouted, and Patsy gave a little scream of excitement as they all scurried off to hide.

Billy's game proved to be terrifically fun, and now they played it every visiting day, unless it rained and they were stuck inside with Aunt Rita. They never tired of it, and only two slight alterations were ever tried, only one of which became permanent.

The first occurred when Patsy declared that she wasn't going to play anymore. It was unfair, she said, because her legs were smaller and thus she was always the one caught first.

"Oh, Pats, shush!" Nora had said irritably. "Why can't you just get along?"

"No!" Refusing to move, Patsy plopped down on one of the oak tree's roots and pulled the top off of a dandelion.

It was Billy, in the end, who had cajoled her back by declaring that she would be his assistant whose job it was to guard the prisoners.

The second was when Lyle asked to be the wizard, a suggestion Billy merely laughed at until Celia insisted. It wasn't the same at all, however. Lyle ran about and tried to find them, alright, but he didn't have Billy's dramatic flair.

Nora could not remember a time in her whole life when she had laughed so much. Visiting Day, which had once been such a source of sadness, had become the day she looked forward to the most. She didn't even mind the obligatory chat with Aunt Rita. Nora rather enjoyed listening to the older woman's many edifications and pearls of wisdom, no matter how impractical. For example, what need did she or Celia have of advice on which gloves to wear to the symphony, which annuals were the best to plant in a south-facing yard, what was considered an acceptable dish to bring to a pot-luck picnic, what one's attire should be when one's husband returned from work, or which strain of cucumbers made the best pickles? Still, while Celia seemed unappreciative, Nora found them fascinating.

As much as Nora had wanted Aunt Rita to be an ogre, she was actually rather nice, even if she appeared to be completely blind to her own son's antics. Billy was the type that could "charm your socks off" as Ma would have said, and he had certainly succeeded in charming his own mother.

Lyle, on the other hand, could do nothing right. More than once, Nora wondered if the real reason Aunt Rita had taken Lyle in was to be a permanent whipping boy for Billy. If Lyle suspected the same, he didn't show it. Like his sister, he seemed to take everything in stride.

The other person Aunt Rita did not seem particularly fond of was Patsy, who could never sit still and engage in polite conversation for any length of time, causing Aunt Rita to ultimately suggest that Patsy wait outdoors with Lyle and Billy. This arrangement suited Patsy, who would much rather roam about the grounds than be stuck inside with "ole' Aunt Rita." Indeed, Patsy had become quite attached to Billy, following him everywhere and never wanting to leave his side. Worried that she was becoming a pest, Nora told her not to bother Billy so much.

"I'm not a pest," Patsy pouted. "I like Billy. And he likes me!"

Nora wanted to say more, but she held it in, trying to convince herself that Patsy might be finally getting a little better. She rarely talked back to Mrs. Morris now, or to any teacher, really. In fact, she barely spoke at all, which was surely a good thing, wasn't it? It meant less chance of her getting in trouble, although, she still got thrown into the Carrie Cort on a monthly basis.

Once Patsy had been thrown into the dungeon for stealing a paperweight off of Mrs. Morris's desk! When Nora had asked her later through the wall why she had done such a stupid thing, Patsy had responded, "But I didn't steal it, Nora." She sounded so convincing that for a second, Nora almost believed her. "I just wanted to look at it," Patsy clarified.

Nora sighed. Did Patsy really not have any common sense? She had turned seven, but still seemed as babyish and unaware as ever.

"Patsy, look. You can't just walk off with other people's things; they think you're stealing them."

"But I wasn't. I was going to put it back."

"But no one knew that, did they?"

Silence followed.

"And anyway, even if you were to pick something up to look at, *never, ever* touch anything of Mrs. Morris's! Don't you know that by now? How many times have I told you this?"

"I didn't know it was hers," Patsy said in a small voice.

Heavens above! Nora wanted to scream. "Well, whose *did* you think it was?" she asked irritably. "On Mrs. Morris's desk, in Mrs. Morris's office, in Solomon Cottage?

"I don't know."

"Oh, Pats. What am I going to do with you?" Nora exclaimed and slid down the wall of the coal chute to keep vigil.

Over and over this scenario would repeat, Nora sitting on the basement's earthen floor and doing her schoolwork by the little light afforded by the small window cut high into the stone wall. She would stay there until she had to get back for bed check. Patsy would inevitably cry, begging Nora not to leave her alone in the dark, but there was nothing Nora could do. Later, when she was sure Mrs. Morris was asleep, she would slip back down. Knowing Patsy was too afraid of spiders and snakes to sleep, Nora would whisper the stories that Ma used to tell, though it was getting harder and harder to remember them. Sometimes she just made them up herself. Eventually, they would somehow both fall asleep, or Nora would, anyway, luckily waking in time to crawl back into her bed before Mrs. Morris discovered she had been gone.

Whether in the Carrie Cort or not, however, Patsy was a terrible sleeper. Oftentimes she would get out of bed and wander about, still asleep. Once Nora had awoken and found her gone completely! After quickly searching the cottage, Nora had dashed outside, where she finally found her in the little woods behind the cottages, walking and mumbling, her doll in her arms and her white nightgown billowing around her, making her look like a little ghost.

"Patsy! What are you doing out here?" Nora cried, grabbing her about the arms.

Patsy had been staring straight ahead, as if she was asleep with her eyes open, but startled when Nora grabbed her. She took a few moments to focus on Nora and then looked around confused.

"I'm talking with Ma," she said simply. "She's right here with me." She gave a little gesture to the air beside her. "Don't you see her, Nora?"

Goosebumps instantly covered Nora's neck and arms. "Come on, Patsy," she said roughly, pulling her along. "We've got to get back in bed."

After that chilling incident, Nora switched their bunks, making Patsy sleep on the top. It took Patsy a little while to get used to the new arrangement, falling out several times, but it at least kept her from wandering, especially with Nora sleeping below her like a faithful guard dog.

She still cried out for Ma sometimes, and Nora would have to get out of bed and shush her, or sometimes even climb up into her bed to cradle her, just as she had done at the shelter when Ma was out working all night.

And then there was the schoolwork. As expected, Patsy did terribly. Nora had been trying to teach her the alphabet ever since their days in the shelter, but to no avail. Even now, despite Nora going over and over the letters, Patsy seemed unable to retain which one was which for more than a few seconds. Nora despaired. Surely Patsy's teachers must realize the level of Patsy's deficiency? Or had Patsy been able to hide it? Under Nora's constant tutelage, she was getting better and better at hiding things.

The one thing Patsy did excel at was art. It was the one time when Patsy seemed to come fully awake, her normally drowsy eyes wide and bright. And now that they were at the Park Ridge School, with paper and crayons and paints, not just a dull pencil or a rock scratched along a patch of cement, Patsy had flourished.

"She's quite good," Mrs. Hanley, the art teacher told Nora. "Even for one so young."

"Thank you, miss," Nora said, stunned that Patsy was being praised for something, and looked at what her sister was working on. It was a painting that resembled some sort of body of water—maybe a lake or an ocean. It *was* quite good, Nora judged, for a seven-year-old, anyway.

"What are you going to do with Patsy while you're gone tonight?" Celia asked now, startling Nora from her thoughts.

Nora didn't answer and clutched her books to her chest. The last time she had gone to a Girl Scout meeting, Patsy had turned on the faucets in Solomon, letting them run endlessly. Thankfully, one of the other girls noticed and turned them off before Mrs. Morris had found out. "I'm not sure—

"Nora!" called a voice from across the quad.

It was Agnes, one of their friends from Solomon, the same girl, incidentally who had discovered the faucets. She was running, which Nora was sure meant nothing good.

"Nora," Agnes said, stopping abruptly in front of the two girls, bracing her hands on her knees to catch her breath.

Nora felt a chill instantly surround her heart. "What is it?"

"It's Patsy," the girl panted. "She's gone."

CHAPTER 14

September 1932

The last person to have supposedly seen Patsy was a girl named Esther, Agnes reported, who claimed to have seen her walking toward Solomon. Nora and Celia accordingly took off in a run toward the cottage and began looking in every nook and cranny they could think of, which was difficult to do covertly as Mrs. Morris was still in her back office. They even searched the area behind the cottage, thinking maybe she was playing or hiding back amongst the crates of garbage, but to no avail. The fact that her doll was also gone from under Patsy's pillow made Nora's chest tighten into a knot.

Finally, after more than thirty precious minutes had passed, Celia finally convinced Nora that they needed to solicit the help of some of the other girls. They all fanned out, then, even into the woods, trying to find the missing Patsy without bringing any attention to it. Somehow, though, the rotten Priscilla caught wind of the situation and promptly ran to report it to Mrs. Morris.

As predicted, Mrs. Morris was furious—particularly as it threatened to interfere with her supper—and gave orders for the girls to search the other cottages. After nearly another hour had passed and still no Patsy, she reluctantly gave up the search.

"That's it!" Mrs. Morris declared, throwing up her hands. "I suppose I have no choice but to report this to Mrs. Harvey. And she won't be happy—I can tell you that." Her face twisted into the most severe scowl Nora had yet seen as she pointed a long, bony finger at her. "You're to blame for this, my girl. I told Mrs. Harvey she should have been sent to Emery. But, oh, no—you said you'd be responsible for her. Well, look what's happened," she snarled. This is *your* fault, and I'll not take the fall for it. I've a mind to lock her in the Carrie Cort for a month. You'll both be sorry you ever stepped foot in Solomon."

Mrs. Morris stomped out of the cottage then, Priscilla and her friends nearly tripping on themselves to keep up with their infuriated mentor. Priscilla looked back just once, a smirk on her face as she stuck out her tongue at Nora.

Nora watched them go, her face burning with both guilt and hatred.

The remaining girls quickly dispersed as well, telling Nora and Celia that they were off to search the main hall one more time, though it was obvious they merely wanted to hear Mrs. Morris's report to Mrs. Harvey.

"Celia, what am I going to do?" Nora cried, throwing herself onto the front room sofa.

"Do you think she left the grounds?" Celia asked nervously.

"I don't know." Nora let out a deep groan. Why was Patsy always disappearing? From the time she could walk, Patsy always seemed to be wandering away. Ma said it was her gypsy blood, but Nora never understood what that meant. Pa hadn't been a gypsy, had he? And besides, with blond hair and blue eyes, Patsy didn't look like a gypsy. Regardless, Nora was forever losing Patsy. It hadn't been too difficult to keep tabs on her at the shelter, though Nora didn't really remember much of those days. According to Ma, they had lived there for almost a year after Pa died.

If she tried hard, she could remember a long room with cots lined up along the wall. Ma had a cot, and she and Patsy had slept on the floor beside her. They had kept their stuff, which wasn't all that much, under Ma's cot. On their left was a kind lady who had a baby like Ma, but she couldn't remember who had been on their right. The women who ran the shelter, "nuns" Ma called them, were mostly nice, but they made Ma get a job. There was a very old woman there, Mrs. Bartkowicz, who was supposed to watch Nora and Patsy while Ma was gone, but mostly she fell asleep, and then the two little girls would roam about until they got tired.

After their time at the shelter, they had moved to the one-room apartment on Hirsch Street. It was called the Hirsch Hotel, but it wasn't a hotel, just a place for working people. It was populated mostly with men, and there weren't many children about. Ma told them not to leave the apartment when she was at work, which wasn't so hard in the beginning, as Ma worked nights and would always be home by morning.

But then Ma started working as a waitress, and Nora, almost seven, eventually grew so bored during the long days that she would bundle up Patsy and take her outside. At first, they played in an empty lot two blocks down with an assorted gang of children, but they eventually grew bold enough to walk to Humboldt Park.

Humboldt Park was a paradise, so immense that it took weeks and weeks and weeks for Nora and Patsy to explore the whole thing. There was even a lake, big enough for people to take out little boats. Nora, eager to play with the other children, would often run ahead, Patsy trailing after her on her chubby legs, calling, "Wait for me, Nora! Wait!"

Usually, Patsy stayed by Nora's side, but sometimes Nora would look over and find Patsy gone. She was usually close by, but one time, Nora had found her all the way down by the edge of the lake. Patsy was just staring at it, as if in a trance, the chilly air gently ruffling her blond curls, and Nora had the horrible feeling that if she hadn't come upon Patsy at that exact moment, she might have ventured in.

Terrified by the thought of it, Nora had refused to leave the apartment for a week after and instead sat in the window, watching the bigger girls in the neighborhood playing hopscotch on the street below. Finally, after several days of watching, it occurred to Nora to sneak down while Patsy napped.

Her experiment worked without a hitch, and she was so relieved to have made it back to the apartment before Patsy even woke up that she decided to try it again. And again. And then every day. It was perfect—her playing hopscotch, or sometimes jump rope, on the street below with Patsy safely tucked into bed up in the apartment.

One day, however, Nora lost track of time. The girls had started a jump-rope competition, and Nora had made it all the way to the last round. She was congratulating the winner when it occurred to her that Patsy must surely be awake by now. Dashing into the building, she ran up the stairs, her feet pounding on the thread-bare runner. Before she even got to the fourth floor, however, she was stunned to see Patsy coming out of Mr. Richardt's apartment, one flight below theirs.

Mr. Richardt was an older man with a balding head and large birthmark covering the whole left side of his face. He had glasses and a nervous tic in his left eye, and he was always saying hello to them. Ma had warned them never to talk to him. Sometimes, though, when Ma was gone, and they were sneaking out to the park, Mr. Richardt would open his door and offer them a cookie or ask them if they wanted a cool glass of milk. Patsy always said yes, but Nora would look the other way and pull Patsy along behind her.

Dust motes floated lazily in a lone ray of sun from the one small window in the stairwell as Nora stood staring at the scene before her. In the flash of a second, Mr. Richardt's nervous eye caught hers before he quickly closed his door, leaving Patsy standing in the hallway.

"Patsy!" Nora scolded, suddenly coming to life again and rushing up the last few steps. "What are you doing? You know you're not s'posed to talk to Mr. Richardt. What will Ma say?"

Patsy began to cry and then to visibly shake.

Nora grabbed her hand and tugged her toward the last flight of stairs. "Come on," she urged, but Patsy seemed unable to move. "I won't tell Ma, okay?" She herself was worried about what Ma would say if she found out that Nora had left her alone.

Patsy only sobbed all the more.

"Come on, Patsy!" Nora urged, softer this time, and was about to really pull her when she noticed a little trickle of blood running down the inside of one of Patsy's legs.

"Oh, Patsy! Did you fall? What happened?" Nora asked, really worried now. Ma would be furious.

Patsy, her face ashen and her big eyes wide as she clutched her little doll, just nodded, tears still rolling down her face.

"Come on, Patsy," Nora said gently, lifting her up in her arms, which wasn't hard—she barely weighed anything. "Why didn't you tell me you fell? It's okay. I won't tell Ma, okay? But you don't tell either? Promise?"

Patsy merely sniffled and laid her head against Nora's chest.

"Promise not to tell, Patsy."

A stray memory of that day floated to the surface of Nora's mind now as she watched Celia pace back and forth. She hadn't thought about it for a long, long time, having tucked it safely away, as something about the incident had never sat right with her. She was careful never to sneak out again while Patsy was sleeping, but a few times she had strangely found Patsy standing outside Mr. Richardt's door, staring up at it as if mesmerized. That was also around the time, Nora remembered with a sudden burst of panic, that Patsy began hiding away in tiny, dark places . . .

Tiny, dark places.

Nora felt her stomach convulse so tightly she thought she might be sick. Oh, poor Patsy! She stood up and ran to the pantry.

"Where are you going, Nor?" Celia called. "We've already looked in there."

Nora didn't answer and instead grasped the dull, iron ring of the door cut into the floor. It was heavy. Nora struggled, pulling with all of her might until the door hovered precariously midway. Celia rushed to help her, adding a push so that the door finally banged open. Nora began to doubt her latest theory. How would Patsy have managed to open the door on her own, much less close it again? Maybe she opened it just a crack and slipped through?

Nora peered down into the darkness. Mrs. Morris, having once discovered Nora studying by the faint light afforded by the one window, had ordered Mr. Ackerman to board it up, so that now only a few chinks showed through the sawed-off planks.

"I don't think she's down there, Nora," Celia whispered.

"Well, it's worth a try. Patsy?" Nora called into the darkness. She gripped the rail and carefully made her way down into the musty black. "Patsy?"

Nora thought she heard a movement and froze.

"Nora?" whispered Patsy.

Nora's heart flooded with relief as she leapt down the rest of the stairs and threw open the for-once unlocked door of the Carrie Cort.

"Patsy!" Nora cried. "She's here, Celia! I found her!"

"Oh, Nora! I'll run and tell Mrs. Harvey!"

Nora heard her bang out the cottage's front door and turned her attention to her sister. "Patsy, we've been looking everywhere for you!"

"I'm sorry, Nora. I'm sorry."

Nora knelt next to where Patsy was sitting, her knees pulled up with her arms around them. "Why on earth are you down here? Everyone's looking for you! Even Mrs. Morris!"

"Oh, no!" Patsy sobbed, burying her head in her arms.

"Did . . . did something bad happen?" Nora asked gently, her mind alarmingly straying to the memory of Mr. Richardt again.

"Oh, Nora!" Patsy wailed. "I broke Mrs. Morris's clock!"

"You broke her clock?" Nora asked, incredulous that Patsy would have dared to even touch Mrs. Morris's prize possession—a clock she had purchased at the world's fair last year. But on the other hand, Nora was relieved it wasn't something worse. "Patsy, how could you?"

"I didn't mean to, Nora! I just . . . just wanted to touch it. Feel it. I've done it lots of times. But this time . . . it just dropped."

Nora closed her eyes, trying to think. It was bad, yes, but hiding away in the Carrie Cort? It was so silly! Suddenly, though, her eyes shot open at the sound of hurried footsteps. *Oh, no!* How was she going to get Patsy out of this mess!

Nora heard someone try to repeatedly pull the light bulb chain.

"Why is this light not working, Mrs. Morris?" asked a crisp, unfamiliar voice.

"It . . . it must have just burned out," Mrs. Morris said nervously.

Liar! thought Nora. All the girls knew that Mrs. Morris refused to change the bulb to enhance their fright. "Here, Mrs. Harvey, take this flashlight."

Mrs. Harvey! Nora scrambled to her feet. She had never actually met Mrs. Harvey, only seen her at a distance across the dining room. She heard footsteps on the stairs now, and then, before she could do anything, a flashlight beam shone in her face. Nora shielded her eyes and moved to stand protectively in front of Patsy.

"What is the meaning of this?" Mrs. Harvey demanded, indicating with a flick of her wrist that Nora should move. Nora obliged, though Patsy remained sitting on the dirt floor, her face still buried in her arms. Mrs. Harvey paid surprisingly little attention to either of them and instead continued to shine her light on the walls and ceiling of the coal chute and then the boarded-up window. "What in God's name do you think you were doing, Mrs. Morris?" Mrs. Harvey's lips were drawn so tightly that they appeared white.

"I . . . it's just when the girls are naughty," Mrs. Morris stammered. "You have no idea how bad they can be. They're the devil's spawn. 'Specially those two," she said with a nod toward Patsy and Nora.

"Do you have any idea what would happen if the State found out about this?" Mrs. Harvey hissed. "This is exactly the sort of thing that got us shut down in Evanston! You are dismissed, Mrs. Morris. I'm not about to lose my job. Not to mention what would happen to all of these girls if this school closed."

"Dismissed?" Mrs. Morris asked incredulously. "What do you mean 'dismissed'?"

"You know very well what I mean, Roberta. Pack your things. You're relieved of duty."

"But . . . but surely you can't be serious?"

"I'm very serious. Get out. Now!" Mrs. Harvey commanded.

Mrs. Morris stood there for a few brief seconds, silently opening and shutting her mouth like a fish. She shot a bitter dagger at Nora and Patsy before storming up the stairs, the knot of girls huddled there noiselessly unraveling as she passed through.

Mrs. Harvey turned back toward Nora and Patsy, then, and Nora felt as if she might throw up.

"Stand up," Mrs. Harvey commanded Patsy, who after a few seconds, wobblily got to her feet. "Are you the one that disappeared?"

Patsy remained frozen until Nora gave her a shove. Patsy gave a slight nod.

"Why?"

"She was frightened," Nora blurted, sweat beginning to trickle down her back.

"Of what? Mrs. Morris, no doubt?"

"Yes, she . . . she was afraid for me. I . . . I broke Mrs. Morris's clock. I shouldn't have been touching it, I know . . ."

"Nora!" Celia said faintly from somewhere on the stairs.

"I broke it," Nora continued, louder now, "and Patsy was afraid for me, and she ran and hid. And she . . . she didn't mean to scare everyone. She fell asleep, that's all. We're . . . we're sorry to have caused all this trouble, Mrs. Harvey," she mumbled, fiercely biting the inside of her cheek to keep from crying.

Mrs. Harvey looked carefully from one to the other. "Touching a teacher's or staff member's personal belongings is strictly forbidden, as I'm sure you know, girls," she finally said sternly. "However, I'm sure this has been punishment enough." Her eyes darted over the Carrie Cort again. "We will forget the transgression just this once, but see that you are more careful in the future."

"Oh, yes, Mrs. Harvey!" Nora gushed. "Thank you! It won't happen again! I promise!"

"See that it doesn't," Mrs. Harvey said briefly. "There's nothing more to see here, girls," she announced to the gaggle still quivering on the stairs. "Get back to your cottages now. Go on. I said now."

Without another look back, Mrs. Harvey trudged up the stairs herself, the girls scattering before her as she went.

CHAPTER 15

November 1932

Things changed dramatically after the departure of Mrs. Morris, who didn't even bother saying goodbye and instead simply left in the middle of the night. The next morning, Mrs. Harvey herself appeared in the cottage, saying that not only was the Carrie Cort to be torn down immediately, but that *she* would be taking charge of Solomon until another matron could be found. Likewise, Mrs. Harvey had declared that from this point forward all cases of discipline would be routed to her.

The girls were at first terrified to have Mrs. Harvey as their new matron, temporary though it was, but they soon discovered that she was by far a more lenient mistress than they could have imagined. For one thing, she promptly did away with morning inspection, and secondly, she provided ice cream sundaes after dinner every Saturday evening, which, Agnes whispered once, was her trying to make up for all the abuse they had suffered. Whatever the case, Nora was glad of the respite. In fact, Mrs. Harvey was so accommodating and kind that for one long afternoon, Nora considered confiding in her about her worries regarding Ma. In the end, however, she decided against it. There was nothing Mrs. Harvey—or anyone, she felt certain—could do. She at least had Aunt Rita, she told herself, which was better than nothing.

Another visiting day had rolled around, and Nora sat across from her benefactress on the ancient horsehair sofa next to Celia, blowing on her cup of cocoa, but wishing she were outside with Billy and Lyle and Patsy, whom, she noticed after a furtive glance out the window, were playing in a big pile of leaves. Normally, Nora enjoyed Aunt Rita's many lectures, but today she was having a hard time focusing on the chosen topic, which was the proper way to preserve peaches. Nora felt antsy and uneasy, though she couldn't put her finger on why. Patsy had been acting strangely this morning, too, saying over and over that Ma was coming.

Nora had resisted the urge to yank Patsy's hair as she wove it into tight braids. "No she's not, Pats. How many times do I have to tell you this?"

"But she is, Nora." Patsy tried to turn her head to look at her. "She really is."

"No, she's not. Just behave today," she said giving one braid a tug. "Then we can play the game later."

"Put bows in my hair!"

Nora sighed. "I don't have any bows. You know that."

"Yes, you do. You have those blue ones."

"I only have one. I lost the other one."

"Oh. Well, I'll have one, then."

"What are you going to do with one bow, Pats? You've got two braids."

"Just give it to me, Nora. I want to look good for Ma."

"Oh, fine. Have it your way, then. You always do," Nora snipped and bent down to look under her bed. She drew forth a little bag, which she riffled through until she found a tiny blue bow. "Here."

Grinning, Patsy grabbed it and clipped it to the top of her head. She looked ridiculous, and Nora fretted about what Aunt Rita would say if she saw her this way. Oh, what did it matter? More than likely, Patsy would forget about it in an hour, and Nora could secretly remove it before anyone noticed.

Nora looked back at Aunt Rita now, determined to concentrate.

"You must make sure to remove every bit of skin from the peaches before you bottle them, or the whole jar will turn foul and—"

"Nora DeLorenzo!"

Nora jumped and looked over at the parlor doorway, where Mrs. Dubala stood with her hands thrust impatiently on her hips. Aunt Rita stopped talking and looked over, as did several other family groups.

Nora swallowed hard, dread filling her. Had something happened to Patsy yet again? She had left her outside to play with Billy and Lyle . . .

"Yes?" she answered feebly.

"You have a visitor," Mrs. Dubala barked, and then, before Nora could really take in the full meaning of this announcement, the wispy figure of Ma stepped from behind Mrs. Dubala's bulk.

Nora had imagined this moment a hundred thousand times, but this had never been one of the variations. It was like seeing the dead come to life, and Nora felt a deep, dark wound split wide open.

"Ma?" Nora asked, her voice strangled.

"Nora!" A big smile spread across Ma's face, like the sun cracking the horizon.

Nora felt the urge to run to her, but her legs somehow wouldn't move.

"Nora!" Ma cried again, this time holding out her arms.

At the sight of Ma's open arms, Nora's legs finally began to work, and she took a few tentative steps before breaking into a run. Ma's arms wrapped around her, crushing her against her bosom, and Nora tried hard not to cry. As she breathed in Ma's lovely familiar scent, she thought her heart might be in danger of breaking.

"Oh, Ma," she sobbed. "Where have you been? Why didn't you come?"

"Well, I'm here *now*, Nora," Ma said softly as she squeezed Nora tight. "You're so big!"

Ma, on the other hand, felt skinnier than Nora remembered.

"I can't believe how big you are," Ma said, kissing her on the head. "Where's Patsy?" she asked, releasing Nora and looking toward the couch, where Aunt Rita and Celia sat perfectly still.

Nora was suddenly mortified. Celia's eyes were kind, but Aunt Rita's eyebrows were raised to never-before-seen heights. Nora felt her face burn in shame. She hadn't ever imagined Aunt Rita meeting her mother. Someone like Aunt Rita would instantly be able to tell what her mother really was.

A scarlet woman.

Nora had never told anyone what Mrs. Morris had called her mother, not even Celia, but she had also never forgotten. Only once, when the gang lay breathless on the ground beneath the old oak tree, had she cautiously broached the subject, asking if any of them knew what a "scarlet woman" was.

"No," Celia answered first. "Why?"

"What about a 'lady of the night'?"

"Never heard of that one, either."

"I know what it means," Billy said from where he was lying on his back on the grass. Patsy was lying near him. "It's a woman who sleeps with men for money."

Sleeps with men for money? Nora thought of Olson.

"Yeah, you know. To do the business," Billy added with a grin, raising up on his elbows.

Nora wasn't exactly sure what this meant, but a guess began to hover in the back of her mind.

"No," Patsy said in her baby voice. "A lady of the night is a *fairy*. I saw one once."

Billy laughed. "Yeah, sure you did, kid."

"Why do you want to know?" Lyle finally spoke.

"It's just something I heard," Nora said nervously. "It doesn't matter."

Nora had promptly suggested another round of the game to ensure the subject was dropped, but it haunted her for weeks after. Is that what her mother was doing all those nights? Sleeping with men for money? *How could she!*

Panic filled Nora's chest. Besides the fact that her mother was so horribly shameful, she remembered telling Aunt Rita that her mother was very ill and that's why she never came to see them. And yet now here she was, making a liar of her, she thought with a quick lick of anger. But no, she countered, she had done that all herself.

Flustered, she grabbed Ma's hand and pulled. "Come on, Ma!"

Ma easily resisted. "Aren't you going to introduce me to your friends?" she asked, giving Aunt Rita and Celia a little nod of greeting.

"No, Ma." Nora pulled harder. "Come on!" She knew this was not the ladylike approach Aunt Rita would have advised, but she couldn't think properly. She was desperate to get them out of this room.

"Alright, Nora! You're going to pull my arm off!"

Nora finally succeeded in pulling Ma into the little foyer, but there were still people mingling about. Mrs. Dubala had returned to the desk and looked to be writing something, but Nora could not be sure. She pulled at Ma again, wanting to get her alone—outside maybe? But Ma had paused to examine the class pictures on the walls.

"You in any of these?" she asked, pointing to them.

"Ma! Come on!" Nora said, tugging her towards the main door.

Nora didn't stop until she got Ma outside on the main walk and then promptly dropped her hand. Ma did not seem to notice the slight and instead looked at her with such love that Nora almost melted right there on the pavement. How dare she look at her that way, as if nothing whatsoever was wrong! Hot tears appeared in the corner of her eyes.

"Where have you been?" she asked, hoarsely.

"Well, now, honey, I had to work, you know that. And I didn't have a way to get all the way out here."

"But you just left us here!" She was dangerously close to sobbing.

"Well, Mr. Cohen told me that this was a real nice place," she said with a quick glance around. "That you had ballet class and everything."

"Ballet!" Nora almost shouted. "And who's Mr. Cohen? One of . . . one of your *customers*?" Nora thought she might vomit.

"Customers? From the Sunshine? No, honey, he's the lawyer in charge of our case. He told me not to disturb you."

"Not to disturb us? And you listened to him?" Nora cried, her leg beginning to tremble.

"Well, I told you, Nora. It's not like I had much of a choice."

Ma's face was scrunched. Oh, why was she making this so hard!

"Fact is, I did come visit one night. I looked in on you. Through the window. Bet you didn't know that, did you?"

"You were here?" Nora cried, angrily wiping a tear that had managed to escape. "How come you didn't come in, then?"

"Well, I tried to, but one of the ladies here, a Mrs. Morris, told me it wasn't the proper day and that I would have to come back a different time. I tried to explain, but she was a real tough cookie. Just about broke my heart to drive away. That's the God's honest truth. But Jerry was real good about it."

Nora wasn't sure which was worse—Ma driving away with some man named Jerry, essentially abandoning them to their fate, or that Mrs. Morris had apparently sabotaged her mother's one attempt to rescue them. Nora had the urge to slap Mrs. Morris and wished with all her heart that she was still employed here so that she could do just that.

"I couldn't help take a peek though," Ma went on. "And I saw you were clean and you looked fed. You both looked happy."

"Happy? But you—"

"I started working on Lou then to let me have at least one Sunday off." She gave Nora a big smile, as if . . . as if it all made sense. As if everything was okay now . . .

"But . . . but what about my letters? Didn't you get my letters? How come you didn't answer them?"

Ma sighed. "Well, I tried, but I'm not all that good at letters, Nora. I find it hard."

"Hard! But weren't you worried about us?" Nora could barely keep her voice from cracking.

"'Course I was worried about you. Night and day, I've been worried about you. Don't you know that?"

"No," Nora mouthed, unable to speak, and covered her face with her hands.

"Nora," Ma said gently, touching her shoulder and then wrapping her arms around her. "Come here, my poor girl."

And at the touch of Ma's hand, Nora felt a huge release. Like it was a game of Wizard, and she had finally been rescued. She began to cry in earnest.

"Nora, don't cry. I'm here now," Ma said gently and led her to a battered little bench under an elm that was growing too close to the sidewalk, the roots of which were causing it to buckle. Nora buried her head in Ma's lap. She was sure this was not ladylike, but she didn't care. Ma's touch was so soothing, so intoxicating, that Nora felt she might die. She *wanted* to die, if she were honest, so that this moment would never end. Maybe she *was* dead, she thought for a brief second.

"Where's Patsy, honey?" Ma asked, then, completely shattering the illusion that Nora was actually in heaven.

Who cared where Patsy was? For once she hoped Patsy was well and truly lost. She didn't want to share Ma—even for one second.

"I don't know," Nora said, sitting up slowly and wiping her nose with the back of her hand. "She's around here somewhere."

"Haven't you been looking after her, Nora?" Gertie asked with just a hint of reproach. "I was counting on you."

Nora stared at Ma, feeling the sting of her words as if she had been slapped. How could Ma suggest such a thing? After all that she had endured for Patsy: comforting her, minding her, searching for her, teaching her, lying for her, keeping vigil outside the Carrie Cort. New, raw tears flooded Nora's eyes at the cruel injustice of Ma accusing her of being negligent, when *she* was the negligent one! Nora broke down into horrible convulsing sobs.

"Nora, come on, now." Ma rubbed her back again, but it had lost its soothing effect. "It's okay now. It's okay."

Nora continued to sob, unable to stop.

"Come on," Ma said. "I can only stay a little while, so let's not waste it with tears, should we?"

The fear that Ma would disappear again abated Nora's sobs just a little. Wearily, she sat up again, and Ma silently handed her a handkerchief. When she saw that her gray eyes held tears, too, a new pit of despair opened. She didn't want Ma to cry! For once, she needed Ma to be the strong one. For once, *she* wanted to be the one being cared for and comforted.

As if Ma could read her mind, she gave Nora a smile and ran her hand along Nora's face. "It's okay now, Nora. I'm here now."

Nora's eyes closed involuntarily, and she longed to crawl into Ma's lap as she had when she was a very little girl, but before she could even move, her momentary peace was shattered by a piercing call from across the quad.

Nora opened her puffy eyes to see Patsy on the edge of the orange and red woods, the air seeming to quiver around her. How could Patsy even see this far? It was unnatural.

"Ma!" Patsy shouted again and broke into a run. Her braids had come undone, and her golden hair flowed out behind her as she ran across the grassy stretch, abnormally fast, as if she were perhaps some little animal or maybe even herself a fairy. She crossed the distance in no time, and as she leapt into Ma's arms and wrapped herself around her, there was no reproach, no sadness, no questioning, no anger, just pure joy.

Ma laughed and twirled and kissed her repeatedly on the side of the head. "Here's my Patsy," she said, flashing Nora a smile, inviting her to join in the happiness. "Here's my girl."

Nora watched them in their joy, but found she no longer shared it in quite the same way. She had been allowed to hold it for just a few moments before it had somehow all leaked out. Wasn't Patsy going to reproach Ma at least a little?

"Come on," Ma said, shifting Patsy onto her hip, despite the fact that Patsy was seven, and holding out her hand to Nora. "I've got someone I want you to meet. He's waiting out in the car."

"Who is it?" Patsy asked absently, absorbed in twirling a bit of Ma's hair around her finger.

"Well, his name's Jerry. He's one of my customers, and he was kind enough to give me a ride out here."

"I don't want to meet him!" Nora blurted. "I . . . I just want you, Ma. I just want to be with *you*!"

Ma set Patsy down and put her arms around Nora. "Nora!" she admonished gently. "A big girl like you. There's nothing to fret about."

Nora pressed her cheek against Ma's middle, squeezing her tight. She was already ashamed of her childish outburst, but she didn't like the sound of yet another man in Ma's life.

"Come on, now," Ma urged. "We'll surprise him."

Reluctantly, Nora let herself be led all the way out to Prospect Avenue, which ran in front of the school. It seemed wrong to be out here, as if she were breaking some kind of rule, and she felt vulnerable and exposed. She looked back at the main building. It was the first time she had seen the school from this perspective since they had arrived that gray and wet afternoon.

"Come on, Nora!" Ma admonished, albeit gently. "Stop dragging your feet."

Ma led them to a big, blue car parked a little way down the street. Nora peered curiously at the man inside. He wasn't at all what she was expecting, which, she supposed, was some version of Olson. This man, however, looked different. Curly brown hair, skinny neck, protruding Adam's apple.

"Hey, Jerr!" Ma called.

"Finally," the man said without looking back at the little group. "Thought you said it'd only take a few minutes." He folded up the newspaper he had balanced on the steering wheel and turned to look at Ma. "What's this?" He pushed his hat back onto the crown of his head as he sized up the two girls, his face one of obvious annoyance.

"Well, this here's Patsy," Ma said, setting her down finally. "And this is Nora." Nora was surprised by the eagerness in Ma's voice and felt her stomach clench a little.

"Come, on, Gert. We ain't got no time for this. We've got to get to the track." He glanced purposefully at his wristwatch. "I told you that."

"I just thought you might want to meet them, Jerr," Ma said, her voice slightly irritated now. "We've come all this way."

"I told you before, Gert. I ain't gonna be no dad."

"I didn't say anything about that," she snapped back. "You might at least say hello."

Jerry let out a deep sigh. "Hello, girls. Doin' good?" His gaze passed over them quickly before he returned it to Ma.

Nora felt like little more than a piece of trash, blowing down the street. In fact, she wished she *could* blow away. She glanced over at Patsy, who was sucking her thumb. She felt the urge to knock it out of her mouth, but then realized it didn't matter. Nothing really mattered. She had Ma back, finally, but she suddenly understood that she wasn't going home.

CHAPTER 16

June 1942

Gertie

"Jerry!" Gertie shouted, though she knew he couldn't hear her in here. Frantically she again rifled through the contents of her sewing box that she had dragged out from under her bed, not pausing to brush off the accumulated dust. Where was it? It had to be in here . . . he couldn't possibly have found it, could he? Her fingers flew through buttons, cards of needles, scraps of fabric and old letters, as sweat trickled down her back.

Finally, Gertie stopped, closing her eyes and biting her lip so hard it hurt. It wasn't there. It was gone. How could he have stolen her money once again? Tears formed in the corners of her eyes at the raw betrayal. Again!

"Jerry!" she shouted, throwing the sewing box on the bed and stomping to the front room of their brick bungalow on Pratt. "Jerry!"

Jerry lowered the paper he was reading in his ratty plaid armchair by the front windows, the air above him filled with rings of pipe smoke. "Yeah?"

"How could you, Jerry?" Gertie cried. "That money was for Nora's graduation! You know I've been saving that since even before me and you got together."

Jerry tossed the paper to the side and had the decency to look at least a little uneasy. "Now, look, Gert," he said, pointing his pipe at her. "I'm gonna pay that back. It's just that I lost pretty bad last week, and I needed it to try to win it back. You know how it goes." He gave her a shrug.

"Damn you, we've got to be there in a couple of hours! What am I going to do now!" Gertie moaned. She wanted to kill him, to lunge at his throat and scratch him—something. But what good would it do? She gave him another scowl and retreated to the bedroom.

"She'll understand!" he called to her.

"No, she won't!" Gertie said, more to herself than to him, and sat on the spilled buttons, covering her face with her hands. Nora, she knew, would be disappointed. She had a way of always making Gertie feel guilty when she turned up to visit, which, granted, wasn't very often. Nora never seemed to understand how much she had to work. *And* she had to make a home for Jerry. Nora didn't seem to understand how terribly hard it had been for her to start over.

Gertie had ended up telling Jerry everything the night he had first driven her to the Park Ridge at a bar called O'Malley's on Devon, and afterwards she had gone home with him. In the morning she took a bath and put on her uniform, sponging off the dirty spots before he drove her to the Sunshine. That was the beginning of their relationship, such as it was. Gertie had made sure, during their first conversation that night at O'Malley's, that there was no secret wife or crazy mother in the attic.

"Nope," he had said, "what you see is what you get."

And he was right. Jerry was as ordinary as they came. He worked the press at the Tribune, feeding paper onto the drums. He was good to Gertie for the most part, and over time, Gertie grew to love him in a certain way. Enough to marry him after dating for eight months.

After a while, it had just seemed like the natural thing to do. Gertie was tired of being alone, tired of living in a one-room apartment in a sleazy hotel, tired of looking at Patsy's pictures that Nora had mailed to her. Upon first receiving them, Gertie had delightedly hung them up with a bit of cellophane tape on the walls of the kitchen, but then they had spilled out into the living room and even into the bedroom. In the beginning, they had been a comfort to her, making her feel as if the girls were still somehow with her, but as time had gone on, they began to make her sad and despondent, though she didn't have the heart to take them down. Finally, however, when every last space of wall was covered, she agreed to marry Jerry, after which she had no choice but to remove them all, carefully folding them and tucking them away.

Jerry had inherited his parents' modest bungalow on Pratt, and though it needed a lot of repairs and the interior was very dated, it felt like a palace after the Hirsch Hotel. But unlike the monstrous McPherson place, this one felt manageable. She could make this into a home, she decided, and she could likewise manage being married to Jerry. He was not Olson by any stretch, but he was not Lorenzo either.

He had wooed her by taking her fishing and bowling and to see a show at the Davis every Friday night. Saturdays were usually spent at O'Malley's with his friends and their wives or girlfriends. He was relatively easy to please, as long as she put dinner on the table, kept a clean house, ironed his shirts, and had sex with him weekly. He made it clear that he ruled the roost, but he was good for a laugh, and he didn't care when she broached the subject of wanting to update a few things.

"You do what you want, Gert. You do what you want," he would say over the newspaper.

In general, however, he was used to getting his own way, and he had a spoiled, lazy streak. But didn't all men? Gertie had reasoned. Occasionally, she would catch him winking at one of the waitresses at O'Malley's, and he didn't hide the fact that he enjoyed ogling well-dressed or well-endowed women on the street, but he was faithful, as far as she knew, and he never laid a finger on her, which was saying a lot. And he wasn't a drunk.

But he did have one flaw that he had managed to hide until about six months into their marriage. He was a gambler, and not a very good one at that.

He was forever losing money. He never gambled so much that he lost the bungalow or the car, but enough to never have much spare cash and to always be late on the bills. If any money did happen to come his way, he immediately gambled it away again. Poker was his game, though he sometimes bet on the horses, too.

Gertie had discovered his problem one Saturday morning when the coal man had turned up with a bill for the past three months' supply and a warning that no more would be delivered until it was paid. Early on in their marriage, they had decided that Jerry would pay all the bills and that Gertie would manage the household and any repairs out of her wages. But here was the coal man, standing on the front stoop. Gertie had hurriedly gone to the closet to get some money from her handbag, only to discover, after a frantic search, that it was gone. She returned to the front door, her cheeks burning, with only an apology and a promise that she would have the money next week. With a heavy sigh, the man had tucked the bill back into his plaid shirt pocket, his thick dirty fingers suddenly reminding her of her father. "Gonna be a cold winter for you folks," he said with a shrug. "I'll be back next week. But if you don't have the dough, I'll be chargin' interest."

Gertie had shut the door on him and fiercely turned to Jerry, who was standing there looking sheepish. "What the hell is going on here?" she shouted. "And what have you done with my money?"

"Now, Gert. Don't you get all high and mighty with me. Truth is, I lost it in a poker game. But I'll make it up to you, doll. Don't you worry."

"Don't worry? Are you out of your mind? Gambling? That's a fool's game if there ever was one. How long have you been gambling?"

"Since I was seven."

Gertie just stared at him, her chest heaving. Oh, God, *not again*. She had chosen wrong yet again. Realizing that there was nothing left to say, she went to the credenza, grabbed her still-open handbag and threw it at him. "Here, have it, you bastard."

After that, Jerry was good for a while, and Gertie began to hope that perhaps he had changed. But, as it turned out, it was only a brief hiatus, possibly brought on by a rare episode of guilt. Once the cat was out of the bag, so to speak, he was less careful, and many times Gertie was forced to bail him out and pay the bills out of her wages. Several times, their electricity had even been shut off. *And,* she had to have enough to buy groceries each week to put a good dinner on the table, or he would complain.

She quickly figured out how to supplement by digging up most of the back yard and planting vegetables and even some berry bushes. Oddly, she found it a sort of solace, bringing her back to her childhood when she had weeded not only Maman's garden, but sometimes Signe's. It was difficult to save, but Gertie managed to put away a certain amount each week for the girls, though it meant going without herself. She rarely bought anything new and simply patched what she already had.

In the very beginning, and for a long time after, she held a secret, almost subconscious hope that her marriage to Jerry might mean that the girls could finally come home. Now that the girls were both old enough to be in school all day, Gertie could work and be home in time to make dinner for them. Maybe even help them with their homework, though she wasn't sure how much help she would really be in that department. She had brought it up to Jerry once or twice, usually after they had had sex, when she knew he was most amenable.

"Now, Gert, you know I don't like kids. Never have. Anyway, we've got the dogs," he would say, referring to his two German Shepherds. Gertie had never really grown to like either of them, as they were just as stubborn and bull-headed as Jerry, frequently making messes in the house and digging up corners of her garden.

"I know, Jerr," she would say, running her fingers through his chest hair, "but they're real good girls."

"That may be, honey, but we can't afford kids. Let's let well enough alone. Your girls are happy where they're at; you've said so yourself about a half a million times. So why should we change things? You're always wanting to change stuff. Let well enough alone," he would say, giving her breast a little tug.

Gertie went through varying degrees of emotion regarding Jerry's rejection of bringing Nora and Patsy to live with them and often angrily wondered what would happen if she became pregnant. Though bringing another child into the world was the last thing she wanted, she sometimes perversely hoped it would happen, just to see if the tables might turn. But she never did, and, ultimately, she was thankful. A small part of her, however, resented Jerry for a long, long time, hating the fact that he so easily rejected the thing closest to her heart. For almost a whole year, she tried to get Jerry to come along with her on her visits to the Park Ridge, thinking that if he just got to know them better, he might change his mind. But he wouldn't budge.

"Now, Gert, you know I have my Sunday schedule," he would tell her.

Ah, yes, his precious Sunday routine—up early to fish, come back home, have a bath, read the paper from cover to cover while smoking his pipe and waiting for her to cook him a roast dinner. Certainly, that *was* more important than visiting her girls, she thought bitterly.

So, she went alone. Each month, she would try to bring the girls something—some zucchini bread she had baked or maybe some flowers from the garden, and though they politely thanked her, Gertie never felt it was enough. Patsy seemed always glad to see her, but Nora, after that first visit when she had cried in her lap, had never really warmed to her again.

Perhaps she was imagining it, but Gertie got the distinct feeling that Nora almost resented having to spend visiting day with her. She had caught her several times looking wistfully over to where her friend, Celia, and her aunt—Ruth was it? Rita?—were seated. More than once, Gertie had suggested they join them, but Nora always refused. It made Gertie try all the harder, but the more she seemed to try, the more Nora remained aloof. Monica at the Sunshine advised her to wait it out, that Nora would surely come round eventually.

At one point, Gertie had tentatively revealed to the girls that she and Jerry had gotten married, but even that was met with muted emotion.

"That's nice, Ma," Nora finally managed, though her face held nothing but reproach. And maybe pity?

"How come we didn't get to go?" Patsy asked.

Gertie shifted uncomfortably. "Well, no one was invited, you see. It was just me and him. Real simple. Why have a big fuss?"

Neither of the girls said anything, but Gertie's eyes were on Nora. "He's got a real nice house," she said to her. "It's one of those bungalows. Remember? The ones we used to point out sometimes on walks."

"That's nice."

"I was thinking that maybe you could come see it sometime. Just for a visit. Maybe at Christmas?"

Patsy opened her mouth to speak, but Nora spoke over her. "We can't, Ma," she said. "We have to stay here for Christmas. There's a lot going on."

"I'd like to come," Patsy piped up, and Nora gave her a shove with her elbow.

"We can't, Patsy. You know it's not allowed," she hissed. "And anyway, there's the play? Remember?"

"But Agnes and Winnie got to go home for Christmas last year." Patsy gave her a crooked pout. "You know that's true, Nora."

"No, it isn't!" Nora insisted, throwing Gertie a guilty look, one which threatened to crush her completely.

Later, on the bus home, she cried silent tears at the realization that her daughter would rather spend Christmas in what was essentially an orphanage than come home with her.

Gertie stepped into her sturdy heels, smoothed down her pink dress, and then pinned on the matching pink hat she had just brushed this morning. In all the years that the girls had been at the Park Ridge, this was the first thing that Nora had ever invited her to, and she was determined not only to go, but to look nice. Proper. She had insisted that Jerry attend as well, threatening to stop his dinners for a week if he didn't. He had accordingly put on his brown suit, grumbling all the while, but now she almost regretted it. She was fuming, and she wasn't sure she could sit that long beside him on the drive out to Park Ridge without screaming. She had no gift for Nora! She paced around the bedroom, the thought of showing up empty-handed nearly driving her to despair.

Well, she resolved, finally snatching up her pink gloves off the little vanity, she would just have to find a way to make it up to her. *And,* she further resolved, she would get even with Jerry. This was the last time she would allow him to steal what was rightfully hers.

June 1942

Nora

"Jeez, Patsy! You scared me!" Nora hissed, watching Patsy climb through one of the bedroom windows in Solomon. "Were you out all night again?"

Patsy laughed as she landed on both feet and pulled back her long, blonde hair. "Guess so," she said, kicking off her shoes. Patsy still hated shoes.

"You're gonna get caught one of these days," Nora warned.

"Probably."

"Were you with Billy again?"

Patsy's face lit up with a sheepish smile. "Yeah. You should come sometime, Nora. You study too much."

"Well, you don't study enough."

"Why should I? It doesn't mean anything. You know that as well as I do. We'll either get factory or waitress jobs when we get out of here. That, or get married."

"You know I plan on being a secretary." Nora straightened her belt.

"You're such a wet hen, Nora. Why don't you ever live a little?" Patsy threw herself on the bed of some girl named Wilma. She dug a cigarette out of her handbag and lit it, blowing smoke toward the bunk above.

"You can't smoke that in here! Mrs. Bosworth is sure to find out."

"No, she won't. She's deaf and stupid and nearly blind," Patsy said, puffing away.

Ever since the "Mrs. Morris affair," as the girls now called it, something seemed to have snapped inside of Patsy. She no longer cared about rules or schoolwork or punishments or anything, really. She became a sort of wild child, doing just as she pleased. And perhaps because Mrs. Harvey felt a generous amount of guilt and/or fear when she learned the full extent of Patsy's past incarcerations in the Carrie Cort, she had a tendency to never be heavy in her treatment of Patsy's many infractions, a fact which only encouraged Patsy to be all the more daring.

It was a situation that baffled and infuriated Nora. Not only was it grossly unfair, but sometimes the other girls would make snide comments about her sister being Mrs. Harvey's pet. As if Nora could help it!

"Listen, Patsy," Nora said sternly, waving away Patsy's cloud of smoke. "I hope you're not going to ruin today for me."

"Oh, yes. It's your big graduation. How could I forget?"

"I know it probably doesn't mean anything to you, but it does to me," Nora said in a slightly hurt tone.

"I know, I know!" Patsy sat up. "Here," she said, reaching into her handbag. "I got you this." She thrust a small bottle of whiskey into Nora's hands.

Nora just stared at it. "Where'd you get this?" she asked, stunned. "Billy?"

"'Course it was Billy. But *I* paid for it."

"I can't take this!"

"'Course you can. And you don't even have to share it with me. You and Celia can drink it later to celebrate. Or maybe you and Lyle." She gave her a little wink.

Nora blushed. "He's not like that, and you know it."

"He comin'?" Patsy asked, inhaling so deeply that her right eye squinted shut.

Nora shrugged. "I think so."

"What about Ma?"

"She's supposedly coming, too. And bringing Jerry, I think."

"Oh, goodie!" Patsy said wryly as she snuffed out her cigarette on the windowsill. "We'll finally get to spend time with Daddy."

"Stop it, Patsy. You said you wouldn't ruin it."

"I won't!" Patsy flashed that charming smile of hers.

"Anyway, knowing Ma, she probably won't show up," Nora said.

Patsy stared at her for a few moments. "You're too hard on her, Nor," she said gently. "She tried her best, you know."

"Did she?" Nora asked. "Well, anyway, I've got to get going. I've got to find Celia before the ceremony."

"That what you're wearing?" Patsy eyed Nora's pale blue dress.

"Yeah," Nora said, smoothing the skirt. "Why? Is it not right?"

"No, you look nice." Patsy gave her another wink. "You go on. I'll catch up."

As Nora hurried across campus to the main building, where she knew Celia was helping set up refreshments, Patsy's words continued to form an uncomfortable knot in her mind. She knew Patsy was right, that Ma had probably tried her best, but it was still hard to accept the fact that she had never taken them back home.

Well, Nora resolved, she wasn't going to let thoughts of Ma ruin today's happiness. She was graduating at the top of her class, and Mrs. Harvey had already spoken to an employment agency on her behalf. It didn't really matter if Ma came or not, she told herself. She had learned long ago not to need her. She loved Ma, of course—what kind of daughter would she be if she didn't?—but she didn't need her. *This* was her family now and had been for a long time, she thought, watching her fellow Park girls scurry by.

Graduation was always the highlight of the year, carrying as it did a flavor of victory. The juniors were in charge of decorating, and Mrs. Harvey always provided a large budget. And while each senior girl was required to sew her own graduation dress, the school bought them each a beautiful orchid corsage, as well as a Waterman fountain pen and monogrammed stationery as a parting gift.

Nora poked her head into the dining hall, where a flurry of girls were hanging streamers, sorting through boxes of programs, and carrying huge vases of lilacs, the official school flower, to and fro.

Nora finally spotted Celia at the far end of the room, a clipboard in hand as she spoke to one of the younger girls.

"Hey! Don't you look swell!" Celia said as Nora approached.

"You, too!"

Celia had constructed a buttery yellow dress, and it suited her.

"You just couldn't stay away, could you?" Nora asked, nodding toward the clipboard. "This isn't your job this year, you know. You did it last year."

"I know, but their class is smaller than ours, so I thought I'd give them a hand."

"You just want to be in charge."

"That, too," Celia said, then shouted at a girl at the other end of the hall. "Not that one! The other one!"

"Want help?" Nora asked.

"Not really. But I'm glad you came over." She gave Nora a mischievous smile.

"Why?"

"Someone's here to see you." Celia gave her a little wink. "Out back."

"Lyle?" Nora's stomach clenched a little. "What's he doing here so early?"

Celia shrugged. "I'm sure you can guess. And it ain't just to see his sister. Why don't you go find out? He's waiting for you."

"But why wouldn't he just talk to me later at the party when—"

"Girls! Slow down!" Celia shouted and began walking quickly to where two younger girls were attempting to carry trays of glasses. "I've got to go," she called over her shoulder. "I'll find you later. Tell me all the details!"

As Nora watched her instruct the girls, she thought for the hundredth time about what a great teacher Celia would be. But Celia was determined to be a nurse, probably because it was what Aunt Rita wanted. They had stayed up many nights discussing it, Nora trying hard to persuade her, but Celia remained resolute. Aunt Rita was difficult to defy, even though she had become less and less of a presence in their lives. She still occasionally came to visit—alone, now that they were all too old to play Wizard in the Woods and the boys both had jobs—but she often begged off, claiming one ailment or another, the most popular being her varicose veins. When she did come, she seemed preoccupied with telling tales about Billy and Lyle.

Much to her bitter disappointment, Billy had left school at fifteen to take a job on the railroad. It was surely Lyle's wayward influence, she had said more than once, though Lyle himself remained in school until he graduated and took a job as a clerk in an accounting firm the very next day. Lyle further angered her by moving into a rooming hotel, which Aunt Rita predicted spelled certain disaster. "He says it's because he doesn't think it's fair to live off our generosity any longer, but I know the truth! I know what he's up to!" Billy, of course, still lived at home, though he spent much of his time at the local tap.

Out of the original three, only Lyle continued to routinely visit. He did not own a motorcar, and though Aunt Rita repeatedly told him he was welcome to borrow theirs if he replaced the gasoline, Lyle never took her up on her offer, preferring instead to make his own way out via an elaborate system of trolleys and buses and then walking the last mile to the edge of town.

At first Lyle simply came to visit Celia, but lately he had sought out Nora just as often. It was Celia who suggested that perhaps Lyle had eyes for her, a theory which Nora, her face flushed, had declared to be "utter rubbish." Since then, however, Nora had caught him looking at her in a way that lent itself toward Celia's suspicion. Nora denied having any feelings at all for Lyle, though if she were honest, she wasn't sure. He had always just been there, like a friend or a chum or a neighbor. Certainly not someone to fall in love with.

As Nora rounded the corner of the main hall, the pea gravel crunching under her quick steps, she spotted Lyle standing by the crumbling bird bath at the garden's center. Like the sickly rose bushes that surrounded it, Lyle stood tall and spindly, anxiously gripping his hat and pacing back and forth, his eyes focused downward as if deep in concentration.

"Lyle?" Nora called out, shielding her eyes from the bright sun.

Lyle's head jerked up, and he pushed his round glasses back onto the bridge of his nose with one finger, as was his habit. "Oh, hello, Nora." He gave her a shy smile.

"How'd you get in without an escort?" she asked, looking over her shoulder.

Lyle shrugged. "Everyone's too busy today to pay any attention. Let's get out of the sun, should we?" He nodded toward a bench planted under a magnificent old oak tree.

Nora flushed, unsure of what to do. "Well, it's nice of you to come for the graduation, Lyle, but I'm a little busy at the moment to sit and visit."

"Yes, I . . . I know." He scratched his head nervously. "I know this is your big day, but I just wanted to ask you something."

"Can't it wait till later?"

"Well, it's kind of private." He looked back at the bench.

Nora let out a little breath of resignation and marched over to the bench, her mind racing. She hoped this mysterious communication wasn't what she suspected. Why did he think of her that way? Why couldn't they all just still be friends?

"So, what's all this about?" Nora said, trying her best to keep her voice light. "You're scaring me!"

"Listen, Nora." He fingered his hat. "I'm going to join up. As soon as I turn eighteen."

"Join up?" This was certainly not what she had been expecting.

"I've got to, Nora. I can't sit by. I've got to do my part. You see that, don't you?"

Nora considered. With the bombing of Pearl Harbor just five months ago, and the president's sudden declaration of war, the whole country had transformed into a veritable war machine almost overnight. Only last week, Mrs. Harvey had held an assembly explaining that the school, in compliance with the new Office of Civilian Defense, would be participating in mandatory blackouts and air raid drills and that they could expect less food as rationing went into effect. The last time she and Celia had walked into the little town of Park Ridge itself, Nora had been surprised to see how many shops boasted posters of a stern Uncle Sam, pointing a menacing finger and promoting enlistment.

But Lyle? He seemed like the *least* likely boy—man—to ever be a soldier. He was quiet and precise, considerate and almost overly polite, especially when he was nervous. Nora had never once seen him be confrontational, even to Billy at his worst. He was as gentle a soul as Nora could ever imagine.

How could he possibly go off to fight? Suddenly she felt very alarmed.

"Say something, would you, Nora?"

"Does Celia know?" she asked tentatively.

"Not yet. I wanted to tell you first."

Nora stared at his light brown eyes and noticed that they held flecks of hazel. How had she never noticed this before? "Why me?" she finally asked.

He looked over at the bird bath and then back at her. "Can't you guess?" he asked quietly.

Nora swallowed hard. So he *did* have feelings for her. She wasn't sure what to think. What to feel. Every time Celia had brought up the subject, she had pushed it away, not wanting to even consider it.

"I . . . I don't know what to say," she fumbled. "Are you sure, Lyle? Sure you want to be a soldier? It's just that . . ."

"Just that what?"

"Just that . . ." She had been about to say that he just didn't seem like a soldier, but she stopped herself.

"Look, Nora." He awkwardly placed his hand on top of hers. "I was hoping you might write to me. You know, be my girl, maybe," he said wistfully, giving her a look she had never seen before from him. Gone was the shy, skinny kid with whom she had played a hundred games of hide-and-seek, replaced by a man—a real man—who sought a different type of thing now. Despite herself, she felt a little stirring in her heart. Could she possibly grow to love Lyle?

With the slightest, tiniest movement of his thumb, Lyle rubbed the side of her hand, sending an odd thrill through her whole body. It was a tiny gesture, but with it, she felt an unexpected crack in the walls it had taken her entire child-hood to build.

"Nora?" he asked gently.

Nora swallowed hard and searched his eyes one last time. "Yes, Lyle. I'll write to you. If you really want me to."

A giant smile erupted across Lyle's face. "Gee, Nora. That's swell." He leaned toward her, and Nora, fearing that he meant to kiss her, hurriedly stood.

"I should get back."

"Oh, sorry," he said, obviously flustered. "Yes, I shouldn't keep you." He stood up and offered her his arm. "I'll walk you over."

Nora took his arm, feeling nervous and flushed as they walked back toward the main grounds and tried to work out exactly what she felt. Well, she supposed, there would be time enough to figure that out through their letters, though the thought of him going off to war made her feel ill. She glanced over at him. His eyes were locked on the ground, but his face held a small smile. It made her feel oddly happy, content.

She jumped, then, when they rounded the building's corner and nearly collided with Ma, Patsy, and a man she assumed must be Jerry, if she remembered correctly. She had only met him once—the day Ma had turned up for the first time and had led them out to meet him. He hadn't even gotten out of the car that day, simply said "Hello, girls" and flashed them a false smile, just as he was doing now.

Nora retracted her arm from Lyle's, though it was obvious by the little wink Patsy flashed her that she, at least, had noticed.

"Nora!" Ma cried. "Here you are! Don't you look nice! You look so grown up. Doesn't she, Jerry?"

Jerry looked her up and down and flicked his cigarette as he gave her another false smile. "Good seein' you, Nora. Been awhile."

Jerry looked exactly like he had when she met him ten years ago, and, like then, Nora got the distinct feeling that he would rather be anywhere right now than here. She gritted her teeth and wickedly wished they hadn't come at all. It was ruining everything.

"Who's this?" Ma asked, smiling at Lyle.

Lyle opened his mouth to answer, but before he could, Nora blurted, "This is my friend, Lyle. Celia's brother." Nora did not dare look at Lyle's face, not wanting to see if he was hurt by her not introducing him as something more. Instead, she plowed ahead. "This is my mother," she said with a gesture, "and this is her husband, Jerry."

"Well, your stepfather, I guess," Ma corrected weakly.

"I wouldn't go that far, Gert," Jerry said, focusing on crushing his cigarette underfoot. "Nora's all grown-up now, aren't you?"

"Jerry!" Ma cried. "You said you'd be on your best behavior!"

"I *am* on my best behavior, Gert."

Nora got the distinct feeling they had been arguing. This was just what she needed!

Nora looked over at Patsy, who could barely suppress a grin. Of course, she found this amusing.

"So what's your plan after graduation?" Jerry asked.

Nora glanced at Ma, as if the answer lay with her. Ma, however, suddenly became interested in something in her handbag, which told Nora all she needed to know. It wasn't as if Nora expected, or even wanted, to go live with Ma and Jerry. Still, it stung that Ma did not even at least offer.

"I'm not sure yet," Nora answered.

"I had . . . *have* a gift for you, Nora," Ma said eagerly. "It's just that I . . . I left it at home." She gave Jerry a deep scowl.

"It doesn't matter, Ma," she made herself say, doubting whether there had ever really been a gift.

"No, really, Nora, it's a real good gift. I've been saving—"

"Well, I should probably take my seat now. They're going to be starting any minute." She again put her arm through Lyle's, who didn't seem to know what to do. "I'll find you after, okay?"

She could see the hurt in Ma's face, but she didn't care. Patsy, too, looked disappointed in her, which further annoyed her. This was not at all how she had envisioned her graduation day, and even as Lyle led her past the lilac bushes to the rows and rows of chairs set up on the main quad, at the end of which a small stage had been erected, she could not help but be irritated. She had just wanted to have one perfect day.

Well, she sighed, as she took her seat, Lyle striding off toward the spectator's section, she supposed she couldn't have everything, could she?

CHAPTER 18

September 1942

Gertie

Gertie rifled through the mail that had been left in the dented black mailbox on the front of the house, praying that it would be here today. She nearly swore when her initial search yielded nothing. Instead, she pulled the stack out and carefully went through them all again. This time, she nearly gave a squeal of delight. It was a letter from the Department of Defense addressed to Mr. Gerald Munson. With any luck, this was his notice to report for duty.

Gertie placed the letter on the top of the stack and hurried back into the house. This was her revenge for him stealing and gambling away the one hundred dollars she had saved for Nora's graduation. So far, she had re-amassed sixty-two dollars, fifty of which she planned to give to Nora as soon as she saw her next. The rest she would continue adding to, so that when Patsy graduated, she would have enough for her, too.

She and Jerry had argued all the way to Park Ridge that day, Jerry swearing as he drove that he would "pay it back, God damn it!" That she should "give a guy a chance" and "what right had she to keep money from him in the first place?" Gertie had given as much back to him by calling him a "rat" and a "weasel" and even a "good-for-nothing bastard."

He had begrudgingly handed her a crumpled six dollars the following week, and another eighteen the next, but after that, he just sort of forgot about it. But Gertie didn't, and she couldn't seem to let it go. It wasn't just about the loss of the money, it was about the loss of respect from Nora. As she had saved the money, week after week after week, Gertie had begun to convince herself that this money would be a sort of peace offering, a small recompence for the life Nora had been cheated out of, though Gertie never admitted this out loud.

Over the years, she had never ceased bragging to anyone who would listen about her girls being at a fancy school in Park Ridge. Still, Gertie knew the truth, and she knew that Nora knew as well—she could see it in Nora's eyes whenever she visited. It was a judgement of sorts, and worse was the fact that Gertie felt she deserved it. She *was* a bad mother. There was no getting around it. But this grand gift, this graduation money, had been her way of trying to make it up to her. To both of them, really.

Jerry had destroyed all of that, however, all of that work and sacrifice, in the space of just one night. Gambling it away as he had was almost worse than setting it on fire—giving it over into the grubby hands of some equally idiotic man who just so happened to have been dealt higher cards than Jerry. It was monstrous! And every time Gertie thought about it, she felt sick.

She could not forget how Nora had waved away her explanation about the gift at her graduation, as if she didn't believe her or, worse, care. Perhaps she shouldn't have said anything at all. Yes, that probably would have been better. Saying that she had a gift but hadn't brought it just highlighted its absence. She longed to tell Nora the truth, that Jerry had stolen it, but she didn't want the girls to have a bad impression of him, not that he deserved it. But Nora's potential disapproval or disgust or even anger toward Jerry would have been easier to take, Gertie realized now, than what Nora had instead dished out, which was apathy, as if Gertie's very presence or anything that she said or did made the slightest difference at all.

That was the heart of it, Gertie realized. The essence of the pain. That the girls didn't really need her and didn't really care. Patsy always had a kiss and a hug for her on visiting days, but she was flighty and ethereal and would eventually wander away, leaving her to sit with the grim Nora, who struggled, she could tell, to come up with conversation. Often Gertie was sick at heart at how it had all turned out, her beautiful little girls despising her.

Once in a while, usually after a drink or two with Jerry, she would grow brave enough to try to fathom it all out, to understand how it had all gone wrong. Sometimes she still blamed Lorenzo or, alternately, Olson and his miserable wife, but now she mostly blamed Jerry. It was *his* fault, she decided, that this rift had occurred between her and her girls. If he had let them come live with them when they were younger, and if he hadn't been a gambling good-for-nothing, she could have given them a secure home and none of this would be happening now.

Which is why it was shocking when, after things had cooled down between the two of them following the graduation debacle, Jerry had oddly suggested that maybe the girls *should* come and live with them after all. Patsy could finish out high school at Sullivan, and Nora, too, could live here and work. Why not? he had said casually one morning, only briefly looking up from his newspaper.

Gertie could tell by now when he was up to something, and she was immediately suspicious, though she couldn't think of what his ulterior motive might possibly be. Why now? After all these years of her begging? Because he saw how beautiful they were? How accomplished? How grownup? Had he simply envisioned them all these years as crying little brats, and now that he saw that they were quite lovely young women, had he changed his mind? Or was it a way to ease his guilt over stealing her money? Did he think that allowing the girls to come home would make up for it, or that she would then forget about his debt to her?

There was admittedly a small part of her that was more than a little excited by his suggestion, but she made herself be wary. Jerry often said things but never did them. Still, he continued to bring it up over the next few weeks and months, seeming more and more eager each time.

Finally, she decided one day to mention it to the girls at the Sunshine. Linda, the woman who had more or less taken Monica's place as her best friend after Monica and her husband had years ago moved to Indiana, could always be counted on to be direct and outspoken, and this time was no exception.

"He's tryin' to dodge the draft, Gert. Ain't that obvious?"

"Dodge the draft?" Gertie asked as she wiped one of the back tables. "What do you mean?"

"Sugar, don't you know nothin'? Used to be if you was married, you wouldn't get called up. But now they're talkin' 'bout callin' up married men, too, unless they have kids or someone dependin' on them. Not just a wife."

Gertie paused in her wiping and let this sink in. *What a rat!*

"He's kind of pushin' it, though, ain't he?" Linda continued from behind the counter. "I mean, Patsy's already sixteen, ain't she? She hardly a kid."

Gertie tossed her rag in the bucket. It made perfect sense, of course. Here she was, afraid that he was perhaps some sort of pervert (her latest theory), when really he was just a coward. Gertie always thought of Jerry as being older than her, but he was in fact six years younger, only thirty-one. He could still be drafted, and Gertie felt a stab of hurt that he had tried yet again to deceive her.

All day at the Sunshine and all during the long bus ride home, she stewed about it, so that when she walked in the front door, she was no longer sad, but fuming. How dare he try to use her girls for his own convenience? Gertie knew it was wicked, but she wished he *would* be drafted, then she might be rid of him.

She was further infuriated when he didn't bother to come home on time for dinner that night. She waited a good forty-five minutes and then ate hers, leaving his to crust over on the table beside her. She did the dishes and then picked up his plate to put it in the oven to keep, but then changed her mind and tossed it back onto the table, a few of the peas rolling off onto the tablecloth.

When he did stumble in, several hours later, she could smell the booze from across the room. She watched as he tried to toss his hat on the coat rack and missed. It landed with a soft thud on the floor, and he stared at it for a few moments, swaying. Finally, he turned from it and walked toward where Gertie was standing in the middle of the room, her arms crossed, her cardigan wrapped tightly around her.

"You look mad, Gert." He staggered closer. "Why are you always fuckin' mad at me these days?" he slurred, his right eye squinting shut. "Where's my dinner?"

"Admit it."

"Admit what?" he said, walking past her toward the kitchen.

"Admit that your idea of having the girls come live with us is to get out of the war. That's right, isn't it?" she called after him.

"This it?" he called. "Why the hell didn't you put it in the oven?"

"Jerry!" she shouted, following him to the kitchen where he stood staring at the crusted-over food, his hands on his hips.

He picked up the plate, sniffed it and then tossed it back onto the table. "Smells like shit," he slurred.

"Admit it!" she yelled.

"Admit what?" he said, swaying again.

"Admit you wanted the girls to come live here so you could stay out of the war!"

Jerry's face went blank as he considered her accusation and then gave a late little shrug. "So? I don't want my head blown off. Marchin' about this way and that. No thanks."

"But it's your duty! Don't you want to fight for your country?" she asked incredulously, forgetting about the girls for a moment.

"No," he said, slowly shaking his head. "Why the hell do you think I married you?"

Gertie hugged the letter to her chest now and took a deep breath. He was still in the kitchen finishing the ham sandwich she had made for lunch. She wanted to run in and thrust it in his face, but she made herself walk slowly—left, right, left, right.

He was reading the paper. God, why was he always reading the paper? He took a personal interest in it, as if he were the editor-in-chief or something, not some jerk who fed the paper onto the drums. Gertie wanted to scream at his inflated ego. *Well, let's see how he'll fare in the South Pacific or tramping through some forest in Europe.* Carefully she placed the letter on the table to the side of his plate and then casually walked to the sink.

"Letter for you," she said, turning on the tap to fill the sink with water, holding her breath all the while, waiting for the explosion.

For several agonizing moments, Jerry didn't do anything but continue to slowly turn the pages of the newspaper.

"Aren't you going to open it?" Gertie finally blurted.

"What?" He looked up at her absently.

"Aren't you going to open your letter?" Gertie asked with a nod toward it. "Looks official."

Jerry glanced at the letter lying on the table and let the paper slide from his fingers.

"What's this?"

Gertie didn't answer but picked up a pot and let it sink into the bubbly water. She could hear him ripping open the envelope and pulling out the insides.

"What the fuck?"

Gertie looked over at him and reveled in his ashen face and his furrowed brow. "What is it?" she asked innocently.

"Jesus fucking Christ, I'm being drafted." He tugged at his chin angrily. "There's got to be some mistake," he said. "I got a deferment! I have dependents!"

Gertie's cool eyes held his frantic ones. "Do you?" she asked innocently.

"Yes! I told them I did. It's only a matter of time before the girls move back. Didn't you write to that Mrs. Harvey or whatever her name is?"

"No," she said coolly, wiping her hands on her apron. "But I did stop by the recruitment office over on Clark and told them all about you."

"What?" he said hoarsely. "You did what?" he asked, more incredulously now. The chair scraped painfully against the floor as he stood. "You fucking bitch!"

"Turns out two can play your game, Jerry. You're to be a soldier after all. And then my girls really can come and live here with me while you're away fighting for us. And now you know why I married *you*."

CHAPTER 19

September 1942

Nora

Nora glanced nervously at the clock one more time. She was sitting at a desk outside of Mrs. Harvey's office, though not as an errant student, but as Mrs. Harvey's personal secretary. It was not a job she ever envisioned herself doing, nor did Mrs. Harvey seem in particular need of a personal secretary, but Nora was glad for it just the same. More than glad, actually. Grateful. Without it she wasn't sure what she would have done.

After graduation, she had gone on many arranged interviews in the city, but each time, Nora was either not offered the job, or she found one reason or another not to take it. Finally, after almost a month, Mrs. Harvey invited Nora into her office for what she called a little "heart-to-heart." It was natural and completely understandable, she said, for some girls, especially those who had been here for so long, to be reluctant to leave. Was it a case of this perhaps? she had asked. Or did it maybe have something to do with Patsy?

Nora's heart beat a little faster at Mrs. Harvey's surprising perception. She supposed there *was* some truth to her words, she thought, twisting her hands in her lap. This was the only home she had really known, and she couldn't imagine living anywhere else. But it was Mrs. Harvey's second suggestion that was probably closest to the truth.

She simply couldn't leave Patsy. It wasn't just that she loved Patsy with all her heart, almost as if she were her own child, but who knew what kind of trouble Patsy would get herself into without Nora being there to rein her in? Every time Nora thought about it, about moving away without Patsy, she suffered a small episode of panic.

Patsy, meanwhile, who was oddly aware of Nora's internal struggle, predictably laughed it off in typical Patsy fashion. "For God's sake, Nor, don't worry about me. Get out of here! See the world; do something! I'll be alright. I'm not a little girl anymore, you know. Fly away, Nor. Fly away while you can."

But Nora seemed unable to do so. Dutifully, she had gone on interview after interview, but her wings, she found, had somehow been clipped over the years, damaged beyond use, though they looked perfectly fine from the outside.

In the end, Mrs. Harvey managed to come up with a satisfactory solution, at least for the time being, anyway. She offered Nora a job as her personal secretary in exchange for continued room and board and an almost non-existent salary. She suggested that Nora take some time to think it over, but Nora insisted on accepting the position immediately. She knew Mrs. Harvey was doing her a very great favor, and she thanked her profusely, telling her that she would not be sorry, that she was determined to be the very best secretary. And she was, though a large percentage of her time was spent *not* engaged in secretarial work, but on helping the various matrons to get their classrooms ready for the next school year.

Still, Nora didn't mind. She was allowed a bedroom up on the third floor of the main building with the other staff members, mostly the kitchen help and the cleaning women, and she delighted in being able to go into town any day she chose. For the first few weeks, she frequently did, though she had nothing much to do when she got there. Still, it felt very grown up to walk down Prospect Avenue alone and stop for as long as she wanted in front of the shop windows. She could come and go as she pleased, though it never occurred to her to visit Ma. The only time she ventured out, besides to stroll through town, that is, was to see Lyle.

Lyle had remained a faithful constant over the summer, continuing to show up every visiting day until Nora had gently reminded him that he could come and see her *any* time, as often as he wished. Lyle had given her a sheepish grin. "Oh, yeah. I guess I should have thought."

Since then, they had developed a kind of routine, which consisted of him coming out to Park Ridge every Tuesday for a show at the Pickwick and an ice cream after. And twice he had persuaded her to come to Riverview in the city, where she had ridden a carousel for the very first time. There was also a fun house with freaks and other oddities that he was determined to see, but she refused, saying that that was all just trickery and a waste of good money.

Nora tried her best not to get too caught up in it all. They were in a sort of bubble, she reminded herself, waiting for him to turn eighteen so that he could enlist. She continually tried to keep a check on her emotions, but she found it hard, as she was in truth falling deeper in love with Lyle as the weeks went on.

She looked at the clock one more time. He should be here any moment. Lyle's birthday had come and gone last week, and today was the day he had chosen to report to the army recruitment office to enlist. His plan was to come out to see her afterwards, when he could present himself to her as an official private in the United States Army. She had suggested he simply telephone to let her know how it had gone, but he had insisted, saying that he would surely be in need of moral support and would welcome a chance to hold her hand.

So far, holding hands and some intermittent kissing had been the limit of their physical intimacy. Nora found she rather enjoyed kissing Lyle, though she was always careful to stop them before they got carried away, though it wasn't really required all that often, as Lyle was usually a perfect gentleman. There was only one time when things almost got out of hand.

It had happened at Riverview. They had gone in the evening to see it all lit up, and the amusement park, they discovered, took on a whole different feel after the sun went down. There was a jumpy electricity in the air, one that made them feel excited and daring. Lyle bought some popcorn and convinced her to go on the Ferris wheel, during which she tightly gripped his hand and buried her head in his shoulder.

Afterwards, when they were safely on the ground, he had led her beyond the park's big gates to the path that ran along the Chicago River. They could still hear the park's music floating in the hot air as they walked, and at one point, they stopped to look over the railing at the black water below. Unexpectedly, Lyle pulled her to him and kissed her, right there in the open! It was a risqué move for Lyle, who normally saved his kisses for their private goodbyes. Nora was stunned, and not a little aroused, and soon found herself returning his kisses, her heart speeding up to a dangerous pace. He was oddly passionate tonight, and Nora felt parts of her body respond in a way they hadn't before, especially when his hands roamed along her back and then grazed her bottom. She let out a small gasp, which he seemed to take as a cue to stop. He took her hand, then, and led her off the path and into the dark and mostly deserted picnic grove.

"Lyle, where are we going?" Nora asked, but Lyle didn't answer and continued on to a small stand of walnut trees and pulled her down onto the grass. They sat there looking at each other for several moments, after which Nora finally opened her mouth to protest, but before she could, Lyle began to kiss her again. Despite her initial hesitation, she soon relaxed, her passion quickly returning. She was eager now, willing, though a part of her was anxiously wondering if anyone could see them. This consideration quickly flew out of her head, however, when he broke his kiss and began to nibble her ear and one hand grazed the side of her breasts. Gently he caressed her until she let out an embarrassing little moan, his kisses on her neck flooding her with passion. She knew what they were doing was dangerous, and yet she couldn't seem to stop. When she felt his hand move lower, however, she gasped.

"No, Lyle!" she said, making herself pull away.

"Nora!" He was breathing heavily. "I'm sorry. But I love you; you know that, right?"

"But Lyle, we can't. It isn't right. And, anyway, not out here in the open."

"I wasn't going to go that far," he said raggedly, kissing her cheek and then her earlobe.

Nora felt herself wavering.

"What if I get killed in action? What if I don't come back?" he asked between kisses to her neck.

"Lyle, don't talk that way!"

"Nora, we have to face reality. It's a real possibility."

He began kissing her lips again, and she felt a warm flush race through her. What he was saying made sense . . . but when she felt his hand move inside of her blouse, his fingers touching the bare skin of her breast, a real alarm went off in her head.

"Lyle!" she murmured, pulling away again. "Not until . . . not until we're married," she said. Instantly, she regretted it. He had never really asked her to marry him. "I mean . . . *if* we ever get married," she added hurriedly.

"Course I want to marry you, Nora." He stroked her cheek. "But not until I come back."

"But why? I don't mind."

"Because." He sat up awkwardly and looked at the lights of Riverview in the distance. "I don't want to make you a widow before you're even nineteen. If I make it back, we'll get engaged. How's that?"

Nora sighed and sat up, too. Absently, she pulled at some of the grass. "Why are you so pessimistic all the time?"

He didn't answer and just kept looking at the lights.

"Lyle?"

"Wouldn't you be if you were me?" he asked, glancing over at her now. "My mom died, my dad left us to fend for ourselves. Everyone thinks I was the lucky one for getting taken in by Aunt Rita and Uncle Carroll, but no one really knows what it was like growing up with Billy. It wasn't all fun and games." He looked back at the lights.

"No, I'm sure it wasn't," Nora said softly. He had never opened up to her this way.

He ran his hand roughly through his hair. "I'm sorry, Nora. I didn't mean to say all of that." He tried to muster a smile. "I didn't mean to upset you."

"It didn't upset me," she said eagerly.

"I know you've had a rough time, too, haven't you? Celia doesn't like to talk about it, but I know it wasn't all fun and games at the school. And here's me going on about my troubles."

"We've both had a hard time," she said, and took his hand, trying not to think about the fact that a new, collective chapter of "hard times" was about to begin with him being away at the war and her left behind, writing letters and hoping they made it, hoping he would come back for her.

The clock read five-thirty p.m. now. It was already half an hour past quitting time, and it was no use just sitting here any longer. Nora looked around the little lobby where she and Patsy had first been delivered all those years ago, as if they were unwanted, damaged packages. It looked different from this side of the desk. She examined the pictures on the wall, again, as a way of distracting herself from the time, and wondered where all of these girls had ended up. Had any of their lives turned out happy?

What was taking him so long? She had already tidied her already-tidy desk and filed everything she could possibly file. She let out a sigh. She supposed she would just have to go upstairs and wait for him there. Mrs. Harvey had already left, so the locking up had been left for Nora. She stood and switched off her desk lamp and then extracted the keys from her top drawer. As she did, she heard someone come into the vestibule.

"Nora?" came Lyle's unmistakable voice.

"I'm in here!" she said, clutching her navy cardigan from the back of her chair. Remember, she schooled herself, be happy for him. *Don't cry.* Be proud of him for wanting to go.

She came out from behind the desk just as he stepped into the lobby. It was dim now, the dying sunlight from the front windows illuminating stray bits of dust floating gently in the air. She wrapped her sweater around her shoulders, steadying herself for his news and hoping that he might not have to leave immediately. She could tell instantly, however, that something was wrong.

"I'm not going!" he said bitterly before she could even ask.

"What?" Nora asked, stunned.

"I'm fucking 4F." He shot her a look of disgust. "Flat feet, apparently."

"Oh, Lyle. I'm . . . I'm so sorry," Nora said, not knowing what else to say, but hardly believing their good luck.

"I can't believe it!" He pounded the thick plaster wall with his fist.

Nora jumped. She had never seen him be violent. Ever. Even with Billy. She couldn't think of a word to say. Well, she could think of *some* things, but she was afraid they might further anger him.

"Now what am I going to do, Nor? I'll look like a damn coward. Everyone already thinks that anyway, I'm sure."

"That can't be true," Nora said quietly. "*I* don't think you are a coward. You joined up the first minute you could. That's not . . . that's not cowardly."

Lyle held her gaze for several moments, seeming to consider something. Finally, he gave a sigh and walked to the window. Outside, girls were scurrying to their cottages for dinner. "What the hell am I going to do?" he sighed. "I've already quit my job. That was stupid, I suppose."

"You can ask for it back; I'm sure they'll give it to you," Nora said, walking toward him. "With all of the men gone." She bit her lip at what was such an obviously wrong thing to say. "You could sign up to be an air-raid warden," she hurried on. "They really need men. I've seen the posters—"

"Billy will have a heyday with this, I'm sure. He's already joined up, of course. Fucking flat feet, of all things! I might as well be called a cripple."

Nora hesitantly laid a hand on his arm. "Oh, who cares what Billy thinks. It doesn't matter."

"But it does! You don't know what he's like."

"Well, don't you care what *I* think?"

As Lyle looked down at her, his face relaxed. "Course I do. You know that."

She returned his look with as much love as she could muster. When he didn't say anything more, she decided to speak. "Where does this leave us?" she asked shyly.

He searched her eyes and then looked away again. "I don't know, Nor."

"But I . . . I thought you wanted to get married."

"Come on, Nora. That was wartime talk. I'm not going to hold you to that. Especially now. After I've been labeled a cripple."

Unexpected tears welled up in Nora's eyes. She had never been *completely* sure about wanting to marry Lyle, but now, at the prospect of not doing so, she wanted it more than ever.

"Hey, why are you crying?" he asked incredulously. "Don't feel bad for me. I'll be fine."

Nora tried to take a deep breath. How could he not understand her tears? "I'm . . . I'm not crying for *you*," she managed to get out. "I'm crying for me. I love you, Lyle. I thought you loved me, too."

"Hey, I do love you." Suddenly he pulled her to his chest and put his arms around her. "Oh, Nora," he said. "Do you really still want to be with me? Flat feet and all?"

"Yes, of course I do," she said, a small smile escaping.

"You really want to get married?" he asked, pulling back so that he could look into her face.

"Well, you never really asked me," she said quietly.

"I didn't?"

Nora slowly shook her head. "Not properly, anyway."

Lyle took one hand from around her waist and grabbed one of her hands. He let out a deep breath. "Well, here goes, then." He looked deeply into her eyes, taking his time. "Nora De Lorenzo, will you marry me? Will you be my wife?" he asked. "Will you take me as your husband, such as I am?"

"Yes," Nora said, unable to stop smiling. "Yes, of course I'll marry you, Lyle."

They spent the rest of the evening strolling about the grounds, talking wistfully about all that lay ahead. It was certainly not the conversation Nora had expected to have with him this night. She had assumed it would be about the details of his unit, when he would be shipping out, where she could write to him. Instead, they were talking about when to marry and how they would live.

Lyle, it seemed, was determined to save enough money to put down on a house before they got married. He wanted to do it right, he said, not like his parents. At first Nora was inclined to say that she didn't mind living in an apartment at first, but she stopped herself the more she thought it through.

It would mean leaving Patsy.

Nora groaned silently. She hadn't thought about how getting married would affect Patsy. Perhaps she could come and live with them, Nora thought as she and Lyle slowly circled the bird bath. But then Patsy would have to quit school and work, which Patsy herself had already threatened to do about a dozen times. Most people didn't finish high school, but she didn't want that for Patsy; if Patsy failed to graduate, Nora felt as though it would be all her fault. No, she had to finish, Nora determined. Besides, she was pretty sure Patsy wouldn't agree to live with them, anyway. Or maybe wouldn't even be allowed to. Who knew what the state ruling from all those years ago really outlined?

No, thought Nora, if Lyle wanted to wait and save money, why not? It seemed the best scenario. It would buy enough time for Patsy to finish school and get settled somewhere—if that was even possible, she thought with a sigh.

Patsy didn't care about anything or barely anyone. It wasn't in a bad way, per se; it was simply that she didn't get caught up in the everyday concerns of life. She had a true artist's spirit, Mrs. Hanley had once said, what Ma would have called the gypsy in her. She had a whole gaggle of boys around her whenever she went into town who fell over themselves trying to buy her a soda or a candy. Nora just hoped she wouldn't end up with Billy, who was annoyingly the one Patsy snuck out most nights to see. Nora had tried to warn Patsy on more than one occasion to not consider Billy a serious contender for marriage, but Patsy always laughed and said, "Poor Nora."

Nora gripped Lyle's hand and told herself not to think about all the things that could go wrong where Patsy was concerned, remembering her accusatory words to Lyle about being pessimistic. Tentatively, she allowed herself to be hopeful. Lyle said he would ask for his job back and maybe look for a second job at night. They would announce their engagement, but it would be a long one, they decided. Nora wished that Celia was still around so that they could both tell her the news, but she had left after graduation to attend St. Luke's Nursing School in the city.

Nora missed her terribly, but so far they had lived up to their promise to write every other week. Nora enjoyed hearing about Celia's exploits out in the world and lived a little vicariously through her. She herself never had much to relate and usually resorted to simply reporting the week's routine, just as she had done with Ma all those years ago, though now she could add little bits of gossip here and there, especially where the matrons were concerned. Finally, she had some big news to share—that their childish dream of becoming sisters was about to come true! But perhaps it was really Lyle who should be the first to tell Celia, as she was the only relative he still had contact with, not counting Aunt Rita and Uncle Carroll, of course. He had no one else to tell. She at least had Mrs. Harvey and all the matrons and the girls at the school. And, of course, she had Patsy, whom she knew would be happy for her, despite being so unconventional herself. Nora was eager to assure her that she wouldn't leave her behind, though she guessed that Patsy would say she didn't care. Almost as an afterthought, Nora realized that Ma would have to be told at some point.

As the minutes with Lyle ticked on, she grew more and more eager to tell Patsy— anyone, actually—her good news. It had grown dark and cold, and they had stepped back into the lobby to get warm. She didn't want to push Lyle away, but he didn't seem all that eager to leave. Instead, he had somehow slipped back into his original despondency regarding his 4F status.

"It's going to be okay, Lyle. You'll see. We need you here—*I* need you. Someone has to stay and protect us all." Shyly, she put her arms around him and kissed him on the cheek. "I know it's wrong, but I'm glad you're staying."

Lyle gave her a sad smile as he wrapped his arms around her waist. He was silent for a few moments, and Nora began to worry that she had offended him.

"Remember all those times you caught me while we were playing Wizard in the Woods?" he asked softly. "I let you catch me."

Nora gave him a sly smile. "No, I let *you* catch *me*."

Lyle let out a little chuckle and bent to kiss her lips. "Alright then." Slowly he released her. "I'll go now. I know you want to tell Patsy."

Nora smiled and folded her arms across her chest, basking not only in his love but at how well he already knew her.

"You'll write to Celia?" she asked, as he reached for his hat on the stand in the corner.

He nodded. "She'll be thrilled, I'm sure," he said wryly, then walked over to give her a last kiss, resting his forehead against hers for a moment. "Goodbye, Nora. I'll make you happy; you'll see."

"I already am happy," she said softly.

He left, then, a mix of bitter sweetness still about him, though he seemed eager enough to begin his new mission, not fighting the Jerries or the Japs, as he had hoped, but preparing for their life together.

Alone now in the middle of the lobby, it suddenly occurred to Nora how odd it was that she was proposed to in the very same room where her life at the Park Ridge had begun. She glanced around at the photos one more time and allowed herself the childish fancy that all the girls were silently cheering for her, happy that at least one of their own had found happiness, before she shook it off as nonsense. Then she pulled out the keys from her pocket, their jangling noise further dispelling any sort of silliness, and locked not only the front door, but the heavy door on that early chapter of her life.

As she stepped outside, she was immediately hit by a gust of wind and pulled her sweater tighter. She looked across the quad toward Solomon. Dinner was long over by now, which meant Patsy would be sitting in the front room of the cottage listening to the radio or trying to get someone to play cards with her rather than have to resort to doing homework.

Shivering, Nora hurried down the steps and walked quickly across the lawn. The closer she got to the cottage, the more excited she was to relay her news, and she began to practice how to say it. She was about to climb the two simple steps to the front door when she saw the glow of a cigarette on one side of the cottage. Nora stopped to see who it was, ready to chastise, when she realized that it was Patsy.

"What are you doing out here?" Nora asked.

Patsy turned to her, nonplussed, almost as if she had been expecting her. She took a deep drag of her cigarette.

"Hi, Nor."

"It's chilly out here! Did Mrs. Bosworth catch you smoking inside?"

Patsy exhaled. "No, I just needed some air."

Nora didn't know what to say. Patsy, she could tell, was in a strange mood; it seemed suddenly not the right time to announce her wedding. Still, she tried. "I've got something to tell you," she began, trying to resurrect her happy excitement.

"Oh, yeah?" Patsy asked, inhaling again. "I've got some news, too," she said with a tiny smile, tossing her cigarette on the ground and grinding it out with her shoe. "I'm pregnant."

November 1942

Nora

"The Park Ridge School for Girls is not a maternity home," Mrs. Harvey said sternly over the rims of her glasses.

"But why? Isn't this a school for girls from broken families?" Nora pleaded, shifting uncomfortably in one of the two hard-backed chairs in front of Mrs. Harvey's desk, as if she were again an errant schoolgirl. Patsy sat beside her but was thoroughly unengaged with the conversation unfolding and was instead absently staring out the window. Nora had finally forced her to come and confess her expectant state.

"Yes, Nora. We've been through this all before," Mrs. Harvey said with a little sigh. "But policy is policy, which I did not write. That's up to the board. I'm merely the administrator, and I have to follow the rules just like everyone else," she added, looking directly at Patsy, who was still looking out the window. "Besides, we don't have the facilities to handle the birth, nor the adoption, for that matter."

Patsy suddenly stirred. "There isn't going to be an adoption," she said quietly.

"Well, there has to be. You won't name the father, so I assume that means there's not to be a wedding. How else will you support it? You can't possibly keep it."

"Yes, I can." Patsy's voice was calm. "I'm going to go live with my mother. You can't stop me. I'm sixteen, so legally I can leave."

"Is that true?" Nora asked, turning to Mrs. Harvey. "That we can leave at sixteen?" How had she not known that? And how did Patsy know it?

"Yes, it's true," Mrs. Harvey said quietly. "I did say that to you not long ago, Nora. Just after graduation."

Nora did remember this vaguely, but at the time it hadn't sunk in.

"Have you spoken to your mother?" Mrs. Harvey asked Patsy. "About this plan? About your . . . situation?"

"Yes, as a matter of fact, I have. She's all for the idea. In fact, she says she was just about to ask us to come back anyway. That means you, too, Nora."

"Did you really, Patsy?" she asked in a low voice.

"Yes, I did," Patsy said with an annoyed tilt of her head. "I wrote her a letter. I can write, you know, when I want to."

"But what about Jerry?"

"He was drafted apparently."

"Drafted? Isn't he too old?"

Patsy shrugged.

Nora looked at her shoes, trying to take it all in.

"Well, I guess that's our answer," Mrs. Harvey said matter-of-factly. "I will begin the necessary arrangements. When do you plan to leave, Patsy?"

"I hadn't thought about it, really. Tomorrow?"

"Tomorrow!" Nora shot Patsy an incredulous look.

Mrs. Harvey's face turned grim. "I know you've never liked it here, Patsy, but I'll need at least a week."

Patsy flashed one of her famous smiles. "I like the Park Ridge all right, Mrs. Harvey. You know that. But my time here now is over, and I need to move on. Ma's waiting for us. Well, for me, anyway. I guess it's up to Nora what she wants to do."

"Yes, Nora," Mrs. Harvey put in. "You are very welcome to stay. You're doing well in your job, and I quite like having your assistance. And I like having you about. I enjoy your company." She said this last part softly, kindly, which only made this the more difficult.

Nora bit the inside of her cheek. As much as the two of them told her she had a choice, she knew she didn't really. She could never leave Patsy. A feeling almost like rage welled up in her at the unfairness of it all. Patsy should be the one feeling trapped by a pregnancy out of wedlock, not her! How could Patsy have been so stupid?

Her initial shock after Patsy had blandly delivered her announcement had turned to anger with Patsy and then ultimately with herself. She should have kept a closer eye, should have tried harder to put a stop to it. But on the other hand, trying to stop someone like Patsy was like trying to hold water in your hand.

Patsy seemed remarkably unaffected by her shameful state. There was only one time when she became even just a little emotional, and that was when she confessed to Nora that Billy was the father of her unborn child.

"Are you sure?" Nora had asked.

"Of course, I'm sure," Patsy had hissed. "What do you take me for, Nor?"

"Sorry. I just—"

"I love Billy, Nora. I'll always love him."

Nora had been tempted to blurt out how stupid that was. To be in love with Billy of all people. "Does he know?"

Patsy shook her head. "He'd already shipped out by the time I figured it out. He said he'd write, but you know Billy. He hasn't yet, so I haven't been able to tell him." Rare tears hovered about her eyes.

Nora put her arm around her little sister's shoulders. "It'll be okay, Pats. Don't you worry."

But Patsy's momentary sadness was not the same as worry, and she continued to go about life as if she hadn't a care in the world, leaving Nora to worry for the both of them. Sometimes she wished she could be like Patsy for just one day—light and free.

Nora forced herself to look back up at Mrs. Harvey, sweat trickling down the back of her neck. "No," she said hoarsely, "I'll go home with Patsy."

It was Lyle who drove them to Ma's house on Pratt. Nora felt terribly guilty asking him to help, but he claimed he wanted to. And in the end, she was more than glad of his calming presence. Nora's insides were churning the closer they got to Ma's, and she felt she might actually be sick when Lyle rolled up to the curb and put the old Ford truck he had recently purchased into park.

Patsy immediately jumped out, leaving Nora alone with Lyle.

"Want me to come in?" he asked softly, his arm resting on the big steering wheel.

She looked over at him and felt a fresh wave of love.

"We could announce our engagement," he suggested with a sly smile.

Nora shook her head, unable to speak.

"You sure you want to do this?"

Nora cleared her throat and nodded. "Come on, before I change my mind," she croaked. She climbed out of the truck, and Lyle followed, lifting her cases out of the back.

"Want me to help?" he asked, squinting in the sun.

"No, it's okay."

"Come on, Nora!" Patsy called, already halfway up the sidewalk, her suitcase in hand.

"S'pose I should go." He kissed her on the cheek. "I'll telephone you. Good luck."

Nora felt an increasing sense of panic as she watched him swing himself back into the truck, grind it into gear, and then rattle down Pratt, as if he were the last vestige of her old life and somehow not a part of her new.

"Come on, Nor. It'll be alright," Patsy called cheerfully, having already climbed the cement steps. Nora turned her gaze to the brick bungalow in front of her. It looked identical to all the other bungalows on this street. She tried to internalize that this was her home now, not the brick buildings of Park Ridge.

Ma greeted them with tears and hugs and a plate of cookies, as though they were little children who had just come home from school after a particularly long day—a day that had lasted nearly eleven years. Nora looked around with curiosity, surprised by how neat and tidy everything was. For some reason she had never pictured Ma as a tidy housekeeper.

She was surprised when Ma showed them to their own individual rooms, saying that the baby could stay in Patsy's whenever it arrived. As the three of them stood in the doorway, looking at the twin bed and the little cradle next to it, Patsy exclaimed that it was perfect.

"What's this?" Nora asked, gently pushing past Patsy and heading to a far wall where a painting was hung. It was one of Patsy's.

"Do you like it?" Ma asked, looking eagerly at Patsy.

"Oh, Ma, you didn't have to hang that up. That's old."

"But how did you get it?" Nora asked.

"A Mrs. Hanley somebody or other, Patsy's art teacher, sent it to me. Wasn't that kind?" Ma was beaming. "Come on, I'll show you your room now, Nora!"

Wordlessly, Nora followed her, feeling a rare, unsettling jealousy. Had any Park Ridge teachers ever sent Ma *her* work? Her work that had made her the top student of the year? But what would they have sent? An essay?

"Here you are, Nora," Ma said, gesturing awkwardly. "I gave you the bigger room. Not by much, but it's something."

Nora stepped in and, after a quick look around, tried to muster a smile. "Thanks, Ma. It's nice."

Ma suddenly wrapped her arms around Nora and held her close. "I know it can't be easy, Nora. But I'm so happy you're here. I'll try to make it nice for you."

"Oh, Ma." Tears stung her eyes. "It *is* nice. Truly."

Nora was surprised by how quickly they fell into a routine. She was further surprised when Patsy immediately went out and found a job as a cocktail waitress at the Shangri-La, just around the corner. Certainly not the job a pregnant woman should have, Nora judged, but her concerns, as usual, fell on deaf ears. Whenever Nora brought it up, Patsy merely laughed, while Ma just sort of ignored it. In fact, Ma had yet to say one word of reproach about Patsy's shameful condition. She just went along with it, as if it was the most natural thing in the world. It wasn't as if Nora really wanted Ma to be angry or scornful to Patsy, but surely Patsy deserved at least one disapproving conversation? And shouldn't they be discussing what was to happen after the impending birth?

In the months that followed, Nora tried hard to not only squelch her fears about how Patsy was really going to take care of a baby, but also to start over where Ma was concerned. She supposed that Patsy was right, that Ma had tried her best, even if she *had* made some terrible choices. But given she was practically raised in a coal mine, what did she expect?

And Nora could tell that Ma was trying, too. She allowed Nora her privacy when she wanted it, saying nothing when Nora sat alone in her room to read or to write letters to Celia or Mrs. Harvey. And she didn't stop her from coming and going as she pleased, even when she was out with Lyle.

Eventually, Nora told Ma about her plans to marry Lyle. She had kept it a secret at first, wanting to hold on to something from her past life that was hers alone, but, as time went on, she figured that she might as well. Patsy would probably spill the beans soon anyway.

It was an early February afternoon, and random flakes of snow were materializing every so often. Patsy was at work, and she and Ma were making an apple pie. Ma was rolling the dough, and Nora stood beside her, peeling the apples.

"I'm going to marry Lyle," she said, keeping her eyes on the edge of the paring knife as she moved it around the apple.

"I thought as much." Ma was silent for a few moments. "Is he good to you?"

Nora stopped peeling. "Yes, of course he is. I wouldn't have chosen him otherwise."

"When's it going to be?" Ma had not taken her eyes off the dough.

"Probably next year some time. Lyle wants to save for a house."

"But what if he's drafted, Nora? Maybe you should wait. Stay with me and Patsy until the war's over at least."

Nora sighed. "He's not going to be drafted, Ma. He tried to join up first thing, but he's 4F."

"Oh, Nora!" Ma's head jerked up. "That's lucky, isn't it?"

Something squirmed inside of Nora. "Well, I guess so, but *he* doesn't feel that way. Not everyone's Jerry, you know."

Ma looked as if she had been slapped. "That's not what I meant," she said.

"I know you didn't." Nora let out a deep breath. "I'm sorry."

Ma continued rolling the dough. "Well, I'm happy for you. I'm proud of you, you know, Nora. I just wanted to say that."

Nora went back to peeling her apple, her throat aching.

A week later, Nora invited Lyle to come to dinner. He was nervous, she could tell, dressed in his good suit, but soon enough they were all laughing, Patsy and Nora relating, mostly for Ma's benefit, stories of how they had played in the woods behind the school.

"And the four of us ended up together. Isn't that strange?" Nora asked no one in particular as they finished their roast pork dinner.

"It isn't strange. It's fate." Patsy flashed a smile and took another drink of her wine, her other hand resting on her rounded belly.

"I wish Celia were here," Nora said wistfully. Lyle took her hand under the table and with the other raised his glass.

"To absent friends and family," he muttered.

Ma and Nora raised their glasses in unison and repeated his words. Patsy, however, raised hers "to never-ending love."

Patsy's baby arrived without fanfare on a mild May morning. She had declared ahead of time that she wanted her baby to be born at home, surrounded by all those who loved him (she always called the baby a him, claiming she knew it for a fact to be a boy). Patsy was remarkably calm during the labor, and the midwife Ma had arranged to come delivered a healthy baby boy without fuss or complication. Patsy began nursing him immediately and declared his name to be William Warren Williams.

"Warren?" Ma asked, her face deathly pale. "Why Warren?"

"I don't know," Patsy said with a little laugh. "It just popped into my head."

"Well, I don't know if I care for it all that much."

"Why?" There was a trace of hurt in Patsy's voice; Ma usually went along with whatever they wanted.

"Oh, I don't know." Ma twisted her hands. "I just . . . I knew a Warren once is all . . . It's not that lucky of a name, I don't think."

Patsy suddenly laughed. "There's no such thing as a lucky or an unlucky name, Ma. It's just a name like any other."

"I s'pose you're right," Ma said reluctantly. "I'm being superstitious, I guess. Don't mind me. He's beautiful. Aren't you, Billy?" she asked, stroking his downy cheek.

As it turned out, Patsy was a natural mother. She seemed to always know just what little Billy wanted, anticipating his needs before he ever got a chance to cry. She fed him constantly and told him beautiful, elaborate stories even though he was only a tiny baby. Often, she kept on with the story long after he was asleep, which Nora was secretly glad of. They were quite interesting.

Patsy carried Billy everywhere, the way she used to carry her doll, never putting him down, which was fine for her, but it made it terribly hard on both Nora and Ma whenever Patsy was gone, requiring them to hold him constantly or he would scream bloody murder. "He's got a real good set of lungs, doesn't he?" Ma would say, propping him on her shoulder and patting his back as she paced the floor.

"I think he's spoiled," Nora complained. "Shouldn't he be able to be put down sometimes?"

"Well, maybe," Ma answered distractedly, continuing to sway with him in her arms. "Patsy was like this, though, when she was his age. Cried terrible, she did."

"Now, I just fed him, so he should go to sleep pretty soon," Patsy said softly, coming into the room as she slipped on her coat. She had gotten her old job back at the Shangri-La. "I should be back around two."

"I don't like you working so late." Ma's face was one of worry. "Why don't I try to get you in at the Sunshine?"

"Ma," Patsy said, kissing her on the forehead, "we've been through this a million times. I can make more at the bar, and then I can be home with him during the day. It's perfect. Now, I'm going. I'll be alright."

"If you wait a few minutes, Lyle can drive you," Nora whispered. "He should be here any minute."

"No, I've got to go. I'm going to be late as it is. Bye." She gave Billy's little head a brush of her lips and then left the room. A minute later, the front door opened and closed.

"You going to be alright with him here alone?" Nora asked softly.

"'Course I am. I've been practicing laying him down in his bed." Ma shot her a sly grin.

Nora tiptoed out of Patsy's room and went to her own to finish getting ready. Lyle had promised to take her to the Aragon tonight, and she was thrilled. She had always wanted to go dancing. He wasn't much of a dancer, he said, but he was willing to give it a go.

After putting on some lipstick, she surveyed her image in the little vanity Ma had put in her room and decided she needed a little something extra. She pulled out the pewter broach Lyle had given her for her birthday and was just pinning it on when the doorbell rang.

"I've got it!" Nora called out softly, not wanting to wake Billy. Briskly she walked through the front room, picking up the coat draped across the back of the sofa as she went. She slipped an arm into one of the sleeves as she opened the door with the other.

As expected, it was Lyle, but Nora could tell right away that he wasn't himself. He was standing there grimly in his good suit.

"Hello, there," she said, trying a smile out on him. When he did not return it, she began to worry. "What's wrong?"

"Can I come in?" he asked with a nod.

"Yes, of course." She stepped aside.

With an effort, he walked past her, removing his hat. "I have some bad news, I'm afraid, Nor."

"Hello, Lyle," said Ma, coming down the hall, still patting Billy. "Don't you look nice!"

"What is it, Lyle?" Nora whispered, putting a hand on his arm.

"Aunt Rita's just telephoned me. They've not long received a telegram." He looked from one to the other of them. "I'm sorry to be the bearer of bad news, but I'm afraid that Billy's been killed in action."

March 1944

Gertie

Absence had not made the heart grow stronger; it had hardened it, as it was, at least where Jerry was concerned.

Having suffered a gunshot to his foot, the war was now over for Jerry, though it certainly wasn't for Gertie. The unfairness of it all rankled her. For months, even years, women all around her were getting telegrams telling them that their son or husband or fiancé was killed; why not her? She knew it was a wicked thought, but why couldn't *he* have died instead of Billy? Instead, he had been wounded, which meant he was coming home early. She had heard stories about men shooting themselves in the hand or the foot in order to get sent back home . . . She dared not accuse Jerry of something so cowardly, but neither did she put it past him.

When he had initially shipped out, Gertie had not even gone to the train station to see him off. They had said their goodbyes, such as they were, in the front room of the house,

Jerry vowing that he would get even with her for reporting him to the draft board. Gertie had managed a little laugh, though her insides were squirming. How did he manage to turn everything around? It was *him* who should feel guilty, not her!

As it turned out, his revenge took the form of long letters written from where he was stationed, somewhere in Italy, in which he not only informed her that he had taken up with a local Italian woman, but also very vividly described their many sexual exploits. Linda at the Sunshine had helped her read the first few, and that had been enough. They had sickened her, and even Linda, who had seen a thing or two, seemed surprised by their content. Eventually, Gertie had learned to disregard them completely. If he wanted to take up with an Italian whore, fine. She could care less. She had the girls back, and she was determined that nothing was going to mar her happiness, especially now that little Billy had come along.

She had initially been crushed when she learned Patsy was with child out of wedlock, but she had managed to push it aside. After all, who was she to judge? And, truth be told, she had been worried about having to help Patsy take care of a new baby. But all of that had changed the moment Billy was born, the instantaneous love she felt for him surprising and overwhelming her. She genuinely delighted in caring for him, despite the fact that her nightly rest was now jeopardized. But what did a sleepless night here and there matter? When she was younger, she had craved sleep, fantasized about it, begged God for it, but now she often found it difficult most nights anyway.

No, she didn't mind being up with Billy. What she felt for him was something different and rare. It wasn't just that he was a boy, the son she never had. It was that she had the emotional luxury to cuddle and spoil him in the way she hadn't with her girls, living with Lorenzo or in the shelter or at the Hirsch Hotel and constantly worrying about where their next meal would come from. She had fiercely loved the girls, but a part of her had always been distracted by simply having to survive. She had spent most of those years living in fear, which meant she never really got to enjoy the girls, to immerse herself in their being. Having little Billy was a different thing altogether. For one thing, she wasn't afraid now, even of Jerry, despite his frequent outbursts to "Shut that fucking kid up!"

Jerry had been livid, of course, when he arrived home to discover Nora and Patsy and a wailing baby living in his house. He had skipped the pleasantries and gone straight to bed, where he remained for almost two days. When he finally emerged, he demanded a big breakfast and told Gertie that she was crazy if she thought they were staying.

Gertie had remained silent as he wolfed down his eggs, her lips white from biting them as she poured him some more coffee.

"Yes, they are, Jerry. They're staying here."

Jerry stopped chewing. "What did you say?"

Gertie cleared her throat. "I said, they're staying."

"Did you forget whose house this is?" He tossed his fork down, dislodging the bit of egg he had just stabbed.

"It's part my house, too, Jerry. I pay the bills now."

"Oh, I see," he said bitterly. "You think you're lady of the manor because you pay the coal man? I'm over there fucking risking my life, getting shot at every fucking day—thanks to you—and you're back here lapping it up, taking over my house? No, I don't think that's how it works. It's *my* name that's on the mortgage."

"Things change, Jerry. That's the way life is. My girls and Billy aren't leaving, and that's that," she said, trying her best to keep her voice steady.

"Yes, they are!" Jerry roared. "I'm not raising someone else's brats."

Gertie gripped the edge of the table to keep from shaking. "Fine," she said, making herself meet his eyes. "Then I want a divorce."

"A divorce! On what grounds? Gambling? Fat chance."

"Infidelity, for one thing," she said calmly. She wasn't sure how she was standing up to him this boldly. Perhaps it was because she had been rehearsing this speech for months every night as she paced the floor with Billy into the wee hours.

"Infidelity?"

"The woman in Italy? Josienne was her name, as I recall. Did you already forget about her?"

"That was nothing. Spoils of war and all that." He pulled a cigarette out of the pack that lay on the table. "Anyway, you can't prove it."

"Oh, really? I kept every letter you ever sent."

"I'll say I made it all up," he retorted, lighting it.

"Listen, Jerry. If the girls and Billy go, I go. You can sit here and rot all by yourself. Then you wouldn't have anyone to cook and clean for you. That's all I really am to you—a glorified maid. So, you decide."

"You wouldn't dare. You have nowhere to go. When I met you, you didn't have a pot to piss in."

"I mean it, Jerry."

He stared at her for several moments before heaving himself up from the table. Awkwardly, he grasped for his cane and leaned on it heavily. "Can't a man enjoy breakfast in his own house?" he snarled. "I'm going out."

"Good. Don't come back!"

He surprised her then by spinning back around, his hand lifted to strike her. Gertie saw it coming but resisted the urge to move and instead lifted her chin.

"Go on, hit me. Give me a reason to call the cops," she spewed. "Because I will."

Jerry, his face red and his nostrils flaring, eventually lowered his arm and merely gave her a little shove. "Bitch," he muttered and walked out.

As soon as she heard the front door bang, Gertie let herself breathe.

In the months that followed, Jerry thankfully spent less and less time at home, often walking down the street to O'Malley's and spending the afternoon on a barstool. When he *was* at home, he was a constant fixture in his armchair in the front room, from which he launched a steady stream of criticisms and complaints at whomever was coming and going. Other than that, he ignored the girls completely, which was relatively easy given how busy they both seemed to be.

Nora spent most of her time working at Sears, Roebuck, where she was proudly employed as a secretary, or else out with Lyle. They had named a date for their wedding, May 1st, which was earlier than Gertie had originally understood it was to be. She knew that Nora would never succumb to having relations outside of marriage—she had primly said as much one day—so Gertie knew that the sudden acceleration couldn't be because a baby was on the way. And what about wanting to save for a house? Even with Lyle working as a clerk in an accounting firm and a security guard at night, plus whatever Nora's salary brought in, Gertie calculated that they couldn't possibly have amassed the down payment already. So why the sudden haste?

It had to be Jerry's cantankerous presence, Gertie eventually concluded, which infuriated her. Nora leaving would mean he was getting his way—partially, anyway, though she was sure he'd rather have Patsy and Billy be the ones to leave. Gertie tried on several occasions to bring up the subject with Nora, but Nora always acted like she didn't know what she was talking about. She was sullen and moody these days, and Gertie was sure it had to do with Jerry. How could it not? He brought everyone down.

The one thing Nora *had* wanted to talk about, however, was little Billy, or Wren as they had taken to calling him. Since Billy's death, Patsy couldn't seem to be able to utter that name, even in connection with her own baby, so she began to call him Warren. Gertie, however, had quickly shortened it to Wren, which somehow stuck, especially because he sort of did resemble a wren, a little mite of a thing that barely grew despite his mouth always open to be fed.

Gertie was surprised by Nora's desire to discuss him. Nora obviously loved little Wren and did her share of helping care for him, but she was not all-consumed by him the way Gertie was. Well, that was natural, wasn't it? Gertie mused, as Nora had so many other things on her mind.

"Have you considered," Nora said, looking pointedly at Wren in Gertie's arms as they sat in the kitchen one day, "that Wren has another set of grandparents? Lyle's Aunt Rita and

Uncle Carroll? They don't even know that he exists! Don't you think they should be told?"

Gertie clutched Wren to her chest. She hadn't thought of that. Good God, she hadn't thought of that. What was to be done? She couldn't possibly give him up the way she had the girls. She couldn't possibly go through that again. Surely, they would want to take him from her, wouldn't they?

"Why?" she asked, panic beginning to encircle her heart.

"Well, for one thing because Billy was their only child, Ma. Wren's their heir, so to speak. And don't you think that it would bring them some comfort? To know that a part of their son still lives?"

"No! I don't. That will just make it worse for them."

She sighed. "Ma, they should at least know. You can't just keep him for yourself. He's *Patsy's* baby, not yours."

Gertie did not know what to say to this. Of course Wren was Patsy's baby, but Patsy was not around so much these days. They had all been brought low by Billy's death, but Patsy had been devastated by it, inconsolable. For months, her only source of solace seemed to be little Wren, but gradually even his kisses and cuddles were not enough. Eventually, Patsy had begun to go out more and more with friends after work, sometimes staying out all night, though Gertie didn't dare tell this to Nora, who somehow didn't know, or did she? Gertie was pretty sure Jerry didn't know, either, as he slept so deeply, the large quantities of alcohol he drank knocking him out to the point he never heard anything that happened in the night *or* in the early morning, for that matter.

Gertie was not inclined to scold Patsy for her actions, for many reasons, but she felt she should at least caution her. "Patsy, you need to be careful," she had frantically whispered to her one morning as she slipped in the back door. Patsy's hair was tousled, and she smelled of cigarettes and beer.

But Patsy had only given her a weary smile and cupped her cheek with her tiny hand. "Poor Ma," she said and kissed her on the forehead before tiptoeing to her room.

"Was this Lyle's idea?" Gertie suddenly asked. "That we should tell them?"

Nora shifted uncomfortably. "Well, I don't know if it was *his* idea, but we've certainly talked about it."

Gertie felt sweat forming on the back of her neck. "Is he . . . is *he* going to tell them?" Gertie squeaked. Why was Nora looking at her that way? As if she was so wrong . . . But what good would it do to tell them? *Let sleeping dogs lie.* Wasn't that what her own mother had often said? "Why do you have to be such a goody-two-shoes, Nora?" she blurted before she could stop herself.

Nora looked as if she had been slapped, and Gertie instantly regretted her words. Why had she said that?

"Nora, I'm so—"

"No, he's not going to tell them, Ma," Nora said curtly. "He doesn't think it's his place. That's up to you. You have to do what you think is right. You and Patsy, that is." She stood abruptly and moved toward the back door.

"Nora, wait—"

"Where *is* Patsy, anyway?" she snapped. "She's never here anymore."

"She's out somewhere." Gertie glanced at the clock on the wall. She had no idea where Patsy was.

Nora shot her a look of disgust and yanked open the back door. She paused, though, before stepping out, her hand still on the doorknob. "You know," she said, turning slowly back around, "you and Patsy are just the same. All you ever think about is yourselves!" she said bitterly, her voice gaining surprising volume. "You're selfish to the core!"

"Selfish?!" Gertie felt as if she had been struck. *Selfish?* She had never done one selfish thing in her life! "Nora, how can you say that?"

Nora was staring at her in that awful way she sometimes did, her nostrils flaring and her hands on her hips. "Ma, you're the most selfish person I've ever met! You . . . you just ran off— ran away from your family with *a carnival worker?* What were you thinking? I'm sure they were worried sick about you—probably for years! And why? Because of some wild impulse? You know, you say that Patsy has gypsy blood, that she takes after our dad. But maybe she takes after *you*! Ever think of that?"

Gertie was stunned, unable to think of anything to say or do. Even when Wren began to fuss, she sat immobile, staring at Nora.

"I won't even get into the whole Olson episode," Nora steamrolled on. "But why on earth you would take up with a married man is beyond me. So that you could have a warm body in your bed?" she shouted. "We weren't enough, of course. And then, after your kids get taken away because of it, you just abandoned us there? Didn't come to see us for what was it? Six? Seven months? While you were here doing what? Sleeping in? Did you ever think for one second what that was like for us?"

Gertie could see the angry tears welling in Nora's eyes.

"So, yes, I'd say you were selfish, Ma. The definition of selfish. The tragedy is that you don't even know it."

"Nora, I—" Gertie said weakly.

"I don't want to hear it, Ma," Nora said tiredly. "I have to go. You and Patsy do what you want with Wren, but don't blame me later," she grumbled and banged out the door before Gertie could say anything more.

Wren began to wail, then, and Gertie, her own eyes filled with tears, wrapped her body around him and held him tight, Nora's words wounding her over and over. She wished she could explain everything to her, that it wasn't like that, not really, but she had gone now, and she wasn't sure she would ever be able to get out the right words. Gertie kissed Wren's little head. At least she had him. She kissed him again. And again. No one, she resolved, as she kissed him a fourth and a fifth time, was going to take him from her. No matter what Nora—or anybody—said.

December 1952

Nora

"Mom, is Dwight and Sharon going to be there, too?" Kurt asked from the backseat of the Oldsmobile.

Nora sighed. How many times had she answered this question? "I think so, honey."

"What about Uncle Wayne?" Kenny, the older of the two boys, asked. "Will he be there?"

"I hope not!" said Kurt. "He smells like old cheese."

Nora heard Kenny giggle.

"Boys!" urged Lyle. "Let's not say mean things on Christmas Day."

"But that's not mean, Dad," said Kenny, innocently.

"But he *is* a liar, ain't he, Dad?" Kurt asked. "He didn't really play for the Cubs, did he?"

Nora turned and looked back at the kids. "When did he say that?"

Kenny shrugged. "He's always saying stuff like that, ain't he, Dad?"

"*Isn't*," Nora corrected.

"Well, I wouldn't put too much stock in what Uncle Wayne says," Lyle said, turning onto Pratt. "Why don't you two look out the window? See if you see any of Santa's elves that got left behind."

"Left behind?"

"Well, you never know," he said, giving Nora a wink, "they might have fallen off the sleigh."

"Ooh!" both boys said in unison and each pressed their faces up against the backseat windows.

"Yes, good idea." Nora shot Lyle a look of exasperation; she didn't remember ever talking this much as a child.

"So what *is* happening today?" Lyle asked in a low voice.

Nora shook her head. "I have no idea. Ma says that Patsy convinced Wayne to come."

"She shouldn't have bothered. He ruins every family party." He was silent for a few moments. "I thought they were finally getting a divorce."

Nora sighed. "Who knows with Patsy? It's always on and off. She says they've been getting along lately. Maybe she's just waiting until the holidays are over. The one I feel sorry for is Dwight. Half the time he's with Ma and Patsy, and half the time he's with Wayne in his stupid cabin up north. At least he leaves Sharon behind. It's such a mess," she said, looking out the window herself.

She was glad Ma no longer watched her boys. As soon as they were in school, she had put an end to it. She had been reluctant to give up her job at Sears when Kenny was born, neither had Lyle insisted she do so. After months of thinking it over during her last trimester, Nora had tentatively approached Ma to ask if she might consider watching *her* baby as well as Wren. Ma had been *thrilled*, literally thrilled. Nora had her doubts about how Ma would handle a toddler and a baby, but she seemed to manage fine, that is until Jerry had had a stroke. It was only mild, but it left him incapacitated enough that Ma had quit the Sunshine. Nora and Lyle paid her for her watching Kenny, and then a bit more when Kurt came along; after all, Ma needed to have some kind of income, and she was pretty sure that Patsy never gave it a moment's thought.

Looking back, Nora sometimes regretted her decision to have had Ma watch the boys, as she was sure that Kenny and Kurt had probably seen and heard things there they shouldn't have, but what was done was done, she told herself. She couldn't change the past; all of them knew that, none more so than poor Patsy.

Even before the one-year anniversary of Billy's death, Patsy was already pregnant again. Some guy named Wayne Keifer, whom she had met at the Shangri-La. With just the right amount of swagger, Wayne had gallantly offered to marry her, and Patsy accepted, though Nora tried to tell her that she was making a mistake. In typical Patsy fashion, however, she had plowed ahead, saying that she loved him enough and that little Wren needed a dad. Unfortunately, as Kenny had so neatly summed up, Wayne was indeed a liar, as well as a deadbeat and also a drunk. Patsy had always been fond of a drink, going all the way back to the Park Ridge when she would smuggle it in somehow, but it wasn't until after she married Wayne that she began drinking heavily and often.

When they first got married, they'd lived at the house with Ma and Jerry for almost a year before Ma's "tone" started getting on Wayne's nerves whenever he and Patsy cracked open a bottle of vodka. Ma tried to like Wayne, Nora could tell, but she would frequently go on and on and on about him when Nora came to pick up Kenny. Eventually, Wayne got it into his head that he and Patsy and Dwight should probably move out, which caused immediate panic in both Patsy and Ma, though for slightly different reasons.

Ma hastily exclaimed that there was no need to move out, though Jerry, on the other hand, offered no resistance to Wayne's proposal, as he had already told him, despite his limited capacity, to "get the fuck out of my house," on numerous occasions.

Patsy's alarm was not necessarily about leaving Ma, truth be told, but about leaving Wren, who was evidently not part of Wayne's equation. It was no secret that Wayne did not like Wren, though everyone hoped that he would eventually warm to him. But as time went on, Wren began to look more and more like his maternal grandfather, dark-haired with dark eyes.

"He looks like a little shithead," Wayne would say. "Must look like the bastard that raped you." Though Patsy had repeatedly told him she had *not* been raped by Billy, Wayne had somehow convinced himself that this is what had happened. He apparently couldn't tolerate that his wife had been willingly touched by someone else. In the end, Patsy simply gave up trying to tell him otherwise and just let him believe his own story.

It was Nora who had eventually convinced both Ma and Patsy that perhaps moving out might be a good thing. Nora was sick to death of Wayne belittling Wren, routinely calling him "shithead"—and she didn't even live there! She wanted to scream every time she heard it. How Patsy and Ma allowed him to talk to him that way, she didn't understand.

"You're only moving six blocks away, Pats," Nora tried to say gently.

"I can't choose between my two sons," Patsy whimpered, a small tear rolling down her cheek.

"Don't say that," Ma said anxiously. "You won't be choosing. Don't say that."

"You can still drop Dwight off here every day while you're at work," Nora urged. "And you'll see Wren then. I'm afraid, Patsy," she added when Patsy still seemed unconvinced. "Afraid of what might happen. Wayne's unpredictable. You never know what he might do to Wren. It makes sense. He'll be happier here."

"Wayne would never hurt him!" Patsy exclaimed, uncharacteristically angry. Quickly, she wiped her eyes and left the room, leaving Nora and Ma to just sit and look at each other. In the end, however, Patsy agreed to go and likewise to leave Wren behind.

Wren, for his part, seemed unaffected, which made sense as he had been cared for by Ma pretty much from the moment he was born. He even called Ma "Mama" sometimes, even *before* Patsy moved out. This infuriated Patsy, and she corrected him whenever she heard it, *and* Ma, telling her to have him call her Grandma, not Mama. Ma insisted she *did* correct him, but what did it matter? He would figure it out eventually, she said.

Nora had hoped that things would be better for Patsy once they were away from Ma and Jerry and Wren—even Lyle had said as much—but it was hard to tell. It seemed to start off okay, though Patsy still spent most of her time over at Ma's, but it gradually went downhill, especially after poor Patsy had two miscarriages in one year. She lost so much weight that Nora began to suspect they might be in danger of losing Patsy herself.

But then Patsy surprised everyone by eventually giving birth to little Sharon, though she was early and only four pounds, just as Wren had been. Ma urged Patsy to stay home and rest, but Patsy ignored her and was back on her feet and working as soon as she could, dumping off little Sharon at Ma's along with Dwight. Money was apparently a constant struggle for Patsy and Wayne, and only once, when she was drunk, did Patsy confess to Nora how little they really had and how much she and Wayne fought because of it.

Wayne worked construction, but it was never steady, and he refused to get a side job. Instead, he just drank more during the times he was off. Patsy, meanwhile, had taken Ma's old job at the Sunshine (Wayne forbade her to go back to the Shangri-La), and even sometimes cleaned offices again at night, but they still barely made ends meet.

Finally, it all came to a head one April night about nine months ago, and after a particularly bad fight, Wayne had walked out in the middle of the night.

Patsy immediately telephoned Nora, crying, saying that Wayne had disappeared.

"Who is it?" Lyle asked groggily, coming down the stairs to the kitchen, where Nora, her hair in curlers, stood in the dark, talking to Patsy on the wall telephone.

"It's Patsy," she said quietly, holding her hand over the mouthpiece. "Wayne's left, apparently."

Lyle sighed and ran a hand through his rumpled hair. "What do you mean 'left'?"

Nora shrugged. "What did you say, Patsy?"

"Want me to talk to her?" Lyle asked.

Nora frowned and shook her head, still listening to Patsy. "I know. It's okay, Patsy; just go to sleep. I'll come over in the morning. No, it'll be alright. He's fine, I'm sure. Yes, okay. Yeah, I know that. Okay, yes, I'll be there tomorrow. Are you *sure* you're okay? Alright, then. Bye. Bye," she said again and then hung up.

"What happened?" Lyle asked, scratching the stubble on his chin.

"They had a big argument. Wayne's drunk, of course. He took off."

"Is she hurt?"

Nora gave him a sad little smile. His concern for Patsy always touched her. "I don't think so. I guess I didn't ask."

"Want me to go over?"

"No. Come on; let's go back to bed. We can sort it out in the morning," she said, wishing that she could "rescue" Patsy as easily as they had done in the game in the woods—simply with a touch.

Nora herself went over in the morning, sure that there was nothing really wrong, but was outraged when she saw that Patsy had a black eye.

"Has he ever done this before?" Nora demanded.

"Once or twice, Nor. It's not a big deal. I'm more worried about *him*."

"Why? I'm sure he can take care of himself."

"But what if he's been in an accident?" Patsy said, biting her lip.

Nora felt that this would not be such a bad thing, but she didn't say so.

As it turned out, two full weeks and three days later, Wayne condescended to telephone Patsy, informing her that he was staying at his cousin's fishing cabin in Fox Lake. Patsy had never heard him mention this cousin before, or the fact that he even liked fishing, but she didn't care. She was simply glad that he was safe. She asked him when he was coming back, and he told her he didn't know.

As the weeks went on, however, Patsy began to struggle under the weight of having to care for everything. She fell behind on not just the rent, but on all of the bills. Eventually, she decided to try to telephone Wayne at the number he had given her to tell him that she was almost out of money and that if he didn't come back soon, she would have no choice but to move back in with Ma. Wayne's response, apparently, was "do whatever the hell you want."

"What's a divorce, Dad?" Kurt asked from the backseat now.

"Children should be seen and not heard, young man," Lyle said into the rearview mirror with mock sternness. "Do you know how many times I was told that as a kid?" He turned around and looked at them briefly. "I would have been smacked by Aunt Rita for less than that. Now," he said with a small grin, "best behavior today. Best manners. It's Christmas day, don't forget."

"Yes, Dad!" they both said in unison. Nora looked at her boys, dressed in their new Christmas outfits. They could almost be twins. They both had the same thin blond hair, parted perfectly down the side, and big brown eyes and dimples. They were truly her joy in life, and as they tumbled out of the car, she offered up a prayer of thanks that she had been so blessed, not just with them but with such a good husband. She had so much more than poor Patsy, she reminded herself, and she resolved to be a better sister to her. She tightened the belt of her coat and tried to put all judgment from her mind as they walked up the sidewalk.

"Hello!" Ma called from the front step, opening the door before they even got there. She must have been watching from the front room window, though the shiny aluminum Christmas tree took up much of it. "Here's my two boys!" She squatted down and opened her arms wide. Both Kenny and Kurt ran to her.

"Merry Christmas, Grandma!" they shouted and let themselves be hugged.

Dwight and Wren and Sharon suddenly appeared behind her.

"There you are! We've been waiting for you!" Dwight said. "How come you're late?"

"We had to go to church first," Kurt said.

"Better you than us!" Nora heard Dwight say under his breath.

Ma either didn't catch it or chose to ignore it. She wrapped her arms around Nora. "Merry Christmas, honey! Don't you look lovely? Hello, Lyle!" She reached for some of the gifts off the stack he was carrying. "Here, Wren, you take these. Put them under the tree." Wren obediently took the stack but hesitated for a moment.

"I'll help!" Dwight grabbed a few and ran from the room before Wren could even turn to go.

"Be careful, Dwight!" Nora shouted, still standing on the front stoop. "Some of those are breakable!"

"Come in, come in," Ma said, stepping aside and opening the door wide. "Merry Christmas, Lyle! Come in. My, don't you boys look fancy," she exclaimed, looking at Kenny and

Kurt in their navy wool short pants, jackets, and ties and caps. "You two make a perfect picture! Reminds me of that fancy school you were at, Nora. Fancy dress and nice manners and all that."

Nora sighed. Ma was forever going on and on about the Park Ridge, as if it were some exclusive boarding school and not a court-mandated institution for poor or troubled girls. It was a fantasy that Ma seemed to indulge in more and more the older she got, which Nora suspected was a reaction to the guilt she must still feel. Nora had tried to tell her over the years not to feel guilty, that it was just something that had happened. "It's all in the past now, Ma. And, anyway, it wasn't such a bad place. In the end, I really liked it. You don't have to feel bad about it anymore." Each time she said it, Ma seemed to understand and accept Nora's words, but eventually she would just revert to her own version of the story.

Nora and Lyle followed Ma into the front room where all the kids had run ahead and were gathered around the shiny tree, staring eagerly at all of the presents. Nora smiled at their excited faces, but she couldn't help but note that Dwight was hardly dressed for the occasion, sporting his brown school sweater and a disheveled tie. Sharon was not much better in a sleeveless pastel-pink dress that was more suited to Easter than Christmas. Wren, likewise, had on an old sweater that was too big, the sleeves of which he was constantly pushing up. Nora sighed. Neither Patsy nor Ma seemed to care if the kids were dressed or groomed appropriately. Wren's clothes always looked too big for him, and Nora wished he could have opened her and Lyle's gift early, as it was a new shirt and tie.

Though Wren supposedly looked like her father, he was nothing like the stories she had heard about Lorenzo. Nor was he like Billy, who had been chatty and charming and wild. Shy and nervous, he was tiny for his age, with dark, soulful eyes that seemed to cut right through a person. He didn't learn to talk until he was four, and Nora used to wonder if he was mentally deficient in some way. Ma, however, would hear none of it. "There's nothing wrong with him!" she would exclaim, bouncing him on her knee. "He's a smart little thing!"

"I didn't say he wasn't smart, Ma, just that he should be talking by now."

"Nonsense!" Ma said. "You're perfect, aren't you, Wren?" she cooed, rubbing his chubby cheeks.

It turned out that Ma was correct; Wren astounded everyone once he got to school, where his teachers commented that he was exceptionally talented, gifted even. There was clearly nothing wrong with his brain; he was just, well, awkward. He had no friends and was frequently bullied. Dwight, meanwhile, was always trying to steal the attention from him, which Wren didn't seem to mind, and in this way, he reminded Nora a little of Lyle as a child. Always running in Billy's shadow.

Nora tried to catch his eye across the room. "Merry Christmas, Wren!" she said, but he only looked up at her apprehensively. "Did Santa come?" she asked gently, hoping he still believed.

She saw him nod, but then Dwight hopped in front of him. "He came to me, Aunt Nora!" he said excitedly.

Nora forced herself to smile. "Did he?" she asked. Dwight was not her favorite, and it was hard to like him. It wasn't just that he looked exactly like Wayne with his stringy orange hair and freckles, it was that he could never sit still. No matter how many times he was corrected, even punished or smacked by Wayne, he was perpetually moving, like an excited puppy. The difference, however, was that puppies eventually outgrew their excitement, but Dwight never did. He just got worse.

"How about you, Sharon?" Nora asked over Dwight's bobbing head. She had orange hair, too, but finer features. She was pretty, like Patsy. She gave Nora a tiny smile and put her finger in her mouth.

"All of you, sit down on the davenport!" Gertie called, her voice tinkling with excitement.

"Can we open presents now, Grandma?" Dwight asked, sitting on Wren for a moment before squishing himself between Kenny and Kurt.

"No, but I'm going to give you each a special stocking that Santa left behind! Now just wait a minute!" Gertie said, reaching for something from behind the tree.

"Ma, I thought we were going to eat first," Nora said, taking off her coat. What was it about Ma that she was so crazy about the grandchildren? She was like a woman obsessed! Maybe it was because she was such a crappy mother, Nora thought unkindly.

"We are, we are!" Ma exclaimed as she lifted a box from where it was hiding in the corner. "But I have to give them *something*! Look at them, the poor things! They can't be expected to sit around and do nothing. It's Christmas, after all!"

As Nora watched Gertie pull out an old box that appeared to hold five overflowing stockings, she tried not to think of all the Christmases she had spent alone with Patsy in Solomon Cottage

"Which one's mine, Grandma?" Dwight squealed, banging his legs excitedly against the sofa.

"Now, now. Just you wait," Ma said with a laugh, though Nora did not find anything about Dwight's behavior amusing. "Did I ever tell you the story of the elves and the white witch?"

"No, Grandma!" Kurt said.

"Is it scar-wy?" Sharon asked, her finger still in her mouth.

"Well, not really, but it's a good one!" Ma said excitedly, as if she were one of the children herself.

"Is it a Christmas story?" asked Wren softly, and Ma give him a look of such intense love that Nora thought her heart would break at the sight of it. Wren had always been, and still was, Ma's favorite. There was a deep, deep love there, a bond between them that could not be broken, and Nora, despite everything, was happy that they had each other. They needed each other.

Ma kissed him on the head. "Sort of," she said gently. "You'll see. But first!" She looked down the row at each of them. "The stockings!"

"Where's Patsy?" Nora asked as the kids squealed, but Ma did not respond, so busy was she with passing out the stockings and watching the kids discover the delights inside.

"Come on, Lyle," Nora said. "Let's go through."

Patsy was stirring something on the stove as they walked into the kitchen. Wayne was mixing two drinks at the table, which he now held out to Nora and Lyle.

"Merry Christmas!" he said cheerily. When they hesitated, Wayne held the glasses up a little higher.

Nora finally took hers, as did Lyle.

"It's a little early for a drink," Lyle said, looking at the wall clock.

"Come on! It's Christmas! Anyway, don't tell me you cops don't have a nip every now and then." He gave Lyle an obvious wink.

"I'm not a cop, Wayne," Lyle said with a sigh. "You know that."

"Almost a cop, though. Close enough." Wayne clinked his glass to Lyle's.

Nora walked to the stove and gave Patsy a kiss on the cheek. "Merry Christmas," she said happily. "Need help?" she asked looking over the various pots. "Ma making turkey again?"

Patsy nodded. "Yeah, we'll need help in a couple of minutes when we're ready to dish up." She seemed sad. Maybe she and Wayne had been fighting again, though Wayne seemed jovial.

"Where's Jerry?" Nora asked.

"Sleeping, I think," Wayne said, as he took a drag of his cigarette. "He'll come out later. You know how he is."

"So, how's the cabin?" Lyle asked Wayne, taking a sip of the rum and Coke. "How long you been back?"

"Came back last week." He nodded toward Patsy. "Said Christmas wouldn't be the same for the kids if I wasn't here, so, you know." He shrugged and took a drink.

"Well, I suppose the fishing's done for the year anyway. Lake froze over yet?"

"Oh, it's frozen, alright. Been ice fishing now."

"Yeah? What you catching?"

"Blue gills mostly. Some Crappies."

Lyle simply nodded and picked a nut out of the dish on the table. "That's good."

Nora was trying to think of something to say as she tied on an apron when she saw Wren appear in the doorway.

"What do you want, Shithead?"

"Wayne! Don't say that!" Nora scolded.

"Yes, Wayne," Patsy added. "I *told* you."

"Well?" Wayne stared at Wren as if he had done something terrible.

Wren directed his frightened gaze at Nora. "Grandma says she wants all of you to come in," he said and then disappeared as quietly as he had come.

"What the fuck does she want now?" Wayne mumbled.

"Wayne!" Patsy cried.

"Come on, Wayne. It's Christmas," Lyle said. "Long day ahead. Let's not ruin it." He nodded toward the front room.

Wayne thrust his cigarette in his mouth and picked up his drink, sloshing some of it on the tablecloth. "It's always something," he muttered, but he obediently followed Lyle out.

Nora clasped her drink and was about to follow, too, when she felt Patsy's hand on her arm.

"Wait a minute, Nor," Patsy said, tears in her eyes.

"Oh, Patsy!" Nora set her drink back down and wrapped her arms around her sister. "Don't let him get to you," she said, rubbing her back. She felt Patsy shudder in her arms, as if she were crying in earnest. "You definitely need to fill your plate today," Nora said. "And have an extra slice of Christmas cake. You're skin and bones!"

Patsy pulled back but held on to Nora's arms. "I've got cancer, Nora," she whispered. "But don't tell. Don't tell Ma."

CHAPTER 23

October 1960

Gertie

Gertie woke with a start. She had had the dream again. Again! It was becoming maddening. Every night now for almost a week. What did it mean? It had to mean something. She wondered if she should tell Nora. But then again, Nora would probably just dismiss it, as she did most things.

It was the same as it had been when she was a young girl, only now it was clearer, more in focus, which didn't make sense. You would think it would fade over time, not get clearer. It was always a boy, or maybe a young man, calling to her to wait, to take him home with her. He was always in distress, though the background changed over the years. As a girl, the boy in her dreams had seemed to be lost in a fog or in a storm, perhaps. Now he seemed lost at sea. Maybe not the sea, exactly, but a big pool of water. She couldn't tell what it was.

As a girl, she had vaguely sensed that the boy's name was Warren, and now she felt certain of it. But that didn't make sense. Surely, it couldn't be the Warren of her girlhood, but she didn't know any other Warrens . . . except her grandson, she remembered uneasily. Yes, that was true. Wren's real name was Warren. But it couldn't be *him* in her dreams. How could she have dreamed about her grandson as a young girl? Maybe she was going crazy. Nora was always saying that she was getting more and more forgetful . . .

Well, it was true, she thought, as she sat there in the armchair by the front window where she had been dozing, again. She *was* forgetful. Sometimes—*many* times, actually—she forgot that Patsy was dead. She would reach for the telephone to call her, or she would open her mouth to shout into the next room for her before she would remember, and then reality would rush in and punch her full force in the gut. Her beautiful little girl, gone. And if that blow was not fatal in and of itself, Dwight and Sharon leaving had very nearly finished her off.

Not even a week after Patsy's funeral, Wayne had turned up to collect them as if they were forgotten pieces of luggage. Gertie had been completely taken off guard by his sudden interest in taking them permanently to live with him at his cousin's cabin. It didn't make an ounce of sense. Nothing made sense. Gertie concluded that Wayne could only be acting out of spite. Both Nora and Lyle had tried to talk to him, but he was resolute. Desperate, then, Gertie had not been too proud to beg him—to literally beg him on her knees—to let her keep them. He let her grovel before him for several moments.

"You really want them that bad?" he asked, irritably.

"Yes, Wayne, please!" she pleaded. "Please don't take them from me. They've just lost their mother. Give them a little time, at least. Please. If not for me, for them."

"You saying I'm not a good dad?" he asked hotly.

"No! It's just that they're used to it here. Used to their school and everything. Please, Wayne."

Wayne stared at her, and for a few precious seconds she thought he might give in. But he crushed her, then, as he snuffed out his cigarette. "Nah, I'm takin' them."

"But they're my grandchildren! You can't just take them from me. Please, Wayne; I don't think I could take it again."

"You'll get over it. Anyway, Jerr's on his last legs; why don't you take care of him? And you'll still have Shithead. You can keep him; he ain't mine."

The next day, they were gone. It happened so fast. Gertie had gotten up early to look through their cases one more time, wanting to make sure they had everything. She made herself pretend to be happy and excited, saying what an exciting adventure they were about to go on. Sharon believed her, of course, happy to finally be included on a trip with her father to the mysterious cabin that so far only Dwight had been privy to. Dwight, on the other hand, was less enthused, probably because he knew what awaited them. "It's nice," he had said once of the cabin, "but it's not like home."

Gertie tried to keep these words out of her head as she made them pancakes and bacon. Before they were even finished eating, however, Wayne had turned up and told them to hurry up and get their things. Everything turned to chaos, then, and all the little things Gertie had been planning to say and do were lost in the shuffle. Before she knew it, she was hugging them goodbye, telling them that she was sure they would see each other very soon. As she hugged Sharon, though, she bit her lip so hard it drew blood in order to keep from crying. She forced herself to smile as she stood on the porch waving to them, trying hard not to be swallowed up by the fear that she would never see them again. At least when Nora and Patsy had been taken away, it had been to somewhere good. A proper fancy place. Not some godforsaken cabin with a drunk of a father. Her only hope was that Wayne would tire of them and bring them back. Yes, perhaps he would bring them back, maybe even next week, she thought as she watched the car turn onto Western and then disappear.

She stood leaning on one of the square wood posts of the stoop for several moments before finally turning and going back in. She was almost surprised to see Wren still sitting at the table, his plate untouched. In all of the excitement, she had forgotten about him. And Dwight and Sharon hadn't even said goodbye to him! They had forgotten!

"Oh, Wren," Gertie said going over and giving him a hug. "Guess it's just you and me now."

"I'm sorry, Gram."

"Sorry? For what?"

"Sorry it's just me. It should have been me that left, not them. I'm the one that doesn't belong."

"Oh, Wren! Don't ever say that! Don't you *ever* say that, you hear?" she said, tears rolling freely down her cheeks. "You're my special boy; don't you know that? And no one's ever going to take you away. Ever. You can be sure about that."

Wren didn't say anything.

For almost a month Gertie continued to live on the hope that Wayne might bring Dwight and Sharon back any day. She jumped every time the telephone rang, hoping that it was Wayne, telling her the good news, but it never was. Once, she had ventured to telephone *him*.

Gloriously, the call actually went through. Wayne answered and put each of the kids on briefly so that Gertie was satisfied that they were at least okay. But hearing their little voices crackling across the line was somehow worse, she realized, than not hearing them at all, and she therefore resolved never to call them again. It was too painful—for her and for them, she thought. Wren offered to write a letter for her, but she had already been down that road. It wouldn't matter anyway, she told him.

What did anything matter, come to think of it? she thought, crying one day in the armchair after Wren had left for school. And then it suddenly hit her full force that *her daughter* had died. Never mind Dwight and Sharon being gone. *Patsy had died!* How had she forgotten that? Somehow, her reaction had been delayed, but now she was completely swallowed up with grief. How many times could a person be swallowed by darkness and still live? Wasn't there some Bible story about a man being swallowed by a whale and still being alive? Perhaps that was her; she wasn't sure.

The next several months were a blur. Nora started coming every day. Gertie didn't remember when or why, but she just did. She didn't remember cooking or cleaning or even if Wren went to school. Jerry also died somewhere in there, but she barely gave it a thought. It was only one day that she walked into the room where he had been lying ill for months that Gertie seemed to wake from whatever fog had consumed her to ask, "Where's Jerry?"

"He died. Remember, Gram?" Wren said softly, taking her hand.

"He did?"

"Yeah, Gram. Remember the funeral?"

"Was I there? Or was I sick, maybe?" she asked, desperate to remember.

"No, you were there, Gram."

She looked down at him and wrapped her arms around him. "What would I do without you?" she asked, fear racing through her as she gave him a kiss on the head.

As time went on, Gertie came back to herself in fits and starts, though there was always a whiff of sadness about her now that no holiday or birthday or even Wren could ever blow away. Nora still came every day, although now she brought Kenny and Kurt with her, which Gertie eventually began to look forward to. Nora was different than she had been before Patsy's death, but Gertie couldn't put her finger on how.

One day she had found her standing in the doorway of Patsy's room and had reached out to put her arm around her, but Nora had stepped away from her grasp, albeit gently, and told her to go check on the boys.

But the boys didn't really need checking. They were getting so big. Kenny would be fourteen in January. Besides Wren, he was her favorite. Kenny reminded her of how Nora *used* to be, trusting and happy and helpful. Well, she supposed Nora was still helpful, it was just that she now did things with more of a frown. And there was always a price to pay for Nora's help.

Gertie preferred it when Nora sometimes simply dropped off the boys while she did errands. Then she and the boys would spend the afternoon playing games or doing a puzzle for hours until the room grew dim around them. Sometimes, Kenny and Wren would work on a model airplane while Kurt watched *The Mickey Mouse Club*. It made Gertie happy to see them together; they seemed more than cousins, almost like brothers.

Eventually, Nora would reappear, bustling in with a bag of groceries, and would throw off her coat and immediately tie on an apron.

"So, what have you all been doing this whole afternoon?" she would ask briskly, unpacking the bags. Sometimes she would scold Gertie for not starting supper, but most times she just stepped in and started it herself.

"Ma," Nora said one day, as she stood mashing potatoes on the stove. "You've got to start getting out more. Why don't you start going to church? You can come to St. Constance with us if you want."

"I don't know." Church had never really appealed to Gertie. She sometimes went on Christmas and Easter, but not always even then. Church was a place of judgement, she always felt, and she had no need of extra guilt. She already had plenty of that. Enough to last a whole other lifetime and beyond.

"The Women's Club always needs help selling concessions at bingo. Why don't you do that? Or the Altar and Rosary are knitting blankets for the poor. You could do that."

"I haven't knitted in years, Nor."

"Well, maybe it's time you started again," Nora said, turning from her task to look at her. "You need to get out of this house sometimes. Or go back to work maybe. You're becoming a hermit."

Not this again. "I try to Nora," she faltered, "but my nerves get to me. I find it hard to even step out on the porch sometimes."

Nora merely sighed and continued stirring.

Gertie went to the small kitchen window and looked out at the garden she had planted so long ago. How had it gotten so overgrown? It looked terrible! Maybe she and Wren should go out there tomorrow and tackle it . . .

"And Wren needs something to do besides sit in the house with you," Nora continued. "That's not normal, either. He's pale and gaunt," she said in a low voice. "He needs to be outside more, playing baseball with the neighborhood kids or something."

"He doesn't like baseball."

"Ma! He has to do something."

"He does plenty!"

"With his *grandmother*. That doesn't count. He should have more friends than just you and Kenny."

Gertie hoped that Nora would drop the subject, but she annoyingly did not and continued to periodically offer suggestions as to things Wren could get involved with. Gertie should have expected as much. Once Nora got an idea in her head, she would never let it go. And Gertie supposed Nora was right. Wren *was* losing weight. Barely anything fit him anymore.

Finally, she agreed to swimming at the Y. Wren seemed to like the water, and he claimed to be interested in the concept of learning to swim. The problem, however, was how to get him there and back.

The truth was that she was terrified of Wren being out of her sight. She dared not tell Nora that Wren sometimes *did* want to go out and play with the kids in the street, but Gertie always pleaded with him to stay with her, not to leave. It was a request that Wren always gave in to without complaint. He would simply say, "Okay, Gram. Let's stay in." He would stand at the windows for hours, though, staring, his eyes holding a far-off look, even if there was nothing out there. It was as if he could see something that she couldn't. That was just it. There were things about Wren that Nora didn't understand.

For one thing, Wren was a wanderer. That's one of the reasons she began to keep him inside with her from little on. When he was a toddler, she had been in the habit of taking him to the park in the mornings, but she was forever losing him. Once she had lost him for nearly an hour. She had run through the park, searching for him, even resorting to grabbing people to ask if they had seen a little boy. Finally, she had found him hiding in a lilac bush.

As he grew older, Wren began asking her if they might someday go on a trip, to which she always said no. Yes, he was a wanderer, she could see and concluded that he must take after Lorenzo, that he had the gypsy blood in him. The thought startled her. Could he really have the gypsy blood? Besides his dark hair and dark eyes, however, he didn't seem like Lorenzo in any other way. Wren was soft and sensitive and—what was the word?—intuitive? Like he could sense things about people or how they were feeling. It was uncanny the way he seemed to be able to predict what she was going to say before she even said it.

And he wrote poems. Long twisting poems filled with longing and love and loss, woven with the desire to leave, to explore, to see and understand, to find peace. He was like a sad caged bird, resigned to his fate like one of the birds the miners would take down to test the air. These thoughts filled her with dread, however, as usually when the cage was pulled back up, the poor bird was dead.

Sometimes, Wren would read his poems to her, and she oftentimes found herself crying at their beauty, filled with images of Maman, or, she hated to admit, Warren.

But it wasn't just she who thought they were good. Wren's teachers did, too. A Mr. Doyle, his English teacher, had telephoned one day to tell her what an exceptional writer Wren was. He had asked if there was any other writers or artists in the family and Gertie had replied no. It was only after she got off the phone that she remembered that Patsy had been an artist! How had she forgotten that?

Every day when Wren left for school, a small part of her was terrified that he wouldn't come back, yet every day he turned up like clockwork, and she would relax for a few hours before it was morning all over again. And now, here was Nora forcing him to go to the Y. She could tell that Wren didn't want to, but that he didn't want to disappoint his Aunt Nora. Oh, why did Nora have to interfere all the time? Why couldn't she just keep herself to herself? How on earth was he to get to the Y and back?

It was Wren who had convinced her that he could walk it on his own. It was only two blocks, he reminded her, his hand comfortingly on her shoulder. "Shorter than my walk to school, Gram."

In the end, Gertie had given in, but she walked with him the first day and sat outside waiting for him. As the weeks went on, however, she became more comfortable with him going alone, tricking herself into thinking that he was merely going to school each time he walked out the door and that he would be okay. Still, she would sit in the front room window with a cup of coffee, staring down Pratt until he rounded the corner. She supposed she should do something useful while she waited, like knit a blanket or whatever Nora had suggested, but she found she couldn't keep her eyes from staring down the street. It was difficult, though, just sitting. Sometimes her eyes would close for a few minutes, and then the dream would inevitably invade her mind . . .

Perhaps Nora was right. Maybe she should get out and do something. But what? All of Nora's suggestions sounded reasonable, but Gertie couldn't get enthused about any of them. She was numb. She had no emotion anymore—only fear. Tonight's parting from Wren had been particularly difficult.

"That all you're wearing?" Gertie asked, giving the front of his thin corduroy jacket a little brush with her knuckles. "I don't think you'll be warm enough."

"I'll be fine, Gram. I don't have far to go."

He was as tall as her now, and as he looked into her eyes, she thought she saw something there. A hesitancy, maybe. Or was it a sadness?

"Why don't you stay home tonight?" she asked, a quiver in her voice. "It won't matter if you skip one night."

Wren remained silent, looking at her, as if he were considering it. "No, Gram," he said quietly. "I have to go. It's supposed to happen this way."

"What's supposed to happen?"

Wren gave his head a little shake. "It doesn't matter." He bent and kissed her cheek. "Goodbye, Gram." His voice was hoarse. "Just remember . . . just remember that I love you. That I've always loved you."

"Oh, sweetie. I love you, too," she said, overwhelmed by the soft way he had about him and gripped his hand in hers. He left it there for a moment or two, then pulled it slowly from hers and gave her a last smile.

It wasn't until he had slipped out the front door and turned to give her a wave, which he never usually did, that the familiar hum of fear returned.

CHAPTER 24

October 1960

When the telephone rang, it was well past dinner time. Gertie woke with a start, blinking and trying to figure out where the ringing was coming from. She looked around, confused. She was in her chair in the front room. Where was Wren? Why didn't he get it? She glanced out the window. It was dark. What time was it?

"Wren?" she called. The phone rang again. "Wren?" she said louder and stood up unsteadily. Wasn't he back yet? She made her way to the front hall where the big black telephone sat atop a doily on the side table. "I'm coming," she muttered. It must be Nora. Who else would be this insistent?

"Hello? Nora?"

"Mrs. Munson? Gertrude Munson?"

The voice was *not* Nora, nor was it one she recognized, and tendrils of fear began to encircle Gertie's heart. "Yes?"

"Mrs. Munson, this is Officer Grenz. I'm afraid I have some bad news. There's been an accident."

"An accident?" Gertie croaked. *Oh, God, no. Please, no!*

"Yes, involving your son. He—"

"I don't have a son," she interrupted, allowing herself one second of hope that perhaps this call was some sort of a mistake, a mix-up . . .

"Well, your grandson then? Or nephew? We found his identification in a locker. William Williams. 2324 West Pratt Boulevard? That mean anything to you?"

William Williams? Why did that sound so familiar? Frantically, Gertie rummaged through her disheveled mind until something finally surfaced. *Oh, God,* she thought, her stomach clenching. That was Wren's actual name. She had forgotten...

"Yes," she said hoarsely, "that's my grandson. We call him Wren."

"Well, whatever the case," Officer Grenz went on, "seems he slipped in the pool at the local Y and hit his head. Suffered a pretty severe head injury. He's been taken to Ravenswood Hospital by ambulance, but I should tell you, Mrs. Munson, he's in pretty bad shape."

Nora stayed with Gertie at the hospital for the first three days, though since only one person was allowed in the room at a time, she spent a lot of it on a worn couch in the waiting area. Lyle came periodically, bringing sandwiches no one ate, as well as Kenny and Kurt, who left each time in tears.

Gertie never left Wren's side except to go to the bathroom. She sat in a hard chair by his bedside, sometimes dozing from exhaustion, but mostly holding his hand and stroking it, or standing over him and caressing his head and his face.

According to the lifeguard on duty at the time of the accident, Ted something-or-other, Wren had gotten into an altercation of sorts with two boys who frequented the Y pool.

"They were always pushing or shoving him, but the kid would never fight back. Couple of times I had to break it up," Ted explained when he one day turned up at the hospital to see how Wren was doing. "All I know is I heard a shout. I look over and I see those two creeps beating it out of there and the kid lying face down in the pool. Circles of blood around his head. I jumped in and pulled him out as quick as I could, but he wasn't breathing. We called the ambulance, and, well, that was it," he finished with a shrug. "I feel terrible about it all." He cleared his throat. "Tell you the truth, I haven't been sleepin' all that much since it happened. He was a real nice kid. Quiet, like. Never did much swimming. Come to think of it," he added, scratching his head, "I don't know if I ever saw him actually *in* the water. Got the feeling he couldn't swim. Just liked to sit by the side and write in that little book of his. I'm real sorry. I sure hope to God he makes it."

The doctors, however, were *not* as hopeful. Apparently, there was much bleeding on the brain, and Wren's lungs were filling with fluid, drowning him from the inside. They were doing everything in their power, they assured Gertie, but still, they grimly advised her to prepare herself.

Prepare herself? Gertie said the words over and over in her mind, as she sat by Wren's bedside, each hour bleeding into the next, but she couldn't seem to comprehend their meaning. Everyone was telling her to prepare herself, even Nora, but she had no idea how to do that. Eventually, though, it came to her that perhaps she had been, in fact, preparing for this for years. She gripped Wren's hand hard, realizing with horror how many days she had wasted envisioning his death, his absence, while he was still alive. Every day that she had spent worrying that something might happen to him was essentially the same as if it had. Oh, how could she have been so stupid? She should have been *living* each day with Wren, not sitting entombed with him in the house on Pratt. Is this what Nora had been trying to tell her?

Wren, please don't die; please don't die! She watched his chest shallowly float up and down.

Why was God punishing her? Did God hate her so much that He had allowed so many terrible things to happen to her? Her child was dead, and now another lay very close to it. But this was not the time to be angry with God, she chastised herself. She needed Him right now, and so she forced herself to set aside her anger and attempted instead to pray. But she hadn't prayed in so long, she could barely remember any of the prayers. Did it matter? She would make up her own. *I'll do anything*, she promised Him desperately. *Give anything, be anything*, if only He would let her have Wren. She knew she didn't deserve it, but she had already lost so much. Was it too much to ask to have this one person?

"Wren," she whispered. "It's Gram. I know you can hear me. Wren, please. Please don't leave me."

Gertie was surprised on the morning of the fourth day to hear a knock on Wren's door, followed immediately by a priest entering the room. He was wearing a long black cassock and a purple stole. He was carrying a crucifix and what looked to be a bible.

"Mrs. Munson? I'm Father Finnegan. I'm here to give Wren his last rites," he said gently. "He's your grandson, correct?"

Gertie froze in terror. "Last rites? He doesn't need last rites!" she hissed. "Who asked *you* to come?"

"I did, Ma," Nora said, coming in now. She walked to where Gertie was sitting and tried to put her hands on her shoulders, but Gertie shrugged them off.

Nora gave a little sigh. "Ma, we should do it now, before it's too late."

Gertie stared at Nora as if she were some strange beast. She searched Nora's weary, watery eyes for some sign of betrayal, but there was none. Just a haggard face staring back at her.

"No!" Gertie insisted. "He's not going to . . . he's going to be alright."

"Mrs. Munson," the priest said. "Of course, it doesn't mean that Wren might not yet recover, but . . . in case he does not," he added softly, "his mortal soul will not suffer. Is this not wise?"

"But he doesn't have any sins!" Gertie cried. "I know he doesn't."

Father Finnegan's eyes flicked briefly to Nora's and then back to Gertie. "All of us are burdened with sin, Mrs. Munson. To deny it is to sin twice."

"Ma, come on. Just let him do it," Nora pleaded. Gertie was surprised to see her chin trembling. "For once don't be so stubborn."

Stubborn? She was the least stubborn person she knew; she had spent a lifetime giving in to other people. "No!" she said defiantly.

Father Finnegan sighed. "Perhaps I should come back later," he murmured to Nora.

Nora stood hesitating. "Why don't we step outside, Father?" she suggested, her head bowed.

The priest obeyed and moved toward the door. "Let me know if you change your mind, Mrs. Munson," he said. "I will be praying for him. And for you."

Gertie watched them leave and burst into tears. Had she made the wrong decision? Oh, why was there always so many decisions to make? She brushed Wren's hair back with her fingertips for the hundredth time.

Oh, Wren! Her favorite boy—her favorite child, if she were honest. She had always connected to him on a level that she couldn't explain. Even as a baby, she had always known what he needed. Except now. Now there was nothing. She couldn't tell what he needed, couldn't reach him. Maybe she *should* have let him have last rites, she worried with a groan, again laying her head down on the mattress by his thigh, a position that was becoming familiar. *Was* she just being stubborn?

"Gram," came a faint voice then, and Gertie's head shot up. Several times over the last three days she had imagined she heard him calling to her, but whenever she had looked, it had turned out to be merely a figment of her imagination. But this time, Wren's eyes were genuinely fluttering a little. They were fluttering!

"Wren?" she cried, her voice cracking. "Wren?" She grabbed his hand with both of hers. She wondered if she should call for the nurse, but she didn't want to leave him.

"Gram?" he asked again, his voice thick and raspy as his eyes finally managed to flutter open.

"I'm here, Wren," she said eagerly and put her face nearer his.

"I need to go home now," he whispered. "You need to let me go home."

"Yes! I want to take you home, sweetie. I want to. Now that you're awake, maybe they'll let you go. I'll go get them, should I?"

Wren shut his eyes and moved his head slightly from side to side, wincing as he did so.

"Oh, Wren! I've been so worried!" Gertie cried, lifting his hand to her lips and kissing it. "I've been frightened half to death!"

"I love you, Gram," he said hoarsely, opening his eyes again and giving her such a look as she had never received from any other human being. He was radiating love, pregnant with it, surrounding her with it. It was as if *he* was taking care of *her*, not the opposite! She couldn't find any words to answer.

"You're going to be okay," he whispered.

"Of course, I'm going to be okay," she managed to say, her voice thick. "And so are you, my boy. Just you wait. You'll be up and running in no time."

"You need to go back home, too, Gram." He squeezed her hand faintly.

"Of course, I will, sweetie. Of course." She almost smiled at his insistence on the obvious. He was clearly confused, probably because of his injury. Well, he would get better. There was no doubt now, and she felt a wave of relief that God had heard her prayer for once. For once, it was really going to be okay.

She gave his hand another kiss and then let it go. "I'd better go get the nurse! I'll be right back," she said, hurrying toward the door.

"Mrs. Munson, to move him now is out of the question. He won't survive the drive home. It's better to leave him," Dr. McCauley said after he had examined Wren. They were standing at the nurses' station, just outside of Wren's room. "He's comfortable, not in any pain. That's the best we can do."

"But he's awake now! You've seen him," Gertie insisted.

"Mrs. Munson, his vitals are very weak; he's not responding as we had hoped. Let me be frank," he said with a deep sigh, "I don't think he has much time. We've done all we can. Spend what little time you have left. Say your goodbyes; now's the time. I'm sorry," he added and looked back at the chart he was holding, turning slightly away from her.

Gertie felt her heart constrict. There was a humming in her head now, and she had a hard time hearing anyone. A part of her understood what the doctor was saying, and yet the other part urged her to act. She knew it would be reckless to take Wren home, just as it had been all those years ago to run off with Lorenzo, or to sleep with Olson, or to take up with Jerry, and yet she felt compelled. But more than that, it occurred to her suddenly as goosebumps rippled down her arms, that the dream was finally being realized. It was obvious. The boy in her dream, telling her to wait, to take him home—it was Wren. All this time, it had been Wren. Wren begging her to wait and to take him home. It all made sense.

But how was she to achieve this? she fretted. It seemed impossible. And yet this was absolutely what she must do! If she could just get him home, he would get better!

"Doctor, please!" Gertie begged. He looked up at her as if surprised she was still standing there. "Doctor, please . . . if there really isn't a chance that he'll . . . he'll make it through, then let me take him home to . . ." Gertie couldn't bring herself to say the word "die." "Let me take him home," she instead repeated. "If it doesn't matter anyway? Please!" Her brain raced frantically, trying to think of how to convince him. "I . . . I have some money. I'll . . . I'll pay you."

Dr. McCauley pinched the bridge of his nose and let out a deep sigh. "This is highly irregular, Mrs. Munson. You'd be acting against medical advice. You'd have to sign several documents saying as much." He looked at her sternly. "Do you really want this on your conscience?"

"Oh, yes! Yes, I'll sign." Gertie could barely breathe she was so filled with hope.

"You do understand, correct? We can't be responsible for what's going to happen."

"Yes, yes, I understand," Gertie said quickly.

"Very well." He gave another sigh. "I wash my hands of this. Nurse!" he said over his shoulder to the nurse who had been listening to the whole exchange. "Make the arrangements."

"Yes, Doctor. But . . ."

"Just do it, Nurse Simmons."

"Yes, Doctor, but there will be a problem with the ambulance. They won't transfer in a case like this."

"Hmm. Yes, I see. Well, do you have transportation?" the doctor asked Gertie.

Gertie bit her lip. She hadn't thought of this. She would have to telephone Nora, but Nora, she knew, would never go along with her plan. "Yes, I'll . . . I'll arrange something," she said. "Thank you, Doctor! Thank you so much! He'll get better; you'll see!"

Gertie hurried back toward Wren's room, wondering how she was possibly going to find transportation—maybe a cab?— when she spotted Kenny miraculously standing outside it.

"Kenny! Kenny, you'll never guess," she called out. "Wren's awake!"

"He is? Oh, Grandma!" he said, hugging her. "Can I talk to him?"

"Yes, in a minute. But why aren't you at school?"

"It's Saturday."

"Is your mom here?" she asked, looking around.

"No, I took the car. She told me to tell you she had to go into the office but that she'll be here later. She thought you might need some company, so she sent me." He gave her a shrug.

"Oh, Kenny," Gertie said, gripping his jacket as an idea exploded in her head. "I need you to do something for me."

"Sure, Grandma. What is it?"

Two hours later, Kenny was perched behind the wheel of the old Buick Lyle had bought just last year. "Grandma, I don't know about this," he said into the rear-view mirror. "I think we should have waited for Mom. Wren doesn't look too good."

"He'll be fine," Gertie called from the backseat, though she was, in truth, burning with worry. Wren was so weak he could barely sit up. He was wrapped in a white blanket from the hospital and was leaning against Gertie, her arm tightly wound around his shoulders. His head was still bandaged, and a little bit of blood was seeping through where his stitches ran across the back of his head. He looked like a war victim. "Try to drive faster, Kenny."

"Why?" he asked frantically. "Shouldn't I be driving nice and slow?"

"We need to get him home fast! Once he's in his bed, he'll be fine."

"Oh, Grandma. I don't know. We shouldn't have done this. The doctor didn't look too happy. Maybe we should drive back . . ." Kenny fretted, turning onto Pratt very slowly to prevent Wren from falling over.

"For God's sakes, Kenny, just drive. He'll be fine."

Kenny went silent then, and all Gertie could hear was Wren's raspy breathing.

Finally, they pulled up outside the house on Pratt, and Kenny threw the car into park and shot out of the door. He ran around to the other side of the car. Gertie slowly pulled her arm back. How were they going to get him inside? she despaired and wished Lyle was here. An orderly had wheeled Wren down to the car and had gingerly placed him in the backseat, but now what were they to do?

"Kenny, do you think you can carry him?"

"I'll try, Grandma, but he's pretty heavy."

"What do you mean? He's skin and bones!"

"Yeah, but still, he's older than me."

It took several tries before Kenny found a position that allowed him to lift Wren, and still he staggered backwards a few steps under the weight, Wren's head flopped against his chest. Gertie hovered near, her arms outstretched in a half-hearted attempt to catch Wren should Kenny drop him. Finally, she turned away and hurried up the sidewalk to open the front door. Once on the stoop, she turned to check their progress and was horrified to see that Kenny had gone down on one knee, halfway up the walk, struggling under Wren's dead weight.

"Kenny!" Gertie called, starting back and wishing she was stronger. Kenny's face was beet-red and sweat was building by his temples.

"Go on, Grandma," Kenny shouted, standing again. "Get the door."

With renewed effort, Kenny heaved Wren up and staggered forward, making it all the way up the two stairs of the stoop before having to rest one more time on bended knee.

Gertie ran ahead to Wren's bedroom and pulled down the sheets before running back.

"Come on, Kenny! Hurry!"

Kenny gave her a nod, and he strained to lift Wren for the short remaining leg of the journey when Wren suddenly opened his eyes.

"Kenny," he said hoarsely.

Kenny paused in his efforts, panting, and went back down onto one knee. "Almost there," Kenny said, trying to give him a smile. "Almost home."

"I know." Wren's voice was calm. "Bye, Kenny. You don't have to be afraid anymore," he said with a ragged smile. Then his head rolled back, and his body went limp.

Gertie, having appeared in the doorway at just this moment, gave a little cry and flew down the steps, sinking to her knees beside them. "Wren!" she called, feeling his cheek with the back of her hand. "Wren!" she said louder and looked up into Kenny's mortified face. "What did you do?"

Frantically, she felt for a pulse in Wren's neck. She grabbed him by the shoulders, wrenching him from Kenny's arms, and shook his now lifeless body. "Wren!" she shouted. "Wren!" She turned to Kenny. "I told you to hurry!" she sobbed, and then buried her face in Wren's chest, letting out a cry so deep and so guttural that it seemed to be coming from a wild animal.

"Wren, no!" she sobbed. "Please, God, no."

October 1963

Nora

Nora pinched the bridge of her nose and tried to let out a deep breath to calm herself. She was always uptight these days. She thought about taking another valium, but she didn't want to. She was worried that she might get addicted to them, though the doctor had said not to worry about that. But she didn't like the way they made her feel. Well, in a certain way she did; they numbed the pain and the anxiety, but she was foggy, then, and loopy, and she needed to be able to think straight.

Lyle would be home soon, and she hadn't even started dinner, though she knew he wouldn't mind. Since she had sprained her ankle last week during their bowling league tournament, she had been hobbling around on crutches. It had taken her a day to master the crutches, but since then she had been trying to still do as much housework and cooking as she could. Lyle had told her not to worry, that they could just have eggs or open a can of soup or even maybe go out for a Chinese.

He was always looking for an excuse to go out for a Chinese. But Nora thought it expensive and also not very tasty. Too salty, by far. And she knew Ma wouldn't eat it.

Nora had a hard time not performing her housewifely duties even when injured. As it was, it caused her extreme stress and anxiety to not provide a lovely home and three home-cooked meals for her family every day of the year, an obsession that had only become more intense once she had quit her job. She had no idea where this passion to be a perfect housewife and mother came from, but it was now part of every fiber of her being, though if she really thought about it, it had gotten worse after Patsy died. All she knew was order made her feel calm.

Endlessly, then, she labored at cooking and cleaning, gardening, canning, making jams, sewing, and volunteering a certain amount of her time to charitable events at church. She made sure that the boys, and Lyle, were always dressed perfectly and that everyone's shoes were shined and their hair trimmed. She decorated the house from ideas that she got from looking through *Good Housekeeping*, the result of which was that she was the envy of the neighborhood, or at least the ladies in her bridge club, who always remarked that she had the loveliest home and the best holiday decorations. Also, she had a reputation for being a wonderful baker, and her lime Jello mold, the one with the pistachios, was always requested by the ladies of the Women's Club at church whenever there was a function. And Nora was good with their money, always clipping coupons, looking for sales and forever putting pennies away for a rainy day. Essentially all the things Aunt Rita had taught so many years ago.

No, neither eggs nor Chinese was a proper dinner, she resolved, and hobbled over to the Frigidaire to get out the pork roast she had bought at Harvey's. They would have roast pork and apples with mashed potatoes and boiled cabbage as she had planned. She didn't think she could manage a pie tonight, however, so she decided they would have fruit cocktail for dessert. Everyone liked that, and it was easy. Just open the can.

She would have to get going, though, as it would take twice as long as normal. It was amazing how something as insignificant as a sprained ankle could affect her whole world. As it was, her foot was currently throbbing, so instead of peeling the apples at the sink, she carried the basket to the table with one hand, while leaning on one of the crutches with the other. She had just positioned herself in one of the chairs when Kenny banged through the back door.

"What are you doing home?" she asked.

"Mr. Novotny said he didn't need me today."

"Why? He always wants you on a Wednesday."

Kenny shrugged and yanked open the Frigidaire. After perusing the contents for a moment, he pulled out the bottle of milk. "I don't know."

"I hope you didn't ask off."

"I didn't, Ma. Jeez." He poured a glass and then took a long drink.

"Why don't you go get a haircut, then, before dinner?" Kenny had taken to letting his hair grow long like some of the more undesirable boys at school. She hated the way it made him look.

"I'm not getting a haircut! I like it like this."

"Well, you know your father's going to complain again."

"I don't care."

"Kenny! Don't you sass, young man," Nora said, wagging her paring knife at him.

"God, Mom, lighten up already. It's just hair," he grumbled.

"Don't you talk to me that way!"

Nora bit her lip in frustration. What was she going to do with this kid? But at nineteen, he wasn't really a kid anymore, she reminded herself. She didn't understand what had gone wrong. He had been such a perfect little boy—so well behaved, such perfect manners, always so eager to please. And now he was essentially a hippie who had barely graduated from high school, spending most of his last two years there talking back to teachers and cutting class. Somehow, he had gotten into Northern Illinois, but at the last minute he decided not to go, much to her and Lyle's despair.

He had also started hanging out with the wrong types of kids. Recently she had suggested that he invite a few of his old friends over for dinner, maybe Eddie or Mike? But Kenny had just laughed and said they were dopes. She frequently smelled alcohol on his breath when he came home late, and a couple of times she had found empty bottles of vodka under his bed—almost as if he *wanted* her to find them. She never confronted him, however, merely put them in the trash can in the garage, shoving them down deep so that Lyle wouldn't notice. And he had taken up smoking as well. Lyle forbade him to smoke in the house, but he lit up as soon as he walked out of the house each day, which she suspected was done to purposely spite Lyle.

It pained her to see how far they had grown apart. They used to be the best of buddies, but now they fought constantly, usually about the war, of all things. It pained her when Kenny accused Lyle of being old-fashioned and strict, when, in many ways, Lyle had become almost a pushover. In her opinion, he wasn't strict enough. Maybe if they held Kenny by a tighter rein, he would behave better, she often said, but Lyle insisted he was more than likely going through a phase they just needed to wait out.

After one particularly bad incident, however, when Nora and Lyle had been called to the police station because Kenny and several other boys had been caught vandalizing the YMCA with spray paint and toilet paper, Lyle had despaired and suggested that maybe they really *should* do something drastic, like send him to military school. But Nora refused to ever send her children away, not after what she had been through, and Lyle had apologized, saying he had forgotten . . .

Kurt had become Lyle's favorite now. Silly and goofy when he was little, he had become quite serious and earnest in high school, eager to get good grades and to please in general. He was an honor student and a boy scout and an altar boy, everything she had once upon a time hoped Kenny would be. Nora had been immensely proud when Kurt was accepted to Notre Dame, but when they dropped him off at Sorin Hall in South Bend, it almost made her despair all the more for Kenny, who seemed to be so dreadfully lost, still at home and floundering.

Many times, she had tried to trace back when the change had occurred in Kenny, and each time, she was led back to Wren's death. That's when *everything* had changed, really. Ma had nearly lost her mind, for one thing. Nora would go to the house on Pratt and find her sitting in the same chair she had left her in the previous day, the food she had laid out untouched. Ma would call her Patsy and ask where Wren was, and Nora would then have to explain that they were both gone, causing a fresh set of tears and even sometimes wailing from Ma, as if she were hearing it all for the first time. Nora despaired about what to do with her and complained to Lyle that she didn't see any other option but to put Ma in a home, that's all there was to it. She couldn't keep living on her own, she argued; she would starve to death, if nothing else.

It was Lyle who suggested that Gertie live with them. Nora hesitated for several weeks, letting the suggestion brew, until finally, reluctantly, she admitted it made the most sense. Of course, Ma should come and live with them, though Ma could be difficult sometimes, Nora knew. She was stubborn and contrary at times, *and* she could be messy. Still, Nora felt she owed it to her. More than once, however, after Ma had moved in, it had struck Nora as odd that after so many years of longing for Ma to actually mother her, she was now in the role of mothering Ma, whose confused sadness needed constant care.

Nora wondered if that was perhaps the real reason she had hesitated to bring Ma into their home. It was so painful to be around her. Ma was perpetually stuck, spinning endlessly in her tragedies, while Nora was always trying to move past them. It wasn't that Nora hadn't felt each tragedy as they happened—Patsy dying, and then Wren, but she had no wish to perpetually dwell on them. They had been bad enough to live through the first time.

She felt sorry for Ma, of course. She couldn't imagine what it was like to lose a child, and yet she wished that Ma could just once in her life think of someone besides herself. After all, she did not have a monopoly on tragedy and sorrow. Did Ma for one moment realize the crippling grief she herself had felt at the loss of Patsy? She had lost her beautiful little sister, who, truth be told, had been like *her* own child. There were days when thinking about the loss of Patsy nearly stopped Nora's heart. But no, of course Ma did not realize that. It was beyond her capacity.

For a long time after Patsy's death, Nora had not wanted to go on. She couldn't imagine living in a world in which Patsy did not, and at the funeral, she had had to fight an overwhelming longing to simply lie down next to her sister in the casket, to wrap her arms around her and go to sleep next to her, as she had so many times before. No matter that she would be buried alive.

Instead, she had felt Lyle's gentle arms come around *her*, and he led her back to her seat, where she buried her head in his chest as the casket lid was closed. When the priest raised his hand to give Patsy a final blessing, Nora found she couldn't even mouth the response. Patsy had finally wandered beyond her reach, beyond her ability to find her and bring her home.

Despite Lyle's loving grasp that day and many after, Nora felt herself sliding into a black hole, a vortex of unrelenting grief. They had traded positions, she and Patsy. Patsy was free now, in heaven, while she had taken Patsy's place in the Carrie Cort. But why? That was the question that kept repeating over and over in her head. Why had Patsy deserted her, when Nora had never once deserted *her*?

Eventually, Nora stopped being sad and instead drifted into a state of weary emotionlessness. Except for anger. She still felt *that*, but, then again, she had always felt that. She allowed herself to wander in this barren landscape for a very long time—months—before she realized that Lyle and the boys needed her much more than Patsy's memory did or even Ma.

How had she lost sight of this?

At that point, she determined that she needed to package up her grief and set it firmly behind her. It was a method of self-preservation she had learned long ago, and she was surprised that Ma had apparently not, continuing instead to wallow in her sad grief, unable to move past it. Kenny, too, Nora eventually realized with a sinking heart, was the same. This partially infuriated her, but it also confused her. He and Wren had been close in a certain way, but not enough to warrant this kind of a reaction. Why could he not get over it?

The night before Wren's funeral, Kenny had been inconsolable, crying and ranting that it was all his fault. Nora had reassured him over and over that it wasn't his fault at all. How could it possibly be his fault? Lyle, too, had tried to hug him and tell him that Wren hadn't been going to make it either way. That there was nothing anyone could have done.

"But Grandma said he should have died in the bed where he was born, not on the front stoop like a dead bird," Kenny had sobbed.

"Well, don't listen to Grandma," Nora had scolded. "She's out of her mind right now!"

Kenny sobbed louder. "That's all my fault, too!"

Eventually they had gotten him to calm down, and at the wake the next day, sitting in the front row at the funeral home, he seemed to fragilely be holding it together, though he was deathly pale and his right knee jiggled endlessly. Nora spent most of the time either sitting by Ma, who was a wreck, or greeting various guests and making small talk. Finally, she found a moment to sit down next to Kenny, still sitting forlornly in front of the casket. He hadn't moved an inch.

"It's okay to cry, honey," she said, but Kenny didn't shed a single tear.

In the days and weeks that followed Wren's funeral, Nora thought that Kenny had mastered his sorrow and his guilt, but she soon began to realize that he was not quite the same boy as he had been before. It was if her little boy had died as well, and this new Kenny had come to take his place. Not only was he more sullen and quick to anger, he quit the football team and even stopped going to the Student Affairs Club, of which he was the vice president. Instead, he went to anti-war demonstrations, where Nora was pretty sure he smoked pot. Nora had tried talking to him countless times, but it was as if he had put up an impenetrable shield. "Just leave me alone, Mom," was his constant response.

Kenny let the Frigidaire door bang shut and pushed his empty glass across the counter toward the sink. "I'm going in to talk to Grandma," he said with a scowl. "At least she doesn't nag me," he said and slunk off down the hall.

Nora was about to scold him, but she bit it back. "Tell her I'll bring her some tea in a little bit," she called wearily instead.

Kenny didn't answer, but she heard him knocking on Ma's door. It opened now, and she could hear *Gunsmoke* blaring on the little black and white television that Lyle had hooked up for her. Nora had never understood her mother's predilection for Westerns. How many times could a person watch them? It was the same story over and over.

CHAPTER 26

October 1963

Gertie

Gertie heard a knock and opened her eyes, surprised that the room was dark. She was sitting in a rocking chair by the window, but she couldn't tell if it was dusk or dawn. How long had she been sleeping?

She had been having the dream again. She had it almost every time she closed her eyes. It was getting more and more real by the day. Now she knew for sure it was Wren. She could see him clear as day. He was no longer sad, no longer calling for her to wait for him. "You have to go home," he always said now. "He's waiting for you." Each time, Gertie would try to ask "Who?" but she could never get the words out before Wren disappeared. If only he would stay longer!

She heard the knock again.

"That you, Wren?" Gertie called eagerly. "Come in!"

The door opened, and Gertie was surprised to see Kenny.

"Oh, it's you, Kenny! What are you doing here? Did Wren let you in?"

"Yeah, it's me, Grandma," Kenny said. "Why are you always sitting in the dark?" he asked and switched on the light.

"Oh!" Gertie exclaimed, shielding her eyes. "That's too bright, Kenny! Turn it off!"

Kenny obeyed and ambled over to the T.V. "Mind if I turn this down?"

"That's better," she said, lowering her hand. "No, go on. Turn it down."

Kenny obliged and then plopped onto the end of her bed, bathed in the glow of the little T.V., and drew his legs up under him.

"How was school?"

"I don't go to school anymore, Grandma."

"Why not?" she asked, peering up at him. Why did he have whiskers?

"I graduated, Grandma."

"That old already?"

"Yeah," Kenny said with a grin.

"I never much liked high school myself," Gertie mused, thinking back to Eddyville. "Ingrid always liked it better than me. But we were lucky to go, I reckon. Lots of kids didn't."

"Yeah, I know. You told me that," Kenny said.

"Did I?"

"Yeah, a few times."

"Well, what are you gonna do now?"

Kenny shrugged. "I don't know."

"Well, you better think of something, or you'll have to go down the mine."

Kenny laughed, but Gertie didn't see what was so funny. The mine was a terrible place!

"What was the mine like, Grandma? Did you ever go down?"

"Go down the mine? No! Girls weren't allowed. But who would want to? Turned you black as night, it did. Looked just like the coloreds when you came up. Only the whites of your eyes showed. I could barely recognize my own Pa when he came in at night. Used to frighten the life out of Maman when he turned up like that. Sometimes, if the pump outside the mine froze, and the men couldn't wash up then, you see, so they had to go home and wash. Poor Maman," Gertie said and oddly felt like crying.

Suddenly, Gertie had a memory of her mother's white aprons and of the clothes hanging on the line, snapping in the breeze. She could almost taste her mother's strawberry scones, fresh from the oven. More memories began surfacing, then, and she desperately wished she could go back. Just one last time, to see them all again. Is this what Wren had meant in her dream? Oh, God, was *that* what he meant?

She struggled to stand.

"Grandma! What's wrong?" Kenny asked, unfolding himself from the bed and holding out his arms as if to catch her.

"I want to go home," she said.

"You mean back to *your* house? On Pratt?"

Gertie thought for a moment. Weren't they at the house on Pratt? Well, it didn't matter. "No, back *home*," Gertie insisted.

"You mean Iowa?" Kenny asked, his eyebrows oddly raised.

Iowa? Gertie thought for a moment. Is that where home was? Yes, that was it. Iowa! "Yes, I need to go back there."

"But why, Grandma? I think everybody back there is probably dead by now."

"No, they're not all dead. Not everyone."

"How do you know?" he asked. "And anyway, why do you want to go back *there*?"

"I just do," Gertie said, balancing herself by leaning on the edge of the dresser. But how was she to do this? Wren couldn't drive, and Nora would probably say no, that she couldn't take off work. She looked at Kenny. She would rather have Wren go with her, but Kenny would do. "Will you drive me there?"

"Me? Drive you all the way to Iowa?" he asked with a laugh, folding his legs back under him, and leaning his chin on his hand as he looked at her.

"Yes! You know how to drive, right?" she asked, and then an image of him driving a car while she held Wren in the backseat seared through her mind. Frantically, she pushed it away. "'Course you do," she mumbled. "I remember."

"I know how to drive, Grandma, but I don't think Mom or Dad will just let me have the car to cruise over to Iowa. They're pretty strict, if you haven't noticed."

Were they? Gertie mused. She hadn't, in fact, noticed. She must try to pay more attention. What was wrong with her these days?

"But we have to go back. It's very important!" Gertie urged, taking a few shuffling steps toward the door and grabbing hold of one of the bed posts.

"I'll take you, Grandma, but we've got to figure out how to get the car. I'll ask Mom, but I'm pretty sure I can guess the answer."

"Where is she, anyway? Is she still at work?"

"She quit work about five years ago, Grandma. Remember?" Kenny asked, his voice sounding impatient for the first time.

"Did she really?" she asked, truly perplexed.

"Did I really what?" Nora asked, hobbling in with one crutch and carrying a steaming mug with the other. "Ma, why are you out of your chair without your cane? Sit down now, and I'll put this on your table. Kenny, help her, would you?"

Kenny made a slow move to scooch off the bed, but Gertie turned on her own and shuffled back. "I've got it," she said, placing her hands on the chair. Once she fell heavily into the cushioned seat, Nora set the mug on a doily next to one of the crosswords Nora always set there. As if she would ever be interested in a crossword! Words were already crossed enough in her mind.

"Did I really what?" Nora asked again, taking a step back and looking from one to the other.

"I was just reminding Grandma that you quit work a while ago."

"Quit work? That was years ago. Why are you thinking about that?"

"I'm not really," Gertie said, weakly waving her hand as if to dismiss the subject.

"Grandma wants me to drive her to Iowa," Kenny said with a small grin. "So, can we borrow the car?"

"Drive to Iowa! Why?"

"Grandma wants to go back and see where she grew up, I think. Right, Grandma?"

"Yes, that's it." Gertie gave him a thankful nod.

"Ma, all those mining towns are shut down now. The mines are closed, and the towns are gone."

"Gone? What do you mean?" Gertie asked, deciding to challenge her. You had to have your wits about you to challenge Nora. "A whole town just can't disappear, Nora."

"They're abandoned, Ma. They're ghost towns."

"Ghost towns?" Kenny asked. "Like a *real* ghost town? Like out west? The OK corral and all that?"

Gertie saw Nora give him a disparaging look. "You know what I mean, Kenny."

"Not really, Mom. Why can't we go? I'd like to see it. You're always saying I should get interested in something, aren't you?"

Nora paused, and Gertie could tell she was genuinely considering it. "What about your job? And we can't just take the car; Dad needs it to get to work."

"We'll go on a weekend," Kenny suggested.

Nora sighed. "I don't know. This doesn't make any sense, Ma. What brought this on? More than likely you'll forget about it by tomorrow."

"No, I won't, Nora! Wren keeps telling me I need to go." She saw Nora give Kenny a look, but she ignored it. Nora was always giving someone that look, as if to indicate that she was crazy. Usually, it was directed at Lyle. "If one of you doesn't take me, I'll take the bus!" she threatened. "You can't stop me, you know."

Nora sighed again, shifting her weight on the crutch. "All right, Ma. We'll go. Just as soon as my foot is better."

"No, Nora. I need to go now! I can't wait that long."

"Yeah, Mom. Why do we always have to do everything on *your* schedule? Just let me and Grandma go. You stay here with Dad."

"Watch your mouth, young man," Nora said sternly. She was silent for a moment, as if thinking. "Well," she finally muttered, "I suppose I could rearrange my sewing circle for this weekend. And Dad could have Chinese one night, and I could make up a meatloaf for him for another night," she mumbled to herself.

"Mom, we'll be alright by ourselves," Kenny urged. "You don't have to go."

"No, you're not going alone. I'm coming with you."

"Ah, jeez," Kenny muttered.

"But you'll have to do the driving, Kenny. I won't be able to manage with this foot."

"When can we leave?" Gertie asked anxiously. "When can we go home?"

CHAPTER 27

October 1963

Nora

The drive to Eddyville, Iowa, took longer than Nora expected. For one thing, Ma had to stop almost every hour to go to the bathroom, and then as they were passing through Dixon, Illinois, Kenny had declared himself hungry and convinced her to stop for lunch at a little diner. Nora had packed them a lunch—sandwiches and potato chips and some of the chocolate chip cookies she had insisted on making for Lyle before she left—but they decided instead to have a hot meal for lunch and save the sandwiches for dinner. It wasn't what Nora had planned, but she admitted that it was probably a better idea, as, now that she thought about it, there probably wouldn't be any places to eat near Keystone, which was way out in the middle of nowhere, or had been, that is, once upon a time.

She still couldn't believe she was doing this. The more she had thought about it after initially agreeing, the more it seemed a fool's errand, and she had said as much to Lyle late one night in their bedroom. Lyle, annoyingly, thought it might be a good idea, essentially repeating what Kenny had said about it being a step in the right direction that he was interested in something again. And that he was willing to drive, Lyle had pointed out.

Nora sighed. This was true. Nora couldn't remember the last time Kenny had asked for the car. Lyle had even offered it to him the night of his senior prom, but he had turned it down with a snide laugh, saying that he wasn't going to the dance, that it was for squares. But shouldn't that be a cause for concern? Nora mumbled, bobby pins in her mouth, as she sat at her little vanity, pinning her hair up in curlers. Should she really be entrusting their lives to him on a three-hundred-and-fifteen-mile drive when he hadn't driven in ages? But Lyle hadn't seemed concerned, saying that it would be good for Kenny to have the responsibility. He was more worried about the car making it, given that the carburetor was on the fritz again.

"All the more reason not to go," Nora said, turning to look at him. "This is crazy! I don't know why I let myself be talked into this. I'm going to put my foot down!"

"You just don't want to be stuck in a car for six and a half hours with your mother," Lyle said with a wry grin.

"Well, would you?"

"Honey, maybe it would be good for you." Now he was using his soothing voice.

"Good to be trapped in a car on its last legs with my mother, driving to the middle of nowhere because my dead nephew told her she needed to go?" she asked, irritated, screwing on the lid of the Dippity Do.

"Well, at least you'll have Kenny along," Lyle offered.

Nora gave him a look. "Yes, so we can argue the whole way? You're right, that makes it so much more appealing."

Lyle just looked at her, his head tilted to the side a little, which was what he always did when he was being self-righteous. "Let me rephrase, then. Maybe it will be good for *them*."

"Well, don't you think it would be better to wait until you get the car fixed and my foot gets better?" Nora asked, throwing out one last argument.

"I can look at the car tomorrow," Lyle offered. "But aren't you supposed to be on those for a few more weeks?" he said, nodding at her crutches propped against the wall. "I wouldn't wait too long. Pretty soon it will be the holidays, and after that, you risk bad weather. You don't want to be driving in a blizzard."

Nora let out a deep breath. He was right, of course. He was always right.

"Fine," she said. "We'll go this weekend."

As it turned out, Kenny was proving to be a fairly competent driver. He took a little while to master the gears again, but by the time they left the city limits, he was driving smoothly.

Nora sat beside him in the front seat, her crutches in the back with Ma, and tried not to let her nerves show. She glanced over at him. He had the window slightly cracked for his cigarette smoke to escape, and the wind lifted his hair every so often, making him look like a little boy again. She let her eyes fall to his black turtleneck and beaded vest and jeans. How had he become a hippie? He reminded her of Patsy, who would have been the perfect flower child. She had just been born in the wrong era. Maybe that was it. Poor Patsy.

Nora looked out the window and watched the scenery, such as it was, pass by. There was not much besides endless brown fields, drying corn, broken up only occasionally by a field of hay or a pasture with cattle huddled under a lone tree. Nora stared at them and wondered why they didn't spread out more. Or were they huddled there for shelter? But did they not realize that there were no more leaves on the tree to protect them?

After nearly six hours, they finally whipped past a sign that declared Ottumwa five miles away and Eddyville thirty. Nora felt a surprising little flutter in her stomach.

"Slow down, Kenny!" she said. "Why do you have to drive so fast?"

"Why not, Mom? There's nothing out here. And I've told you a million times, stop calling me Kenny. I'm not a baby."

"Well, I can't help it." Nora looked back out the window. Maybe they should stop in Ottumwa. In truth, she was a little curious to see it, as she had been born there. Ma had never said much about their life there, other than to say they had lived in a creepy old mansion with a big black spider who sat spinning tales the way a normal spider spun webs. The spider lured many an unsuspecting person in and then held them prisoner for long periods of time, even years, until she had gotten what she wanted out of them.

"What did she want?" a five-year-old Nora had asked one day, rapt with attention.

"Yeah, whad 'id she wan?" Patsy had added, her doll at her nose.

"Sometimes she wanted their treasure," Ma had said cryptically, "but mostly she wanted their souls."

"Do you want to stop in Ottumwa, Ma?" Nora asked, turning back to look at her.

"Ottumwa?" Ma asked, looking out the window in a surprised way as if expecting to see it. "No!" she said, sitting back, "we need to get to Keystone."

"Well, the sign didn't mention Keystone and neither does this map."

"Well, maybe it's not on the map."

"This is a brand-new map, Ma," Nora said irritated. "I just bought it at the diner back in Dixon."

"Maybe we should just keep on the road, Mom. Stop in Eddyville."

Nora studied the map again. "Was Keystone closer to Eddyville or Oskaloosa?" she asked Ma, turning around again.

Ma did not immediately respond, which did not bode well. "Eddyville, I think."

"Let's just head there, Mom."

"Fine, but it's getting late, and we should probably start looking for a motel."

"Motel?" piped up Gertie. "We can stay at the house."

"Ma, there might not even be a house left. Don't you understand that?"

"'Course there's a house there, Nora!"

"Mom, just ignore it," Kenny said, turning off the highway.

After about thirty more minutes, they rolled past a sign that read, "Welcome to Eddyville—Miner's Paradise." Kenny drove down the town's main street, slowly for once. There was the usual assortment of shops, a bank, the town hall, a couple of churches, a gas station, and rows of shabby little houses. There were no traffic lights, however, and before they knew it, they were surrounded by fields again.

"Guess we missed it," Kenny said with a grin, rolling the car to the side of the road.

"Well, we'll have to turn around." Nora arched her neck to look back at the little town.

"Yeah, that's obvious, Mom." Kenny did a U-turn.

"Pull into that 76 station," Nora said. "We'll have to ask."

Kenny obediently pulled in and parked. Slowly, he peeled himself out of the car, flicking his cigarette as he did. As he stretched, Nora got out and bent over to speak to Gertie, still in the backseat.

"You stay here, Ma, okay?" Nora said through the crack in the window. "We'll be right out."

The man behind the counter was as fat as he could be, with only a little tuft of gray hair on the top of his head. He looked Kenny up and down with disgust and then spit out his tobacco. "Can I help you folks?"

Nora spread out her map. "We're looking for Keystone," she explained.

"Ain't gonna find it on that. That's one of them mining towns that folded. Nothing left out there. Few shacks is all."

Nora sighed.

"Whatch you want out that way, anyway?" His eyes narrowed a little.

"We're looking for the town my mother grew up in. She moved away when she was young, and she wants to see it again. I told her it was foolish, but . . ." Nora gave a little shrug.

"What's her name?" the man asked, rubbing his chin.

"My mother? It's Gertie, or Gerda, I suppose. Gufftason was her maiden name."

"There's an Ingrid Anderson still livin' out there. Think she was a Gufftason, if I'm remembering right."

Nora didn't remember if Ma had a sister named Ingrid.

"Think she was," the man mused. "There was a whole lot of 'em. You can drive out there if you want. Might not hurt."

"How do we get there?" Kenny asked.

The man gave him another distrustful look before he finally answered. "You take this main road out of town, right?" He wagged his thumb over his shoulder. "Until you come to a sign that says, 'Henderson Street'. You take a right there and go a couple of miles. Then the road's gonna bend to the left, but there's a split at that point. You take the split. With me so far?"

"Yeah, I think so," Kenny said.

"You keep going on that road for about five miles or so. Pretty bumpy cause it's full of ruts. That takes you along a ridge, see, and then it dips down," he said, gesturing with his hand. "Follow the dip into a little holler. And that's it. That's where Keystone used to be. Tucked right into that holler. You'll see a few shacks here and there, but most of them either blew over or were torn down and used for firewood by the ones that stayed. Old Ingrid lives out there, I'm pretty sure. If she's not who yer lookin' for, though, maybe she knows where they went."

"Thank you," Nora said. "We really appreciate your help."

"Yeah, thanks, man," Kenny said flippantly. Nora shot him a dagger. Why did he have to talk that way?

"Are there any motels here in town?" Nora asked, trying to fold the map neatly.

"No, ma'am. Have to go back to Ottumwa for a motel."

Nora sighed. "Okay, thanks."

"Good luck," the man called as they left the shop. "Need a fill up?"

"We'll stop back," Kenny called.

"Suit yourself."

"Did I ever tell you about Patsy Montana?" Ma asked from the back seat as the car bounced along the dirt road the man from the gas station had instructed they follow. This was not ruts; this was more like ditches, Nora thought frantically. The rain had obviously eroded the road over time, and no one, apparently, had been out to fix it. Well, thought Nora, if there wasn't a town out here, why send men out to fix the road? Maybe they should turn back, she thought, one hand on the door handle and one braced against the ceiling of the car. After all, it was getting late. The sun was already beginning to set.

"Did I?" Ma asked again, as cool as a cucumber.

"Ma, this is not the time! We're trying to concentrate on the road!"

"I loved Patsy Montana, you know," Ma rambled on. "You never hear her on the radio now. But that's who I named Patsy after. Did you know that, Nora?"

"Kenny, slow down!"

"I miss Patsy," Ma said sadly, and Nora felt a pang of guilt. She was about to turn around and address her, but Gertie spoke again. "Why didn't you bring her back from Park Ridge, Nora? Why did you leave her there?"

Nora sighed. She wished she had brought her valium and tried again to remember why they were making this pointless journey. In the end, however, she found she couldn't think of a single reason. She wished Lyle was here. He would be so much better at handling all of this. She felt the car descend.

"Think we're almost there," Kenny said, peering through the windshield.

They had begun their descent into the "holler" the gas station man had described. Thank God. The hill was rather steep, however, and Kenny was obliged to lean on the brakes almost the whole way down. How would they ever get back up? Nora worried, but it was too late now. They were almost at the bottom.

The town, if it could even be called that, was just one street long. A few abandoned buildings still stood along the road, though they were in varying degrees of decay and disuse. The roof of one had fallen in, and none of them had doors. Likewise, the glass in the windows was either broken or gone altogether. Beyond these stood a few houses, more like shacks or hovels. Piles of rubbish lay everywhere, and even in the fading daylight, it did not resemble any of the ghost towns of the west that were depicted on *Bonanza*. Those had a certain quaint charm to them, being, after all, a television set in Hollywood, but this was nothing like those at all. This was ugly and rotting.

Kenny drove slowly. "Far out, man," he said. "This is radical."

The second to the last house at the end of the street was the only one that seemed to have living inhabitants. A glow came from the windows, and smoke trickled out of a pipe thrusting through the roof. Kenny rolled the car to a stop in front of the house and threw it into park.

"This must be the place. Recognize it, Grandma?" Kenny asked, turning around to look at her. Nora did as well.

Ma leaned forward to see out the windshield. "Yes, this is it, I think," she said with a smile. "It's a little different, but this is the house. This is where I grew up."

Nora looked over at Kenny, who gave her a slight shrug.

"Might as well," he said. "This is what we came for, right?"

He and Nora opened their car doors at the same time and got out. Kenny came around to help Gertie get out. She needed her cane, and Nora heaved herself up on her crutches. They looked like a sorry lot, Nora realized, as they hobbled toward the front door. She tried to rehearse in her mind what she would say if someone actually answered the door. She had thought of several options on the way down: "Hello, my name is Nora Graves," or "Is this the old Gufftason place?" or "Hello, do you remember a Gertie Gufftason?" She was interrupted, however, by Ma.

"I don't know if I can do this, Nora," Ma said behind her. She turned to see Ma stopped dead in her tracks in the dirt road, Kenny at her elbow. "I feel one of my spells coming on," she said. "Maybe we should come back another time . . ."

"Come back another time?" Nora exclaimed. "No, Ma. We're here now. We've come all this way. It's too late for you to get cold feet."

Before Ma could respond, however, the door of the house opened swiftly, and a rather large woman filled the space. The glow of light behind her made her look almost like a divine personage.

"Who is it?" she asked, peering into the darkness and holding what looked to be a rolling pin in a threatening manner.

Nora was just about to speak when she lowered it.

"Gerda?" she asked. "Is it you?"

The woman stepped outside, breaking the divine illusion, and hurriedly approached Gertie.

"It's really you, isn't it!" she said excitedly, throwing her thick arms around Gertie's frail body. "Oh, Gertie! I knew this day would come! I knew you'd come back some day."

Aunt Ingrid, as the woman turned out to be, welcomed them into what was a surprisingly cozy little home considering that the outside looked like a rundown shack. It reminded Nora of something out of one of the fairy tales she used to read to Kenny and Kurt. It was like stepping back in time. There was no electricity, and no modern conveniences could be seen anywhere, not even a telephone. There was a long table in the middle of the room that looked like it had been made by hand and which Ingrid now gestured them toward. They arranged themselves around it while she bustled to put a couple of logs in the woodstove in the corner. She disappeared then into what was presumably the kitchen while a young woman went around and lit more lamps and candles, several of which she placed on table. Ingrid introduced her as Anna, one of her granddaughters.

"They all take turns staying with me," Ingrid explained "but I don't really need looking after. Fit as a fiddle, I am," she said, bringing out some steaming cups of coffee and setting them down on the table. "But I like the company." She had snow-white hair tied up in a bun on the top of her head, several wispy strands of which hung down and framed her plump, red cheeks.

Ingrid looked at Ma again then and reached out to give her another embrace, as if she couldn't believe she was real.

"Nothing's changed," Ma chirped. "It looks just like it did when we were little," she said, her eyes brighter than Nora had seen them in a long time. "I can't believe it, Ing. You've kept it perfect."

Ingrid gave her a big smile, her front teeth sticking out like a rabbit, and then disappeared back into the kitchen, followed by a demure Anna. Nora took a sip of the coffee and looked around, marveling at the fact that she had stepped into her mother's childhood world. Had it really not changed since 1923?

When Ingrid and Anna reappeared, each carried a small platter of homemade bread, hard sausage, and cheese.

"Is that Hushallsost?" Gertie asked excitedly, pointing to the cheese. "I haven't had that since I was a girl!"

"It certainly is," Ingrid said proudly, placing her hands on her hips and surveying the table. "I make it myself, like. Well, dig in, dig in," Ingrid encouraged, wiping her hands on a dishtowel draped through the belt of her big house dress, which, except for the size, looked exactly like the ones that Ma usually wore.

Tentatively, Nora reached for a piece of bread and the Swedish cheese and took a bite. Normally, she wasn't a lover of cheese, but this was soft and very mild and reminded her almost of butter. Whatever it was, it was delicious.

"The sausage is deer," Ingrid said. "My son, Dick, makes it. Try it," she urged Kenny, "it's real good. Cut him some, Anna," she said to the young woman.

Anna sliced off a piece and handed it to Kenny. Nora expected him to refuse, but he instead took it and tried a bite.

"It's good," he said, surprised, and gave a grateful nod to Anna, who blushed and pulled her long blond hair behind her shoulder before taking a seat at the table with them.

Apparently satisfied that they were enjoying the food, Ingrid made one last trip into the kitchen and returned with a green mason jar filled with what looked like sliced peaches. "These are the last of my peach preserves," she said, setting them on the table with a thunk. "I was saving them for Christmas, but we're going to have them tonight!"

"Oh, no! Don't open them on our account!" Nora nearly choked on a sip of coffee. "Please . . . Aunt Ingrid." It felt strange to call her that. "Please keep them for Christmas, honestly."

"Indeed I won't!" Ingrid exclaimed. "It's not every day that my sister returns from the grave. You're like a regular prodigal's son," she said with a grin at Gertie, "'cept you're a woman." She gave a hearty laugh. "I wish Maman was here to see you," she said with a touch of sadness. "She would have loved to have seen you one last time, Gert."

"I know," Ma muttered. "I wish I could see her one last time, too." Her voice wavered. "I thought maybe she might still be here. But I guess that was foolish, wasn't it? To think that she'd still be alive?" Nora could see tears filling her mother's eyes.

"Well, never mind," Ingrid said soothingly. "She can still see us. I'm sure she's still here with us. I hear her rattling around all the time, though Anna here don't believe me."

Anna did not respond to this, but Nora saw her shoot Kenny an embarrassed glance.

They continued to eat and drink, Ingrid eventually unearthing a bottle of plum wine from somewhere in the pantry. It was quite horrible, but they all still drank it, though only Gertie and Ingrid had more than one glass. The two of them did most of the talking, Ingrid sitting at one end of the table and Gertie sitting very close to her, their chairs nearly touching as the two sisters tried to relate, in the space of an hour or two, all that had happened in the last fifty odd years.

Ingrid told them about her husband, Tom, who had died about two years ago, and that she had four children and fifteen grandchildren, and even a great grandchild on the way. Briefly, she spoke about the mine closing and how everyone in the town had gradually left, although not many of their siblings went far. Most still lived within a seventy-mile radius of this house, though both Arnie and Felix had passed away. Only one, Carl, had left the area and lived somewhere near Denver. And then there was Gerda, of course, who had gone away and never come back. "Until now." She reached out and squeezing Gertie's hand for probably the fiftieth time.

Nora listened carefully here, expecting Ingrid's next words to be of reproach, but they surprisingly were not. It baffled her. Shouldn't she be at least *a little* angry with Ma? According to Ingrid, Ma had never once written, not even to let them know she was okay or that for a couple of years, she was living not twenty-five miles away in Ottumwa! Nora didn't understand it. But Ingrid seemed not to care about any of that. She seemed simply grateful to have her sister back. As if she really had come back from the dead. Nora wondered what it would feel like to have Patsy back from the dead . . . But it was too much to think about, too painful.

She tried to focus on what else Ingrid was saying. She found it fascinating to hear this woman talk, her aunt, about a whole family, *her* family, whom she had never known. Again, she found it hard not to be irritated with Ma—they could have come and lived here when Ma was struggling after their father died. But would it really have been better than the Park

Ridge? She wouldn't have met Lyle or had Kenny and Kurt, of course, but . . . but maybe Patsy would still be alive. Or had she always been destined to die young? Regardless, Nora felt her old anger rising.

She tried to swallow it down with another piece of cheese, and took another sip of her plum wine, trying hard to listen to what Ma was saying. She was telling her side now, relating all that had happened to her in the last fifty years, and, oddly, she was more lucid than she had been in years. For once she was not confused about Patsy and Wren being dead, or about what year it was, or what had happened to Dwight and Sharon. Some days Ma seemed to think that Dwight and Sharon were at the Park Ridge. Each time, Nora had tried to explain that they were with Wayne in Fox Lake and that the Park Ridge School for Girls was no more. That it had been torn down in 1962 and replaced with a strip mall. Nora knew because she had once gone back to see Mrs. Harvey, but she was gone.

And anyway, it didn't do any good to try to explain things to Ma. It never did any good. Ma just believed what she wanted to believe. Nora hadn't the heart to tell her that Dwight was a drug addict and that Sharon, though only twenty, already had three children with three different fathers. Even if she did, Ma would just forget it by the next day. Nora knew this wasn't right, suspecting something must be wrong with Ma's mind and had eventually taken her to a doctor. After only a brief examination, however, the doctor had folded his arms across his chest and given Nora a weary look.

"What do you expect?" he had said with a shrug. "She has high blood pressure, osteoporosis, a weak heart, and she's old. She's been through a lot. It's probably the beginnings of dementia."

"But she's only in her sixties," Nora argued. "That's not exactly old."

"Well, sometimes it starts early. Not much you can do. You can either have her live with you or put her in a home."

That's when Lyle had insisted she live with them. But he didn't have to put up with her all day. There had been a small part of Nora, though, that had hoped that when Ma came to live with them that she might snap out of it, but she didn't. Ma definitely had her good days, but there was no rhyme or reason, no pattern to her confusion. She seemed to have some strange attachment to Kenny, but that was probably because half the time she thought he was Wren.

So it was strange to hear Ma speak clearly now to Ingrid about what her life had been, to hear it all from her mother's perspective instead of her own. About Lorenzo and Olson and Jerry and Patsy and Wren and Dwight and Sharon and, of course, herself and Lyle and the boys. She even trotted out the old story of the Park Ridge School, but she didn't, for once, glorify it the way she usually did. And for a moment, Nora felt sorry for Ma, the way Patsy used to, remembering how Patsy would always remind her that Ma had had a hard life.

Finally, Nora realized, with a yawn and a resultant shake of her head, that neither of the two old women were speaking any longer. The two sisters were just gazing at each other, tears in their eyes as they grasped each other's wrinkled hands. As touching a scene as it was, Nora took it as a cue that they should leave. Her ankle was throbbing from not elevating it all day.

"Ma," she said, wincing with pain. "We should probably get going. We have to drive back to Ottumwa yet tonight."

Gertie looked up at her as if she were a little child. "Already?" she asked. "But we just got here!"

"We've been here over two hours, Ma. It's getting late. We don't want to overstay our welcome. We'll come back tomorrow. If that's okay, Aunt Ingrid," she said, giving her a quick glance.

"Come back tomorrow?!" Ingrid exclaimed. "Drive back to Ottumwa? Don't be silly! You can stay here with us! It's no trouble, is it, Anna?"

Anna shook her head and looked at Kenny.

"Oh, no, Aunt Ingrid! We couldn't possibly stay here. Honestly. We don't want to impose. You've been so generous already. Really." Nora reached for her crutches and attempted to stand.

"I haven't seen my sister in forty-two years!" Ingrid boomed. "And I'm not about to part from her just yet. Besides, it's going to snow in a minute."

"Snow?" Nora said, hobbling toward a window. "It was clear as a bell before." She bent to look out into the darkness.

"Well, it's going to snow just the same."

"In October?"

"Let's just stay, Mom," Kenny said. "They said it's alright. I'll sleep on the floor. I don't mind."

"No need for that," Ingrid said. "Gertie can sleep with me. And Nora and Anna can sleep in the spare room. You don't mind sharing, do you?" Ingrid asked Nora. Not waiting for an answer, she looked at Kenny. "And you can sleep on the couch. That okay?"

"Sure," Kenny said with a grin. "Beats the floor."

"Anna, go get some blankets," Ingrid instructed, as she began to gather up the plates.

"But I didn't say we were staying!" Nora exclaimed.

"Come on, Mom. It's all settled," Kenny urged. "We don't really want to drive back all that way, do we?"

Nora sighed. It made sense, but she felt uncomfortable taking advantage of people who were basically strangers. She tried to remind herself that they were her family and suddenly felt very weary. "Oh, alright," she acquiesced. "Thank you, Aunt Ingrid. It's really very kind of you. Here," she offered, hobbling back to the table to try to help the older woman gather the dishes, "let me help."

"Ach! This won't take a minute. Anna can help me. You'd better sit down and get that leg up. Go on," she encouraged, nodding toward an armchair. "Kenny, you pull that stool over so she can put her foot up. That's it," she said, directing them as if they had known each other all their lives. "Take that afghan there, put that under. That's it."

She picked up the nearly empty cheese and sausage platter and carried it to the kitchen, then returned with a dishcloth and began wiping the table. Nora marveled at how much spryer her aunt seemed than Ma, even though she was only a year or two younger and much heavier. Ma seemed positively elderly in comparison.

"How'd you hurt your foot?" she asked Nora as she wiped.

"Bowling. My husband and I are on a league."

"You should put the salve on it. I'll get it out later, if you want."

"Salve?"

"It's an old family recipe. Very secret. Only old Aunt Ida still knows how to make it. It can cure anything."

"Even a sprained ankle?" Nora couldn't help asking skeptically.

"It really is true," Anna said, carrying out a pile of neatly folded wool blankets and sheets and set them on the couch.

"Tell them about the pitchfork thing, Grandma," she said, as she began to make up a bed for Kenny.

Kenny stood awkwardly beside the couch. "Do you need help?" he asked quietly. "I can do it."

Nora saw Anna shake her head, almost seeming puzzled by his offer, but was distracted when Ingrid began speaking again.

"Oh, yeah. That was old Clem. He would have been your great uncle. Pa's brother who came to live with us for a while. Ran a little farm down the way and one day accidentally drove a pitchfork into his foot. Went right through the boot, it did. Well, they tried putting a cow patty on it, but—"

"Cow patty?" Kenny interrupted.

"You know," Ingrid answered, "cow poop."

"They put cow poop on a wound?" Kenny asked incredulously.

"Well, that's what people did back then. Had to be fresh, though, so they chased the cow around until it pooped, then they smeared it on Clem's foot. Didn't get any better, though. Got worse, in fact, as you'd imagine. Doctor said he was going to have to amputate, but Clem begged him not to. Finally, Maman brought over the secret salve. It came down from her side, you see. They put the salve on, and wouldn't you know it, in a week it was healed! The doctor didn't believe it when they told him about the salve. He was convinced they had gone to see a specialist in Iowa City or maybe Des Moines. Kept asking for the name of the doctor. So, you see? It really works. Got that bed done, Anna?"

"Yes, Gram."

"Well, I'm going to turn in. You all can stay up as long as you like. But I have to get up early to do the chickens."

"Thanks, Aunt . . . Ingrid," Kenny said hesitantly. "Where is the bathroom?"

"Out back," Ingrid answered with a nod.

"Out back?"

"Just out the back door. Cross the yard. You can't miss it."

"It's an *outhouse*?"

"Course it is. We don't have no plumbing out here."

Kenny laughed. "Groovy."

"I keep forgettin' you all are city slickers. I guess this isn't just the story of 'The Prodigal's Son,' it's 'The Town and the Country Mouse,' too. Though this is one country mouse who ain't goin' anywhere near Chicago. Come on, Gertie. Ready for bed? It'll be like the old days, us sleeping together. Come on," she urged.

And without a word to anyone and without looking back, Gertie followed her.

CHAPTER 28

October 1963

Gertie

Gertie lay awake in what had once been her parents' bed with Ingrid beside her, just as she used to, all those years ago. They were silent, staring at the ceiling. Gertie longed to ask the question she had held in her heart for so long, but she couldn't think of a way to bring it up. How could she just bluntly ask about a man she hadn't seen for forty-two years and had no reason to ask about, really? But isn't that why she had come? To speak to him? To tell him that she was sorry for how it had all turned out. Finally, she whispered, "How is he?"

"You mean Warren?" Ingrid asked, still looking at the ceiling.

Gertie took Ingrid's hand under the quilt. "Yes, Warren," she finally said. It was the first time she had spoken of him since the day she had left him at the carnival to run off with Lorenzo, the day her life took a different trajectory altogether and sent her flying into a different universe.

"He died. Long time ago, now. Pneumonia, I think it was. Right around Halloween, if I remember right."

Gertie felt a terrible blow to the stomach and wanted to cry. But somehow she had already known this, hadn't she? "When?"

"About twenty-some years ago, I think. Something like that."

Wren would have turned twenty-two this year, she recalled uneasily. "Did he ever marry?"

"No, he never did. Pining for you all these years, I guess." She said it lightly, as if it was supposed to be a joke, but it fell flat.

Gertie squeezed her hand. "I was so terrible to him, Ing. I can't forgive myself."

"For a long time, he asked about you," she said after a long pause. "A year or two probably, always asking if we heard any news. I felt so sorry for him. I was tempted to make something up, tell him you were in California or something, like you used to talk about, having a gay old time, but then I thought maybe that might make it worse for him." She took a breath. "Shame he didn't get married. He would have made someone a good husband."

Gertie felt the tears welling.

"After a while, he didn't ask about you anymore. Never came up to me after church the way he used to. Stopped coming to church altogether as far as I could tell. I never saw him there, anyway. So, one day, I went to him. Went to check on him. At least that's what I told myself, though I think it was because I always fancied him. Did you know that, Gert?"

Gertie bit her lip. "Yes, I kind of thought you might. I'm sorry."

"Well, I finally found him on the front porch of his parents' house, just sitting there all by himself. That's when he told me that he had seen you."

"What?" Gertie looked over at her, but Ingrid's eyes were still locked on the ceiling.

"He said that he had traced you, finally, to Ottumwa. Found out that you were married to Lorenzo and that you had had a baby, a little girl. He went there, apparently, and hung around long enough to actually see you, he said. Wanted to make sure you were okay, and that you were happy."

Gertie's heart constricted a little. "He saw me?" Gertie thought back to all the times she had felt she was being watched in the old McPherson place. She had always assumed it was Madre, spying on her, but maybe it had been Warren. But if he had come all that way, why had he not at least said hello? She would have so welcomed a friendly face from home. But she knew the answer before she had even finished formulating the question. He was right not to have spoken to her; it would have made it worse for both of them. He must have believed she was happy, and so he had left. But how could he have believed her to be happy? Hadn't he been able to see her sorrow and her misery? But even if he had, what could he have done about it? He was too honorable to have tried to take another man's wife, she knew, a fleeting image of Olson flickering through her mind.

"I didn't see him for a long time after that. Years, I think. He was in prison for a while."

"Prison!"

"Killed a man in a bar fight, apparently. All the way up in Chicago. Funny you both ended up there, isn't it?"

Gertie let out a little choking noise and felt her heart slip out of rhythm. She should probably get up and get her pills, but she didn't think she could physically move. Had Warren . . .? She couldn't even finish the thought. It couldn't have been him. It had to be some sort of coincidence. But she didn't really believe in coincidences anymore . . .

Oh, poor, poor Warren. How he must have loved her, and yet she had thrown it all away. Thrown it away for a dirty life with Lorenzo. It pained her to think how gullible she had once been. How she had been tricked by both Lorenzo and Roman. Lorenzo was a scoundrel, to be sure, but somehow Roman seemed worse to her. She had thrown away her life based on what a man in a turban and a purple cloak had told her.

There is a man in your life. He will promise you things, but you must not listen. You must run away from him before it is too late. I see much sorrow and suffering.

Gertie had not thought of Roman's words to her in years, and yet now, as she lay next to her elderly sister, it occurred to her that he had not lied after all. Roman, she saw, had tried to warn her, just as Ingrid had, but she hadn't listened. *Oh, how could she have been so stupid?* For years she had been content to blame Lorenzo and then Olson and then Jerry and even God for her woes, but now she saw that it had really been her own fault all along. Her own stupid fault. The realization threatened to crush her, squeeze the very life out of her, and for a moment she thought she might die, right here in this bed. There might be worse things, she considered. It might be nice to die in the same bed as Maman . . .

"Gertie?"

Gertie wiped at the tears rolling down her cheeks. She had forgotten for a moment that she was here with Ingrid. Poor

Ingrid. She had deserted her, too, she thought, feeling yet another stab of guilt. How many stabs did it take before you died of your own sorrow? How many times could one be crushed and still live? Still *want* to live?

"Why didn't you come back before now, Gertie? I've missed you terrible."

Gertie's throat ached. "I guess because I was ashamed, Ing."

Ingrid squeezed her hand. "You did the best you could, Gertie. You made mistakes, sure, but we all have."

Gertie let out a little sob.

"I'm sorry your daughter died, Gert, and your grandson, but you still have Nora. And four other grandchildren, right? That's something right there; some people in this world don't have anyone. Like Warren, for example.

Yes, Gertie mused, she still had Nora. But Nora had never seemed to need her love as much as Patsy. Patsy had always been a lost sheep, her own prodigal child. *Like mother, like daughter*, she suddenly realized. Maybe that's what bound Patsy to her so fiercely. A memory resurrected itself, then, about how she had bargained with that awful woman who had come to take the girls away from her. It was a memory that she hadn't thought of once since the day it had happened, but now it was crystal clear. She had offered the woman Nora if only she could keep Patsy. *Had she really done that?* Yes, she *had*, she realized with horror. She had offered one for the other. Had Nora heard her? *Oh, Nora, I'm sorry!*

Gertie's body was covered with a thin sheen of sweat now. Madre had cursed Nora, Gertie remembered, but it was *Patsy* who had died. It was Patsy who had been lost and never found. There would be no rejoicing in heaven.

"Why'd you stay here, Ingrid?" Gertie asked, her voice hoarse. "Why not at least move to Ottumwa or Des Moines or Iowa City with the others?"

"Can't you guess?"

Gertie remained silent.

"Because I was waiting for you," she said, rolling over on her side and kissing her on the forehead. "I knew you'd come back some day."

CHAPTER 29

October 1963

Nora

The snow continued to float down relentlessly and quietly pile. Nora sat looking out at the ghost town beyond.

Had it really only been three days? In some ways, it felt like a lifetime, like they had somehow always lived here. She had felt it the moment she walked in that first night, when the hair on the back of her neck had stood up.

It was like they were living in a museum diorama. "Mining Cottage, Southern Iowa, circa 1920" is what the label would have read. Nora had thought the town horribly ugly when they first drove through it, but the snow had magically transformed it into some kind of quaint Dickensian Christmas village. How did snow have this power? How did something so light and fluffy and innocent—something that was essentially just water—have the power to trap them?

She had panicked on the first day of the snow, ordering Kenny to get out and shovel and to clear off the car. Grumpily, he had obliged, but Aunt Ingrid had laughed, saying it was a waste of time. "No one can get up that hill in the snow. You'll just have to wait it out."

Regardless, Nora had hobbled from window to window, anxiously watching Kenny dig. She was worried sick about Lyle. There was no phone with which to let him know they would be delayed, and no way to get to one. Kenny tried, in his usual crass way, to reassure her, saying, "Dad will figure it out, Mom. Just relax. Jeez."

As it turned out, Nora had no choice but to simply give in and attempt to relax. There was simply nothing she could do in this situation. She even allowed Aunt Ingrid to liberally apply the mysterious salve to her ankle, which Nora thought peculiarly generous, considering it was apparently so rare and precious. The salve was thick and black and smelled like tar, and Nora was certain it was nonsense, but, oddly, after only about a day, it seemed to be doing the trick. Perhaps it was merely that she had spent most of the day lying on the couch with it elevated while Ingrid brought her cups of tea and homemade soup. Whatever it was, after two days she was able to finally walk for little bits of time without crutches.

Ingrid brought her magazines to read, all of which were delightfully old, some of them dating back to the 1940's. Occasionally she read something so hilarious that she couldn't help but read it aloud. "Listen to this one," she called to no one in particular. "It's an advertisement for silverware!

Choose Your Silver as You Choose Your Husband.
A lot of things count, of course, when you're choosing a husband as a lifetime proposition.

But two essential qualities always stand out above the rest: He must be a man of character. And he must be a man you know you'll grow even fonder of as the years roll along. Apply that same measure when you make another lifetime choice—the choice of your silver—and you'll surely decide on *sterling*."

"Ha!" Nora said with a laugh and flipped through more pages. "Or how about this one:

War's First Christmas Brings Men in Uniform back to London's Night Spots.
The first Christmas in "the rummiest war the world has ever seen" went off far better in England than in Germany, when in a better day came most of the world's Christmas customs. On this page are to be seen some of the holiday festivities around wartime London. Four out of five men in most night clubs were in uniform."

"Rummiest?" she said, looking up. "I've never heard the war called that, have you, Ma? And look at this! Bread was only ten cents a loaf!"

Even Kenny seemed to have relaxed. He was almost like a different person. Like he used to be. From time to time, he helped Anna bring in wood to keep the stove running and even offered to chop more. Aunt Ingrid tut-tutted this suggestion, however, pointing to the stacks of wood beyond the outhouse that her son, Dick, had piled up for her for the winter. She thanked him, though, and instead suggested that perhaps he and Anna get out the checkerboard.

Since then, he and Anna had played about a hundred games on a little table placed in front of the fire. Just yesterday, Anna had offered to teach him chess. She was a very pretty girl, Nora assessed, but definitely not Kenny's type. Not that it mattered anyway, since they were second cousins. A relationship was certainly out of the question. And yet, Nora thought she detected a certain flirtatiousness on Kenny's part that made her smile.

"Checkmate," Anna said, pulling her hair back with one graceful swipe.

"Not again!" Kenney groaned.

Ingrid and Ma were nowhere to be seen.

"Want another game?"

"How about a walk instead?" Kenny glanced at the windows.

"Now?"

"Why not? I need to stretch my legs."

"Well, I guess so." She began gathering the chess pieces. "But I don't know where we'll go."

Nora was just about to suggest they try the road, but then Kenny said, "Why don't you take me to see the Carrie Cort?"

"The Carrie Cort? What's that?" Anna's brow wrinkled.

"Isn't that the name of the mine around here?"

Anna laughed. "No. Where'd you get that idea?"

"I'm sure that's what Gram told me the mine was called. Isn't it, Mom?"

"I have no idea," Nora said, glancing back at her magazine. "But it's not the Carrie Cort, I can tell you that." For a moment she was tempted to tell the whole story, but she didn't feel like putting forth the effort. What did it matter? Kenny probably wouldn't believe her, anyway.

"She must be getting it confused with something else." Kenny scratched his chin.

"Yeah, I guess. The mine around here's called The Paradise," Anna said, standing and pushing in her chair.

"Can you take me there?"

"If you want," she said with a little shrug. "It's not that exciting."

Nora watched as they bundled up. She couldn't imagine wanting to go outside right now. "See ya, Mom." Kenny gave her a brief wave before turning his attention back to Anna and slipping out the door.

Nora sat watching the fire for a few minutes, wondering what Ma and Aunt Ingrid were up to. It was so awfully quiet. All she could hear was the crackling of the fire. Knowing she would doze off soon if she kept sitting there, she made herself get up.

Standing now, Nora decided to hobble over to the little table in the corner, littered with photographs in a variety of sizes. She had glanced at them when they first arrived, but she had never really studied them. They were plopped haphazardly on top of the lace tablecloth with seemingly no rhyme or reason, no pattern, and Nora had the overwhelming urge to rearrange them. Some of them were posed professional shots taken at a studio, but most were candid snaps, some even having the grainy, greenish hue of a cheap Polaroid. Graduations, birthdays, vacations. Snapshots of a life. A life she had never had. All these years, Nora thought grimly, as she picked up a few of them, there had been a whole family here whom she could have known and loved if it hadn't been for, well, for Ma.

For her pigheaded stubbornness. Why else would she have stayed away all this time? Embarrassment? Shame? Nora could feel the old twinges of anger rising up and tried to quickly squash them before they got out of control. She was an old hand at it by now.

Nora glanced out the window, where the meager winter afternoon light was beginning to fade. But why had Ma run off in the first place? She knew the answer of course, but in all honesty, she didn't like to think about her father. She couldn't really remember him. As a very little girl, she had liked to imagine him as a sort of Ali Baba character who ran the most beautiful carnival on earth, but as she got older and Ma spoke of him so disparagingly—when she spoke about him at all— his image had slowly tarnished to the point she had finally become ashamed that her father had been nothing more than a carnie.

"You got everything you need?" Ingrid called from across the room. Nora jumped and quickly set the photograph she was holding back in its place, feeling as though she had been caught snooping.

"Sorry! No, I . . . I was just looking at all the photos."

"Ah!" Ingrid said, wiping her hands on her apron as she came closer. "I should change some of them out, really. Put in new ones."

"It's a big family," Nora mumbled, looking back at them now.

"Well, there was eleven of us kids, so there's sure to be a lot of grandchildren."

Ingrid then proceeded to point out who each person was despite the fact that Nora hadn't asked her to. At first Nora tried diligently to memorize who belonged to who, but after a while she gave up. It was too difficult, especially as some of the photos were over a decade old.

Eventually there was only one left. It was a large sepia print in the very back, which Nora was pretty sure was the original whole family. Nora had so far avoided looking at it. Gingerly, Ingrid lifted it from its place and handed it to her.

"That's us."

Forced to look at it, Nora obligingly tried figure out which one was Ma.

"That's Maman and Pa. Pa was in the Swedish cavalry as a young man. Did you know that?"

Of course she didn't know that. Ma had told them nothing. Nora stared at the man sitting ramrod straight, a grim look on his cheerless face.

"And that's Maman. She was a lovely woman. Too bad you couldn't have met her."

"Yeah, too bad," Nora said, staring at the woman and noting that she looked so much younger than the man sitting beside her.

"She used to tell us all the time about the green meadows of Sweden where she and her sisters would wander among the cornflowers. Their dresses, she used to say, were made of linen and always fresh and clean and their aprons the purest of white. This is one of hers." Ingrid lifted a corner of the apron she wore. "What I never understood is if it was so wonderful back in the old country, why'd she come live here in the grime and the muck? Coal dust covering everything. Keystone was terrible back then."

Like mother, like daughter, Nora thought sadly.

"That's your Ma." Ingrid pointed to a gangly little girl in the front row. "And that's me." She pointed to the plump girl next to Ma. "I was always a chubby one." She gave a little laugh. "That's Bjorn," Ingrid said, pointing to a stern-looking young man at the back, "and there's—"

But Nora wasn't really listening. She was staring into her mother's eyes, trying to read what lay behind them, trying to see her as not her mother, but simply as a little girl, with her own dreams and sadnesses and fears.

"And that, of course, is little Felix," Ingrid said, pointing to the baby on her grandmother's lap.

"He's one of the ones that passed away, right?" Nora asked, coming back to the conversation.

"Yeah. He never was real strong. Born too early, we all reckoned. They say he was only two pounds. The midwife told Maman to put him in a little box and keep him warm in the oven, and wouldn't you know it, it worked. Eventually he got strong enough to latch on."

"That can't really be true, Aunt Ingrid."

"It sure as heck is! I remember it. He was always sickly, though. Pa said that they should have just let him die. He didn't really mean it to be cruel, but Felix heard him say it one morning while Pa was milking, so he ran away. At first no one thought much of it; after all, how far could he get? But as night drew on, Maman was sick with worry. It was Gertie that found him, believe it or not. She was real good at finding things out, was your Ma. Found him out wandering in the woods."

Nora felt a shiver run over her. Just like her and Patsy at the Park Ridge . . .

Nora carefully set the frame back in its spot. "Weren't you even the least bit upset when she left, Ingrid? Or that she never came back?"

"Sure I was upset. So was poor Maman. She cried for days, but, well, she had to get over it. She had too many other ones to worry about. Pa got sick not long after Gertie ran off. Miner's lung, they used to call it. Kept waiting for a letter from Gertie, but one never came."

"Yeah, I know the feeling," Nora said bitterly.

"I had this childish fantasy that she was going to turn up at my wedding as a surprise, but she never did. I think it was the littler ones that missed her the most, tell you the truth. She was always keeping them entertained, telling them stories."

"Stories?"

"Oh, yeah. She was a great storyteller, was Gertie. But you probably know that, don't you?"

Nora sighed. Though Ingrid had been told about her and Patsy's extended sojourn at the Park Ridge, she obviously wasn't connecting the dots that she and Patsy had pretty much grown up apart from Ma. Ma had told them a few stories about the creepy house in Ottumwa, but that was about it. As she stood there, though, she did suddenly remember telling Patsy stories while she was imprisoned in the Carrie Cort. They had started off as Ma's stories—exciting and adventurous—before she had begun to turn them into her own. She had forgotten about them . . .

"You wouldn't think it, though. She was terrible at school. Always getting punished for not being able to sit still, never paying attention. She got the ruler more times than you could imagine, poor thing."

Poor thing? It seemed odd to hear her mother described in those terms. "Where is Ma, anyway?"

"Having a lie down. Awfully tired, she is."

Nora looked at her wristwatch. "Well, she should probably get up. It's almost dinner time!"

"Speaking of, I should go check the pie. You go wake her up. Tell her I made her favorite. That should get her up."

Nora hobbled toward Ingrid's room, a hundred thoughts swirling around in her mind. There were so many things she wanted to ask Ma and resolved to do so at dinner if Ma's mind was clear enough. Sometimes after a nap, she was foggy.

"Ma?" she called, only knocking briefly on her door before poking in her head. "Ma, you should get up now. Aunt Ingrid said to tell you that she made your—"

Nora paused in the doorway. The room was eerily silent, though she could see Ma lying there on top of the bed, no covers, her hands folded peacefully on her abdomen. Within a second, Nora realized that she did not hear Ma's familiar snore.

"Ma!" she shouted, bursting into the room despite the pain in her foot.

She put her hand on Ma's forehead, and it was cold. That deep unmistakable cold.

"Oh, Ma, no!" She gripped Ma's shoulders and shook them. "Ma!" she shouted, though despair was quickly filling her, drowning her from the inside. "Oh, Ma, no. Don't leave me. Please," she whispered as she slid down onto her knees. "Please don't go."

CHAPTER 30

October 1963

Three days later, a small service was held at St. Mary's in Eddyville, Iowa, for Gertie Gufftason De Lorenzo Munson. Nora sat next to Kenny and Lyle, who had turned up yesterday after taking a bus all the way from Chicago to Ottumwa and hitching the rest of the way. Nora watched with detached curiosity as Signe and Kirsten and Bjorn and all the rest of them trickled in, putting faces to the names she had only just learned. A part of Nora was comforted by this instant family, but in some ways, it only intensified her grief.

The potluck dinner after the burial was put on by the ladies of the Bereavement Ministry and held in the church basement, which was cold and musty and looked like it hadn't been painted since before the second World War. Little kids were running all around the place, and the women—her cousins, she supposed—were gossiping and laughing and discussing plans for Christmas. They were kind, asking Nora if she needed anything or if they could help, but there were no tears among them for Ma. Nora respected them for not faking it. And, anyway, it made sense. After all, "Aunt Gertie" had been the black sheep. The one who had run off and never come back, so it made sense that they weren't overly sad. Compassionate, of course, but more so they seemed curious, if nothing else, about their odd cousins from the big city. Every once in a while, Nora caught one of them surreptitiously looking at her and imagined they were trying to determine if any of Gertie's black sheep-ness had rubbed off on *her*. Nora took it in stride. It wasn't the first time she had been judged because of Ma's actions.

Only Ma would find a way to die in such a dramatic way, Nora decided, as she took a bite of the pumpkin pie someone had handed her. Obviously, Ma had not planned her death, but Nora could not help but think that her dying at home would have been so much easier. Nora's friends on the Altar and Rosary would have embraced and helped her in this sad time, the way she had helped so many other parishioners over the years. For one thing, they would have served fried chicken and ham sandwiches, not casseroles, and they would have had memorial cards printed. And she would have for sure chosen different hymns for the service. No doubt Ingrid and her family thought they were doing her a kindness by arranging everything, but it bothered Nora that she wasn't even consulted. After all, it was *her* mother! But, as Nora well knew by now, there was nothing about her mother that she had ever been able to control or influence, including, it would seem, the details surrounding her death.

The excessive snow likewise added to the drama, making Kurt's presence at his grandmother's funeral practically impossible. Lyle thought that they should telephone him, but Nora said no. He would just make some foolhardy attempt to get here, and she knew he had finals coming up.

The one Nora felt the most sorry for, besides herself, was Aunt Ingrid, who genuinely mourned the loss of the sister she had gotten back for only three short days. Aunt Ingrid spent most of the service crying and excessively coughing. She practically shriveled before their eyes and suddenly seemed older than her sixty-odd years as she sat hunched at one of the card tables, staring at her plate of mostly untouched food. As soon as the dinner was over, she took to her bed, where she apparently remained for several weeks. It didn't surprise Nora much when, about a month after her mother's funeral, she received a telephone call from one of her new cousins, Donna, who told her that Ingrid had passed away. Apparently full of cancer, Donna said. None of them knew it, though the doctor said she must have had it for a long time. "Just goes to show," Donna had chirped over the telephone, "appearances are deceiving, I guess."

What *did* surprise Nora about her mother's death was Kenny's reaction. He seemed remarkably unaffected by his grandmother's passing, which seemed odd given his behavior at Wren's funeral. He had been close to Gertie, especially since she had come to live with them, and he wasn't as distraught as she thought he might have been. He was sad, of course, but it became quickly obvious that his attention was elsewhere.

"Mom . . ." he said to her as they sat on the couch together in Ingrid's house, the day after Ma's funeral. Ingrid was in bed, and they were somehow the only other two there at the moment.

Kenny took her hand and squeezed it, something he had not done since he was a little boy when they would walk hand-in-hand at the park, the same park, coincidentally, where she had taken Patsy and held her hand as they crossed the busy streets. God, they were only five and seven then, Nora marveled.

"Mom," Kenny repeated.

Nora looked into his eyes. Suddenly, she knew what he was going to say.

"You're not coming back, are you?" she asked softly.

Kenny shook his head gently. "No, I don't think so," he said. "How'd you know?"

She gave him a sad smile and bit her lip, hoping she wouldn't cry.

"I'm sorry, Mom," he said hurriedly. "Sorry for everything. I've been a shit son."

"You haven't been a shit son, sweetie. Don't ever think that," she said, her throat thick as she wrapped her arms around him. She held him for a few moments. "Is it Anna?" she asked, pulling back.

"Partly." His gaze fell to his hands. "But it's more than that. I feel like I . . . like I belong here. That I can do something here. Be something."

"Like what?" Nora asked, trying not to be skeptical and wondering what he could possibly do here that he couldn't in Chicago.

"Like be a writer maybe."

Nora tried not to sigh. She knew Lyle wouldn't like this answer, but what did it matter? Kenny seemed happy and at peace for the first time in a long time.

She ran her fingers through his newly shorn hair, courtesy of Anna. He looked so much younger with short hair, and it pained her to remember what a happy little boy he had once been. It was another thing Nora had frequently blamed Ma for—taking away his happiness by using him in her stupid scheme with Wren. How could she have been so short-sighted? So irresponsible?

"I'll miss you," she said hoarsely.

"I know, Mom. But it might not be forever. Who knows? I'll write to you. And I'll come back and visit."

Nora gave him a weak, unbelieving smile.

"I'll come back for Christmas; how about that? When Kurt's home. And maybe I can bring Anna? If she wants to come, that is."

Nora did not answer but leaned over and kissed him on the cheek.

The next day, she and Lyle drove home alone. There was nothing left to do.

It was strange walking into the house without Ma or Kenny. Though neither of them had made much noise, it was still eerily quiet without them. She put her case down on the floor in the hallway and ran a bath, not even bothering to unpack. Then she went to bed and slept for almost twenty-four hours, only waking to go to the bathroom or to get a drink of water.

In the days that followed, she felt empty and blue, wandering around the house, doing little jobs and trying to get interested again in cooking, though it wasn't the same with just her and Lyle. She found she missed Ma, or missed the idea of her, anyway, and realized that she had been doing that all her life. Missing her, or the idea of her. She kept thinking about how odd it had been that Ma had not seemed confused at all when they had been in Keystone.

Well, Nora told herself, they say the mind can do strange things. Maybe Ma had some sort of sixth sense she was about to die? Was that why she had been so insistent to go back? Because she wanted to die at home? Like a homing pigeon or an old dog? Well, whatever the case, she was gone, a fact Nora had to remind herself many times in the coming month. And she found she missed Kenny, too. She tried to appreciate that she didn't have to listen to his sarcastic comments, or pick up after him, or tell him to turn down his stereo, or worry about if was up to no good, but it was strangely lonely without him.

As time wore on, Nora found ways to distract herself during the days, inventing all sorts of little projects around the house, but at night, her sorrow always found its way back. She tried to hide it from Lyle, but she suspected he could sense it. He got in the habit of putting the radio on, loud, every night, as a way to perhaps block out the silence. That or he was beginning to go deaf.

It was Lyle who finally suggested that she get out of the house more, maybe get a part-time job. Nora wasn't sure she wanted to be at someone's beck and call again, but she knew that she was in danger of turning into Ma, sitting alone in the house all day with nothing to do. At Lyle's urging, they returned to the bowling league, and Nora likewise pushed herself to go back to attending the Women's Club meetings at church and even took on the position of treasurer. Likewise, she joined a card club and took up quilting, which was something she had been wanting to do for a long time. Still, however, the darkness lingered.

The ladies in her card club put it down to grief. It took a long time to get over a death, they counseled. Nora politely agreed with them, but of course she already knew that, didn't she? Ma's death seemed like nothing compared to Patsy's and even Wren's. But how much tragedy could one person experience and still stay sane? she worried. The ladies at the Women's Club, on the other hand, put Nora's apathy down to depression over the last child leaving. It was common, they said, and she would soon get over it. But as much as she missed Kurt and Kenny, she knew that that wasn't quite it, either.

Kurt rarely wrote to her, but Kenny surprisingly did. Long letters, in fact, in which he poured out his heart, telling her how much he appreciated everything they had done for him and apologizing for all the grief he had given them in return. But mostly they were filled with expressions of hope and love, which were almost too difficult for Nora to read, like a light that was too bright to look at. They had gone to a peace rally in Washington, him and Anna, he wrote. They had hitchhiked across the country and found it to be exhilarating. He had also found a job at the mine office in Ottumwa. (What was his obsession with the mines? Generations of family trying to get out, but him wanting to go back in.) And he was writing on the side, he mentioned almost as a footnote. He had gotten a couple of stories published, of which he was extremely proud.

He was obviously in love with Anna; he mentioned her constantly in his letters. The two of them had taken up residency in the shack after Ingrid had passed, and no one there seemed to mind that they paid no rent or that they were living together without being married. It bothered Nora, but she knew she was an anomaly these days. No one believed in anything anymore; all the old standards were falling by the wayside. Once or twice, she had mentioned her disapproval on one of his visits back, but Kenny had just laughed.

Was that all she was anymore? A joke? Or a nag? Recently, however, Kenny had written that he had a "big announcement" to make the next time he came home, and Nora found herself hoping it was their engagement. She was fond of Anna, and she thought she would be good for Kenny. Look how much he had already changed. Initially, Nora had been worried about them being second cousins, but according to Lyle it was legal and perfectly acceptable for them to marry if they chose. Well, she supposed he was right.

"Why don't you make it into a sewing room?" Lyle asked.

"Hmm?"

"Gert's old room. Why don't you clean it out and make it a sewing room? Save you bending over and ruining your eyes like that." He nodded at the quilt she had splayed out in front of her.

"I'm perfectly happy sewing out here on the couch with you," she said through her teeth, biting off a piece of thread.

Lyle was silent for several moments, and Nora assumed he had begun reading again. "Well, how about a nursery, then?" he asked quietly.

Nora's head shot up. "Nursery?"

"Yeah, you know, should any grandchildren happen to appear."

"Well, I think that's a bit premature, isn't it?" she snipped, though, to be honest, she felt a quick stirring of something in her chest.

Lyle caught her eyes, his face relaxing into a smile. He shrugged. "I don't know. Kenny did say he had a big announcement, didn't he?"

Oh, God, thought Nora. Was *that* the announcement? It would be just like Kenny to do everything backwards. Nora looked back at the quilt. She wasn't sure she was ready to be a grandma.

"Do you think that's what it is?" She stared at Lyle through her sewing glasses, which made him appear blurry. "Has he told you anything?"

Lyle laughed and stood. "Do you really think he'd tell me something before you? I'm going to make some tea. Want some?"

Nora shook her head and made a few more stitches. She was agitated now, and it irritated her. What if Kenny and Anna really *were* expecting? Probably not, she reasoned. Anna had too much sense about her. But if they were getting married soon, a baby in the near future was not so unrealistic. Perhaps she *should* convert the room. It would make a lovely little play-room for grandchildren. Nice east windows. A big closet. She could paint it. Maybe a nice yellow. Yes, and she could make some cute curtains. She would have to get all of Ma's stuff out of there, though . . .

Yes, she thought, folding up the quilt and putting her thread and shears and squares of material back into her sewing box. It was time to clean that room out.

"I think I will have some tea, Lyle," she shouted toward the kitchen, and for the first time in a long, long time, going all the way back to before Patsy had died, Nora felt a flush of real hope.

The following Monday morning, Nora made a big breakfast for Lyle before he left for work and then busied herself clean-ing it up. She stared out the little kitchen window above the sink and noted how many leaves had fallen off the maple in the back yard, seemingly overnight. Perhaps she should go out and rake them, she mused, but then immediately scolded herself. She had already procrastinated enough by insisting on making a big breakfast, though Lyle had tried to protest, saying his waistline didn't need it. He had already had to convince her that she likewise didn't need to make a batch of cookies, another idea she had woken up with.

No, she thought, glancing at the calendar that hung by the back door. Kenny and Anna were coming in a few weeks, and she wanted to surprise them. She was looking toward the future, and Ma's old things had nothing to do with that. The sooner they were gone, the better, she thought, reaching for the stepstool behind the pantry door. Most of it would simply be tossed in the rubbish bin. Why had she put this off for so long?

Nora was shocked, however, by the musty old-lady smell that hit her when she walked into the room. She immediately cracked open one of the windows to let some air in, despite the frigid temperature outside. Her eyes fell to Ma's bedside table, and she hastily gathered up an empty glass, as well as a half-eaten cookie (no wonder they had ants!) and the untouched stack of novels Nora had set by her little lamp. Nora had tried to get Ma interested in reading to pass the time, but none of the books she brought her seemed to appeal, even the Westerns.

Well, she no longer needed to try to amuse her, Nora sighed, as she began to strip the bed and then to rummage through the dresser drawers. Having decided ahead of time to simply donate everything to the St. Vincent DePaul Society, she began to stuff all of Ma's old dresses and cardigans and polyester pants into the boxes Lyle had brought in from the garage before he left for work. After that, she brought in the vacuum, the mop, and the dust rags and began to clean.

By early afternoon she was finished. Well, almost finished. She stood surveying her work, trying to imagine the room as a nursery so as to muster the strength to tackle the few remaining boxes sitting forlornly on the closet's top shelf. Nora stood looking at them, her hands on her hips, knowing that this is where the real work lay. They were the only things Ma had brought with her from the house on Pratt, and Nora knew they contained all of the little pieces of rubbish Ma had collected over the years. Nora had no desire to sift through them, dredging up all of the emotions she had spent so much energy locking away, but it had to be done. She sighed and dragged the stepstool over. Carefully, she grabbed the smallest box first, an ordinary shoebox, and carried it to the bed, sitting down heavily on the bare mattress.

Nora sat with it for a few moments, just looking at it and working up her courage. Finally, she took a deep breath and removed the lid.

It was filled with what looked like pages of poems, all of them by none other than Wren. Nora picked up a few and read through them, but she had no idea if they were any good. She had never enjoyed poetry. All that symbolism and deeper meanings. She didn't understand it. Why not just say what you meant? Why wrap it in superfluous words and phrases? She was tempted to throw them out, but then hesitated. They were all that was left of Wren, really. She set the box on the bed, thinking that maybe Kenny might like to have them.

Nora went back to the closet, this time removing what looked to be a large hat box from some place called Linden's. She carried it across the room and sat on the bed, balancing it on her lap. There was a faint address printed on the edge of the box, marking it from somewhere in Eddyville, Iowa.

It appeared to hold a pile of clothing.

Carefully, Nora pinched the shoulders of what looked to be a black dress and lifted it out of the box. It *was* a dress, from the twenties, she guessed. She laid it on the bed and then drew out a black cloche hat, black gloves, and even a pair of black heels, crumpled up at the bottom, the leather cracked and brittle. What on earth? Why would Ma have had such an ensemble? And why had she kept it? Had there been a special funeral she had needed to attend back in the Lorenzo days? Surely it wasn't her wedding dress, Nora mused, but it was the only other thing she could think that it might be. She knew that women back then didn't always have the traditional white wedding gown, but black? Nora sighed, wondering what to do with it. It seemed a shame to throw it away. It looked like it belonged in a museum.

She folded it back up neatly and put it in the box. She would decide later what to do with it. She looked back toward the closet shelf. Only one box left. One box? Was that all? She was suddenly filled with a rare pity for her mother. She sat for a few moments, staring up at the last box. Instinctively she knew that this was the one that held all of Ma's personal mementos, and Nora was just as afraid of what it might *not* contain, she realized grimly, as much as what it did. How much of Nora's childhood was stored in that box? Maybe none.

With a sigh, she stood, the floorboards creaking.

It was heavier than she had expected, and she nearly dropped it in the process of bringing it down. When she finally made it to the bed, she looked at it curiously. This one had been taped. Gingerly, she pried it open and peeled back the cardboard flaps.

She felt her neck muscles relax as she picked up the item on the top. It was an old Christmas program from St. Constance from the year when Kurt had played Joseph in the nativity play. She looked over the cast of characters, recognizing many of Kurt's little friends. She held it, wondering what to do with it. The point of today's task was to get rid of rubbish, she reminded herself, but, like Ma, she was hesitant to throw this little piece of the past away. She set it on the hat box; she would decide later.

Next, she lifted out what looked to be an old report card of Dwight's from second grade. Nora quickly skimmed it. All C's and D's, one F. How could he have gotten an F in second grade? Nora read the teacher's comments: *Easily distracted, class disrupter, has trouble following direction, frequently talks out of turn.* Nothing positive, Nora thought with a sigh. Nothing like "sweet boy," or "tries hard,"—the things that teachers usually added to soften the blow of an otherwise bad report. Nora set it on the bed on the other side of her, effectively starting a trash pile. That was one thing that could certainly be tossed.

Next, Nora lifted out a stack of what looked like homemade birthday cards with "Happy Birthday, Grandma!" scrawled across them in varying degrees of proficiency. Nora smiled sadly to herself as she read through them, absorbing their childish messages of love. She couldn't possibly throw away any of these, she decided, and placed them on top of the Christmas program.

Nora reached deeper into the box until her fingers grazed the bottom. She could feel various trinkets and pulled them out, one by one, but they were nothing of note: an old brooch, a tiny ring with a purple stone, a rosary in a little linen bag, and a pair of gilded clip-on earrings. Nora wondered what the significance of each of them had been. There was also an envelope which looked to contain every ticket stub from every movie Ma had ever gone to. Why would anyone keep these? Beneath that envelope, she found another, this one oddly filled with various newspaper clippings, all of them featuring someone called Patsy Montana. Nora thought she remembered Ma mentioning Patsy Montana from time to time, but she didn't realize her mother had been such an admirer. She wondered why. Did it have something to do with her obsession with Westerns?

Nora hesitated and then placed both envelopes on the trash pile, which so far only consisted of Dwight's old report card. Maybe she should have waited until Christmas when the boys were home to go through this box. They might have found the contents more interesting than she did. Or maybe they would want some of this stuff? But that was silly. What would either of them want with newspaper clippings or an old ring? Besides, she was on a mission now, and she needed to get through it.

Her fingers rifled through more programs and various receipts, the significance of which was difficult to fathom. As she lifted a big pile of them in an attempt to see if anything of real interest was going to turn up, she spotted a stack of letters, pinned together with a paper clip. These looked interesting. Nora pulled them out and examined the postmark on the top one: Palermo, Italy. They were addressed to Mrs. Gertie Munson, and from the military look of them, she guessed that they were Jerry's letters home from the war. She felt a mild stirring of excitement that she had finally found something worth investigating.

Oddly however, only the first two appeared to have ever been opened. The other . . . ten, maybe? . . . were still sealed. Maybe they had arrived after Jerry had already come home? In either case, wouldn't Ma still have opened and read them?

Nora pulled the top envelope out from under the paper clip and gingerly pulled out the paper inside. It was indeed from Jerry. It was not very interesting, just a note to say that he had made it safely to Italy. There were no proclamations of love or care or affection at all, which, Nora supposed, didn't really surprise her. There had never seemed to be much love between the two of them, and more than once Nora wondered why they had ever gotten together in the first place. She had asked Ma one time, and her reply had been "because he had a car." Nora had always assumed that was a joke, but maybe it wasn't? But how could Ma have been so shallow as to marry someone because he had a car?

She opened the other one. This one was longer and surprisingly more descriptive. Nora settled in for a good read, her curiosity piqued.

July 26, 1944

Gert,

> *The joke's on you I suppose, as I couldn't have landed a better station. Our platoon has been assigned to patrol and guard Malta, which is on the beautiful Mediterranean. The war is nowhere near us, just a bunch of diplomats. It's a paradise here - plenty of food and wine, not to mention women. Their men are all off fighting, so it's up to us to keep them company, if you know what I mean. Sarge doesn't mind; looks the other way. The woman I've taken up with is called Josienne, but I call her Josie. She don't seem to mind. Doesn't speak much English, but that don't matter where love is concerned. Unlike you, you*

old crone, she likes it when I make love to her until it hurts. How do you like that, you bitch? Serves you right for ratting me out to the draft board. You wanted me in the war, well here I am. They say that all is fair in love and war, well so be it.

Nora stopped reading here, her mouth agape. *What the hell?*

And since I know you can barely read and write, my revenge is sweeter because maybe this is being read aloud by someone else, probably one of your bitch friends at the Sunshine. How do you like that? Hope you feel humiliated. And one other thing, I've directed my army pay to be put in a separate bank account, so good luck fending for yourself. I hope you starve. And don't even think about bringing your two brats to live with you while I'm gone. I'm sick of you asking about them. Don't try anything funny; Charlie next door is watching the house for me."

Your loving *husband,*
Jerry

Nora sat, stunned, her shoulders slumped as she tried to absorb the contents of the letter that lay slack in her hands. She read it through one more time, unsure if she was more shocked by Jerry's vulgar behavior or the fact that he felt the need to write about it so descriptively. No wonder Ma hadn't opened the rest. But how had something like this gotten through the mail? Didn't the army censor the mail back then?

Oh, poor Ma, Nora thought, folding the letter back up. What she must have gone through with him. And then for him to come home and she having to wait on him, especially after he had had a stroke. Nora felt herself shudder, thinking about all the times she herself had waited on him or brought him things. But there was one other detail in the letter that jarred her, in fact, more than Jerry's adulterous bits . . .

Could Ma really not read?

Nora read that part of the letter again, her mind speeding up to a frantic pace as she tried to resurrect any memories that might support this accusation. Could it really be true? she wondered and thought about how she had never actually seen Ma reading a book, or consulting a cookbook, or even doing a crossword. But why save all of these things, then, all of these papers and mementos and newspaper clippings? They obviously meant something to her. But did that mean . . . ?

Quickly, Nora rifled through the rest of the contents of the box, searching for the thing, she suddenly realized, that she had been desperately afraid to find, or not find, as the months since Ma's death had slipped by—her letters to Ma from the Park Ridge.

Nora shoved the remaining layers of paper to the right and then the left, hunting, until she finally found what she was looking for. There they were. A big stack of them, tied up with a ribbon. All the lonely letters of a lost little girl, begging for her mother's help. Nora felt her lip begin to tremble just a little. As she pulled them out, she noticed that they had at least all been opened. Surely Ma had been able to read something so simple, hadn't she?

Nora fingered the pale blue ribbon, trying to decide whether to read them. She had no desire to dredge up all of those sad feelings, but on the other hand, she couldn't just set them to the side and move on. She knew she was going to have to read them, at least a few. She took a deep breath, as if preparing for a battle, and untied the ribbon. It fluttered to the ground, but she didn't bend to pick it up.

She examined the top envelope and pulled out the thin sheet of paper. Eagerly her eyes drank in the sight of her own childish handwriting. It was dated April 12, 1932. *"Dear Ma,"* it read. *"Where are you? How come you haven't come to get us? We are sad without you. Love, Nora and Patsy."* Nora placed it back in its envelope and pulled out another. This one was dated a week later. *"Dear Ma, Please come get us. It is very bad here. Patsy keeps crying, and I can't get her to stop."* Then another one. *"Dear Ma, Please come get us. I will be good from now on if you come. I am sorry if I was bad."*

Nora stopped reading, her heart breaking, though she wasn't sure at this point for whom. The little girl in the letters, afraid and abandoned in a strange place, or the mother who received such desperate pleas from her child but who was unable to do anything about it? She wasn't sure who deserved the most pity. For once she allowed herself to really imagine herself as Ma, getting such heart-wrenching letters week after week. Worse, what if she really hadn't been able to read them and had needed someone at the Sunshine to read them to her? Fretting all night about what might be in them? Or maybe she had asked a neighbor? And not only could she do nothing to help her children so far away, it now seemed quite possible that Gertie didn't know how to write back.

Nora groaned. Could Ma's not being able to read maybe have had something to do with why they were taken in the first place? "Refusal to show up at court," Mrs. Harvey had once told Nora. Well, what if Ma had not been able to read the notices? Oh, God, the sorrow of it. So many lives ruined, essentially, because of something so stupid. For a moment Nora found it difficult to breathe, but she forced herself to calm down. To concede that *her* life, at least, hadn't been ruined. Things happened for a reason, she counseled herself. For example, if she and Patsy had not been sent to the Park Ridge, she wouldn't have met Lyle and had Kenny and Kurt. And there *was* a point at which she had been free to leave the Park Ridge, but she had chosen not to, having grown so close to Mrs. Harvey, and even, oddly, to Aunt Rita.

Suddenly, a lone memory entered her mind. How Ma had wanted them to come home for Christmas that one year and how Nora had so cruelly rejected the offer.

"Oh, Ma!" Nora whispered. "I'm sorry!"

Ma, she finally conceded, had done the best she could. Nora had of course always known that on the surface, but now she really felt it. It wasn't Ma's fault that her best had sometimes fallen short.

She had no desire to read through any more of the letters; it was too painful. But she knew she had to, and so she dutifully picked up the next one.

In one letter, she described her new friend, Celia, and Nora enjoyed reading about their meeting through her eight-year-old eyes. In another there was a mention of Billy and Lyle. Nora read it eagerly, hoping for more, but they were only listed in passing. Besides a sometimes curious tidbit or two about Patsy, there was not much else of interest. As the years went on, they became more infrequent and quite tedious, really. Just dutiful lists of what she had done during the week, an inventory of sorts. There was absolutely no emotion in these last ones at all; they weren't even signed "love," anymore, just "sincerely."

When she finally finished the last one, Nora had no idea how long she had been sitting there. The room was growing dim, so she assumed it must at least be late afternoon. She bent forward and picked up the ribbon. As she carefully retied the stack, she glanced over at the box and wondered if she had the strength to keep going. She was tempted to put off the rest for tomorrow, but a part of her just wanted to finish. Surely, there couldn't be too much left.

With a deep sigh, she reached in and pulled out what seemed like another stack of receipts and programs. She gave it the briefest of skims before placing it all on the rubbish pile. Finally, at the bottom was a stack of what looked to be drawings. At first she assumed they were drawings from the grandkids, but upon closer inspection, Nora found that they were all of Patsy's old paintings! All of the paintings and drawings that Nora had dutifully mailed to Ma before she had given up trying to get Ma to come. With a sad smile, Nora noticed the discolored tape in the corners, which meant that Ma must have hung them up. But there were more, here, Nora realized as she slowly flipped through them. Ones that she had never seen before. These were much more accomplished, more skillful. They must have been from later years. Had Patsy sent them on her own? Or had Mrs. Hanley? She flipped one of them over and saw Patsy's unmistakable handwriting scrawled across the back. "To Ma, to brighten your day. Love, Patsy and Nora." Another one read: "Saw the sun today and thought of you, Ma. Painted this to let you know we love you." Each had a cheery message of encouragement and love for Ma that, reading them now, made Nora feel all the sadder. She was touched that Patsy had always included her in the salutation; it was as if Patsy had picked up the task of writing to Ma just as Nora had abandoned it. But how had she known? Nora wondered. But maybe she hadn't; maybe it was a weird coincidence . . .

She read through Patsy's messages again and for a moment selfishly let herself imagine that Patsy was speaking to *her* instead of Ma, and she suddenly felt in danger of crying. With a heavy heart, Nora moved to set them to the side, wondering what she should do with them, when she noticed that there was one more wrapped in its own tissue paper. Nora pulled it out, wondering why it had been segregated. Carefully, she unwrapped it and sat, spell-bound.

It was a picture of two girls, their arms raised above their heads, twined together until they formed into branches of a tree, which had leaves of every shade of green. Nora had never seen so many versions of green. She knew she was no art expert, but this was unlike anything she had ever seen before. It was beautiful. Stunning, truth be told. It was by far the best thing that Nora had ever seen, and something inside her stirred. Carefully, she turned it over.

At the top was a title: *The Prodigal's Return*. Below that was a note that read, "I would offer this as a gift to you, Ma, if it weren't already your gift to me. The girls in the painting are me and Nora, of course, but the tree is you. We both miss you and love you, Ma. Someday we'll be together."

Nora felt tears pooling in her eyes, and her heart further skipped a beat when she saw that there was an envelope taped to the back upon which was printed: "To Nora". A note to her from Patsy? She could hardly believe it! How many times did one wish to stumble upon a letter, a note . . . a word . . . of love from beyond? Such a gift was rare, and yet here one was, sitting in her hands. A letter to her from Patsy!

With trembling fingers, she carefully peeled the note off of the picture, trying not to rip it, wondering how long ago Patsy had written it and how it had gotten into the box in the first place. Finally, Nora managed to remove the envelope, and her hand shook a little as she ran a fingernail under the flap, gently prying it open. Inside was a plain white notecard. Nora quickly pulled it out and opened it.

"Dearest Nora," it read. "Somehow, I know that you will be the last of us to remain, and so this painting comes to you. Of its artistic merit, I can't say, nor do I really care. But that shouldn't surprise you. It is meant instead to be a missive of love, to remind all who see it, or maybe just you, that love transcends all."

Nora stopped reading for a moment, shocked at Patsy's eloquence. She had never talked like this. Sadly, she rarely spoke at all. Reading this note was almost like reading something from a stranger.

"I never thanked you for all that you did for me, all the sacrifices you made, how hard you tried. It has never, not even for one day, gone unnoticed by me. My regret is that I never told you. I know that I was many times a great burden to you and for that I am sorry. Truly. I also know that many times you judged your situation to be unfair. You weren't wrong in that, and many times I wished that I could change it for you. But do not too much envy the prodigal his wanderings, as that road is full of its own sorrow and death, though it might not look that way to the family left behind. It is a life that is not so easy and carefree as you might imagine. The role of the older brother in that old story is always imagined to be dull and boring and dutiful, but appearances, as you know, can be deceiving. It does not look that way, at any rate, from the view of the poor prodigal. To him, his brother's place looks to be one of privilege and safety and love. What is it that the father in this story says to his firstborn? Something like, 'I *know* you are the good son, and *everything* I have is, and always has been, yours.' This is not a light statement, Nora. Think about it.

"And who's to say who's who in this story? The truth is that each of us at some point or another have been the father, the prodigal, and the older son. All of us have squandered our inheritance and then regretted it, all of us have been angry and judgmental, all of us have rejoiced in the finding of a lost child, the dead resurrected. Poor Nora. You were always the one playing the parent, but now it's time for you to really *be* the father in the story. It's time for you to forgive Ma, forgive me, and especially to forgive yourself. It's not as hard as you imagine. And then we can have a time of rejoicing. No more pity, no more anger, no more fear. I have had the benefit of being wrapped in your love my whole life. Now wrap *yourself* in it and live the life that has been given to you. You are free! But then, you always have been free, you just didn't know it. I love you, Nora. Completely. Never forget that. Everything I have is yours. Until we meet again, I remain, your Patsy."

Tears poured down Nora's cheeks as she set the note aside, and for the first time since Ma had died, she wept. Really wept. Nora sobbed for what felt like hours, letting Patsy's words settle over her like some sort of magic salve of their own.

She was still curled up into a ball at the top of the bed, the note still in her hand, when she heard a light tap on the door. It was Lyle.

"Why are you sitting here in the dark?" he asked, switching on the light.

Wearily, Nora sat up, the various contents of the box sliding toward her.

"You look terrible!" Lyle said, as he gently pushed some of the things to the side and sat down beside her. He handed her his handkerchief. "Going through your mom's things?"

Nora blew her nose and nodded.

"Rough, huh?" he asked, rubbing her back.

"You could say that." She gave him a weak smile.

"Anything interesting?"

Nora paused. Where should she start? "I don't think Ma knew how to read," she finally said.

"That doesn't surprise me."

"But . . . but how did she manage all those years at the Sunshine then?" Nora asked, as if *this*, out of everything she could have said, was the most pertinent question.

Lyle shrugged. "I guess she must have figured out some kind of system to get by."

"I've been such a terrible daughter," Nora groaned, looking down at Patsy's note.

"No, you haven't." Lyle put his arm around her. "Nobody's perfect, Nor. I've been trying to tell you that for a long time." They sat in silence for a moment until finally Lyle spoke again. "Anything else?" He glanced at all of the stuff on the bed beside them. "Looks like a lot."

"There was a letter from Patsy. To me," she said, holding up the notecard half-heartedly.

"Ah. That explains it. Want to share it?" he asked, kissing her forehead.

"Not right now." She looked at him then and felt an overwhelming feeling of love, like she had back in their early days, only stronger, if that was possible. "You know what? You're a sterling kind of guy."

Lyle's brow crinkled. "What's that mean?"

Nora patted his cheek. "Just something I read once."

Lyle smiled, his big easy smile.

"I want to have a party when Kenny comes home," Nora said.

"A party? For what?"

"To celebrate."

Epilogue

Gertie opened her eyes and saw him. Finally, she could see him clearly. It was Warren . . . or was it Wren? For a moment, they almost seemed to be the same person . . . No, she decided finally. There was no doubt. It was *Warren*.

He was standing there by a split-rail fence. The same fence, she somehow knew, where she was supposed to have waited for him all those years ago. She wanted to run to him, but a stab of regret passed through her and she couldn't move. He smiled at her, and she felt infinite love and patience. Again, she tried to move but couldn't, and she realized now that it had never been him that had been stuck or lost, it had been *her*. She looked around, half expecting to see fog or a storm or the woods or the sea.

But there were none of those things. Nothing to obstruct her vision or distract her, nothing to confuse or trap her. It was like she was standing in a meadow. There were flowers all around, and everything was vividly clear. The colors were brilliant, and a heavenly perfume soaked the air, like lilacs maybe. It was daylight, but Gertie couldn't see the sun. The temperature was perfect, the kind so perfect that it isn't noticed at all. She began to feel an overwhelming sense of peace.

She looked back at Warren. It struck her as odd that he looked just as he had. He was even wearing the same plaid shirt he had been wearing at the carnival that day. And he was so young! How could that be?

Suddenly she felt old and vulnerable and immeasurably sad. She had thrown him away, thrown away her youth, thrown away her home.

"Warren, I'm so sorry, "she tried to say, but as soon as the words materialized, they dissipated upon hitting the air, as if they were evaporating as quickly as they formed.

He smiled at her. "Hello, Gerda. I've been waiting for you," he said lovingly, though his lips didn't move. Somehow, she simply knew what he said, like she could read his mind and he hers. She was shocked that there was no reproach in him at all.

"Oh, Warren." The longing to tell him how sorry she was and to explain what had happened was almost unbearable, but each time she opened her mouth, her apologies evaporated.

"I know, Gerda. None of that has any meaning anymore. That part is over now. Are you ready?" he asked gently. "Ready to begin our new life together?"

She wanted to go with him, be with him, never leave him, but she somehow knew that if she went with him now, there would be no turning back. No return. She was suddenly stabbed with a bolt of fear, though of what she didn't know. Making a mistake? Judgment? Retribution? Punishment for the mess she had made of her life? How would she be able to explain herself?

Warren seemed to sense her hesitation and held out his hands. She stared at them. The hands of a young man. She wanted to weep. The longing to go to him was intense, and yet her fear was nearly as strong. She felt as if she were in danger of ripping in half. Every fiber of her being began to vibrate. Inch by inch, her fear was creeping into the background, only to be replaced, sadly, by shame. She didn't deserve to go, she suddenly felt. She didn't deserve to be with Warren, not then and not now.

Still he kept his hands outstretched. They never wavered. She looked into his eyes, which were strangely large and blue, almost like a lake, like a lake she had seen in a painting once . . .

She had no idea how long she stood there. She had no concept of time. Maybe it was a minute, maybe an hour, maybe an eternity . . . Still he stood before her, patient and waiting.

You are loved, Gerda, she heard him say directly into her mind. *You are loved, don't be afraid.*

She let his words wash over her, go through her, become part of her somehow, and finally, after what felt like a lifetime . . . she let go.

She let everything go.

All of her fear, all of her sins, all of her mistakes, all of her regrets. As she stood there before him, feeling naked and exposed, she was having a hard time remembering what she had been so upset about, so worried. It was over now, just as he had said.

Without further hesitation, she raised her hands and laid them gently in his.

At once she felt a warmth and a tenderness shoot through her, a happiness that she couldn't explain. She felt light . . . young again, just as he was. No aches, no pains, no sorrows of the heart. Only joy. Only peace. She sensed that Patsy was near, and Wren, and Maman. She longed to see them.

Warren kissed her on the forehead and smiled.

Let's go home.

Acknowledgements

First and foremost, I'd like to thank the indie publishing community for giving me the courage and the support to take the next big step in my writing career. It's been a pleasure and an honor to be counted in your number.

It would take pages to list every single person who has given advice and answered my newbie questions during the publishing of this book, but there are a few to whom I would like to give a special shout out: Valerie Taylor, Kari Bovée, and James Conroyd Martin. Thank you for showing me the ropes and so graciously sharing with me that which you have spent years learning.

I'd also like to thank the Self-Publishing Formula crew, specifically Mark Dawson and James Blatch. It was only after listening to their podcast week after week that I gathered the courage to take the plunge into the indie world. Besides giving extremely useful tips and examples, they provide something even more valuable—hope. Hope that not *every* part of the publishing world is broken; hope that authors can *absolutely* take control of their own careers and be successful. So, thank you Mark and James for being a beacon to so many authors and for showing us a different way forward.

On the technical side of things, I'd also like to thank my editor, Andrea Robinson, who stepped down from the big leagues to help me see a clearer vision for this book and for gently helping me to sculpt it into the best version of itself. Thank you for really "getting" the book, Andrea, and for believing in it. I'd also like to thank Stuart Bache at Books Covered for the gorgeous cover, Danna Steele for formatting, Leo Bricker for proofreading, Yolanda Facio for website and newsletter assistance, and Bizzy Schorr for graphic design. And thanks, as usual, to my beta crew: Otto, Marcy, Amy, Margaret, and Susan for reading rough copies and for sharing your unique insights.

I'd especially like to thank my three children, Nathaniel, Owen, and Ellie, for encouraging me to follow my dreams and for understanding my need to work very early in the mornings, late at night, and usually on family vacations, too. I love you more than I can say. But I'd especially like to thank my husband, Phil, for believing in me and encouraging me not to give up when it seemed the only option left. Thank you for always knowing just what to say when I really need it most. You, to me, are everything.

Author's Note

Gertie, Nora, and Patsy's story is based on a tale I heard while working in a nursing home some thirty years ago. One of the residents, the woman who would become Gertie in my book, told me her life story, which I found utterly fascinating, so much so that when I was fishing around for an idea for this book, it came right back to me. I've changed all the names and fictionalized some aspects, but most of it is true. There really was once a young girl from southern Iowa who ran off with a carnival barker in the 1920s, had two little girls who were taken away by the state, and eventually got them back years later.

This story is their story.

What took creativity was imagining how each of them—Gertie, Nora, and Patsy—would have felt going through what they did. How it felt for each of them to be the mother and the child, the lover and the loved, the prodigal and the redeemed. But then again, each of us probably already knows this in our heart. I hope I got it right.

Two liberties that I did take with the story's timeline involve The Grand Ole Opry and Patsy Montana. In this story, a young Gertie listens to The Grand Ole Opry on her neighbor's radio in 1923, though that program did not officially begin broadcasting until 1925. Likewise, in 1923, Patsy Montana, a real-life country singer, had not yet produced a record. She did not hit "stardom" until the 1930s and '40s. I hope you will forgive these two slight variations to the truth, which I felt were necessary to make the story work.

Book Club Questions
for The Fallen Woman's Daughter

1. This book is very much about mothers and daughters. Who is who in the story? Discuss the various mother-daughter relationships found throughout, including Aunt Rita and Celia, Nora and Mrs. Harvey, Mamen and Gertie, Nora and Patsy, Gertie and her girls, or any others you spotted.

2. Who did you most identify with in the story—Gertie, Nora, or Patsy? Who do you feel is the most "motherly" of the three?

3. Could you understand Gertie's desire as a young girl to escape from Keystone with Lorenzo? Did you see this as realistic?

4. At one point, Nora yells at Gertie: "Ma, you're the most selfish person I've ever met! You . . . you just ran off— ran away from your family with *a carnival worker*? What were you thinking? I'm sure they were worried sick about you—probably for years! And why? Because of some wild impulse? You know, you say that Patsy has gypsy blood, that she takes after our dad. But maybe she takes after *you!* Ever think of that?"

5. Whom do you think Patsy takes after, and why was she so "ethereal" and artistic? Did she inherit the "gypsy" spirit, or was she simply affected by what happened when she

was four at the hands of their neighbor, Mr. Richardt? Was she in actuality as sensitive as her own son, Wren, but had no other way of dealing with her feelings but to "check out" of reality?

6. Nora is quick to blame Gertie for many of the bad things that happened to them, but how much of this do you think is projected guilt over the bad things that happened when she was "mothering" Patsy, such as the Mr. Richardt incident, Patsy getting locked in the Carrie Cort, frequently disappearing, and eventually becoming pregnant while at the Park Ridge?

7. Gertie is constantly bragging to the girls at the Sunshine that her girls were at the finest school ever. Why do you think she did that and discuss the irony of Nora's feeling that it actually was a wonderful place that she didn't want to leave.

8. Was it realistic that Nora wanted to remain at the Park Ridge and that she was resentful of Gertie when she did finally show up?

9. Discuss Nora's longing to be the perfect mother and housewife. Why do you think that was? Do you think Nora is too judgmental? Discuss her feelings when she meets Aunt Ingrid and the long-lost family in Iowa.

10. Discuss the differences between Nora and Lyle's relationship with Gertie and Patsy's. How and why are they different?

11. Discuss Gertie's reaction to Patsy coming home pregnant? Why do you think Gertie embraced her situation?

12. There are several "paranormal" elements in this story, such as Roman's abilities, Gertie's continuous dreams about Warren, and, of course, the epilogue. Discuss whether these are believable and name any others you spotted in the story. (Hint: Wren's abilities, the old woman who tends Madre, Patsy knowing when Ma was going to arrive at the Park Ridge, etc.)

13. Discuss Gertie's relationship with Wren. Do you think she was right or wrong to remove Wren from the hospital? Discuss its impact on Kenny.

14. Were you disappointed that Kenny decides to return to Iowa instead of returning with Nora to Chicago? Discuss his fascination with the mines.

15. Were you surprised by Gertie's inability to read? Discuss how this shaped the course of her life.

16. Do you think it was wrong for the lawyer, Mr. Cohen, to advise Gertie to stay away? How would the story have been different if she had ignored him? Was he yet another man who steered her wrong, or was he wise to advise her to leave the girls alone?

17. Was Gertie wrong to report Jerry to the draft board?

18. Were you surprised by Ingrid's story about Warren killing someone in a bar fight in Chicago? Did you guess that the victim was Lorenzo?

19. Did you at first believe that Olson was a good guy, even though the first line of the book is: "This was all Olson's fault." Discuss how he contributed to Gertie's downfall. Gertie is very much a victim of her own circumstance; discuss the various men she chose and why.

20. Discuss how each of the main characters—Gertie, Nora, and Patsy—each represented the three figures in the Prodigal Son story (the father, the good son, the prodigal son) at different points in their lives.

The Henrietta and Inspector Howard Series

If you liked this book and would like to read more by Michelle Cox, try her seven-book historical mystery series set in Chicago in the 1930s.

Winner of over sixty international awards, the series has been praised by *Library Journal* (starred), *Booklist* (starred), *Publishers Weekly*, *Kirkus*, and various media outlets, such as PopSugar, BuzzFeed, *Redbook*, *Elle*, Brit+Co., *Bustle*, *Culturalist*, *Working Mother*, and many others!

"Henrietta and Inspector Howard make a charming odd couple, mixing mystery and romance in a fizzy 1930s cocktail."
—**Hallie Ephron**, *New York Times* bestselling author

"Henrietta and Clive are a sexy, endearing, and downright fun pair of sleuths. Readers will not see the final twist coming."
—Library Journal (starred review)

Read free with Kindle Unlimited (KU):
https://amzn.to/4vfvmoH

Stay Connected

Sign up for Michelle's newsletter for alerts about new releases, free books, events, and fabulous giveaways. Be the first to know when the next Merriweather novel is available!
michellecoxauthor.com/newsletter-signup

— • —

Buy Direct and Save

You can explore all of my titles (including vintage covers) and available formats at a
Discount!
in my online shop:
michellecoxauthor.com/shop

A HAUNTING AT LINLEY At Castle Linley, Henrietta and Clive must unravel a murder, a supposed haunting, and a web of shocking family secrets to save the estate from ruin and expose the true culprit behind the sinister events.

A CHRISTMAS AT HIGHBURY Henrietta and Clive return to Highbury for the holidays only to find themselves swept into a festive whodunit when gifts (and a necklace) go missing at a glittering Christmas ball.

THE MERRIWEATHER SERIES

MATCHED IN MERRIWEATHER Forced to abandon her glamorous 1930s Chicago college life, Melody Merriweather returns to her small hometown to save her family's struggling general store, where she unexpectedly finds herself entwined in matters of the heart.

UNCOVERED IN MERRIWEATHER Kate Kerwyn, aka "Indian Kate" embarks on a quest to uncover her true family and identity, while Melody returns to Chicago to try to resurrect her old life.

SEDUCED IN MERRIWEATHER When aspiring pianist Bunny Merriweather falls for a charming stranger, it falls to her sensible sister Melody to pick up the pieces—while quietly losing her own heart.

STAND-ALONE TITLES

THE FALLEN WOMAN'S DAUGHTER Based on a true story, this sweeping saga follows three generations of women—from a young runaway in 1920s Iowa to her daughters and grandchildren—through love, loss, and the long-buried truth that finally lets the past be put to rest.

About the Author

Michelle Cox has always been obsessed with stories of the past and has spent a lifetime collecting them. She is the award-winning author of historical fiction, including **the Henrietta and Inspector Howard** series, **The Fallen Woman's Daughter**, and **The Merriweather Series – Jane Austen in Wisconsin**. Cox also pens the wildly popular, "Novel Notes of Local Lore," a weekly blog chronicling the lives of Chicago's forgotten residents.

She lives in the northern suburbs of Chicago with her husband, an assortment of children who continually leave and then come back, and one naughty Goldendoodle. Unbeknownst to most, she hoards board games she doesn't have time to play and is, not surprisingly, in love with both Cary Grant and Jimmy Stewart. Likewise, she is happily addicted to period dramas and big band music. Also marmalade.